EAGLE SCOUTING

Dawn Leger

Wally,
Thanks for your support!
Dawn Lyn
2014

Published by Lefora Publishing

To the victims of terror, wherever and whenever it occurs.
We are all diminished by the violence that exists in the world,
and we are all responsible for finding a way to rise above and end it.

❧

Acknowledgments

Thanks to my partners in Lefora Publishing LLC, Dave Fortier and Chuck Radda, who are also members of Chimney Crest (C.C.) Writers, along with Michele K. Boyko, Frank DeFrancesco, Linda Lynch, Don Paglia, and others who have come and gone over the years. This group deserves thanks for their constructive criticism and support, especially through multiple revisions of the last sections. Thanks to my personal proofreader and arbiter of all things literary (and not), Alice Leger; to Kimberly Kiniry Lynch, for her excellent suggestions and help with book design and promotion; and to a wonderful group of readers, some of whom reviewed this manuscript multiple times: Denise Joy Scoppetta, Isabel Cueto Brady, Joanne West, Patti Ewen, Judith Giguere, Susan Haworth, Craig Minor, Carol Ann Laga, and Lori Birnbaum. Thanks to Eileen McVicar-Schnyder, who created the original cover art, and Lindsay Vigue Photography for the author photo. I appreciate the unofficial "Kickstart" support from arts patron Mr. Wally Barnes. I owe a great debt of gratitude to my late friends Beverly and Jack Bain, and their daughter Karin Bain Kukral, for the use of their home in Naples, Florida, which has been a place of retreat, reflection, and incredible productivity over the past 20 years. I am truly grateful that Karin continues to share this resource with me since her parents' passing. And finally, thanks to Frank Wheeler, Jr., for his support.

Raoul

WHEN HE REGAINED CONSCIOUSNESS, the man called Ismail found that he could not move his limbs. Head covered in black fabric, a grimy piece of cloth taped in his mouth, he strained against the ropes, checking at the same time that his legs and arms were still attached and working. His ears roared, and then—suddenly—everything was quiet. He lifted his head a bit, trying to hear something, anything, but only caught the creak of a floorboard. No one else seemed to be in the room. Once he calmed his quaking heart and slowed the blood pulsing against his eardrums, Ismail could tell there was no one nearby—but muted voices carried into the room through the heating vents.

More tugging, and then the distinct sound of a door opening. Window shades dropping. His two captors wore hair grease that he could identify by its distinct smell, a favorite of some of the local Arab men. He pulled away when he felt cold metal touch his leg, and he clenched his muscles against the expected pain. He was naked, he felt the chill of a breeze across his body. A hand removed the ropes from his ankles, and Ismail prepared to scissor his legs and fight for release. A loud laugh erupted from the other side of the room, then a gruff voice—did he recognize it?—grunted, "Are you going to let this little man get the best of you?" There was a quick flash of light, the sting of a needle, and Ismail fell into darkness again.

When he awakened later, the room appeared silent and dark again. He was chilled, dizzy from whatever they'd shot him up with, and tied down at all four points again. The air conditioner blew a soft coolness across the room, and goose bumps dimpled his bare chest. The door creaked open.

There was a scuffle of fabric against the floor—they were in stocking feet—and then Ismail's blindfold was abruptly removed. The three men surrounding the bed looked familiar to him—but his brain was not functioning at its peak and he found it necessary to stay focused on breathing. The thinnest man, possibly the youngest, stepped forward when another pushed his arm. He was wearing a long plastic apron and a welder's mask, which Ismail noted with interest rather than alarm.

The youngster looked back over his shoulder, hesitating. There was another glint of metal, and then the rubber-covered hand pulled the exposed penis taut. The boy grunted when he sawed the scalpel through the flesh, moving aside when a spurt of blood obscured his work. Ismail's body, a bit slow to react to the assault, arched upwards in distress. He felt no pain, not yet, just the throbbing warmth of the blood flowing across his legs and pelvis. The kid held up the prize.

Sweat flowed into Ismail's eyes—perhaps mixed with tears—as the third man held his hair and roughly removed the tape and cloth from his mouth. Before he could swallow properly, however, the man roughly stuffed the flaccid member between Ismail's gasping lips and slapped the tape back on. Ismail heaved and bucked and fought against the taste of blood and then vomit, the three men standing cross-armed around the bed as if witnessing an ordinary and somewhat boring event. The young one, without his bloody apron and mask, looked greenish as he worked his face muscles into a stolid pose.

"*Calm yourself,*" Ismail thought as he tried to focus. "*Calm, calm, calm.*" He frowned, concentrated hard on the word, calling upon his military training to push down the rising tide of panic. Struggling to breathe through the nose, Ismail could sense the slowing beat of his heart—not because of his efforts to calm it, but apparently because there was a rapidly decreasing amount of blood left to pump out.

Sparkling white streamers danced across his field of vision, and at first he was afraid of another slash of the silver blade. There was no more cutting, however. In a moment, he relaxed into the cool blackness that lapped at the edges of his consciousness.

"Take it off," the Leader instructed, and duct tape stripped the dry skin from Ismail's lips. He wanted to spit but there was nothing left, just the slow inhalation of one last breath. The severed penis flopped in his mouth like an extra tongue, lolling out the corner. He had neither the strength nor even the will to spit it out.

Ismail was able to turn his head an inch and caught the older man's smile as he turned away. Who was he? The question fluttered across the last synapses of Ismail's brain. He was familiar—The Leader.

"Everything clean? Roll up that prayer rug; he won't need it anymore," the Leader said, slapping his gloved hands together. It was cold in the room, the air conditioning humming in the corner. "Let's go."

He winked at the body splayed on the bed, the pallid skin against the crimson mess of the sheets. Ismail's eye fluttered one last time, just at the edge of the clean white shimmer overtaking his vision.

"See you in hell, Ra-oul." The door closed. It was September 8, 2001, and the men had work to do.

Clara

I PROMISED MYSELF, SITTING on the barstool the afternoon after my brother's funeral, that it would be only once, that all I wanted from Guy was just a taste—at first, it seemed that just a kiss, a test to see if the electricity that had flashed between us was real, the heat I'd felt ever since the first moment I saw him across the room and then the obligatory conversation—don't I know you from somewhere? Where did you go to school, what year?—was just a mating dance leading to the actual moment when he touched me and we really danced, right there in the Eagle's Club under the gaze of the old drunks and guys dressed in blue shirts with names like "Joe" and "Butch" embroidered over filthy pockets bulging with cigarettes and pencil stubs, holding up the bar with their leaning potbellies and unfocused eyes, and I knew that a kiss would be absolutely necessary, just that and nothing more than a taste, although when I closed my eyes and felt his hand on my lower back, and imagined him naked, the red hairs flowing smoothly over that impossibly flat stomach, erupting in a glorious chorus of thick pubic hair that must herald the presence of what had to be a thick, red cock and then, interrupting my wet revelry, the question—circumcised or not?—that always came up, so to speak, at these moments, and oh how I wanted to see, actually to taste and experience, the uncut penis of my imagination, pulling the skin away to reveal the glistening red head whose very ripeness was a quivering piece of fruit I must nibble cautiously and then suck upon and finally encompass with my entire being, and then he looked at me, the slow lazy look of a man who knows you want him, and I felt it then, no, not the bulge I'd been expecting or the muscle flexed with the tension of our chemistry, no, I realized there was a ring on his left hand, and I felt my stomach lurch with the absolute certainty that I could not have this man and the realization that I would, in fact, fuck him. The ring actually sealed the deal as I felt my breathing quicken in anticipation.

This familiar exercise had never taken place in the town I used to call home, and that ratcheted up my interest in this red-haired, freckle-faced Frenchman. That and the fact that, since September 11 and the chaos of lower Manhattan, since the murder of my brother, I had lost my bearings. The best way I knew how to ground myself was against the foreign and familiar pelvis of a man.

Raoul

HE KNEW THIS TOWN, its hidey-holes and back trails, like the roadmap of lines on the palm of his hand. Even after being away for years, the familiar feeling of the gravel and sand, the scrubby woods and the poorly maintained neighborhoods, came back to him with ease. Raoul had been in Jerome for several months now, no one the wiser about his nightly comings and goings. Certainly no one in his family knew he was in town, and only the man he reported to was certain where he was.

The day had been warm, a clear and crisp fall day that made a person remember all the Septembers past when school meant a new beginning and the opportunity to make money—and fun—raking leaves all over town. It was too early for the foliage, but with nightfall coming earlier, Raoul's meanderings around town were easier to accomplish. A brilliant half moon lit up the sky as he slipped onto a pier and clambered aboard an old boat that he'd equipped with a powerful, strong, and well-camouflaged engine.

Once the anchor was up and the boat was safely out of sight, Raoul pulled off his 'rican boy uniform—slouchy jeans, bad-ass tee, and black Puma cap. Rolling the clothes into a garbage bag for use on the return trip, he slipped back into the all-black ensemble of the new urban terrorist. With the addition of a woolen pakol, a smudge of kohl under each eye, his Ismail persona was back in business. He pulled the boat close to the shore on the outskirts of town, where a buoy had been placed to hold a rubber raft. With night vision glasses, Raoul scanned to make sure the coast was clear, slipped into the raft and paddled quietly to the dark side of a hulking warehouse on the water. The final run-through meeting was scheduled: in it he hoped to gather enough details to make a report that would stop whatever was being planned here. After months of lying low, training in hand-to-hand maneuvers, the group was approaching D-Day.

Several new faces were among the familiar gathering. Apparently many separate cells had been training in other locations, and some had now come together for the last briefing. The men had been selected for their nerves and dedication to the mission—expressed as "teaching a lesson" to the American devil. Raoul kept his eyes low and grunted when someone pushed against his arm.

"Ismail, hey." Mohammed smiled.

"No names," Ismail said quietly. "Remember? No names."

"Oh, yes, yes. I keep forgetting." Mohammed chuckled. "But we're among friends here, right? I mean, in public, yes, but here? No problem."

Ismail grunted again and slid away from his talkative frien
the background and watch the crowd. His dark eyes flashed, anc
the wall when the Leader called for quiet.

"Check with your team leader to get your directions for later.
training exercise, and then we move into place. Any question
leader. Time is of the essence now, and Inshallah, we will meet _   _ ... heaven."
With that, the man turned away and gestured with his left hand. In the right, he held
a stubby pistol.

"One more thing—a lesson." He gestured again. "Bring him here."

Mohammed was escorted to the front, his feet hardly touching the ground. He
had a stupid smile on his face, as if he was expecting some kind of commendation—
and that was the expression he took into the afterlife as the Leader dispatched him
with a single shot to the forehead.

"Anyone else need a lesson? We are in a battle here, and we cannot allow the
weakness of one to affect the strength of our mission. Now, go." He raised the gun
and fired a single shot into the roof as the group scattered, looking for others in
their squad while avoiding eye contact with anyone in the room. Raoul felt his
bowels tighten, as they did whenever he was ready for action.

Clara

I SAT ON THE stool for about half an hour before touching the beer that had appeared before me. I had fled from the house, away from the wailing woman who used to be my mother but who had, in the forty-eight hours since my brother's murdered body was discovered in the apartment above her own, proclaimed herself alone in the world and the mother to no one. My three sisters and I were simply the girls whose presence was a practice round for when the important one, the boy, had been born some twenty-eight years ago. I don't mean to be harsh; we all loved him, my sisters and I as much as my parents; and he was the baby to all our attentions, especially when my father's midlife crisis propelled him from our little apartment on Main Street and into the arms of a younger woman. I was not much older than Raoul, but I always thought of him as Mijo—*Mi hijo,* my child, the name we all took to calling him when we passed around the squalling baby night after night and then later, when we patched up his boo-boos and searched the neighborhood for him, "Mijo, Mijo!" until he'd emerge, sheepish, from some other woman's kitchen, cookie crumbs soiling his rosy cheeks and rumpled clothes. Who knew that our attentions, our games with dress-up and dolls, would lead to the smirking disclosure from the police that Raoul was, in fact, dressed in "women's undergarments" when they found his mutilated body. I guess we all assumed that his exploits in the Navy Seals, his machismo in whatever combat the government assigned, was vindication that my father's predictions and threats were unfounded: growing up in a house of all women was not going to ruin Mijo.

My father worked at the naval base for years as a dishwasher. Living in the shadows of a transient world, friends came and went with a regularity I took for granted until I left home and discovered people who'd had friendships for their entire lives. At least we stayed put in town and didn't have to move around the country all the time. Our roots were the church and each other, with girl- and boyfriends passing through like the measles or mumps: everyone had to get them once in a while, but eventually you got over it and got back to normal. Only Marisol had trouble with the "getting over" part, constantly falling in love with enlisted men and the young wives who often accompanied them, causing fear and outrage from my parents with every true love she announced at the dinner table. After Maria got knocked up and thrown out of the house, I was wary of men and the heat they provoked. One by one they got in trouble and got married, my sisters, leaving me and Raoul to stand by Mama until the Navy got him hooked and I ran away. Mama started a keen on the day he enlisted, his eighteenth birthday, a wail so bone numbing and sad that all the dogs in the neighborhood joined in the howling. She cried for days, past even the day he boarded a ship and headed to sea, the day I threw my suitcase into the back of my Vega and headed South on I-95. That was the last day my mother spoke my name, as far as I know. Now instead of calling me by my given name, Clara, I'm simply known in the family as *ese*, "that one."

They found Raoul's body three days after his death, according to the preliminary reports based primarily on the staggering number of flies found in the room. Mama had complained for two days about the constant buzzing she heard, and Carmen, the good daughter who lived in the building next door, dismissed the complaint with her usual shrug and rolled eyeballs. She checked the refrigerator for spoiled goods after noticing a strange smell in the apartment, gave Mama a few more of her stash of Valium, and turned up the afternoon programs while fanning her with a church bulletin. It was perfect fall weather, brilliant blue skies with the occasional fluff of white drifting by, the second week of what would turn out to be a long September in 2001.

On the third day, the eleventh day of September, when the buzzing was unrelenting and there was a definite weight to the smell, Mama saw the stain. She'd been glued to the television all morning, watching smoke and flames and bodies falling, and then the towers themselves toppled, and in the middle of it all, a rusty drop fell from the ceiling.

I was waiting for the subway at Forty-Second Street, checking my messages and trying to discover what was delaying the train. Before the realization of the drama playing out just a few miles south at the World Trade Center, I indulged in a short daydream about how perfect September was in Jerome, about the cool breezes that sometimes came in off the Sound to flutter the curtains in Mama's little apartment on Main Street, and how the days like this always made my heart skip with joy.

I came out of the subway station in a crowd of disbelieving people, my cell phone buzzing before abruptly going dead. I recognized my brother's number, and I knew it was not good. Most people getting calls from their family on that day were accustomed to their relatives checking in when disaster struck, but that was never the case for me. Through years of service in the FBI, when all kinds of crises affected me and my surroundings, never once did my phone ring with a call of concern from my family. Never. This time, again, it wasn't them checking on me. I found out later that it was the police pressing the redial option on Raoul's phone.

I don't know anything about biology or chemistry except in the purely sexual and therefore metaphorical sense, but I wonder how much blood there is in a human body and how long it takes to drain. I wonder what would take so long for the liquid to soak its way through a cheap mattress, a plain wooden floor and some thin insulation, through the ceiling tiles and finally, painfully and yet inevitably, to drip once —and only once—precisely onto the framed picture of Raoul himself centered above the massive RCA television in Mama's living room. I probe these thoughts much like a child is compelled to pick at a scab, despite how painful and often physically ill they made me feel. Was it some kind of liquefaction of the body that caused the fluids to keep coming, when most of the blood must surely have pumped out of him when his penis was severed? He didn't die right away, it seems, but bled to death there above his childhood home. I think I'm the only family member, and perhaps the only person outside of the police, who knows the entire story of my brother's death—the penis severed and shoved into his mouth, his arms and feet bound with silk stockings to the iron bedpost. The brassiere and panties—pulled down to his knees—are being tracked by police investigators snickering about what appears to be expensive Belgian lace underwear. I know all the details, or at least I think I do, but I don't accept the theories the police drop casually about motive. They're not even talking about suspects, just cackling like schoolboys whenever local talk shifts from killing the towelheads to discovering Raoul's naked body tied to that bed. I can tell they are not really investigating the murder—and have no intention of doing so.

"We're on red alert here, ma'am," they say to me. "We don't have the resources to devote to a murder investigation right now and anyway, it seems, well, it seems like a crime of passion. We believe that no one else is really at risk for injury, and therefore it's not a high priority at the moment." They shrug: embarrassed about the crime, about their lame excuses not to investigate. When I arrived in Jerome, after a hellish day trying to get off the island of Manhattan, I found the town in a virtual meltdown, everyone and every building locked down tight. Men with machine guns drove through the quiet streets in military jeeps and stood sentry next to barbed wire unrolled along the isolated road to the base.

The Navy police have been around, though. These guys are not the same ones locking down the base and worrying about terrorism. I know those guys—their eyes are almost always flicking back and forth between the blue sky above and the faces around them. These other investigators are hovering on the fringes of our conversations. I know the witch-hunt has begun and will be conducted in deep secrecy. I am afraid that Mama had no clue Raoul was even in town, and I am certainly not going to be the one who tells her. She's linked his death in her mind to the events in New York, believing him to be the victim of terrorists and a casualty of war. I'm afraid that might be closer to the truth than she realizes, but not in a good way.

I had not been surprised to learn that Raoul was working "off the books" for the FBI. The last time I saw him, he told me a little bit about what he was doing, and where. It scared both of us. He'd been posing as a Muslim, an easy task with his dark, ethnic good looks; running with some pretty fanatical characters. He must have been on to something. How he ended up dead in a small town on the Connecticut shore—that's the mystery here.

Back at the Eagle's Club, I felt the power of the blood flowing through the thick veins that crisscrossed Guy's hand and looped under his arm. The coppery hair on his arm glimmered in the flickering neon Budweiser sign over the bar, and I traced the path of his ropy muscles with an unsteady fingertip. The bar was getting crowded, and I thought I heard Raoul's name in the noise. People were nervous, some sad and others pumped up with bravado, ready to enlist and "go over there to whoop some Arab ass."

"Wanna dance some more?" I asked, circling my hand around a hunk of bicep.

"To this?" Guy jerked his head at the sound of rap coming from the speakers. He looked at me, lowering his eyelids and barely moving his lips. "Let's get some fresh air." His breath came close to my ear and I shivered at the promise it held.

The door slammed behind us, and the music was replaced by the mating calls of a thousand crickets.

"Oh, I never hear this in Manhattan," I murmured. "And look at how many stars there are." Planes had just started to fly again and I watched a thin silver line bisect the sky.

I leaned back until the darkness seemed to come closer, and the brilliance of the stars swam in front of me. Guy was slightly taller than I, and his hand was entangled in the mess of brunette curls that tumbled around my shoulders. His slight pressure on my back kept me from falling over as we walked together to the picnic tables. I fit under his arm, my body engulfed in his. My thumb caught his belt loop as he pulled me around to his mouth.

Lying on the grass, looking into the night sky, every hot summer night of my childhood came back: the makeshift tents we created on the roof, the elaborate ghost stories and, later, smoking pilfered cigarettes with Jaime from 2B, drinking whatever he could sneak from the refrigerator. The same sense, I hadn't lost it yet, waiting for something to happen, the magic—all that goddamned Prince Charming shit we'd been spoon-fed as children, and here I was, still waiting. The stars were obscured by the insistence of those lips, the head bobbing over me, and the soft clicking of a zipper being disengaged. A shaft of light cut across the darkness and then a voice, "Guy. Ya out here? Your wife's on the phone," and the slamming door, the night full with our frantic breathing.

Alone again, I listened to the quiet and the crickets humming their little sex songs. "Sex songs," that's what Raoul used to call them; he chanted some rhyme about the birds and the bees and the crickets rubbing their knees. I smiled, thinking sadly about what a sweet little boy he'd been. Mijo. I hadn't been able to recognize him in the blood-soaked body the police found.

The last time I saw him alive, only his eyes and their defiance were the same. I kept flashing back to his face when he showed up at my apartment a few months ago. I tried to shake off the scene—the tense darting eyes of my brother as he asked me for help. His frustration when I dismissed his story as paranoid nonsense, when I'd agreed with his handlers that he was just imagining things.

"Didn't you learn anything from my mistakes?" I'd asked him. I could still see the tension that gripped his jaw as he spat hateful words into the air between us, the stiffness of his proud back as he disappeared into a night portentous with fog and muffled gunfire.

"What happened to you?" he'd asked. "You know how important this is—or at least you did when it was your ass on the line." He turned away then. "Just because you fucked up, doesn't mean that I'm not right," he said, walking away.

"Wait," I'd yelled at his back. "All right, tell me what you need." I'd run after him, tried to pull him back to my apartment, away from prying eyes, where I could talk sense into his stubborn head. Where I could find out what he was up to, and try to limit the damage. He flipped me off and vanished into the darting crowds on the sidewalk.

I shook my head and got up slowly, taking one last look at the stars. I trailed a finger over his tense back as Guy hunched over the pay phone just inside the door. Sliding onto an empty stool, I signaled for another beer. The old man sitting next to me held out his cigarettes. "No thanks," I smiled.

"Heard about your brother," he said. "Sorry for your loss." He did not meet my eyes.

"Did you know Raoul?" I asked.

"Can't say that I did," he replied. He looked away and inhaled deeply.

No one spoke, no one looked at me. The patrons seemed intent on watching the bartender dry glasses. Her fingernails each blossomed with a painted yellow daisy floating on a chartreuse background. Guy mumbled into the phone behind me, and I let the beer flow down my throat. I leaned my head on my hand and examined the faces around the bar. A few of the older men looked familiar, faces from the days I'd visited this smoky hall with my father and, much later, with Raoul. There were several white guys, some older and others looking depleted from a day of hard labor. A couple of elderly black men, ashy faced and dressed in shiny black suit jackets, a younger black woman sitting with them, humming cheerfully into her makeup mirror. Two white women, about my age, leaned against the bar near me, one of them unable to focus her eyes as she sipped from a frothy orange drink. The other one tapped on the bar a rhythm unrelated to the music pounding from the jukebox. She snapped her gum and her eyes came to rest on me for a moment and then jerked away.

"What about you?" I asked. "Did you know Raoul?"

She pointed at herself and mouthed "Me?" I nodded. She paused. I signaled the bartender for another beer and turned back to the gum-snapper. She sighed heavily and shook her head. "Yeah, I knew him," she admitted. "He used to come in here all the time, especially in the last few weeks. Seemed like he was here at closing time every night."

"Yep," the bartender chimed in. Her round face was serious, the dark eyes thoughtful. "He was always waiting in the parking lot when I came to open up in the afternoon. Came here every day after work, like most of the guys."

"Was he alone?" I asked.

"Mostly, he kept to himself," she said. "Although…" she paused. "He always got a phone call, almost like clockwork, around ten every night. And then he was gone."

"And you never saw him with anyone?" She shook her head. "Are there any…" *How to say this and be politically correct?* I thought. *Hell, I'm in Jerome, no one is politically correct here.* "Do you have any Arabs around town?"

She smiled, then opened her mouth and said the hateful things I was expecting. "Nah, we had some towelheads around, a pair of 'em got beat up last week, but they's not A-rabs. They're Pakis, I heard. Big meeting about tolerance and all that whatnot down at the churches, but hell, those people would just as soon kill you as look at you, I say. Lock 'em up, just in case." She looked at me, continued. "I never saw Raoul with none of them." She paused again. "He could pass though, he had the same look. He could pass."

The snapper chimed in, cheerfully oblivious to the discussion about terrorism. "That's where he was usually sitting," she pointed to my stool. "Funny you chose that spot, too."

I felt a shiver and looked away. The bartender made some clucking noises and put a bowl of peanuts in front of me before returning to her towel. I could see the local news on the television screen at the other end of the bar, but the sound did not penetrate the other noises in the room. The news took a break from the story about the continuing effort to recover people from the Trade Center site, cutting away to Raoul's picture with the word "Murder" dashed across the screen in brilliant red. I wondered how much of the story had leaked out by now, but I did not want to hear the news in the presence of so many strangers. I'd keep my appointment with Detective Barkowski and hope I could find out if the police had any leads on the identity of the killer.

By now, Barkowski would probably have figured out my relationship to the "deceased," so it was unlikely he'd be as talkative as he'd been when I showed him my press credentials. I shut my eyes against the recurring pictures on the television screen, the buildings falling over and over, a body bag carried out, and a screaming woman covered in ash flashing in the red and blue lights of cop TV. I'd been on the scene downtown when my sister had finally reached me, hysterical. It all ran together in my head now. Which part was the burning hole where the towers once stood, and which was the bloody bedroom where Mijo was being wrapped in plastic? My camera had protected me from the horrors, a professional barricade that kept a distance between the bad stuff and me. How had I stood just outside that scene and talked with the cops so calmly? Tonight I was having trouble just sitting on this stool, avoiding the television and the probing eyes around the bar. I longed to slip my arms around Guy's waist and lose myself in his aroma. I almost got off the stool then, but stopped when I heard the sharpness in his voice.

I looked around. It was my turn to avoid people's eyes. The gum chewer slipped in next to me. "I'm real sorry about Raoul," she began. "I didn't mean to upset you, about the chair and all, you know. I just, well, I wasn't sure about you."

"What do you mean?" I asked dully.

"Well, you know, if you were cool or not, you know?" she moved closer, her sour breath warming my cheek.

"So is there something you want to tell me?" I asked again. I didn't want to alienate her, but I was impatient to get to the point. "Were you friends with Raoul?"

"Oh," she laughed. "No. Not in that way. You know, he was kind of quiet and he didn't really talk to anyone here. I tried though." She laughed again. "He was a real looker, your brother. Man, those eyes. We did spend one night together, a long time ago, but ever since then, it's just been casual, like, you know? He wasn't interested in relationships, I guess."

"I see," I said. I did see, because it had happened for his entire life. All the Quiñones kids shared the same features, but somehow they were more attractive in Mijo. Women loved him; they cooed over his big brown eyes with luxurious lashes and sensually curved brows. They naturally smiled when they saw his dimples, deeply embedded in rosy cheeks that framed the full lips, the perfect white teeth. He was always handsome, from the early days when his head was covered in ringlets, to the shaven head required by the service. He was stubbled, thin, and sallow when I last spoke with him, his cheekbones highlighted by the dark shadows playing on his face. But his eyes were always compelling and attractive.

I jerked back to the woman leaning on my arm. "Listen, ah...what was your name again?"

"Shelly." She stuck out her hand.

"Shelly. Right. Nice to meet you. I'm Clara." I grabbed her hand and pulled her closer to me. "Did Raoul say anything to you? Did you see someone threatening him?"

She shook her head, slowly, and then leaned even closer. Cigarettes and whiskey fogged the air between us. "Well," she whispered. "I think he was in some kind of trouble."

This was not much of a leap, considering he'd just been brutally murdered, but I bit down the sarcasm and patted her arm. "What makes you think that?" I asked.

She shrugged, looked around the room, and then began hunting through her purse.

"Please, if you know something, please tell me," I said quietly. "Even if it's a little thing, it might help us find out who killed him."

"Ha," she said. My head snapped back as if she hit me, and I tightened my grip on her arm. "Here it is," she shoved a filthy piece of paper in my hand.

"What is this?" I turned it over and tried to read the smeared writing.

"He dropped it on the floor the last time I saw him," she said.

"Was he alone? Did you talk to him?" I pressed.

"Nah—he was really out of it that night, hardly lifted his head off the bar," Shelly said. "He was wasted on something before I got here, and he didn't stay too long."

She paused, looking at the bar with unfocused eyes. "He did get a call, I think, just before he left, but I didn't see anyone else with him that night."

"A phone call? On this line, or the public phone?"

"The main number," she confirmed. "Old man Peterson was working the bar that night, I think. He took the call." She paused. "His usual calls, like Marian was saying, he got on the pay phone. This was different, he was real nervous after that call, headed out of here right quick."

"Thanks, thanks a lot," I could've kissed her. "This Peterson, is he here tonight?" I slipped the paper in my back pocket.

Shelly shook her head and sniffed loudly. "Nah, he don't usually stay unless the night bartender don't show up."

"But he's here in the daytime?"

"Yeah, mostly." She was getting agitated. "Got any cigarettes?"

"Oh, no, sorry," I said. "Let me buy you a drink, though." She accepted with a smile and a wave to the bartender.

"Can I bum a couple of bucks off you?" she whispered. "I need a smoke real bad, and I'm tapped out."

"Oh, sure." I put a ten on the counter and watched it disappear along with the shot of whiskey that chased her beer. She wiped her mouth then leaned back over my way.

"You know, he wasn't gay," she whispered.

"What?"

"They're saying in the papers, his murder was a gay thing. But he wasn't, you know, that way," Shelly said. Her eyes would not meet mine.

"I know that. I think someone's trying to cover up what really happened," I replied.

She nodded vigorously. "He fucked a lot of girls in here; he was definitely not gay," she said. "Don't know why they're putting that shit in the newspaper."

I was about to answer when a loud group of twenty-somethings erupted into the bar, and Shelly turned away, preening under the flickering bar light. The talk around the bar turned to war again, the kids bragging about signing up and shipping out. Shelly moved away and I sat alone for a while, finishing my drink. Occasionally I glanced back to check on Guy, who was still hunched over the phone.

I slid off the stool and took a breath, trying to adjust to the rolling floorboards. "Ya okay to drive?" the bartender squinted at me.

I waved my hand vaguely before pushing through the door where gulps of crisp air broke some of the beer frothing behind my eyes. It was easy to recognize the bland sedan with the New Jersey plates. I slipped behind the wheel, taking my memories along with the blaring radio and my taillights flickering down the road back to the hotel.

Raoul

HE FOLLOWED THE GROUP to their corner of the room, where elaborate drawings showed the mechanicals of a building he was unable to identify. Walking around the group, he tried to get a better view of the blueprints, but the Leader was throwing too many other papers on the table that eventually obscured the writing. Mohsen tapped him on the shoulder.

"Come," he said.

"Where are we going?"

He got no response, which was the usual reaction to any question from a member of the cell. A smaller group, most with scarves obscuring their faces, stood huddled at the door. At the center, a tall man whom Raoul had only seen at a distance, watched him join the others and then turned to lead them outside.

Raoul pulled his own *shemagh* over his head and tied it tightly. Only his eyes showed as he followed the group onto a school bus idling in the road. The short ride was quiet, the only sound the creaking of the old vehicle as it lumbered along the dark roads. Before he could get a clear sense of their destination, the bus pulled up to a rusted gate and they were hustled quickly through the opening. Tall trees had obscured what was actually a large open meadow, at the center of which sat a camouflaged passenger jet. It was probably a reject from the 70s, something the military might have kept around for target practice. Raoul followed the group onto the plane.

"This is our last meeting, and we will have a short lesson before leaving for our assignments," said the short man known as Ali. Since there were at least a dozen other men named Ali in the loose group, Raoul had nicknamed this one "caterpillar" because of the single bushy eyebrow that bisected his face. Among the group, the caterpillar was easily the most intense. His counterpart, a silent swarthy man whom Raoul thought of as Lurch, television's Addams' family butler, constantly cleaned his weapon or cracked his knuckles in meetings. He was at the front of the plane, sharpening the blade of a box cutter, when the men took their seats.

"Six of you have been trained to fly and there will be two pilots in each plane. Both will be ready to take over the controls—either as a pair or alone—as soon as the cockpit has been secured. Let's get up in the air and we'll run through the demonstration." He strapped into the stewards' jump seat and knocked twice sharply on the door. The engines roared and the plane took off smoothly, despite its apparent age and what Raoul would have thought difficult takeoff conditions. Obviously the machine had been modernized and its apparent age was part of the ruse.

Over the Sound, the caterpillar unsnapped his seatbelt and barked out some numbers. Five of the seated men rose and entered the aisle as Team 1. This was so different from the activities of the cell Raoul had been working with over the past year that he was on high alert. He figured that his group was either going to be integrated into the elite force or they were about to be used as training decoys.

Most of the other team had weapons—the box cutters—which also made Raoul anxious, since he obviously hadn't been included in the trip as an attacker but a victim. He strained to hear the conversation being held at the cockpit door, but the thrum of the engines blocked out whatever he could have picked up. Abruptly, the men turned and returned to their seats as the second group was summoned. Again, Raoul strained without success to hear their charge. And so it was repeated until everyone was seated again. Lurch remained slouched against the wall, gazing at the activity with hooded eyes. After a moment, he stood.

"All of you others, you will be the passengers in our exercise. Okay, Team 2, let's go," he said, his Arabic thick with a dialect Raoul found hard to identify.

Quickly the second team circled, a few grabbed "passengers" and made their way to the cockpit door. A heavy man put his arm around Raoul's neck and dragged him from his seat. Once in the aisle, Raoul kicked out and in an instant had the man on the floor, his box cutter creased against his neck.

Raoul looked up to see Lurch towering over him as he prepared to loosen his grip.

"Finish him," Lurch ordered.

Without hesitation, Raoul slid the knife neatly across the jugular and turned the man's head so that the blood soaked into the carpet beneath the seats. He dropped the man, pocketed the knife, and stood.

"Here is a lesson. Do not underestimate the passengers," Lurch said. "If you do, you will imperil the mission." He held out his hand for the box cutter, and Raoul gave it to him. He had assumed that the kill would promote him from passenger to predator in this little exercise, but Lurch turned away.

Raoul stepped over the man's body until the caterpillar shouted at him. "You! Drag that man to the back of the plane." Glowering at him, the caterpillar signaled Lurch to join him on the jump seat, where they sat, heads together, for several tense minutes, as Raoul pulled the lifeless body out of sight. A red stain marked its passage, and Raoul was careful not to step in the blood when he returned to his seat.

The two leaders rose, and the caterpillar called for Team 1 to practice their moves. Lurch signaled one of the other "passengers," a young, eager man called Zeki, and handed him the bloody box cutter. He smiled at Raoul as he resumed his seat, slipping the weapon into his boot.

Clara

THE HOTEL WAS THE same low budget place you find in third-rate towns, beige everything embellished with the stale aftertaste of cigarettes and sweat. I'd been in places like this before, on the job, pacing the worn carpet until exhaustion propelled me into the stiffness of over-washed sheets. I'd grown too accustomed to the anonymity of travel, and it made me feel comfortable to recognize the paper seal on the toilet and my favorite brand of soap in the plastic dish.

The white noise of hotel air circulation masked the sounds of life outside the door. We were close to the highway here, not far from the shoreline road with its honky-tonk tourist attractions and stop-and-go traffic, but the vacuum seal on the windows could almost numb the reality that I was sitting less than a mile from my mother's apartment.

After Raoul's death, I joined my sisters at Mama's apartment and spent the night on her lumpy old Castro Convertible. Her abusive torrent upon seeing me there in the morning was enough to send me packing. I'd spent the night rocking back and forth on the couch, alternately looking at the shrine to Raoul on the television console and watching the twin towers fall over and over on the screen below. I had friends there, colleagues, and yet I was numb to the possibility of more death. My clothes smelled rank, reeking of adrenaline and fear. It was hard to comprehend that he'd breathed his last in a filthy bedroom one floor above; he'd lived through some kind of hell just a few feet away. I saw in her wild eyes that death had not altered my mother's feelings towards me. I picked up my bag and left silently. Sometimes, you can't go home again.

The second night, Marisol's couch smelled like the used condom I discovered under the cushions, and I walked out before daylight could illuminate the rest of her crushed velvet palace. I tried to reconnect with her, but it was too hard to listen to the anger spewing from her mouth. Long after she stopped talking and left me alone I was still lying awake, listening to a faucet dripping in the kitchen. Marisol was the only one who told me things, but her words were so wrapped up in rage and misinformation that I couldn't trust them. I tried to stretch out on the couch, but when my arm slipped under a pillow, the slippery coldness of the rubber propelled me to the bathroom. Retching always leaves telltale bruising around my mouth. I looked five years older when I confronted my face in the mirror.

"You should have helped him." Marisol said the words that had been echoing in my head for days. I hadn't told anyone about Raoul's attempt to visit me in New York, but she wasn't criticizing a specific inaction on my part, simply my failure as a sister to save my brother's life. I didn't bother to argue that the sisters in town might have had more opportunity to help than I, especially when I'd seen Carmen's eyes at the church. After two days, I was glad to return to the safety and sterility of the hotel room.

I awakened when the late afternoon sun brightened the window. For a moment, I listened to the rumble of trucks on the highway and wondered where I was. It came rushing back, and I pulled the pillows over my head. It wasn't a dream.

I glanced at the clock, my head clear after my first night's sleep in what seemed to be a lifetime. I peeled off my clothes and tossed them on the floor, then luxuriated in a tub full of hot water and bubbles until my skin wrinkled and my hair frizzed in a halo. I studied my knees, the wrinkly skin there, and darkness and lightness of various parts of the body. Nipples poked through the bubbles; I added more water. Thought about Guy, about fucking him, about the taste of him. I let my head sink under the water and groaned.

Bubble baths were a luxury that I'd never have enough of, growing up in an apartment with five kids, one bathroom, and shared tub water every Saturday night. Only Raoul got his own bath because he was a boy. Mama refilled the tub with fresh water for him and lathered his slippery little body with ivory soap and a thick face-cloth. His was the first male body I ever saw naked. My sisters and I marveled at his tiny little penis, when we first saw it in the diaper, laughed when he peed on the wall, admired his potty training. I tried to imitate him once, standing over the toilet, but I was ridiculed and punished for the mess. I wanted so much to be a boy like Raoul. To be beloved like Mijo.

I shivered. The water was growing cold. I shook my head and tried to scrub away the memories with a thin hotel towel. After dressing, I looked through all the drawers in the little room. Tossing aside the Bible, I hunched over the local phone book and tried to remember names of old classmates.

Longtime friends were hard to find in such a transient town, but I recognized a few names. Uncertain about the last names of my old female friends, I hesitated before picking up the phone. The first few calls were unsuccessful: no one home, no one here by that name, no answer. One last try and I got not only the new number but also the new last name of my old pal Mary Kate. Her father, now retired from the auto repair place on Broad Street, seemed to have nothing but time to spend filling me in on all the gossip.

"What did you say your name was?" he asked two or three times. "Can't put a face to it....Who are your people? It sounds familiar...."

I didn't want him to make the connection between the long-lost friend and the dead Navy Seal on the front page of his newspaper, so I hurried him off the line with profuse thanks.

"Yeah, just tell that daughter of mine to get her butt over here more often," he laughed. "You stop by too—and don't wait for her to bring you by—just come on over and visit."

"Okay, thanks." I disconnected the line. I was exhausted just from speaking with the father, and I wasn't sure I was up to rekindling an old friendship. I looked at the phone for a minute, hesitated, and then dialed a New York City exchange.

"Sam," I spoke as soon as the answering machine finished its spiel. "Samantha, pick up the phone, please. It's Clara." I waited. "Dammit. Okay, here's the number I'm at, and you can also call the cellular. I need to talk with you." I hesitated again, giving her the chance to pick up the phone. "Okay, listen, I know you're pissed at me, but something happened and I really need to talk to you. I know you're probably downtown, handing out sandwiches or comforting firemen or something." I sighed. She was still angry about the last time we spoke, when I'd been critical of her latest artistic experiment. "Sam, I'd like to speak to you, if you can give me a call back. My brother's been killed and I'm in Connecticut and, shit, just call me, please."

I hung up. The walls closed in fast and I dressed in a hurry. I left my clothes in a pile and grabbed my keys from the bureau. The reunion with Mary Kate would have to wait.

Raoul

LIFE IN THE BACK alleyways and smoky bars was easy in Jerome. Although he grew up in this town, as one of the "colored" kids Raoul seldom attracted much attention—except on the sports field, and among females of all ages. He found it hard to believe that the years had erased all recognition, until he looked in the mirror and saw a sallow, thin refugee looking back. He'd been a real gung-ho youngster, all ROTC and buzz-cut hair, so with his hair long and beard grown in, even his own mother would have to look closely to recognize her child in this stranger's face. He brushed his teeth, swallowed two aspirin, and headed for work.

In the middle of the morning, he stopped and stretched. He must have had a funny look on his face, but really it was just an idea that struck him suddenly. He clapped a hand to his forehead.

The foreman looked over at him. "What?" he said. "You sick or something? Get a move on."

"Yeah, I think I got a bug or something," Raoul clutched his stomach, retching. The foreman backed away. He was notoriously squeamish.

"Get out of here then," he said. "Come back after lunch if you feel better."

Raoul acted out the sick routine all the way to the gate. Unused to leaving in the middle of the workday, he pulled a cap low over his eyes and trotted quickly to the shadows of the shore road. Following along, he moved stealthily to the van hidden in the bushes and switched some of his belongings from the gym bag into his hiding space below the floorboards. He lugged his bike out of the back and hopped aboard, the handles of the gym bag looped over his shoulder. Once at the gym, he parked against the back door, used his pass to enter, and stowed the bag in his locker. Changing into some more presentable clothes, he walked to the train station and caught the 10:35 to Manhattan.

"Clara," he muttered. She'd never been a reliable sister, but she was his best bet right now. He tried several old phone numbers and lost the signal as the train neared New Haven. Once there, he watched the passengers come and go on the platform. He looked at his watch, and pulled the cell phone out again as the train slowly left the station.

"Ah, what a nice surprise." A man slipped into the seat next to Raoul. From across the aisle, he recognized the two other men. All three were from the mosque, all three dressed in old polyester suits they'd purchased at Goodwill. Every man in the mosque had one: a special gift from the Leader, to help them fit in.

"Salaam," Raoul nodded to each man.

"Are you taking a trip, my friend?" The man Raoul knew only as Ali smiled and looked pointedly at Raoul's clothing. "Such a nice outfit—perhaps you have a date?"

Raoul laughed along with the others. "Actually, I do," he improvised. "A relative of my uncle has arranged for me to meet a young woman, and her family of course, for a tea. It's just a courtesy," he added. "I have no intention of marrying. But I needed to respect my uncle and could not continue to refuse him."

The other men nodded. "Ismail, let me tell you one thing. This meeting, with your uncle's friend, I'm sure it is nothing. But for us, for our Leader, these days are critical. And he must trust the men around him. You understand?" Ali put his hand gently on Raoul's arm. "I am telling you this now. You should not do anything like this without telling the Leader. From now on, everything we do, we do with his approval. We are all part of one organism, and if one of us goes off alone, all of us can suffer."

Raoul put his head into his hands. "I am sorry. I did not think—I wanted to do this one last thing for my family…" He rocked back and forth for several minutes as the other men discussed the situation with each other. They spoke softly, and he was able to pick up only a word or two.

"What should I do?" he asked. "Can you help me? I will turn around at the next station…No one will even know I left town. I, I will go straight to the Leader and speak to him about this."

The men nodded. "That would be wise," Ali said. The train rocked towards the next station. "And your uncle?"

"I will call him. Thank you. I think Allah sent you to find me today, to save me from making a mistake," Raoul said.

"Ismail, you are a good boy, and very devoted that is sure. But you need to let go of the past, and your family, and all the old ties that keep you from being a true servant of God," Ali said. "You should pray on this, and spend some time in the mosque thinking about the path you are taking. It is a special burden, being part of jihad. You are lucky to have been chosen, but you must be sure. And we must be sure of you."

The conductor announced the station and Raoul quickly rose from his seat. "Thank you," he said, bowing his head to each of the men. "Inshallah, we will meet again." He left the train and hurried into the station. They were following him, he was now certain. Without stopping, he crossed the platform and waited for the train back to Jerome. His world had just gotten much smaller.

Clara

"IT'S NICE TO BE home, isn't it?" Today's bartender was a tiny French Canadian man with a wide smile that revealed a perfect set of pink gums, not a tooth to mar the gosh-darn innocence of his face. I fingered the label of the cold beer he placed before me.

"Mmmn." That seemed to be enough of an acknowledgment.

"I don't really care to visit my hometown," he continued. "Up top Maine, that is. Nothing there but poverty. I just go back for funerals and such." He froze. "Oh, sorry, sorry." I nodded solemnly. No problem.

He recovered quickly, smiling brightly again. "But here, now this here town is a treasure. You got that fancy new hotel and all." He shook his head. The rag moved dirty water along the bar in front of me. I lifted my bottle to clear a path.

"I'm staying at the hotel," I said.

"Really?" He shook his head. "I'd a thought you'd be staying with your ma there." His mouth clamped shut. His eyes wandered and he moved away. "Mmmh mmmh mmh." I recognized the language of disapproval.

I felt Guy enter the bar before I saw his blue eyes fixing on me. "Where'd you run off to last night?" he asked. "Gimme a Bud, Pauloo," he barked to the bartender. "Lemme sign the book."

"Hey there, Gaitan," the bartender pronounced his name the French way.

I leaned in to catch a whiff of laundry detergent on the pressed work shirt. He smelled like sweat, the sharp tang of work and dirt with an undertone of Irish Spring. A swig of beer and the empty bottle was replaced with a fresh one. I suppressed a belch and watched him sign a composition book creased with age, dirt, and bar spillage. "Guy LeBeau." His flowery penmanship reminded me of hours spent hunched over lined paper, sweating with frustration until the ballpoint invariably spat a perfect blue puddle onto the page, and it was crumpled into the trash bin. The tip of his tongue appeared in the left corner of his mouth, forehead wrinkled in concentration.

"So, what happened to you last night?" he asked again, then took a long draught of beer. He looked me over, waiting for a response. The blue of his eyes against the clear whites, and then the deepness of the dark pupil drew me in, and it wasn't until the corners of his eyes crinkled that I answered.

"How's Bambi?" I pulled on the bottle.

"It's Barbie," he corrected me. "And I really don't want to talk about her."

The five o'clock shadow sprouting on his chin was mostly gray, and I noticed then a thin crack bisecting his front tooth. The afternoon sun slanting through the window glinted off his arms, and when he moved, a shaft of light illuminated the gold on his finger. I could hear my heart pounding a beat as I walked across the room. My ears rang with the heavy bass from the jukebox in the corner.

I slipped a dollar bill into the machine and studied the song choices. "There's an awful lot of shit-kicker music around here," I mused. "Sometimes you'd never guess you're in the middle of Connecticut."

"Not much like the big city, eh?" Guy leaned against the machine and waited for the song to start. "How come you're still here then?" he asked. "Why didn't you hit the road right after the funeral?"

I shrugged and concentrated on the music.

"I know you're not here to help your mama, cuz I know you didn't go home last night," he continued.

"So what's your point?" I turned to confront him, and my cheeks flushed from the heat and the beer and the proximity. "You want me to leave town?"

"Nah," he flashed a toothy grin. "You're definitely trouble," he said and shook his head. "But it seems like I've been waiting for trouble for a long time."

Jesus, the clichés were coming fast and furious. I always loved soap operas. I put my bottle on the table and moved in front of him, my fingers hooking the belt loops of his jeans.

"Come on, cowboy," I said. "Just this one dance."

Patsy Cline's "Crazy" was playing, and smoke blurred the edges of the room. We danced. Jean to jean, slow caress of fabric and thigh, the rasp of his cheek against my ear.

I felt Guy's hand press against my back and I relaxed into it. My back and neck were so tense, and my eyes burned from the smoke. "Mmmmnn," I felt rather than heard the satisfaction in Guy's voice, the promise and expectation in one low groan. I tried to let go, to concentrate on the sway of the music and the heat building in the base of my belly, but it wouldn't click. Damned brain.

"Guy," I pulled away a little.

"Yeah baby," he nuzzled closer into my neck.

"Did you know Raoul?" I waited a second. "My brother—the one who…"

"I know who he is," he interrupted.

"So? So you knew him?"

"Nope."

I nodded, waiting for whatever he had to tell me. You learn more by keeping your mouth shut, especially when the person being questioned has something to hide. The song ended, melded into Whitney Houston's decades-old, top selling screech.

We swayed together, sighing. Guy was not going to give me anything. "You know some guy named Peterson?" I prodded.

He pushed his head into my neck as the song ended and was replaced by Aerosmith, definitely changing the mood in the room.

Guy looked at me. "Peterson." I nodded. "The bartender? He's just an old coot, what do you want with him?" he asked.

"He might know something about Raoul," I said. "Is he here?"

He looked around. "Nope." Guy leaned closer and breathed into my ear. I felt my legs go soft and my belly fluttered. What was it about the smell of this man that drove me to distraction?

"Clara." He melted my insides. His tongue flicked my earlobe. I forgot about Peterson, about Raoul. I forgot my own name. The song ended and still we swayed there for a minute. He drew back, looked over my shoulder and then into my eyes. "How about a game?" he whispered.

I followed him to the pool table and watched as he pulled balls from the pockets. This was not exactly what I had in mind as a distraction, but I was willing to play with Guy a little while longer. He handed me a cue and I looked for chalk. It'd been a long time since blue chalk had stained my fingertips, but the slide of the cue on my fingers awakened an almost sensual recollection of hustling in pool halls near the base, pretending to be a dumb local and paying the bills with my share of the pot.

"You break," he crossed his arms and thrust out his hips, rocking back on his heels until I could clearly see the outline of his erection pressed against well-worn denim.

"Are you sure?" I asked sweetly, bending over the table. I looked away from his nod and cracked the cue ball with a force that sent it flying off the table. Old ploy from the hustling days. Never let 'em see you shoot first.

Guy picked up the ball and rolled it along the table, the crinkles deep around his eyes. "Maybe we should make a little wager before we start," he suggested.

"Are you going to try to take advantage of me?"

More leering smiles. What the hell. "Name it," I said.

"Winner chooses."

"Let's go," I agreed. I turned to the bar for another round while Guy preened over his first two shots.

It was a quick enough game, once I decided I'd had enough with the feminine wiles. "Winner chooses," I reminded him.

"What's it going to be?" he asked. The sticks were back in the rack and another pair moved towards the table, emptied of all striped balls and the eight.

"You want to take two cars?" I asked. "Or I can give you a lift back here later."

He paused to light up a cigarette and then squinted through the smoke. "Oh. I have the key to the back storage room…there's a couch in there. Where do you want to go?"

My fingers walked up his belly. "My place." I flattened my hand against his chest, lightly skimming over an erect nipple. "Ready?"

I guess I should have learned by now that men, especially men of a certain age, don't like aggressive women, especially when it comes to sex. I could practically see his cock shriveling up, and I took a breath before he could answer. "Just a sec," I moved away. "Gotta use the ladies."

I figured he might be gone or on the phone when I came out, and I was surprised that he was sitting apart from the other men at the bar.

"Everything cool?" he exhaled and put out the butt.

I nodded and slipped into the chair beside him. We didn't speak for a while, both intent on our drinks and how to back away gracefully from what was clearly not going to happen between us.

"Listen, I got to get home to the wife and all," he shrugged.

"I understand," I nodded. "Family obligations and all that. Yeah. I better be going too; I have to pack."

He nodded. We both looked away at the same time, and then I felt his hand on my knee. "I can't," he began.

"It's okay." I waved away his protestations.

"I'm not shitting you. You make me feel….young, and I don't know, alive again. And I do feel like I've known you my whole life," he said.

I shook my head. "It's okay, I get it—you have a wife and you have to go home. No biggie."

"Let me say this. There's something different. I know you thought I was giving you a line the other night, when I asked if we'd met before, but I really feel that way. Like I know you," he said. He shook his head and tightened the grip on my knee. "I wish I wasn't married, but I am. I wish I could explore this thing with you, because I never had this connection with a woman before."

I had to look away then. The tears came up so quickly that I didn't know quite what to do. It all boiled over, the loneliness and the loss and the longing, and I hunched my shoulders over with my hands tightly clasped in my lap.

"Are you okay?" He leaned closer, his hand warm on my shoulder now.

The kindness, that was too much. And the connection, just like I'd felt it myself. I shook my head, no, I'm not all right, and felt the tears slide down my face.

"Dammit," I muttered. I wiped my eyes and stood up quickly. "I've got to get out of here." I leaned over and kissed him quickly on the cheek. "Take care of yourself, love," I whispered.

There are no graceful exits in these circumstances and fortunately Guy did not sit back and let me leave. I couldn't have driven back to the hotel anyway, and the comfort of his arms around me was absolutely necessary at that moment.

All the tears came out, the anxiety and frustration of the past few days that I hadn't been allowed to share with my family. I soaked through both shoulders of Guy's shirt before I slowed down to take a breath. He silently handed over a much-needed napkin, and I tried to get control of my breathing. His back shielded me from the prying eyes at the bar and I leaned into him.

"I'll be okay," I said. "Thanks."

He rested a hand on my knee and brushed the hair back from my face. Blue eyes searching mine, brow knitted in worry.

"Really," I said again. I tried to smile. "I needed that, I guess."

"You have to take care of yourself," he stroked my cheek with the backside of his hand. "I'm going to worry about you."

"I'll be fine." Maybe if I kept repeating it, I'd start to believe it.

"I think I should follow you to the hotel," he said, sitting back.

I shook my head. No.

Of course, by then we'd moved beyond the sexual tension to a different and scarier place. He followed me to the hotel.

We sat in his car, listening to "pillow talk" on the radio. Hands entwined, windows fogging over. I was so tired and yet absolutely awake, my entire body aching to be touched.

The song changed to "Lady," and Guy reached over and flicked off the radio.

"Not a Kenny Rogers fan, eh?" I asked.

"Wedding song," he grunted, lighting a cigarette. His face was turned in profile as I watched the match flare.

"Ahh."

A car pulled into the parking lot. Silently we watched the couple emerge, then wrap themselves together and walk like a four-legged creature into the hotel. My mind raced, thinking about what to do next, what to say. "Christ, I feel like I'm in high school again."

"Why?"

I was startled. "Did I just talk out loud?" I asked. He nodded. "Oh, sorry," I reached over to grab my bag. "I do that sometimes. Talk to myself. I forget I'm alone, and then I end up doing it when other people are around, and you know, it gets to be pretty embarrassing. And then I can't stop talking—like this—and I have to go before I say something I don't want to say." I pulled the door handle. "Listen, you've been terrific, you really saved my life tonight and I'm, well, I'm glad, about everything." I stood up and bent over into the door. "So, take care and well, have a nice life."

I closed the door and waited for something, a response, the window being opened, his door opening, but there was nothing except crickets and traffic, and I hurried into the beige comfort of my room.

Raoul

AFTER WASHING HIS FACE and changing his clothes, Raoul was back on his customary stool in the lodge, nursing a PBR and pretending to be drunk. No one in this crowd knew him, not one of them realized he had been the high school jock whose four-year record of running rings around the opposition still stood unchallenged ten years later. Nor did they identify him as the brother of the rogue FBI officer whose investigation of gun-running for the Puerto Rican independence movement nearly emptied the town just a few years ago. No, to these patrons he was a loner, a drunken Hispanic who paid as he drank, never bought a round and never, ever, flirted back with the women who were drawn to his dark good looks. His tired air and permanently dirty fingernails identified him as one of their own, in the area that mattered most: he was clearly a working stiff, and sitting at this bar every night was his only relief. They left him alone.

As was his usual routine, Raoul finished two beers, chased it with a shot, and then visited the men's room. The public phone rang once, and he turned around, lifted the receiver, listened, and hung up.

"Night," he mumbled to the bartender, slipping on his jacket. Before she could answer, he was gone. Walking through the back woods on a trail only he knew, Raoul chuckled. He had programmed his computer to call the public phone at about the same time every night. If someone else got to it first and said "Hello," the line was disconnected. When he answered, his own voice cheerfully announced that it was time to hit the road.

In his van later that night, he entered the new information into his coded log-book, stored it in the hidden flap on the bottom of his gym bag, and laid on the thin mattress listening to Urdu language tapes on his Walkman. After midnight, he got up, turned on the small laptop he pulled from beneath the passenger seat of the van, and sent the new information to his handlers. The message bounced back, several times, until Raoul tried the alternative account that had been given for emergency correspondence. Nothing.

At 2:00 a.m., he walked down to the beach and dialed his contact. There was no response. Now he became concerned. Sitting on a log, he rolled a cigarette on his thigh and struck a match on his shoe. Inhaling deeply, he waited for a call back. After twelve anxious minutes, his phone vibrated.

"Yes?"

"It's morning in England," a rasping voice replied.

"Quite so," Raoul chirped. "What the hell is going on?"

"Well, old boy, we've been shut down. Told by the top to refocus and all that. Time to report back to base. Cheerio!"

"Wait. No! I've got information. They're going to hit the World Trade Center. And it's going to be soon." Raoul heard the dial tone.

He dialed again and again, pulling out his notebook to find other contact numbers. Finally, he sighed and pocketed the phone. "I spend a year here and now they want to pull the plug? No way," he shouted at the sky.

He paced back and forth, lighting cigarette after cigarette until his supply was gone. At about 3:00 a.m., he dialed the numbers again, only to hear the same message that the phone had been disconnected. He deleted the number and tossed the phone into the water.

Slowly, Raoul walked back to the van, unlocked the door, and slipped into a sleeping bag. Looking at the sky through the moon roof, he sighed. So, he was on his own. Like his sister before him, Raoul was not hindered by that realization. He'd always preferred to work alone, and this would be no exception. He would continue to play his role with the Pakistani men and see where it led. In the meantime, he needed to find a way to get a message to Washington.

Clara

IT WAS A LONG night, sleepless and airless, and after I emptied the minibar, a little fuzzy around the edges. I've never been married, well, not for long enough to count anyway, and so I felt a kind of angry respect for the institution that was keeping Guy from my bed. Or maybe that was just an excuse, and if he really wanted me, ack—who knew about men? I shook my head over and over, staring at the mirror until my brown eyes burned angrily. I watched the sun lighten the sky over the back parking lot, and I thought about leaving town without understanding everything.

What if I stayed? What made me think I'd be able to figure out all the questions I'd been dodging for years, and find out what Raoul had been doing—and what he knew, and who he talked to—before he died. I'd bombed out of my own efforts to save the world, and I didn't want to let Raoul's death be written off as some kind of tawdry affair. He was doing something important, and someone wanted him to stop. Who? why?—all those questions seemed blurred in the face of the massive disaster in New York. Maybe the answers were there—but then, why was he here, pretending to be a bum, and hanging around Jerome like a lost soul on a bar stool?

I had to face that the bigger questions on my mind were never going to be resolved. It was too late to recreate a connection with my family, and it would be impossible to find my father if he hadn't even shown for the funeral of his only son. Raoul was gone now and I couldn't change what had happened to him, but I could try to find out who did it. I was arrogant, my boss had been accusing me of that for years, and here I was again, thinking that I could wrap things into neat little packages, signed-sealed-and-delivered, when no one else could. No loose ends, I'd been taught back in the academy years ago. That was still my policy, although it was harder to manage as a journalist than a cop.

I unpacked my bag and stripped off my clothes. The pile of dirty stuff was beginning to topple so I shoved it all into a hotel laundry bag and hung it on the door. A hot shower made me sleepy and I rolled into a towel. The phone rang and I jerked awake. "Hello?"

"I can't get you out of my head," Guy whispered.

"Mmmm."

"No, I mean it," he hissed. "What am I supposed to do now?"

"I don't know," I said. "I don't know anything anymore."

"Shit." He hung up.

I studied the interesting pattern on the ceiling tiles for a moment. My heart pounded the way it does whenever the phone interrupts my sleep. The water stains formed and reformed and began to resemble crime scene photographs. I closed my eyes and tried to focus my thoughts, focus on the case rather than my raging hormones, breathing deeply and wishing I'd stuck around for the more than one yoga class.

"Dammit." I rolled out of bed and looked at the clock.

I called the desk to extend my stay in the hotel. "I don't know when I'm leaving," I said. "Give me another week, and I'll let you know my plans."

I warily punched in the phone number Mary Kate's father had passed along. It rang three times and I was about to give up when a familiar voice answered in a way that sent me back about twenty years. "Flannigan's Fish House. What's the catch?"

"Jesus H. Christ, Mary Kate, haven't you gotten tired of that line yet?"

"Hey who the hell is this?" she laughed. "You want some fish or what, Clara Voyant?"

She remembered. Clairvoyant was my moniker in the old days, just as she was Flashy Flannigan, the only girl in Jerome who could catch a fish in the potty river that bisected the town—clean it, cook it over a campfire, and eat it, too. "And she lived to tell the tale," I marveled.

"Bet your ass," she chuckled. "What the hell—Quiñones, is that you? Where you at, kiddo? My pops told me somebody called but he's got a touch of the Al's hammer, so he couldn't sort out who it was."

"Yeah, well, I was kind of vague," I admitted.

"Since when? I never. Nope, the Clara Quiñones I remember didn't know the meaning of the word vague," she grunted. There was a moment of uncomfortable silence, and then she let out a lungful of air. "Oh, Clara, I was so sorry to hear about Raoul. You should've called me, you know? You don't have to be vague with me, no matter what."

"Mary Kate, thanks…I didn't even know where you were living. I just gave it a shot when I called your father," I said. "I've gotten some pretty strange reactions from people about Raoul, you know, so I wasn't sure how he'd react."

More silence. "Anyway," I offered. "I'm here, I don't know for how long."

"Okay," she said. "So, where are you staying—with Marisol? Carmen? Don't tell me you're staying with your mother!"

"Actually, none of them. I'm at the hotel. I tried to be with them, but, well, you know the story."

"Yeah, I remember," she said.

"So, let's get together while I'm here," I suggested. "What about tonight?"

"Oh, huh, well, things are kind of busy around here, let me check," she hesitated.

"You got to check with your calendar or your man?" I sassed.

"Well, in addition to running a business and keeping up with my husband, I have a couple of pain in the ass kids who think I'm their damned servant. Give me your number and I promise I'll call you back later," she said.

Well, at least there was one friend who was still talking to me, I mused as I drove over for the breakfast special at Porgy's place down the road. The crowded room was filled with the loud voices of waitresses sparring with workers. Sexual innuendo interspersed with sports, punctuated by discussion about some local political controversy about which I knew nothing and cared less. There was a haze over the smoking section that drifted into the "non-smoking" room. This, too, was different from Manhattan, where smokers huddled on sidewalks in front of virtually every office building on every street. I ordered a western omelet and coffee, breathed in the forbidden smell of long-abandoned tobacco, and waited for the caffeine to kick in. My stomach soured when I saw a post-mortem shot of Raoul on the front page of my neighbor's paper. He looked like Jesus Christ, but those were not the sentiments in the headlines.

My father's one and only kitchen skill was the creation of huge western omelets, bulging with onions and peppers, a little chopped ham if he had it, and some American cheese just barely melted inside the fluffy eggs. I often ordered it during times of stress. This time my comfort food couldn't distract from the headlines: "No Clues in Sex Murder." I knew the story would leak eventually, small town police being human just like the rest of us, but I'd hoped for a few more days before the fan started spraying the detritus of my family into the public consciousness. I could only imagine the protective shield my sisters would construct around our mother, trying to protect her from the painful truths about her favorite child. My mind wandered to our absent father. I had no idea if Papa even knew about Raoul's death, and with that thought I paid the check and slipped into the perpetual and inexplicable traffic into town.

I had another shot at Barkowski set for 10:00 a.m., and I would have been early except it took ten minutes to find a parking spot. Since when had downtown become so popular? In police headquarters, I got stuck in line behind a man whose red face and breathless demeanor made me nervous. I paced back and forth for a while, and finally dropped onto a cold concrete bench to wait for a satisfactory end to the puffer's quest for information from the monosyllabic cop behind the desk. The lobby of the station was cold and dark, an echoing chamber of wasted taxpayer money. I wondered if they'd updated the courtrooms upstairs, but the lost souls smoking outside the stairwell stifled any urge to explore.

I sat on the bench and thought about my first meeting with the detective. He had taken a long time to study my credentials. His buzz cut hair was so blond it was almost invisible, but it matched nicely with his straight posture and crisp blue uniform. Only the gun sagged on this guy. The chief was keeping a tight ship—no donuts for these cops. When Barkowski finally left me alone I stared into the two-way mirror until the disarray of my hair seemed alive and my brown eyes blurred into smudges.

"Don't look in a mirror too long, you'll see the devil," Mama used to admonish us. *She was right,* I thought as I turned away.

When he came back into the room, Barkowski left the door open and tossed my press pass across the table. "We have no comment at this time," he said. He crossed his arms over the tautness of his torso and waited for my argument.

"I hope not," I agreed. That seemed to startle him. "But I have to wonder who leaked the details I heard on the television yesterday, and the stuff on the front page of the newspaper."

"That did not come from this office."

"No," I interrupted. "It never does."

"I'm not going to argue with you," Barkowski said. "I have nothing further for you."

I stood up and buttoned my jacket. Taking a breath, I willed myself to remain calm. "Officer, I appreciate your position. And I assume that you checked on my background." I looked him straight in the eye. He nodded. "So you know about my work with the feds. I'm a professional. I used to be their top forensic photographer. I think I can help you with this case. I'm asking you to let me try."

"Yeah, but, he's your brother," Barkowski objected. "You shouldn't be here—you shouldn't even look at these pictures."

"But I can help you, and you know it," I said. "Plus, I have connections you've never even dreamed about. And I'll use whatever it takes to find the scum that killed my brother." I leaned towards him. "I'll be back tomorrow morning, okay? And you'll talk with me then."

"You can come back on Monday, but I'm not promising you anything," he shook his head. "I'll have to talk with the chief about this."

"Tell him hi for me," I said. "We went to high school together."

I had stuck out a hand that he first looked at for a beat and then shook.

Now it was Monday and I sat waiting in the lobby. Maybe he was right, and I shouldn't even look at the pictures. But I had to try.

I walked back and forth, my guts churning with indecision. I wanted to see, but I didn't want to know. I needed to do this—for Raoul, for closure; to clear his name, to know what happened. I just needed to know.

In the middle of my pacing, Barkowski appeared and called my name.

"Come on," he buzzed the door. "Chief Franklin wants a word with you." I felt like a prisoner on my way to a cell, but I straightened my shoulders as the door opened.

"Hey, Mark." I forced a smile as the chief looked over his half glasses. He'd been a high school football star, and the years had added only gray sideburns to his lanky good looks. "You haven't changed a bit," I said.

Did he remember the differences between us in the good ol' days, the staggering confidence of the jocks as they sneered at my friends and me, "greasers" huddled by the gym doors puffing on reefer and cigarettes and trying to survive adolescence? I doubt I ever passed his line of vision except as background color to his golden life. We'd never exchanged a single word back in the day.

He hesitated a moment too long before answering. "Yeah, right, Clara," he said. "It's been a while." He motioned towards a chair.

I shook my head and remained on my feet. "What's it going to be, Mark?" I asked. "Are you going to let me help you on this?"

He sighed. "Can you just sit down for a minute?" He looked at me sadly. "I'm real sorry about your brother, Clara, but you're putting me in a bad position here."

"Look, I know there's a conflict." I leaned forward, pressing my weight onto his desk. "But I also know that you don't have the manpower or expertise to solve this crime alone. I can help you. I've done this kind of thing before." I waited until his eyes met mine. "You need me," I said. "Listen. I don't know if you know this, but Raoul was working undercover here and the agency isn't going to claim him. He was onto something here, something big. The military police, they're going to want this covered up real quick, and so no one is going to care what happened to Raoul. I need to do this, Mark." I backed into the chair and sat down heavily. "You've got to let me in on this—we can do it off the record, if you'd feel better."

He shook his head. The muscles in his neck and jaw seemed cramped with tension. "Clara," he said, looking again at the papers on his desk. "If what you say is true, why aren't the feds here, investigating what happened to their guy? With these attacks in New York, we're all on high alert. And now you're telling me your brother was here chasing terrorists? This is not right."

"I know that better than anyone," I said. "But I have to do something. I can't just walk away."

"Okay, tell me something. What are you doing these days? Who are you working for?" I figured he knew the answer so I waited him out. He folded his arms and we looked at each other for a minute. "Say I let you work the case. What makes you think the feds are going to let you anywhere near this? What about your boss? What about your family? How am I going to explain your involvement to the press? Hell, you are the press, lady."

"First of all, I know you've already talked to Hastings, and I know he would be okay with this, because he hasn't called me in." I searched his face for affirmation. "Okay, and I assume he filled you in on the family stuff, and you know that won't interfere with my work. It never has." I waited to see if he was going to push me to discuss my past, or to talk about what I'd been doing recently, but he just tapped his fingers on the blotter.

"So you want to redeem yourself by finding your brother's killer? Are you trying to get your old job back with the FBI?" he asked. "The way it looks to me, it's not going to be so easy." Mark paused, appraising me.

"Look, Clara," he said, exhaling. "I haven't talked to Hastings or anyone else in D.C. I'll be honest with you. I didn't want to tip them off about the case. I don't need any more federal agents running around in my town. And I didn't want them to know that you're sitting on my doorstep asking for a piece of this case."

"I appreciate that," I said. My mind was clicking into overdrive. "Listen, Mark. I think I was one of the last people to hear from Raoul," I offered. "I knew he was in some kind of trouble. Whatever it is, it's not going to be pretty. I know the family is not going to like it, and probably the military brass won't be very happy either. But I'm not going to back away from the truth."

"I don't know." He studied the wall behind me. "The state cops have already been here, and you saw the MPs at the scene. It's not up to me anymore. They've taken all the evidence and shut it down."

We sat silently for a minute, listening to the muted voices in the hallway. "Maybe you don't want to solve it," I said.

He sighed.

"Maybe you want the feds to come in here and take over, so you don't have to do the dirty work," I pushed.

He stared at me then. "Is that what you think?"

"I'm beginning to believe it," I nodded. "I think you have gotten used to presiding over traffic violations and domestic disturbances, and you don't want to get dirty looking into a messy murder like this."

"That's not fair," he said. "We don't have the resources."

"I can help you."

Again, silence.

I gave it a beat, and then pushed at him again. "Do you know where Raoul was living?"

"Yeah," he said slowly. "In the apartment on Main Street."

"I don't think so." I leaned forward. "Doesn't it strike you that the only furniture in the place was that old brass bed? No bureau, no clothes in the closet—nothing in the other rooms. No chair, no couch? Hardly anything in the kitchen, and only a toothbrush in the bathroom. So where did he really live?"

Mark shook his head.

"That was simply a drop site, maybe only set up for the undercover operation. He wasn't staying there, I know it. And when I find his home, I find his stuff—and then maybe I can help you find out who did this," I continued.

"That's a lot of maybes," he replied. "I honestly have no idea where your brother was living, and as far as I'm concerned, the only thing we need is the crime scene. And to my eyes, it looks like a lover's quarrel."

"So you are going to let it go. You're not even going to try and find out what happened, are you?" Our eyes met and held in a long pause. "I know you have no reason to believe me, but Raoul was most definitely not gay. This was not what it seems—it was staged to throw you off. And I guess it worked. You're not going to investigate." I sighed, looking away.

"Clara, are you married?" Mark asked softly. "Have you thought about what this investigation might do to your family?"

I shook my head.

"Well, I think about my family all the time, and I want to protect them. If the crime was sex-related—and I'm not saying it was or wasn't—you don't want that dragged through the newspapers, do you? What would that do to your mother?" he paused. "And maybe you're right. Maybe Raoul's death was related to the terrorist attacks, but maybe it wasn't. I don't want that stuff in my town. I need to protect my town, and my family."

"Protect them from what? From this case?" I laughed. "Mark, you can't protect them from things like this. It happened. Raoul was murdered. Here, it happened here in your little town. And you can't ignore it."

"Let's say it was related to the attacks in New York," he said. "That is so clearly above our capabilities here. I can't take on that kind of investigation. I don't have the manpower, or the expertise. I don't have the money. And the military folks are not going to help us. Hell, they practically threw the case at me when they saw the crime scene. So what can I do?"

"I have the expertise, and the contacts. Let me work on it." There was a long silence. Mark studied his hands splayed on the desk, practically covering the papers there.

"Okay," he whispered.

"Okay? That's it? I'm in?" I asked, jumping to my feet.

"This is totally off the record," he pointed at me. "See if you can find out where he was really living, what he was doing in town. No grandstanding, no talking to the press, no heroics. And if you write about this—well, I'll shut you down so fast."

"Agreed," I said. I almost interrupted him to tell him I was a photographer, not a writer, but I got the message and didn't want to quibble over the details. "Where do we start?" I asked.

"I'll share what I have, but you have to tell me everything," he said. "I mean everything. Even if you find something…unpleasant…about Raoul."

"Absolutely."

I stuck out my hand. "Can I have the file now?"

He passed a binder to me, thick already with autopsy reports and photographs.

"I'll work out of my hotel room," I said. "Here's my cell number. Don't give it to anyone else." I shoved the file into my backpack, took Mark's card with his private number scribbled on the back.

"Call me when you've gone over the reports," he said. "I can meet you outside the office so we don't attract any attention." I could see dark shadows playing under his eyes. This was a big gamble for him, and if word of my involvement leaked out, it would be the end of his career.

"I appreciate this. I won't let you down." I turned to leave. "You won't regret this."

"I better not," he said softly. "I hope you know what you're doing." He was still talking when I opened the door. "I hope to Christ I know what I'm doing."

I stepped into the hallway and leaned against the closed door, hugging the bag to my chest. My heart pounded and I closed my eyes, trying to slow my breathing. I could hear Mark's voice through the door but his words were not clear. An officer came down the hall and I adjusted the strap on my shoulder.

"Can I help you, ma'am?" he asked.

I resisted an urge to smack the youngster. "Thanks, I was just leaving." Steeling myself for the work ahead, I plunged into the brilliant sunshine on Main Street.

Raoul

BEFORE DAWN, RAOUL MADE his way downtown and opened the service door with a master key he'd lifted from the super's belt more than a decade ago. He slid lightly over the stairs, opened his apartment door, and engaged the lock slowly. Shoes deposited by the door, Raoul padded into the small kitchen and poured water and coffee into an ancient percolator sitting by the rusty stove. He flipped up the switch and rinsed the single cup resting in the sink. He dumped a packet of flax, whey powder, and some tofu into a high-tech blender with a banana and a handful of strawberries.

After guzzling the breakfast drink, he stripped and showered, donning the anonymous blue work pants and shirt required for all laborers at the pier. He slicked his curly hair back, tied a tight ponytail, and topped the outfit with a nondescript trucker's cap. Tucking his dog-eared paperback Koran into a pocket, Raoul carried his shoes into the hallway and put them on. His coffee thermos jammed under one arm, he avoided the other tenants and walked to the waterfront via back alleys and woodland trails. By 6:00 a.m. he was seated at the gate, eyes alert behind mirrored shades. He sipped at the coffee, watching as men came and went from the busy industrial park.

"Morning." The usually taciturn Khalid stood next to Raoul. He rose, nodded at the older man. "Tonight, it's important. After work we meet at the mosque. Can you make it?"

Raoul nodded and watched as the older man walked away. Once clocked in, Raoul had trouble concentrating. His heart raced, and he found it difficult to focus on his job as the hours dragged by. Operating a small forklift, he was well away from the heavy lifting that most of the crane operators did, and he was able to take five every so often by idling behind some towering barrels and lighting up a smoke.

At three, the whistle liberated him from anticipation and Raoul joined the flow of men at the time clock. The sun was still high and heat radiated off the asphalt parking lot. No air moved, despite the proximity to the water, and Raoul remembered the "dog days" of youthful Augusts past—days of chasing ice cream trucks and begging for popsicles, days when Raoul watched behind a chain-link fence as his wealthier friends swam in the clubhouse pool. He had learned to keep his cool, even as an adult under pressure, and so he was the only man walking off the grounds each summer afternoon with a dry shirt.

A horn tooted, a truck slowed, and Raoul jumped into the bed, settling among several other workers, all of whom were using their work shirts as makeshift sun hats. He quickly tied his shirt loosely around his cap, the hem tickling his shoulders while it shaded his neck. No one spoke, no one made eye contact. Raoul pulled the brim of his hat lower and watched the others as the truck sped out of town.

They arrived at another ramshackle little airport, this time with a tiny plane that barely held the seven men. The pilot, someone Raoul had never seen before, took off quickly over the bumpy pasture, barely missing a lone pine tree as he pulled hard on the stick. The Leader, a plain-spoken man whose thick accent rendered most of his instructions useless, pointed out various landmarks. They followed the sun, heading west along the shore, until the glimmer of tall buildings took shape through the brown smog.

"Manhattan," the Leader grunted.

Mohammed, the most outspoken of the group, began to regurgitate the ideas heard on Al-Jazeerah television each week. "This is the center of their economic power, the organizations that exploit and impoverish the rest of the world. These capitalist devils take whatever they want, and leave us to feed on the scraps."

The pilot muttered some numbers into the radio and then swooped closer to a busy airport. It seemed a dangerous maneuver to Raoul, who winced at the proximity of the larger jets coming in for a landing.

"This is LaGuardia Airport," the Leader said. "Look closely—see the location is on the north shore of the island. The other airport, JFK, is on the south. You'll be leaving from here, and following this route. Watch now for landmarks. Your best choice is to find the big river and follow it south. Like so."

The plane banked a bit and landmarks became distinguishable: Empire State Building, Citicorp, Woolworth, and then the Statue of Liberty herself. Raoul was quiet, copying the other men, some of whom had obviously never seen these sights and were trying hard to restrain their enthusiasm. Two of the younger men—Raoul thought of them as "the boys"—seemed frightened by the density and activity of the city.

"Look," Fayed said to Hussein, "there are so many flying things in the sky. How can we manage this? We will be hit by the others."

The Leader looked back at them, shaking his head. "Believe me, young man, in the plane you will be flying, no one will be able to stop your mission." He nodded towards the left side of the plane. "Now, see those two towers? We are responsible for the one on the left. Look carefully. You must be able to tell which one to hit."

Raoul's stomach did a somersault and he grabbed for the airsick bag. Turning away, he used the moment to calm his breathing. He knew the target. Now he just needed to get the information to D.C.

"What's wrong, Ismail?" the Leader chided. "Are you ill? I thought you were one of the strongest stomachs in our team!"

Raoul quickly rolled up the bag. "No problem, sir," he said. He knew that any sign of weakness would mean the end of his role with this group, and no doubt the end of his life as well. "I was just getting rid of my gum. You know me, sir—I have no fear of flying. No fears at all."

After a long stare at Raoul, the Leader turned away and spoke softly to the pilot. The plane banked and made another slow pass by the towers.

"See the dark band there—about a third of the way down?" the Leader pointed. "That's the optimal place to target. Don't go too high, it will lessen the impact. And you won't have much time to get lower, although, Inshallah, you will be able to get closer to the center of the tower." He looked back at the men. "Any questions? Anyone need to take another look? Ismail? You got it?"

With a simple flip of his hand, the Leader turned away. The plane banked steeply again, passing closely by the Trade Center before heading out to the open sea. Without warning, the pilot rolled the plane. Several of the men exhaled sharply, but Raoul remained cool. His eyes stayed on the back of the Leader's seat, his hands loose on the armrests. Next to him, Fayed let out a whoop.

"Again!" he crowed, grinning at Raoul. "God is great!"

His words were cut short by the Leader's exclamation: "Allah! If you are chosen, you will fly into paradise to serve Him."

"Inshallah," the group responded in unison.

The Leader glanced back, a little smile on his face, and then whirled his index finger at the pilot again. "One more pass before we head home," he said. Raoul maintained his passive expression, even as he felt the Leader's eyes upon him.

As they flew by the towers again, the pilot dipped his wing.

"Soon they will be rubble," the Leader said.

"Inshallah," Raoul responded. "Inshallah."

Clara

I PARKED ON THE street in front of the funeral home and sat in the car for a minute, looking at the remnants of the West End. A used furniture store filled the windows of what had once been a thriving family pharmacy, and the luncheonette was now a bar with blacked-out windows and a flickering Budweiser sign. The window of the little shoe store held a pawnshop sign taped to a shelf filled with gaudy jewelry and other stolen properties.

I scratched my head and tried to remember the name of the shoe store owner. Walter, I think it was. Every August, just before Labor Day, the entire gang of us would get our feet measured and new shoes fitted, while Papa negotiated with Walter in the back room. While his wife helped pick out shoes and convince us that they were indeed high fashion, Walt would come out, sighing, and lean on the counter. Our card was removed from the battered metal box, notations in red and black covering several stapled layers. As the price of shoes escalated along with the size of our feet, the previous year's bill was often not paid off before the new tally was added. We never got the shiny patent leathers of our dreams, and around seventh grade or so, we started shopping for shoes at the cheaper five-and-dime stores on the main road. I wondered when the store had gone under, but I wasn't surprised that it had.

The street around the funeral parlor was empty but the door stood open, waiting for the next family to stumble inside with their tragedy and grief. In the harsh light of day, my eyes no longer blurry with tears and fatigue, I could see how shabby the old place had become. Carmen had argued with Mama about coming here for Raoul, but she insisted. "We can't afford to go to those mansions on the hill," she said. The "mansions" were only a block from Main Street and yet, miles away in terms of standard of living. The old Widener-Barry Funeral Home, sitting astride the Podunk River (which was hardly a real river but only a trickling overflow of the larger Thames), was where our friends and neighbors always brought their dead. Other Puerto Rican families used it, but most of them chose to send their beloveds home to the island for burial.

"This is my home," Mama had insisted after her sister was shipped to the islands. That was ten years ago; she was still speaking to me then. She had lifted her head from under a black veil to shake a finger at each of us. "Don't you children think you can send me back there and forget about me."

"May I help you?" asked a young man dressed in a conservative gray suit with thin lapels and a starched white shirt.

"Oh, yes," I quickly calculated the advantage of his not recognizing me from the night I'd visited with my sisters. "I am here to settle the bill for my brother. The name is Quiñones."

His eyes flashed as I handed over a credit card and he practically ran from the room with it. The bill, I was not surprised to see, was almost as much as the down payment on a house. As a smart-ass college student, I'd done a little research into funeral costs, and I knew a dirty little secret about the business: this "family" business, the only place the working class thought they could afford, charged almost double their competitors on the hill. In fact, because of changes in regulations and health codes, the Barry family subcontracted with the tonier services on the hill to perform the actual embalming. The caskets sold here were leftovers too ostentatious for the middle and upper class Jerome families, and so my baby brother was now spending eternity in a bronze box that cost more than my first car.

I looked out the back window, a large bay that gave a nice view of the backsides of deteriorating tenements, as well as the trash-strewn banks of the meandering river. We'd fished here as kids with makeshift rods and paper-clip hooks. At night, the river had been a run-away route and a place to drink unobserved. During redevelopment, much of the water had been channeled into pipes and diverted under new roads, but here and there, a small section was still exposed to the elements.

"Did you hear they're trying to uncover the river for recreational purposes?" said a voice at the door. I turned and nodded at the pasty face of Ronald Barry, the class geek who'd taken over his family business. He'd been the source of much derision, but he paid us all back with spooky stories about bodies not yet dead and the use of the river for disposal of body parts and blood.

"Ronald," I reached out to take his hand. "You haven't changed a bit."

"It's nice to see you, too," he said. "Sorry for your loss."

I tried to smile at him, but the sight of my credit card in his hand stopped me. "Is there a problem?" I gestured towards the card.

"Your card was rejected," he handed it to me. "Is there another form of payment you'd like to make at this time?"

"Sorry about that, I must have gone over the limit. Things have been a little crazy, and I didn't get around to the bills. Here, try this one. Can we charge half today, and half in a few weeks? That'll give me time to clear things up, you know?"

There were no pleasantries to exchange after that, and I was happy to leave the dusky place. I walked across the street and looked at the river for a few minutes, then drove away. The car seemed to travel automatically to the Eagle's Club. It was barely afternoon, still early for the bar despite the presence of several men already deep into their beverages. Maybe they never left—who knew? There was very little conversation, and the air was dark with smoke and angst. I drank a cola, asked around for the elusive Mr. Peterson, and headed back to the hotel. The room looked and smelled like I'd been in it for a week, after changing from another one along the eastern side of the building that was too noisy. Housekeeping could not keep up with the level of tension that reeked from my skin, and I called the desk to ask for a fresh change of sheets and towels.

"Yes, Miss," the receptionist answered. "And will you be extending your stay?"

"Yes," I answered sharply. "I spoke with the manager about that already."

"Very good," she said. "Thank you."

The innocuous exchange reminded me that it was almost time to look for another place to stay, but the pickings were pretty slim in Jerome. I dismissed the issue with a shrug and returned to the photographs, studying the blood splatters with a microscope that helped minimize my feelings for the horror documented there. The maid came and went, the room light changed as dusk fell outside, and still I studied the evidence. What was I looking for? In the past, I'd been able to come up with the single shred that turned a case around, but there was nothing here except the blood of my own brother.

When I got back to the bar, I had trouble finding a parking spot and ended up in the shadows behind the club. A couple were either fighting or having sex by the picnic tables, and I felt my pulse pick up the bass from the jukebox when the door opened. My eyes had barely adjusted to the darkness before I saw Guy. It was almost 7:30 p.m. and the place was filled. My eyes sought out his familiar red hair as soon as I walked into the bar. I smiled and walked towards him, but stopped when he turned and glared at me. What the hell.

I swung onto a barstool and signaled for a beer. "Hey Pauloo," I said to the bartender. I'd begun to recognize faces around the bar and was not fooled by their apparent indifference. Everyone in the room now knew too much about me and about my burgeoning romance with Guy.

The cold beer washed over me, and I marveled at how easily I'd abandoned my "chardonnay-snobbery" in favor of America's favorite beverage. The walls of the hotel room had been closing in, after hours poring over forensics reports. The hard shell I put on to study the M.E.'s photographs was threatening to crack, and I was almost giddy with exhaustion and nerves.

From the corner of my eye, I watched Guy finish his beer and speak to the group gathered around a table close to the jukebox. He walked to the bar and placed three empty bottles there. I could smell him next to me and felt heat rising to my face.

"Hey," I said.

He lit a cigarette and exhaled slowly before speaking. "My wife is here tonight," he said quietly. No one spoke; everyone around the bar seemed to be waiting for my reply.

"Do you want to introduce us?" I laughed sharply and then moved my arm so it rested against his.

"You're killing me," he said. "I can't talk to you tonight."

I watched his back ripple with tension as he carried another round to the table. I stood up then, and I saw him frown slightly as I walked to the jukebox. He motioned slightly to the left with his head and the grimace deepened.

I looked at the blond sitting next to him, sipping something pink from a tall glass. From my vantage point, she seemed attractive and youthful. What had Guy said about her? "We don't have anything to say to each other anymore." They'd been high school sweethearts and had to get married to cover an unexpected pregnancy. "I was too young for that," he'd sighed, and at the time I'd felt sorry for him. Now, watching the woman's red fingernails dig into Guy's knee, I wondered about the real story of that marriage.

Barbie laughed loudly at something and leaned closely into Guy's arm. The other man leaned back in his chair, and I immediately figured that he must be Guy's brother. The same face, but with skin stretched tight over prominent cheekbones. His red hair was clipped short, and the same blue eyes burned in an unlined face.

He drank deeply from the frosted bottle, and our eyes met briefly before I turned to the machine. I made a selection and felt someone breathe on my shoulder.

"Like the old stuff?" He smelled like aftershave—a little too much Brut for my taste—and whiskey, with an undertone of something salty. I turned to look into his eyes.

"Not much to choose from here," I shrugged. "Do I know you?"

"No, I would remember you," he smiled. "I'm Noel."

"Like the Christmas song?" I asked, allowing him to take my hand.

"Like the second coming," he replied. "I'd like to show you what I mean." His finger scraped my palm and I took a step back.

"Sorry," I said. "I'm waiting for a friend."

He followed me to the bar where his arm fell across my back. "Come on honey, let Noel bring a little cheer into your life," he murmured. His fingers were playing in the tangle of hair at my neck, and I tried to slip away.

"Hey, slow down," I protested. His mouth was on my ear and I shook my head.

"I am going to eat you until you're begging for more," he whispered. "You're going to love what I'm going to do to your pussy."

I felt my stomach tighten and adrenaline pump through my veins. "Back off," I said. "I'm not interested."

His grip tightened on my arm and I stood up quickly, throwing him off balance. "Back off," I warned again.

He put up both hands and stepped away, smiling. "You'll be asking for it real soon," he said. "And maybe I won't be available when you want it."

"I'll take my chances," I said, turning back to the bar. "Can I have another?"

Noel slapped someone on the shoulder and I overheard an obscene comment that included the words *spic* and *bitch*.

I hadn't heard *spic* in years, and I flashed back on the last time, in this very bar. I must have been a teenager then; captive to my father's strict rules about church-going and silence about the drink he needed afterwards. Papa usually stopped off at the club on the way home, and this time I had trailed inside to wait for him. It was much the same back then, loud and smoky and full of man-smells.

Pauloo brought me another glistening brown bottle. "That Noel, he bothering you?" I think he swore in French; the contempt in his voice sounded like a curse to me.

I shook my head, sipped my beer, and felt my face flush with the memory of my father, standing ramrod straight at the bar. At the time, Papa hadn't responded to the slur, but merely finished his shot and walked away. I looked around, and suddenly I remembered Shelly, and the paper she'd given me, that Raoul had dropped in the bar. I smacked my forehead when I realized that the paper was probably being laundered with my filthy jeans. My heart pounded. Stupid, stupid, I muttered to myself. I was spending too much time drinking, dreaming. How could I have gotten so distracted?

"Hey, Pauloo," I called the bartender back. "You know Shelly, the girl who was in here the other day talking to me?" He looked blank, shrugged. "She's probably early thirties, bleachy blond hair, kind of teased up?" Nothing. "She has a great rack, probably not the originals." I lifted my chest and exaggerated the size with my hands.

"Oh, Shelly!" he smiled. "What about her?"

"Have you seen her lately? Does she come in regular?" I asked.

"Nah, she'll come in on the weekend, when there's dancing and the guys come over from the base," he said. "Why're you looking for her?"

"She knew my brother," I said. "We were talking the other night, and I wanted to ask her something." I smiled. "You don't happen to know her last name, or have her phone number, do you?"

He shook his head. "Nope. She's not a member, usually has some guy sign her in."

"Oh, well, thanks anyway. If you see her, can you tell her to call me? Here's my number." I handed him my business card, with my cell number scribbled across the bottom. He stuck the card on the mirror, between a curled photo of someone's great fishing catch and a magnet advertising a local taxi service. I threw some money on the counter and walked quickly to the door.

My laundry was stacked neatly on the freshly made bed. I checked the pockets of my jeans and pulled out the paper. I could still make out the blue lines of the index card, folded into quarters. I unfolded it, hopeful, yet unsure about what I wanted to see.

A number was still visible, although the ink was washed out in a few places. I dug through my camera bag and studied the paper with a lens. Dialed the number, heard the tape recorded voice ask for an area code. Dammit. I tried a couple and scratched off options on a post-it note.

The crime scene pictures were still scattered around the room, but I could not bear to study the bloody mess again. I let my eyes blur as I slipped the pictures into a pile and covered them with the clinical paperwork that quantified the extent of my brother's demise. Drugs and alcohol in his blood, evidence of healed-over broken ribs, and the old suicide slashes on his manacled wrists. It was obvious he'd been alive when the fatal castration had occurred, conclusions borne out by the splash patterns mapped meticulously on the pages that swam before my eyes.

The phone rang as I wiped my face with a wet cloth.

I hesitated before picking up the receiver.

"Yes?"

"Hey, Clara, it's me." Mary Kate's voice cut through the room. "How ya' doin'?"

She was too cheerful for me to handle at the moment. "I'm okay," I said. I sighed. "Actually, no, I'm exhausted."

"Yeah, I can tell," her voice was a little more subdued. "So you want to get together or what?"

"Gee, not tonight," I hesitated. "Can we do it another time? Like I said, I'm just wiped out tonight."

"Sure," she paused. "So what's going on? What have you been doing?"

I didn't want to go into my little investigation; better to turn the conversation around.

"Just trying to tie up some loose ends," I said. "How about you? Tell me about these kids you're driving around town."

She chattered a bit about her two kids, marriage to a great guy named Joe, and the death of her mother until I was about to scream. "So that's the last twenty years in a nutshell," she concluded. "Or a nuthouse."

She was waiting for a laugh, I knew, but I was not really paying attention. "Well, I'll call you, okay? Sorry about tonight," I said again.

Mary Kate made me promise to call again and seemed reluctant to hang up. "You sure everything's all right? You want me to come over there?"

"Nah, I'm hitting the sack. I'll be fine in the morning," I assured her. "You know, it was seeing Ronald Barry again."

"Oh my God, 'bury 'em Barry'," she laughed, and then stopped short. "Sorry."

"You're right, he hasn't changed a bit. He's still creepy." I agreed. "So, I'll be in touch. And thanks for calling."

I'd barely put the phone down when it rang again. "What'd you forget?" I asked.

"Sorry about the mess." I could hear the music of the bar behind Guy's soft voice.

"Sure." I covered my eyes.

"Are you okay?"

I snorted. "Oh, yeah, I'm just terrific."

"I'm sorry about Noel," he said.

"Your brother is a fucking asshole," I said.

"Look, I can't...."

I cut him off. "Stop it," I said heavily. "I can't do this either." I depressed the button on the phone and returned to the bathroom. The phone rang again and again, echoing in the cardboard room. I nudged the bathroom door shut with a swing of my hips. My hands looked huge underwater, and I studied the blue lines in my wrists until they pulsated with temptation.

In the mirror, my eyes burned deeply in dark circles. I saw Raoul looking back at me. I remembered the night Raoul had cut himself: the jumbled call from the hospital, careening across town to Bellevue, pacing outside the locked psych ward, running towards the haunted look in Raoul's face. The look I saw now in my own face. I shut off the water and let the tears flow.

Raoul

ALTHOUGH HE STUDIED THE Koran faithfully, Raoul could not reconcile the teachings he heard at the mosque with the words he tried to memorize. This congregation, despite their saintly and almost pathologically calm Imam, was totally focused on the virtues of the next world. They hardly cared for their existence on earth, so intent were they on attaining a position in heaven. Raoul supposed the seventy-two virgins might have been an incentive, but since he had struggled with his own demons in the past, he was fascinated by the group's psychology.

The all-male group prayed together daily, after the rest of the small congregation had gone home. Raoul quickly surmised that if the men in this group had wives or families, they were not together in this country. And in fact, the more time he spent with them, the more he realized that they were so far from "home" that most of the men focused more on heaven than earth. Their work lives were monotonous, their home lives spartan and devoid of all pleasure except whatever they derived from prayer. As was their custom, the men prayed five times a day, although the two midday sessions were done carefully. There was no concession for Muslim prayers in their workplace. Raoul found himself mouthing the words along with his fellow workers as he directed his forklift towards the east whenever his phone vibrated the reminder.

The rules became more restrictive as time passed in the group. Where they once simply avoided pork products, lately the food had become more vegetarian. Perhaps on Saturday, a feast involving lamb chops might appear, courtesy of the Leader. But for the most part, they were becoming leaner, hungrier, and more devoted each day. The danger that Raoul felt every time he donned his street identity had become almost unreasonable, and so his visits to the club and his van became shorter each week. Eager to maintain his cover in the bar, Raoul even picked up the occasional girl—never one of the regulars, who might want more than a one-time quickie—and took her, giggling, to his van for some frantic sex.

"That was great," he told each one after a suitable interval. "I'm sorry, but I have to get to work early. Can I walk you to your car?"

Without that, without the nightly shot to help him sleep and the weekly calls to D.C., Raoul thought his own sanity might be compromised by the pressure to release his identity to the service of God. And to the goals of the Leader, which seemed somehow different from the book he pored over at every opportunity.

"Give," the Leader had demanded before last night's meeting. His beefy hand extended until Raoul surrendered his Koran. The swarthy man flipped the pages of the book and then tossed it back to him. "Brothers, see how our Ismail studies his

Koran. Is this the sign of a good soldier in Allah's jihad?" He looked around the room as Raoul nervously fingered the paperback.

No one spoke.

"You are all so quiet. Not sure of tonight's lesson, eh?" He reached again for the book. "This is for children. For women. For those who want to believe, but are not sure. This is not for us. We are the disciples, not the students, eh? We don't need validation from a book. We have the message directly from Allah. We are one, and we are more than words. We are action." He opened the book and split the spine neatly in two, his powerful hands tearing the hundreds of pages as if they were one.

Raoul sat motionless, unsure if he would be torn apart next. Instead, the Leader began pacing the floor, lecturing the group again about the virtues of *jihad* and the rewards that awaited them. Unconsciously, Raoul fingered the scars on his wrist and listened to the drone of the Leader's voice. He remembered vividly the relief of opening the veins in his arms, the way he felt all the anger and disappointment in his life ebb away—until his girlfriend arrived and then the red lights and questions.

"Ismail knows, don't you? You have buried yourself in this book—Ismail?" The Leader tapped his shoulder, interrupting the memory of Bellevue's long corridors.

"Yes, I have listened and learned the way," Raoul intoned. "Allah is my teacher, and I his servant."

"Our quiet Ismail, who is a devoted servant, has already tasted the bitterness of which we speak." The Leader grabbed Raoul's arm and held his hand up. He pulled the sleeve back, exposing the ropy white scar tissue. "What was it for, your dance with death? Disappointment with a woman, perhaps? A handsome man like you. Of course you know that—since you have read the Koran so dutifully—suicide is forbidden by Islam. Suicide—which is the selfish act of giving up the gift of life solely because of a personal problem—this is not permitted. No man will be allowed in heaven that has done this to himself," he said, then shook Raoul's arm and dropped it abruptly on the table. "It's an insult to Allah."

He turned to the group and held his hands up to the ceiling. "Do you understand the difference?" He whirled, taking Raoul's chin in his hand. "Do you see? You were tempted by the devil, but saved by Allah for his glorious mission. You have another chance at heaven."

Raoul closed his eyes and nodded slowly. "I am blessed, and I am thankful. Inshallah, I will be worthy."

"Inshallah," the group intoned. The Leader squeezed Raoul's shoulder. It was not a fatherly or supportive squeeze. It was a warning. He was no longer a student, Raoul understood. He was a messenger. And he had no place to turn, no one to hear his report.

That night, he did not sleep. He toyed with the scar on his wrist, walking back and forth on the beach. At one point, he realized that he was praying, but not to the God he had been brought up knowing. He was praying to their God, to Allah. He stopped abruptly, pulled off his clothes, and ran into the frigid, oil stained water of the Sound. Although it was early June, summer came slowly to this part of the Connecticut shore and the water was as cold as the night air.

Staying under for as long as he could, Raoul felt the blood pounding against his ear drums. He now understood the need for regular contact with the outside, when he was this deep undercover. Maybe he should have gone in, gotten more support—but it was obvious that he was onto something, something really big and dangerous. Frustrated, he knew he had to stay. And yet, he needed to let his handler know what he'd stumbled on. Sure, he had been abandoned, and he was angry about that. His lungs burning, Raoul burst out of the water.

It was still more night than day, the sky barely lighter on the horizon. Although he was cold, Raoul was in no hurry to leave the calming embrace of the Sound. He looked at the stars, allowing his mind to empty and waiting for his breath to slow. All this confusion and fighting over God, he thought. Isn't it all the same? Aren't we all the same underneath? He started swimming languidly, moving parallel to the shore. There was no movement on land, only the haze of neon reflecting off the clouds near the base. He was alone.

He stopped suddenly. "I am alone," he said aloud. In a flash he understood what motivated these men to participate in this terror group, and how easily the leaders were able to manipulate them. They were isolated, they had no money or friends in this country, and their only connection was to this group of men. The Leader had become their father, and they were totally in his thrall. Even Raoul had started to feel it, the isolation and need for approval of the Leader.

Things were moving fast in the group, he knew, and suddenly the urgency to tell someone else what was happening overcame his lethargy. This was clearly more than he could handle alone. He needed to reach someone, to get the word to Washington. He swam faster.

His underwear dripping, knees knocking together with the cold, Raoul walked quickly towards his pile of clothes. He almost stumbled on Metin, who was sitting next to his clothing, going through his pockets.

"What are you doing?" Raoul asked. He held out a hand. "Give me my shirt. I'm freezing here."

Metin threw the shirt at Raoul and silently continued with his excavation of pockets in the jeans. He did not speak while Raoul pulled on his shirt. When he reached for the jacket, Metin handed over the jeans instead.

"What are you looking for?" Raoul asked again, stepping into his pants. "I don't have any money, man. What do you want?"

Metin stood up, Raoul's wallet in his hand. He silently held out the jacket, then opened the wallet and dumped its contents in the sand.

"What did you do that for?" Raoul cried. "Man, what did I do to you?"

Metin flipped the wallet at Raoul. "Watch yourself," he said. He turned and walked towards the road. Raoul watched him, then quickly scooped up his belongings and followed, keeping in the shadows.

Not far from the beach, Raoul watched Metin climb into the back of a rusty pickup. The license plate was distorted, and the driver kept the lights off until he was out of sight.

"What the hell?" Raoul muttered, turning back towards his bike. He rode along the silent streets, shivering in his wet clothes. He expected a dark vehicle to run him down, and by the time he arrived in the alley behind the apartment building, the tension in his neck was unbearable. He crept up the stairs, rubbing the taut muscles as best he could. Once inside, he replaced his damp clothes with warm sweats and settled on his prayer rug. Emptying his pockets, he tried to see if Metin had taken anything. Except for some coins, which may have been lost in the sand, all of his scant belongings were intact. The fake ID and dog-eared union card were together, hopefully enough proof that he was Ismail the laborer. But why had they come checking on him? Someone had been following him. For how long? He shivered.

He glanced at the window. The sun was almost up. He turned on the coffee pot and prepared for another day in the shipyard.

Clara

THERE IS NO TRAFFIC en route to New York City in the middle of the night. The Merritt Parkway is particularly empty, the narrow road twisting under my tires like a tempting snake, drawing me back to the city. I watched for deer on the rolling corners, spotting several gleaming pairs of eyes in the dark woods. The radio hummed with the road, the traffic lights were all magically green, and I pulled onto my street just shy of midnight. The keys slid into the triple-locked door, and my apartment—dusty, airless, and sterile —welcomed my return.

I emptied the corkboard wall in my workroom, piling photos neatly into boxes and moving swiftly to replace the images of war in a doomed place, with a battle lost closer to my heart. The strange pink light that always hung over Manhattan comforted me like an old and heavy blanket that I once found stifling but now embraced. I turned on all the lights in the apartment, snapped on the radio for the white noise of the classical station, and studied the angrily blinking message light on my machine.

The tape rewound squealing the speed of demanding voices in my ear. How long ago had Raoul called this number, was it still on the tape or had it been erased? My fingers drummed the edge of the table as I listened to the drone of work-work-work and then, there it was. I hit the stop button with a gasp. *Mijo.* His voice beckoned me into the darkness. I wandered to the kitchen looking for an ice cube upon which to pour my sorrow.

Brandy clinking cheerfully in my hand, I lay my head on the desk and played the tape again. His voice slurred—was it the tape, or was he already in distress? How to listen objectively, swallowing the guilt along with the panic. The third time I played the message, the shrill ring of the phone interrupted it. I picked up without thinking, part of me hoping to hear the living Raoul on the other end. Maybe this had all been a dream? My heart surged with a childish hope that Raoul's death was only a nightmare, and the call gave me another chance to live it right.

Not so, of course, and who the hell would call me at this hour? I picked up, still hoping for that miracle. Even a call from Guy would be welcome at this point.

It was a breather. Perfect. Slammed and disengaged. Refresh the drink, and try not to look at the photo array, not yet.

It was 4:15 a.m. before I could leave the tape alone, unable to draw conclusions from the eight word message. "It's me. Give me a call, uh, it's urgent." Nine, if you count the significant and loaded grunt in the middle. I pondered that "uh" for close to an hour, watching the pink sky lighten until the birds awakened from their precarious perches below my window. I hugged myself, rocking on the edge of the sofa. Listening to the faraway sounds of my brother.

"It's me." I am thankful, finally, that at least he didn't have to identify himself when he left me a message. At least he knew I would recognize his voice. The distress in the message had to be the wobbly sound of a tape played and recorded too much; the thin breakability that tore at my guts, a mechanical failure. Blame AT&T, the demons at NYNEX, the flimsy fabric of a translucent piece of tape. I turned it off finally. Closed my eyes and tried to think about Guy, but the wide-eyed death gaze of Raoul intruded over and over.

The cell phone rang, jarring and echoing in the room. I looked at it, answered. "Yes?"

"Where the fuck have you been?" a voice exploded from the phone.

Antonio, the forgotten lover, the necessary object. Silence the only appropriate response.

I could hear his heavy breathing. "Sorry," he eventually spoke. "I've been calling. No one knows where you are. I was worried. I wondered if you were in the Towers. I, I was afraid you were." This was new, this neediness.

"Sorry. I should've called." I gave him an inch.

"Are you okay? Were you out on assignment?" He paused again. "Actually—confession time—I called your office. They said you were missing in action. Robby seemed to be concerned, too."

Dammit, he'd crossed a line there. "Oh, really," I murmured.

"Look, I know you told me never to call there."

"My brother died," I interrupted.

"Jesus. Oh my God, I'm so sorry. Was he at the Trade Center? Why didn't you call me?"

"It was kind of unexpected. He was murdered. Not here, in Connecticut. They think it was a couple of days before the attack."

"Do you want me to come over?"

"Whatever."

"I'll be there in five. Jesus." He hung up in mid-mutter.

I stripped then, pacing around the apartment restlessly, thinking about Guy. The smell of him, the feeling of his mouth on mine. The chemistry. Antonio.

Doorbell, quick check of the peephole, distressed yet handsome face. He'd do. We had sex there, inside the door. On the welcome mat, actually. The floor causing burns on my knees as I straddled him. "Poor baby," he whispered once.

"Fuck that." I bit him. My fingers became entangled in his long brown curls, my chin burning against his scratchy beard.

When he was in the shower later, I smoked a cigarette and watched the orthodox guy across the street play with his feet. Every night, I watched him in his BVD's, cleaning what must be endless amounts of lint from between his toes. Or else a wicked case of athlete's foot that he was lucky hadn't traveled up to his knees by now. I sipped a glass of water and let the fluids run from my crotch onto the chair.

I knew he could see me, too. Knew that his chest scratching every morning was solely for my benefit, but if I met him on the street, we'd never exchange a glance.

"Clara, want to talk about it?" Antonio smelled like Yardley's lavender soap.

"Nah," I shrugged. "Thanks for coming, though."

"Where have you been?" he pushed. "Are you sure, I mean, can I do something?"

I sipped, ignored his hand on my shoulder.

"At least call Robby."

I put the glass down, deciding to forgive him for trespassing into my life. I felt it again, the feeling, the need. I'll say it again: There's something about death that makes a person want to have sex, an almost primal itch that must be scratched. Playing games with Guy had roiled me into a heightened state over the past few days.

He was not dressed, just toweled. "Come here," I commanded.

"Oh, Clara," he pulled me into his arms. Probably expecting tears. The man did not really know me that well, I decided.

I pulled the towel away and used it to wipe between my legs. "Come on, Tony, give me a break here," I pushed him down to the couch.

The sun was peaking over the buildings when I unstuck myself from Antonio's leg. Time to get the upholstery cleaned again. Time for Antonio to get the hell out of here.

The cell phone rang again while I was making coffee. "Yes?"

"Hey." It was Guy.

"Hey." I felt something wet drip down my leg.

"Where are you?" he asked. "I've been going crazy here."

"Join the club," I said. "I can't sit around and wait for you all the time."

Heavy sigh. Not fair, I know. Putting the moves on a married man. Best to stick with the immature and commitment-phobic.

Antonio emerged from the bathroom, this time clad in jeans. His abs rippled, but beyond a certain clinical interest, I was done with him. He looked questioningly at the phone.

"I'm in New York," I said. "I'll give you a call when I get back to town."

"Ah." Here comes the explanation: can't call a married man, stupid.

"Oh, I forgot." I laughed, if you can call it that. "I'll see you around then." I disconnected the phone and put it back in the battery charger.

"Everything okay?" Antonio posed by the coffee machine, waiting for the brew to subside.

"Sure," I grabbed a tee shirt from the floor and pulled it on. "Just a friend wondering where I am."

"Look, if you want to talk about it," he started, again.

"No, thanks. I'm all talked out," I took two mugs from the cupboard. "And I really appreciate your coming over this morning."

He smiled, a crooked little smile that first got him into my bed. Well, to be honest, it wasn't his face so much as his gym-hardened body that had propelled me into his life. How many years, how many impersonal, intimate hours had we shared?

"Have some coffee," I smiled then, too. "I'm just going to hop in the shower."

"Paper here?" he studied the fridge. It was empty and he squinted into the blinding box.

"I stopped it last month." I felt sorry for the guy. "There's creamer in the cabinet."

Such a look of gratitude, I had to wonder what he'd do for a morning paper. My inner thighs already ached, but I did a mental check to see if the libido was rested for now. No need to ask for more, although in my experience, one orgasm was never enough. It was too bad that most men were done with one, when I was just getting started. "I'll be back in five."

The water, the slippery soap, the husky recollection of Guy, made for a slightly longer and yet more satisfying shower than planned. Antonio was gone when I came out, as I knew he would be. That was the good thing about our relationship: fucking and no further. Once, maybe I'd entertained delusions about him, but this worked for both of us, although a woman wasn't supposed to settle for a mere sex partner. But I knew his value to me, and it was all between the legs. Not much between the ears interested either of us in the other.

I went out for a paper, just to stretch my legs and clear the booze from my brain. Time to get down to business. I called my friend at the FBI lab and made a date to share my answering machine tapes with him in an hour. Flipped open the laptop and tried to hunt down the phone number without an area code.

It would be nice in these instances to be a computer whiz, a hacker capable of intercepting phone records and background checks. I was not so lucky. No clue, no sidekick. I called Mark on his private line and gave him the number.

"Where'd you get it?" he asked. Satisfied with my explanation, he continued. "What else have you got?"

"Can you get phone records from the Eagle's Club?" Again, the details repeated. "I heard he got a call every night at ten on the pay phone."

"I might need more than that for a subpoena. Let me see," he paused. "The guy's name is Peterson? I think I know who he is. Okay, what else?"

"Nothing much," I admitted. "I've been going over the photos. Have you gotten any of the labs back yet?"

"Nah, takes a while."

"Okay. When can I get into the apartment?"

"What? Why do you want to—oh, never mind. I guess you need to see it."

"I guess."

"I'll have the key for you later," Mark coughed. "Where are you, anyway?"

"New York," I replied. "All my photography stuff is here, and I needed some distance. I'll be back later today. How can I get the key from you?"

He hesitated. "Oh, yeah, I've been thinking about that."

"And?"

"Well, Clara, this is a really small town, and I can't see any way. I mean, if I drop something with your name at the hotel, it'll be all over town by the time I get back to my office."

"Oh." There was a long silence. "I don't believe it can be that bad," I argued lamely.

"It is." Long silence. I wasn't biting. "Okay, let me give you a for instance," he said. "I know you've got something going with Guy LeBeau. His truck has been seen at the hotel, and your car has been parked outside the Eagle's Club for the past several nights."

"Shit." I massaged my temples. "Who told you—are you watching me? Am I being followed?"

"Clara, no. You don't get it. I'm not making any judgments here," he said quickly. "I'm just telling you this so you'll understand. This is a small town. I can't be seen anywhere near you."

"I'll rent a mailbox at one of those twenty-four hour places, and get two keys," I said. "I'll drop off the key—or should I mail it?"

"Noooo," he hesitated.

"Look, I've already been in the department twice, so what's another short visit? I am the grieving relative, after all, and I demand to know what's happening with the investigation." My voice rose, feigning hysteria.

"Okay, okay."

I put the phone in my bag and headed downtown with the tape. I'd tell Mark about it when I had a little more information.

"I don't know what you want from me," Spike said. These techie guys always had interesting nicknames and elaborate tattoos. "This is a really dirty tape."

"What do you mean?"

"It's old, it's been recorded over and over. What are you looking for, anyway?"

"I don't know," I admitted. "Background noises? Anything strange with the voice, you know, like he was drugged or out of breath. I don't know."

"I can't do miracles here, you know," he rewound the tape. "Why are you still using such an old-fashioned machine, anyway? Get yourself digital, would you?"

"I know, I know," I clasped my hands together in supplication. "Please, Spike, do your magic for me."

"Humph."

He listened to it, over and over, until the echoing voice threatened to drive me mad. Turning knobs, snapping headphones, and cocked head. I watched him, a thin Gumby-sort of fellow, completely dressed in black. Shaven head, scrubbed baby face. Thick black half-glasses perched on a pug nose.

"There," he stopped the tape.

"What?"

"Couple of things. Definitely phone booth, you can tell from the quality of the line," he said. "So he's on the street somewhere, not inside because you can pick up car noise in the background."

This was not rocket science, but I leaned forward attentively. "Yes?"

"I think I pick up a boat sound—listen—right there." He manipulated the sliding knobs again. "Hear it?"

I strained. I was afraid that at this point, I'd hear Bullwinkle if he told me to, so I tried to be skeptical. I shook my head.

"Again."

"I'll take your word for it," I conceded. "Now what?"

"Well, if you want me to spend a little time, I can digitize it and probably come up with something more definitive." He looked over the half-glasses at me, head shining in the industrial strength light.

"I don't have a lot of time," I said. He shrugged. "How much will it cost me?"

"I can't say until I get into the lab with it."

I sighed. He always did this, refusing to put a figure on a job beforehand. "Look, Spike, how much detail can you get off something like this? Can you tell me the kind of boat, and the time of day?"

He leaned back in the large leather chair. "Yes."

"Really?" I'd been kidding.

"Well, maybe." He tucked his hands behind his head and smiled. "I'm good, you know."

"Believe me, I know it," I agreed. "Here's my cell number. Call me? Soon?"

"Sure, babe." He snapped back into work mode. "Later."

Raoul

IT WAS TOO DANGEROUS to try a wire, Raoul knew. He had resisted the order to at least get a bug in the meeting room at the mosque.

"No way," he said each time the subject came up. "They will kill me. After they torture me, they will kill me. I'm not scared of getting caught, but it's too big a risk to take right now. I give you everything you need."

There was silence. Raoul heard the snap of a lighter and the slow inhalation of a cigarette.

"You trust me, right? I am not holding anything back, believe me," Raoul repeated.

"You better not."

In his mind, Raoul cursed the legacy his sister had left him in the agency. "I take good notes, and I phone in everything you need to hear," he replied. "Do you want copies?"

"Wear a wire."

The argument had taken place each week that Raoul spoke with his handlers. While it was not always the same person on the phone, the message never varied. The last time they brought it up, Raoul had hesitated. Maybe they were right—how hard would it be to put a bug in the mosque? Later, when he was there for the daily prayers, he looked around and tried to see if it might be possible.

Haluk, one of the burly, silent men who always stood near the Imam, called him over. "What are you looking for?" he asked.

"Nothing," Raoul shrugged.

"I saw you. You have been acting strangely all night. What is it? Did you lose something?" Haluk persisted. "Let me get Orhan, he'll want to know." The Leader, whom no one addressed by name, was walking towards them.

"I, no, I didn't lose anything. I was just worried. I was worried that someone might come in here and, I don't know, plant a listening device or something," Raoul explained. "I like to look around, to make sure nothing is there."

"Why would you think of something like that?" Haluk gestured towards Orhan, who came quickly to his side. "Ismail here is concerned that someone might be bugging the mosque," Haluk said. "What do you think of that?"

Orhan looked at Raoul for a long time, his dark eyes impenetrable to light. "So. A little paranoid, eh?" He clapped a hand heavily on Raoul's shoulder, leading him towards the back. "Who have you been talking to, Ismail?" he asked. "Has anyone been asking you questions, asking anything about the mosque or what we do here?"

"Oh, no," Raoul shook his head. "Nothing like that. No, I don't really talk to anyone else. I just, you know, worry. You hear things people say in the store, or at the shipyard, about us. I wouldn't be surprised if they tried…"

Orhan laughed, again, clasping Raoul's shoulder painfully. "No worries, brother Ismail," he said. "We sweep the building every day. We're perfectly safe here." He tousled Raoul's hair. "But you keep your guard up, that's good. If you hear anything of interest, you come to me, yes?"

Raoul nodded, trying to squirm away from the larger man. Instead, he was pulled closer. "We're all brothers here, and mutual trust is everything. Don't you agree? Don't make me regret inviting you here." Orhan's breath seemed to scorch Raoul's nostrils. The man would not loosen his grip on Raoul's neck. "Zeki—come here. Bring your scissors. This young man needs a haircut."

The next five minutes passed in a painful frenzy as the elder Zeki, who used to barber in the home country but clearly was as rusty as his scissors, chopped Raoul's hair in an uneven bob. When he looked at it later, Raoul sighed, took out his razor, and shaved it all off. With his dark beard growing in, and now his shaved head, Raoul felt closer each day to the men he spent hours with, studying Koran and hand-to-hand combat.

At the shipyard, no one commented on his shorn head, but later that night, in the bar, he felt eyes upon him, voices silenced when he walked to the john. All these months, building his cover here in the bar, and one haircut….

He sat sullenly at the bar, when his musing was interrupted by a hand skimming lightly over the denim covering his thigh.

"Hey, baby." A low female voice caused him to lift his head and glance sideways at the figure sitting very closely next to him.

"You got a light?" she asked.

"Yeah," he reached over and lit the cigarette for her. Their eyes met over the flame. He recognized this one now: Shelly, the girl who'd tried hard to engage him in conversation the first few times he'd warmed this stool. She had abandoned him quickly, moved on to one of the new recruits.

"Hey," she whispered. "What's your name?"

"Raoul."

"You from around here?" she asked. Her fingers moved higher on his leg. He scratched his chin.

"Nope. Just working at the shipyard, passing through," he replied.

"What's the matter, you don't like it here? We can be friendly, you know, if you give us a chance." She smiled, took a long drag on her cigarette and blew the smoke in his ear.

"I'm used to being alone, I guess," he said.

"So maybe you want some company sometime." Shelly mashed out the butt and finished her beer. "I gotta use the ladies. Maybe you can, you know, meet me out back?" Her fingers moved along the line of his crotch, where they danced around.

"Ooooh, a button man," she said. "I just love men with jeans that button." Her left hand traced the line of his bandana, the right still busy below the bar. "So. You wanna take a walk?"

She slid off the stool, but not before giving his hard-on a squeeze.

What the hell, Raoul thought. Might as well get some. He finished his shot, chased it with a swig of warm beer, and went out the front door. Before he could make it around the back corner, he could hear her giggling. In the shadows, Shelly tossed her panties and he caught them handily. One hand stuffed them in a pocket, the other unbuttoned his fly as he approached her. She was splayed open and waiting on the edge of the picnic table.

"Come on, baby," she cooed. He was inside her before she finished the words, and he held her ass while pounding out his frustration. It didn't take long, and when he was done she lay back on the table until her breathing slowed. "Wow," she said.

He smiled as he tucked back into his pants. "That was really nice," he said, handing her the panties.

"Oh yeah," she said absently. "I mean, look at all the stars. Isn't it awesome?" She sat up, slid the panties back beneath her skirt and patted his arm. "You were awesome, too, baby."

He watched her sashay back into the bar, tugging her skirt down in the back. *Women*, he thought. *I have no fucking clue what they are all about.* He followed her back into the bar, paid for another round, and waited for his cell phone to call and release him from this role.

On the way back to the apartment, he thought about Metin, and the paranoia growing among the group. Himself included. He needed a contact. He began composing a list of people he could call, but it was a short one. Without being able to get to Washington, he was totally screwed. He bought a disposable cell phone from the Pakistani convenience store and thought about who to call.

The lights were still on in the apartment below his, so he took care not to make any noise climbing the back stairs. He could hear the laughter from a late night talk show, but that did not necessarily mean his neighbor was awake. More likely she was asleep on the couch, and the chatter of the television was keeping the bad dreams at bay. He prayed for the same release, writing detailed notes about his day in the journal hidden beneath the cardboard floor of his gym bag. He skipped the part about Shelly, although he was not sure about her. Paranoid, he thought. Got to keep it together, man.

He fingered his scar before falling into a deep and dreamless sleep. It was 3:00 a.m. He woke again, at 4:00, the tension filling his body. Someone was in the apartment. He waited, trying not to alter his breathing. It was silent, and then he heard the laugh track from a sitcom filtering up the radiators from his mother's apartment downstairs. He waited.

Could that be it, that he was awakened by a television show? The floor creaked. No, he was not alone.

He sat up, dropping silently onto the hardwood floor. He knew better than any intruder how to avoid the creaky boards; he'd been living like a ghost in this apartment for months now, with no one the wiser.

Another footstep. Raoul reached over and flicked on the light. Metin, shading his eyes, squinted at him from the doorway.

"Hey, cut the lights man," Metin said. "I thought you were awake. I saw lights, figured I would come up and we could talk."

"In the middle of the night?" Raoul sat down on the floor. "I didn't have any lights on. What are you doing, watching the building or something? Never mind, don't answer that." He stretched, looked at the clock. "How about some coffee, man?"

"Sure."

They went into the kitchen. Raoul gestured to Metin to leave his shoes by the door. As he filled the coffee pot with water and the filter with grounds, Raoul studied the younger man. He was nervous, wringing his hands together and looking around nervously.

"Relax man," he said. Hell, I'm the one who should be nervous here, he thought. "So, what did you want to talk about?" he waited patiently, watching the coffee pot and trying to give Metin the space he needed.

"I was wondering. I guess I'm not supposed to ask this, but I was wondering about the scars on your wrists. About what the Leader said." He hesitated. "Is it true?"

"Is what true? The part about me cutting myself? Yeah, that's true. The part about going to hell, well, I don't know about that." Raoul pulled two mugs from the cabinet, sugar packets and spoons from the drawer. "Why do you ask?"

The kid slid down to his haunches, hands dangling between his knees. Raoul could hardly hear him speak. "I was wondering, you know, what it felt like. I mean, why did you do it? Did it hurt? And what happened, who found you? Who saved you?"

"Metin, you're not planning anything, are you?" Even Raoul knew how ridiculous that sounded—after all, they were being trained for a suicide mission. Of course the kid was planning something. "Listen, I don't know what to tell you. Maybe I'm not the right person to ask." Raoul poured the coffee, handed over a mug. "I think maybe you should talk to the Imam."

"Is that how you found religion?" Metin looked up at Raoul. "Ismail, I just want to know. Why did you do it, and what did it feel like? And how did you survive?"

Raoul sat on the floor, leaning back against the counter. He put the hot mug between his legs, held out his arms and studied the scars. "I don't remember much about the survival part," he said slowly. "I was in a bad place in my life, things had happened, and I just lost it. I can't—I don't know how else to describe it to you. I thought it was all over, and I don't remember feeling anything when I did it—or after, when I woke up."

They drank the hot coffee, each immersed in his own thoughts.

"Metin, how can I help you?" Raoul said finally.

The younger man shrugged. "I guess you can't. I don't even know why I'm here. If they find out…."

"Don't worry. I'm not going to tell anyone." Raoul got up, refilled the coffees and looked at the clock. "It's almost time to get ready for work. You want some breakfast?" Metin nodded. "Let me get dressed, and we'll go get a real 'American' breakfast. Eggs, bacon, the whole nine yards," he said. "I think we could both use some food."

After dressing and leaving silently by the back staircase, Raoul led Metin to the Riverside Café, already crowded at 5:00 a.m. with day laborers and Navy personnel, the latter looking like this was the last stop on the way to bed, the former grumpy that their day was just beginning. A French Canadian waitress served them coffee and two specials in short order.

As they ate, Raoul noticed Metin looking at his own veins. "What?" he prodded.

"When you said you were in a bad place, that things happened, what did you mean?" Metin looked at Raoul. "I mean, you don't have to tell me. But, was it a woman? Something like that? Or was it, you know, something like this. What we're doing here. At the mosque."

"Praying, you mean?" Raoul grinned but then he noticed the other man's mortified face. "Sorry, I was just kidding. Nothing to joke about, praying at the mosque." He sighed, stirred more sugar into his coffee. "I had been, how should I say? I was disappointed by someone in my family, and things fell apart at work because of it, and it just went downhill from there. I felt like I had no choice anymore. So what I did, it wasn't like I made a choice—you know, like the Leader is asking us to make. It was more like, you know, the absence of a choice. Does that make sense?"

Metin nodded slowly.

"You can make a different choice, you know. If you're having second thoughts." Raoul looked around. I'm treading on thin ice here, he thought. "If you want to leave, or change anything, you know?" He watched Metin's blush rise into his cheeks. "If you need some money, I can help you, you know, get out of town. Or if you want to go home, I've got some cash I can loan you. There's no shame in it. Really. You can go. I'm sure that not everyone is going to be needed. If you decided. To go. Away, that is." Raoul shook his head. "Just—don't think you don't have any options, kid," he said. "You still have a choice, if you want it."

Metin crossed his arms, working the muscles in his jaw. He shook his head once, then stood abruptly. "I've got to go," he said. "Thanks for talking to me, Ismail. And for the breakfast. See you at work."

Raoul sighed, collected the check and counted out the money. Either the kid was on his way to rat him out, or—who knows? He may have saved the young man's life, or sacrificed his own. He smiled as he stood in the sunshine. Or maybe both. Maybe they were both doomed.

He hopped on his rusty bicycle and whistled his way to work. Ironic, he thought. It should have been painful to remember those bad days, but instead it was almost a relief. Things weren't so bad now, were they? Instead of going directly to the gate, he swerved off towards his hidden van. Without going too close, he checked his security devices: strategically placed branches, some white sand that remained undisturbed across the trail, and a collection of glass jars that had not moved from their perch on the roof rack. No one had found his stuff. Yet.

Not that there was a lot to find here, or that anyone would understand what they were seeing. He'd gotten very good at code in the years since his suicide attempt. When he came back to work, after weeks of scrutiny and talking to shrinks, he was much more careful with his record-keeping. Big sister, who'd encouraged the docs to keep him locked away for his own good, helped the bosses decipher his last notebook. Her way of trying to salvage her own position, he figured. Not one to hold a grudge, he never totally trusted anyone after that.

It had been Clara's screw-up that placed his job in jeopardy in the first place, that drove him to darkness, to the psych ward of Bellevue. When she exposed the Puerto Rican freedom fighters-gun running club, instead of merely proving her allegiance to the bureau by ratting out her hometown and some of her own relatives, she'd also screwed both of their careers to the wall. Every move he made was questioned in the months following that blow-up, and he'd been transferred to the West Coast almost immediately.

All the work he'd accomplished in Florida, gone. All the good will of his superiors, turned into questions. Whose side was he on? Could he be relied upon? No more undercover *gusano*. Before he knew what hit him, he was sitting in an office in Long Beach, wearing a tie, reading email and learning Arabic. Who wouldn't consider suicide under those circumstances?

Clara

I BACKED OUT OF the room and found my way to a Starbucks on the corner. They didn't have coffee shops like this in Jerome, Conn., that's for sure. Get your java at "The Hole," if you can cut through the smoky air and backgammon-playing men hunched over the chipped Formica tables. I ordered a grande mocha frappuccino with a shot of espresso and sat staring blankly at the street until a slurp brought on a sharp pain in the forehead. Ice cream headache.

Years melted away...I remembered Saturday afternoons, rainy days when the five of us were trapped in the house. Papa asleep in the middle of the living room and us kids tiptoeing around him, trying to avoid waking him. Trying to avoid doing chores, huddled over the kitchen table, playing bingo and drinking ice cream sodas. A reward for something, an unusual treat. Raoul clutching his head, grimacing with the brain freeze. "Ay-Ay-Ay!" he'd howled. We giggled, massaging his head, rubbing his little brown cheeks until the pain receded. Mama standing in the doorway, smiling, pretending to shush us, sometimes hissing, "Your father will wake up."

Mijo reached again for the straw, tempting—daring—the pain to come back. We'd laughed, oh, yeah, we'd had a few luminous moments in childhood. I clung to those thoughts, looking at the overpriced beverage in my hand.

The midday crowd slowed my reluctant progress to the looming brick monster that housed my office. I hadn't filed any work for the past week, but I usually had a breather after a big assignment, and the last one had involved international travel so I knew I was still golden.

"Hey." Jude at the reception desk handed over a stack of messages.

"What the hell is this?" I grumbled. I waved the pink papers over her desk. "What happened to the voice mail?"

"Your box overflowed a coupla days ago, so I've been catching your calls." She filed a black fingernail. "Don't be bitching at me. You know what a pain in the ass this job is?"

"Yeah, yeah." I backsided the glass doors and left her talking to the huge floral arrangement on the bookcase.

I didn't have any idea what day of the week it was, but one look at the newsroom and I figured it must be Tuesday. Deadline day. Good, no one would even see me.

"Quiñones!" I heard my name above the din. Just my luck, the boss was out on the prowl when I crawled in. His Oxford-striped shirt was stained with looked like the remains of a Chinese takeout lunch. Khakis ballooned under the too-tight belt, tie askew in that "I'm too cool to be collected" way some men have.

His moist embrace was appropriately brief. He stood back, moved a hair away from my eye and looked me over. "You okay?" Squeezed the shoulder. "Where the hell have you been? I thought for a minute you might've been in the towers, but then I got the photos you sent in. Great stuff, by the way. We ran most of 'em. Hoping for a Pulitzer, tragedy and all that. The whole city's gone fucking crazy. The whole country." He took a breath. "Okay, let's get to it, what've you got cooking?"

I didn't follow when he turned and walked through the cubicle maze, still blathering. I went into my office and shut the door. Counted to ten, eleven, twelve, before he opened it and walked in, still talking. "Clara, wassup?" He leaned over the mess on my worktable. "Where you been? Get anything good?"

"Yeah, yeah, I got lots of shots—hey, how's this angle: the grieving family perspective?" I looked out the window, Manhattan sprawled at my feet. "Yeah, front row seats at the funeral of a murder victim."

"Clara…"

"No, really, Robby, it's a good angle." I faced him, narrowing my eyes. "This could be Pulitzer stuff, dontcha think?"

"Okay," he put up his hands. "Talk to me."

I shook my head and dropped my bag on the floor, myself on the high swivel chair before the window.

"Clara," he started. "I'm sorry about your brother, okay? What do you want me to say?" I stared at him, the short squat physique of the former boxer, topped by a baby face and a cap of red curls. His green eyes darkened and the freckles stood out on his crooked nose. "We're not running any of that stuff. Well, maybe one in the regional section. But that's it. Promise."

"That's a start."

"Okay. Okay, I guess, so, I guess you're not back to work, huh?" he paced, hands pocketed, change jingling.

"No, not back to work. Not here, not yet."

"Not here—wait a minute, where've you been? You're not…" his voice dropped to a whisper. "You're not working for someone else, are you? Freelancing? Selling photos to a tabloid? Newspaper? What the hell."

I hugged my rib cage, fingers fitting in between bones that barely seemed able to hold me together. "No, Robby, no…"

"Oh God," he sat on the couch. "You're working it, aren't you? Aren't you?"

I nodded.

"You can't—you haven't been with the bureau for, how long, you can't…" he sputtered. "Your own brother? You're working his case? This is not right, Clara, really."

"I know, Rob, I know," I shrugged. "What can I do? I can't sit by, I gotta know what happened. I can't tell you much, yet, but suffice it to say, this is probably related to the attacks."

"What? I thought it was, you know, a sexual thing gone bad. That's what the wire had," he said.

"That's what they tried to make it look like," I explained. "I can't give you the details, but he was undercover, and he was onto something, and someone took him out. They dressed him up and made it look like something else. That's all I can say."

He rubbed his face with a thick swipe of a meaty hand. I could hear stubble sanding the calluses on his palm. "You got any proof?" he said, finally.

"You should see these yokels, Robby, honest to God, they're not even working the case." I wondered who I was trying to convince. "Really, Rob, I can't walk away. Not from this. These guys think this is open and shut, and I can't let it happen."

"Remember why you left?" he was pacing again. "Remember how you came here, how long it took to get your head back on straight?" His own head bobbed. "I can't let you do it, Clara, I…"

We stared at each other. He gave up first. "I can't stop you, can I?"

"No."

"And I suppose you won't let me help, either."

"Not now, maybe later…" I walked over to him. "Thanks, Robby. Really. I know what I'm doing. I couldn't live with myself if I let it go, you know?"

"Yeah." We sat on the couch together, and he put his hand on my knee. "There's something else."

"What?"

"You tell me." He reached over and took my chin between his thumb and forefinger. "Who is he?"

"Who—what the hell," I shook him off. "Robby, how do you do that?"

"I know you, chica." He rubbed my hand between his fingers. "I know."

"I'm not going to do this, there's no one, just, just, never mind." I marveled at the psychic abilities of my friend. He shook his head, waiting.

"Dammit, it's just a sexual thing, nothing else," I sputtered. "How do you always know? Jesus."

"It's not just sex."

"Drop it, please, I can't argue with you now." I felt incredibly tired. "I just need to get back, I need to finish this. Rob, let me go and take care of this, and I'll be back and it'll be okay," I promised. I promised him, but we both knew I was trying to convince myself.

"Okay, you call me." He let go of my hand and walked to the door. "Call me anytime, okay?"

"Yeah, I'm sure Chris would appreciate that." I tried to smile. His partner was a high maintenance former model and professional neurotic.

"I mean it," he paused. "And don't go getting your heart broke again, you hear?" He paused. "You're not in any danger there, from these people who killed your brother, right? You take care of yourself out there."

I smiled. He had it right—my heart was in danger. It wouldn't be broken, it was already shattered. A dalliance with Guy LeBeau could only add to the shards. Or so I thought.

It wasn't Guy I was thinking about as I neared the Jerome city limits, however, but Mark. It was too late to find him at the station, but I was too wired to return to the hotel. I parked across from my mother's apartment and watched the shadows move across her window. The apartment above was dark, and I toyed with the idea of breaking in.

* * *

"Girls can't do it," I remember Raoul proclaiming. We were on a MacGyver kick that year, trying to create bombs out of shaving cream containers and break into cars with coat hangers. Crouched before the apartment door, Raoul and his sidekick Carl jimmied the lock with an assortment of screwdrivers and rusty nails. They wouldn't let me near it, and I chewed my fingers waiting atop the stairs. Sweat poured from their faces as I strained to hear the grunted suggestions when they switched positions.

"How about a credit card?" I whispered.

They looked at each other and rolled their eyes.

"That's what they do on Columbo," I hissed again.

The outside door creaked open and we froze, and then lunged for the stairs. Pushing past Mrs. Brimfield, crashing through the door and outside, running down the street and up to the train tracks. Stretching legs, loping along the ties, red-faced and tingling from yet another escape.

We stopped just above the center mall parking lot, the hilltop thick with trees and garbage. Old tattered blankets strung over branches made tents that housed several grizzled bums. No one was around, so we flopped onto the ground and tried to catch our breath.

"That was close," I said.

"Caramba, you're such a baby," Raoul said.

"Yeah." Carl was not very original in those days.

"What do you mean? We almost got caught."

Raoul brushed the hair out of his eyes. "You can't get in trouble for breaking into your own apartment," he sneered.

"So why did you run?" I stood up and brushed off my shorts.

"To get away from you," Carl said, laughing. "Dumb girl."

* * *

I put the car in gear and glided down Summer Street towards the fancy houses.

There was a big white house with a cupola that I'd always loved. Even in the dusky late afternoon light, I could see the careful paint job that accentuated the Victorian details of the massive home. Most of these big old houses were now doctors' or lawyers' offices, with the occasional funeral home interspersed; no one else could afford to live in them anymore. The days of big families and multi-generation households were long gone, and only an active preservation group stood between these painted ladies and a block of condominiums.

I turned down Federal Street and surveyed the decimation of downtown. What used to be a thriving street was a parking lot, which I used. I locked up and crossed to McGinty's. A better class of drinker in here, I wagered.

The large window sparkled with light, and I looked for the red neon lobster that had graced the bar when it was known as Henry's. The wood-paneled walls and shiny bar had replaced what used to be a dark wallpaper and vinyl booth establishment. Steam rose over hot hors d'oeuvres in shiny serving dishes, and men with striped ties lifted brown bottles to their sad faces. That part didn't change, no matter how many bars you went into: the loneliness of the solitary drinker. I ordered a glass of wine and joined the home team.

Baseball loomed like a silent ballet on the large screen television. No one seemed to be watching the flashing images passing noiselessly on the wall. Music played, phones rang, the door tinkled open and shut, and the cacophony of daily life vibrated my eardrums. A male on the make interrupted my internal conversation.

"New in town?"

I wondered if a response was even required for a question like that. I looked guardedly over my shoulder, formulating a reply that wouldn't start with an F.

My retort was cut off by the braying laughter that I would recognize blindfolded. "Hey, chica! Had you going there for a minute, didn't I?" He was all teeth; same as the last time I saw the face, except now there was no fuzzy mop of hair to camouflage the plain ugliness of it.

"Louie, is that you?" I leaned away from his nodding, blinding glee. "Louie Rapture. What happened to all your hair?"

"Hey, that's not nice." His rubber face twisted into a frown, but the eyes were still crinkled in a smile as he tried unsuccessfully to act offended.

"Really, what the hell happened to your face?" I asked, looking closely at the beige splotches that were taking over his previously café au lait skin. He seemed to blush, which would not have shown up in his darker-skinned days. I decided to apologize, but before I could retract my rudeness, his laughter circumvented my effort.

"Sorry, Louie," I shrugged. "I'm having a little trouble with my social graces these days."

"No worries," he cackled. "Pretty soon I'm going to be whiter than most everyone in this damned town." His gleeful pate turned somber. "I was so sorry to hear about Raoul," he almost whispered. "I wasn't surprised, but still…"

"What do you mean?" My spine tingled all the way up to my hairline.

"Oh. You know. The stuff he was into, it was, well…" He wouldn't meet my eyes any longer. "He was into some bad things, Clara, that's all I'm saying. Drugs and stuff."

"Louie, you have to tell me everything," I pressed his arm. "Were you in touch with him since he was back in town?"

"Well, yeah," he signaled the bartender. "Double Dewars, straight up."

I waited. We sat silently, watching the bartender assemble the simple shot of whiskey. "You want another?" he asked me.

"Not yet, thanks." I turned to Louie when the bearded man walked to the other side of the bar. "You have to tell me. Please, Lou."

"Okay, okay." He took a long swig of the liquor. "I heard some things around town. Like he was dealing and that you could get some good shit from him."

"Who told you this?" I asked. "Where was he selling from? My God, what the hell was he doing?"

He laughed, just once, a short bark that betrayed the tough character behind the goofy face. "That's not all."

"What?"

"It doesn't matter, Clara, he's gone now," his voice had changed. "Let's just say he was a messed up guy and somebody took him out."

"I can't dismiss my brother that easily, Louie. You should know that." I let a little anger waver in my voice. "I'm surprised that you can be so hard-assed about it, considering how many times we bailed your ass out of trouble."

He shrugged trying to avoid my eyes.

"Louie, I need to know what you know. I need to know what Raoul was doing, and who he was running with." I pressed.

"Listen," he almost whispered. "I don't think we should talk about this right now." He lifted his head and barely nodded in the direction of the door, where Mark and another man stood in the shadows. "Cops," he whispered.

"Don't worry about it," I said. I looked at his eyes, the heavy lids hooded and shadowed. His jaw was tight. "Okay. Just tell me where I can reach you," I said. "I'm not dropping this."

"Give me a number and I'll call you," he pushed a napkin in front of me.

I scribbled my cell number on it and he folded the paper into his pocket. "I'll get you later, chica," he said smoothly. I lifted my cheek for his kiss. His lips were dry and parched, and he smelled like an old cellar.

I pulled his arm closer. "Don't forget to call," I said, digging my nails into his arm. I pasted a wide smile on my face. "It was really good to see you."

"Yeah, you too," he smiled limply, but his eyes were focused on a spot over my shoulder. "I'll call."

I didn't trust him but I had to let him go. He skirted Mark and his companion and slid into the night. I ordered another drink and waited for an opportunity to speak with Mark. I feigned an interest in the baseball game on television.

"'scuse me, miss." Mark stood next to me and I could feel the heat rising off his body. "Scully? Can I get a couple of drinks over here?" He signaled.

I slid my left hand along the bar and passed the mailbox key to him under a napkin. Mark stepped slightly to the right and folded it into his hand. Out of the corner of my eye, I watched as the paper was slipped into his pocket. I was barely breathing. I almost started giggling, waiting for the password. Just like a character in a bad spy movie.

I took my time finishing the watered-down wine and listened to Mark bid fare-well to his companions. I waited as long as I could, calculating how long it would take him to get to the mailbox place, and when I could stand it no longer, I headed back into the night.

Still in spy-mode, I scoped out the parking lot before pulling in. I wondered which one of us was Holmes and which was Watson. I knew who I wanted to be, always the source of arguments between Raoul and me. There was no sign of Mark, but I waited a few minutes before going inside anyway. I saw a white envelope through the window of my box, and my hand shook as I tried to insert the little metal key. I removed a white business envelope that was heavy with a ring of keys. In the car, I tore it open and unfolded a ruled sheet with neat printing.

Be careful, Mark had written. The building is still under surveillance.

Although I wanted to get in there right away, I appreciated the warning. The lights would probably attract attention, and I wouldn't want my mother to call in the cavalry when she heard footsteps upstairs. I decided to wait. I sat in the parking lot, watching the door of the Mail Room. Darkness had fallen around me and I listened to the thrum of traffic barreling into town on the city's main drag.

Raoul

WHEN HE FIRST CAME into town, Raoul took his time setting up a routine that would cover his presence at the shipyard. He spent some time watching the different groups, the white working-class guys, mostly French Canadians and Irish, who stayed away from the Latinos, who in turn watched the so-called towel-heads with suspicion. There were few African Americans in this town, only the occasional sailor passing through who quickly learned that his presence was not exactly welcome in Jerome. The Spanish guys did most of the physical labor: they were the mechanics and lawnscapers and painters. The Middle Easterners, wherever they were from, worked a variety of menial positions at the shipyard. Occasionally, a family from Pakistan came into town and bought a convenience store, but they never did manual labor. And the whites, they were angry. Their town had been overrun with foreigners, and their resentment grew harder each year. They rhapsodized about the good old days when they held all the good jobs at the yard, when their fathers could become foremen, and when their mothers didn't have to work to make ends meet.

Now they were all in the same boat, and no one was happy about it. Raoul knew this town, its history and people, better than anyone. Of course, he had his prejudices, too, but he kept those close to the vest when making his observations in code and in weekly reports. He'd been sent to follow up some intelligence that had ordnance walking off the base, enough so that the agency had been asked to get involved, though quietly. So, finally, Raoul was back on the East Coast, using both his knowledge of the town, his Spanish, and his recently acquired Arabic to figure out what was happening.

It was mostly small stuff that was missing, some weapons and a couple of hand-held rocket launchers that the Navy was eager to recover. Raoul found some of them pretty easily, simply by snooping around the Rod & Gun Club one night. What hunters planned to do with a bunch of machine guns was beyond him, but the takedown was quick and there was no fallout, so Raoul stayed on the job.

He used his own boat to get around the piers quietly at night and stumbled upon more than a few illicit sex partners. The sight of naked butts flashing along the beach was of no concern to him. One night, when there was no moon and the sky was inky black, he almost got into a shoot-out with a black speedboat cruising around the point. His efforts to pretend to be a fisherman were not successful, and his boat was towed out into the Sound—and away from any ears.

"¿Digame, quien esta? Tell me, who are you, who are you working for?" a man wearing an eye patch asked. Raoul found his black satin shirt, black eye patch, and flashing gold tooth almost laughable, until he saw the big black gun that completed the man's outfit.

"I'm just going fishing, man," Raoul replied, laying on his Spanish accent and lowering his eyelids lazily. "I ain't doing nothing to you-all."

While he stood unsteadily in the black boat, being scrutinized by the Pirate, Raoul's little rowboat was ransacked. "There's nothing here," the flunky called K yelled over. He'd dumped most of Raoul's possessions overboard after he looked through each piece, and Raoul watched his belongings float away in the tide.

"Man, I don care what you all are doing out here. I'm just goin' fishin'. Now kin I go?" he asked.

"No." The Pirate gestured with his gun. "Pull up your shirt."

He did. The man grunted at the sight of his naked chest.

"You a cop?"

"Me? You're kidding, right? Man…" Raoul bent over laughing. He reached into the pocket of his tee shirt and pulled out a joint. "You got a light?"

"Sit here." Another gesture with the gun. "Sit!"

He sat, scratching his nose and trying not to look at the Pirate. Too much familiarity with these guys, and he'd be a witness to get rid of rather than just a nuisance whose boat crossed too close. He studied his thick doobie, tucked it safely behind an ear.

"So. You not a cop. You work for somebody?"

"Yeah, man, I work at the shipyard, same as everybody around here."

"What do you do there?" Gun crossed against his chest, the man was looking more relaxed.

"You know, stuff—move this over here, pile that over there. Stuff," Raoul said.

"And you make good money doing that?"

"Nah, I make shit. But they's no other jobs in this town, man. I work awhile, then I take off. Hang around till I need money, you know." Raoul leaned back a little, trying to mimic the Pirate's pose.

"K, what do you think? This kid knows the water. Maybe we can use him. You know the water, right kid? You're out here all the time, we seen you before. You know the water."

"Yeah man. I grew up here. I know all the currents, the caves, shit like that, man," Raoul said.

"K? What do you think? See kid, we lost our boat guy—you know, the captain of the ship? He had a little accident couple of nights ago, and K here is not so comfortable with the wheel. So we need someone to occasionally, you see, take us around. To do some business. At night. Along the shore."

"What kind of business?" Raoul asked. He looked up at the man standing silent next to him, then back to the Pirate, whose finger was scratching something underneath the eye patch that Raoul hoped not to see.

"Just, some delivery business. No need for you to know details. We can give you a good, ah, wage for this. If you're interested. You want to make some easy money? You know, we'll try you out, see how it goes. Give you a couple bucks to start and if you're a good worker, then we can talk about more. Sound good to you?"

Raoul cocked his head. As he was about to answer, the Pirate swung his gun back towards Raoul's chest. "You just say yes, now, boy," the Pirate chuckled. "You don't want to say no to me. Does he, K?"

K shook his head, pressed his hand down on Raoul's shoulder. "No," he said.

"Okay then," Raoul wrung his hands together. "When do I start?"

"Tomorrow night. Meet us here. Wear black. And don't tell anyone you're coming. If I find out you talked—or if you go to the cops—you won't be going fishing any more. Capisce?"

"Yes, yes, sir," Raoul said. He got up, unsteadily, and turned to make his way to his boat.

"K," the Pirate said, gesturing once again with his weapon. "Frisk him again. Make sure he doesn't have anything on him."

I guess he took that literally, Raoul thought as he swam back to his rowboat. After retrieving his fishing pole, bait box, and cooler, he tossed them into the boat and pulled his naked body up. His clothes had been tossed onto the captain's chair of the speedboat.

"You can get your things tomorrow," the Pirate shouted, laughing as Raoul pulled his oars into place. At least his keys were still on the lanyard he'd hooked under the seat when the other boat pulled alongside.

He shivered to shore, made a beeline for his van, and jotted his notes while wrapped in a thermal sleeping bag. It was summer, sure, but a cool breeze off the water had not just frozen his balls but tightened all the muscles in his back. Morning was going to bring a long day, and an interesting new "delivery" job. He could hardly wait.

"Still in the game," he hummed.

Clara

CARS PULLED IN AND out around me as I watched the activity, wondering why so many residents of this town felt the need to rent boxes. I fingered the note in my hand, no name written, no letterhead to give away the sender. Were there so many clandestine affairs in Jerome?

I put the car in gear and drove to the hotel. The bar, its dark walls dominated by a large sports network poster, was empty save for the bartender, humming tonelessly while he polished glasses.

"What can I do you for?" he asked cheerfully. "My name is Larry, by the by, and FYI." His handshake felt like a piece of fresh liver.

My God, a talker, I thought. Just what I need tonight. "I'll have a glass of white wine—what have you got?"

He showed me a bottle from a vineyard I'd never heard of, and we launched into one of those inane discussions about wine that keep you from enjoying whatever you've chosen to drink. So now I knew that Connecticut is a wine-producing state, and that the recent years of drought have been a boon for the vineyards. He chuckled while pouring popcorn into an old fashioned machine on the counter.

"I can't get enough of this stuff," he said, patting his enormous belly.

"Don't get much business here, huh?" I asked.

"Some nights, we're jamming," he shrugged. "Sometimes a group comes from the base, but you never know."

"Where else do they go?"

He shrugged again. "Who knows? You can't rely on these kids." He shook his head. "They're fickle, not real regulars."

I nodded, sipping the watery chardonnay. It packed a punch, however, and I tried to focus on the big screen television. It seemed like the same baseball game I'd been watching at McGinty's, but how could you tell? My eyes glazed at the green plaid grass and the ubiquitous scratching and spitting of the ballplayers.

"Sports fan?" The bartender was leaning close on his side of the vast wooden partition.

"Nope," I shook my head. "Just killing time." I thought the better of that and added, "I'm waiting for someone."

Seemingly on cue, the door behind opened and a loud couple tumbled in, looking for entertainment.

The bartender moved in for the kill, adjusting the volume on the stereo a couple of notches louder. I focused on the television and emptied a second glass of wine.

"Can we change the channel?" I asked when he came back to refill my glass.

"No, sorry," he frowned. "Management policy—we've got to keep it on one of the sports network channels all the time."

"Why?"

"Management doesn't want the news on, doesn't want to provoke any arguments here. Like I said, once in a while we get a group in from the base, and sometimes they used to mix it up with the locals. But they don't patronize the bar much. I think the officers have their own place on base, and the grunts usually drive into the city whenever they get the chance." Larry leaned closer. "I think we should spruce the place up a little, maybe bring in a band once in a while, that'll help. But what the hell do I know?" he shrugged again. "I'm just the bartender. Popcorn?"

I nodded gratefully and busied myself with wine and overly salted popcorn. Careful not to bite into any kernels, I spit a few unpopped ones into my napkin. An encounter with the wrong end of a handgun during my rookie year with the FBI had resulted in half my mouth being filled with porcelain caps. Who knew how fragile those were? Most of my teeth had been repaired several times before I learned to avoid all hard candy and unpopped corn. I returned my focus to what now seemed to be a soccer game in a very hot place. Coaches paced beneath misted canopies.

I hadn't paid attention to a soccer game since Raoul was named all-state player in the high school leagues years ago. His short, lithe body was perfect for the game, and he was able to run the field for an entire hour without appearing winded. I remember jumping up and down on the sidelines, screaming at the ref when a goal was disallowed.

Afterwards, Raoul tried to explain the concept of offsides to me. "No, I don't think that's right," I'd argued.

He guzzled from a plastic bottle filled with neon colored green stuff. "Clara, it's the rule," he lectured. "When a player gets ahead of the defense…."

"He deserved to get the point if he runs faster than the other team," I finished.

"Ay, chica, you'll never get it," he shook his head.

"You deserved that point," I said stubbornly.

"You're my best fan," he agreed. "Just stop insulting the refs, okay? They don't appreciate it."

"Well, I think he should retire," I pushed. "The old fart could hardly get his fat butt up the field, so how could he see what was happening?" I gestured with my arms as we stopped at a red light. "And how can you drink that sea water?" I asked. "That can't be healthy."

Raoul started laughing and choking on his Gatorade. "Clara, you're the best," he croaked.

*

A tear slid down my cheek when I recalled the laughter we had shared. So many hours we had spent together—driving Raoul to practice, to games, to dates, even to the Navy recruitment office when he was not yet sixteen.

"Sorry, son," the stiff recruiter had said. "Come back when you're eighteen and we'll get you signed up."

Raoul had made me swear not to tell anyone about it, as he stuffed a pile of brochures in his backpack. When he finally did sign up, he was driving his own car, and I didn't know what he'd done until the day Mama found out. I shook my head and tried to focus on the dots moving on the television screen.

I didn't notice when he came in but felt the presence of a man sliding into the seat on my right. I kept my body turned towards the screen and listened while he ordered a beer, "and another drink for the pretty lady." The bartender looked in my direction, and I nodded my acceptance of the drink. I hadn't seen Guy—without his wife attached—for a couple of days and was eager to hear his latest pitch.

"Clara," he spoke softly into my ear, his breath warming my shoulder. "I've missed you."

I ducked my head over the wineglass and waited.

"Where've you been? I've been going crazy."

I turned slowly and looked into his deep blue eyes. They were laced with red lines, and he needed a shave. "I can't stop thinking about you," he said.

"I was in New York, I told you," I replied. "I don't know what you think is going to happen, Guy, but…"

His strong fingers gripped my leg, and I winced. "No, Clara, I need you," he growled. "I know you want me, too. You can't deny it—I know you."

I was a little frightened by the intensity of his stare and the bruising strength of his hand. I put my hand on his chest and tried to get some breathing room. "Guy," I smiled. "I know what you're saying, but I don't want to get involved with a married man." My heart was beating so loudly I wondered if the other patrons of the bar could hear it, but no one was even looking in our direction.

"Guy, please," I whispered.

"Clara," his tongue grazed my ear lobe. "Let's go upstairs."

I shook my head. "I don't think that's a good idea," I began.

"No," he interrupted. "You want me as much as I want you."

The room was suddenly filled with a large group who crowded around the bar and shouted orders to the bartender and insults at each other. I took the opportunity to extricate myself from Guy. His eyes burned and I wondered how long he'd been drinking before stumbling into the hotel. "I'll be back in a sec," I said. I slipped through the crowd and into the restroom.

Locked into a stall, I leaned against the cold metal partition. I'd also had a few glasses of wine—I'd lost count of how many—and I wasn't very steady on my feet. It would be easy to take him upstairs and satisfy the curiosity I'd been harboring since our first encounter. Too easy. I was still rattled by Mark's knowledge of my relationship with Guy. And I had to admit, I only liked sex when it was under my control. Tonight, it didn't feel that way.

There was a knock on the door and then it creaked open.

"Clara, are you in here?" Guy whispered.

I straightened my hair and opened the stall. "Guy, you can't be here," I said. "I'll be out in a minute."

"Is there someone else here?" He looked under the doors. "Come on, Clara, relax."

"Let's go back to the bar," I said. I reached for the door handle, but he pushed me hard against the door. I could feel every inch of him straining along my backside, and I couldn't help but respond. I turned abruptly and took his face into my hands, forcing my tongue into his mouth. His hands slid to my butt and pulled my body into his crotch, and we rocked there, breathless, groping, until I felt someone push on the other side of the door.

"Hey, let me in." A woman's voice accompanied the pounding on the door.

"Just a minute," I said in a hoarse falsetto. I straightened out my blouse and stepped away from the door while Guy wiped his face with the back of his hand. He lifted his eyebrows, and I opened the door.

"Well," a woman with big hair and too much makeup huffed inside. She took one look at Guy and then at me, and before she could say another word, we walked quickly to the hallway. More and more, the time I spent with Guy deposited me back into the idiocy of adolescence.

I shook off Guy's efforts to pull me towards the elevator and went back into the bar. The boisterous bunch had taken over part of the room, and a couple of men in business suits were lolling at the counter, engrossed in the television. I slipped back into my seat and asked the bartender if he could get me a glass of ice water. Worse case scenario, I could use it to cool things off. Guy pressed against my side and I inhaled his musty scent.

"You should go now," I said softly. "It's getting late."

"I can't believe you," he shook his head. "How can you just shut me down like this?"

The bartender came over and asked if we needed anything. I must have had a desperate look on my face, because he stayed in front of us, wiping the counter, even after Guy said we were fine. "Can I have the tab?" I asked.

When we were alone again, I picked up Guy's hand and, fiddling with his wedding ring, shook my head slowly. "Guy, I'm sorry, but you've got to go home now," I said.

He frowned and pulled his hand away. "What's the matter with you? I never know how you're going to be—one minute you're all over me, and the next time we're together, you blow me off," he said. "I'm getting sick of playing games."

That was one way to put the brakes on his ardor. I was alternately titillated and scared by the intensity of his gaze. Without control of the situation, however, I was unwilling to make a move. "Give me a break," I said lightly. "The last time I saw you, Bambi was holding the end of what looked like a very short leash. So don't put this on me."

"Fine," he pushed away from the bar. "I'll see you around, then."

"Fine," I said. I smiled as the bartender placed the bill in front of me, and I added the tip before signing it with my room number. When I turned back, Guy was gone. I sighed and looked up at the television again. I wasn't ready to face the empty room, but it had been a very long day and I was hopeful that sleep would come easily. Perhaps a little assistance was in order, so I ordered a brandy and nursed it for an hour.

The room was neat and impersonal when I finally made it upstairs, and my clothes fell easily onto the floor beside the pile of papers I'd left there. The message light flashed an irritating tempo on the wall until I threw a pillow to cover it.

Raoul

HIS WORK WITH THE Pirate was pretty straightforward. Most nights, Raoul followed the bend of the shore, hiding quietly in caves or lying low while helicopters and Coast Guard boats patrolled the waters. He knew just when to throttle down, to coast slickly into a marsh and dodge the searchlights. More than once, he saved the Pirate from a close call.

"How did you know?" the man demanded once. "I didn't hear anything, and you, pow, the engine cut and you're flat on the deck before I even hear a sound. Are you a cop? How do you know where they are?" He took out the big gun and squinted while sighting Raoul. "So, what's your secret?"

"I can feel them, the vibrations, before I can hear them," Raoul said. "Years of practice, I guess."

"Huh." K and the Pirate whispered to each other, and Raoul pretended to ignore them for the remainder of the night. When the sky was lightening up, he headed towards the cove. "Where you going?" the Pirate demanded. "Did I tell you we was done?"

"No, but the sun is going to come up and…"

"And nothing." The Pirate threw an empty can at Raoul. It clinked across the floorboards well short of its target. "We have to make one special pickup today, so head out into the deep, boy."

"I have to be at work…"

"Shut the fuck up," the Pirate yelled. "I'm the boss here. And if this goes well, you can take the rest of the day off—how's that? Play your cards right and you can quit that stinking shipyard."

The Pirate took the boat out into the Sound. The sky was getting light but the men seemed oblivious to the danger of exposure. They circled around, pulled tight to a deserted boat launch, and idled.

"Go get the package," the Pirate told Raoul. He gestured towards the parking area, empty but for a delivery van puffing black smoke. Not stopping to argue or question, Raoul jumped into the water, swam a few strokes until he felt the rocks under his feet, then slogged up the concrete embankment. He could hear the boat engine idling behind, the squeal of a badly maintained engine in the van he approached, and in the middle, the squeak-slosh of his ruined sneakers keeping time with his misery. It was cold, he was soaked, and this diversion from their offshore business made him jumpy.

"Yo," he knocked on the closed driver window. "Got something for Leon?"

A small man, probably just hitting five feet in height, squinted as he sized up Raoul's dripping visage. "Who are you?" he asked. His low voice convinced Raoul that this was not a kid joyriding in his father's van.

"I'm just the messenger, man," Raoul said. "Got something?"

The window came down, and a small bundle shoved through the window. "Money?"

"He didn't give me anything, just told me to pick up a package." Raoul unrolled the canvas page and peered inside. "Pills?"

"Duh." The window started rising. "Tell Leon that this is a sample. More to come, if he pays the price I asked. That's all."

The van was in gear and moving backwards before Raoul had time to move out of the way. The tire rolled over the tip of his left shoe. "Dammit," he screamed at the driver. "You ran over my fucking toes!"

He limped back to the boat launch, the sack thrown over his shoulder. He gestured for Leon to bring the boat closer, and then he was able to toss the bag and then himself into the boat without taking another swim.

"Fucking guy ran over my fucking toes," he said. He reached down and unlaced the left sneaker. His toes were swelling up, the nail on the big toe already turning black. "Fuck."

Leon chuckled as he gunned the engine and took them out into deeper water. "So now you've met my nephew, Leroy. Good looking boy, don't you think? K, take the rudder. Let me see what we have here." Leon opened the bag, held up a plastic bag with three pharmaceutical size bottles inside. "Nice—good stuff. I told you the kid was going to be a good source for us, eh? We can sell this shit for a lot of dough."

Raoul stopped massaging his toe. "Where'd he get that?"

"Fell off a delivery to CVS last night. My nephew is a regional manager for CVS. He travels all over the state, checking to make sure that stores meet the display requirements, stuff like that. And sometimes, when they aren't up to snuff, he takes a little compensation to look the other way."

"Huh." Raoul grunted. "So now you're going to be pushing prescriptions?"

"Actually, no," Leon said, grinning. "You are."

"No."

"You are. We have our base, you know, the coke and heroin trade. But there's a lot of money to be made selling pills. You're young enough to reach the partiers. You'll see. We're going to have a little party tonight, aren't we K? We rented a room at the hotel, and we're going to send out a notice that there's a pharma party in town. The first time's the hardest." He laughed open-mouthed for a minute. "But once the word gets out, we'll be rolling in dough."

"So what does this have to do with me?" Raoul asked.

"You're going to be our party host. You are young and you clean up pretty good. We'll get you some designer duds, and you will be the next hot thing in Jerome."

"Shit."

"What, I thought you would love this gig. You won't have to work that stinking shipyard job anymore—it's going to be party, party, party all the time for you," the Pirate said.

"No more late night boat rides?" Raoul asked.

"Hey, what about me?" K interrupted. "How come he gets the good gig?"

"You are my boat man, Special K," the Pirate said. "You don't belong on land. You and I, we're meant to be on the water." Leon looked at Raoul's foot. "You gonna be alright to party tonight? Here, let's see if we got anything for that toe—Oh, my, two bottles of Viagra. How about some Darvocet?" He rattled the bottle. "We got some good shit here."

Raoul massaged his foot. This was a good opportunity, he agreed, because he'd been getting nowhere spending nights on this boat. These two characters were obviously not running weapons out of the naval base, and he hadn't seen any signs of other boats during these past few weeks with the Pirate. For a brief moment, he contemplated the ethics of selling stolen prescription meds. *"Hell, at least it's better than pushing heroin,"* he thought. In past operations, he'd done worse—taking the drugs himself, using cocaine, the whole nine yards.

Clara

IMAGES PLAYED IN MY head throughout the night, and I was pacing again when the clock hit 3:00 a.m. I must've had a full hour of sleep, and I woke with a chest-pounding jolt. What was I missing, and what was I looking for? The questions seemed more elusive than the answers, and I took out a pad to start taking notes.

First thing, as soon as the sky was a little pink, I called Spike and left a message on his machine asking for an update. Then Peterson was next on the list, the unknown man who might know something about Raoul's last days. I collapsed back onto the bed after writing as much as I'd learned to date and realizing that I had started running in circles. I had a pretty good idea what Raoul had been doing before he died, but I needed to run down the loose ends before I could let him rest. I was too tired to cry, and too bereft to give myself a break. Echoes of criticism from my mother and sisters rang in my ears, and I wished again that I knew where my father had landed after his abandonment of his progeny. I'd have to run another computer search for his social security number, but each year that passed I was more convinced that the old man was dead, too.

Spike called me back before I'd gotten over my attack of the blues, but his news prompted me to open the blinds and let the sun drench the beige room. "Hey Clara, howya doin'," he chortled. "Got some news for you, and I think you're gonna like it."

"God, Spike, I really need that now," I said. "Tell."

"You got a fax there? I'll send ya some interesting stuff I dug up, howzat?"

"Great, you're the best," I said breathlessly. "Can you tell me what you found?"

"Hang on a sec," he said, cutting me off abruptly. I listened to the dead air, willing him to come back on line. "Come on, Spike, baby," I whispered. Come on, come on.

A dial tone disrupted my mantra and I glared at the phone until it started to beep angrily. "Dammit," I flung the receiver back on the base. "Call back for the fax number," I pleaded. Scrambling across the room, I dug into my bag for his number. What the hell was the fax number, I wondered. I pawed through the hotel propaganda piled on the rickety desk. Papers flew, curses rained, dirty clothes were flung from my bags to litter the floor until I threw myself back on the bed and waited for the phone to ring again. Inevitably, it did, but of course it was not Spike.

"Guy," I sniffled.

"What's wrong?" he demanded.

I didn't answer, but merely sobbed with frustration.

"Oh, shit," his voice softened. "Clara, what's going on? Talk to me, girl."

"I, I'm just. Oh, never mind," I floundered. I was sure he'd be on my doorstep in a moment if I didn't get my act together. "I'm okay, I just had a phone call and I can't find some papers."

"Oh." His disappointment was palpable.

"Um, I need to keep the line clear, okay?" I put on a little girl voice.

"Oh, yeah, sure," he mumbled. "Sorry I bothered you...I just, uh, wanted to apologize for last night...."

"Okay, no problem. Forget about it." I tried to take a light tone.

"Well, I just wanted to be sure..." he hesitated. "Ahh, things are a little blurry this morning and I wasn't sure exactly what happened."

"Oh, I see," I said. There was another uncomfortable silence. What should I tell him? About the bruises on my leg, the rash on my neck? I was floundering as much as he at that point.

"You sure you're okay?"

"Fine, fine, thanks a lot," I said. "Listen, I'll talk to you later, okay? I really need to keep the line open." I depressed the connection and banged the receiver against my head. "Idiot."

The phone rang on the third crack, just as I was about to give myself a concussion. "Yes?"

"Sorry, I had another call and you know how it is," Spike breathed. "What's your fax number? I'll get this to you right away."

I recited a number and thanked him profusely, but he cut me off in the middle, before I could renew my begging for an advance on his discovery. What the hell. I called down to the desk and asked them to bring the fax to my room as soon as it arrived. The shower beckoned.

Dressed and still waiting for the report, I stuffed a pair of latex gloves and plastic bags into my camera bag along with a few rolls of fresh film. I didn't want to leave evidence behind in Raoul's apartment and brought the lunch bags in the off chance that I found something the cops had overlooked. I rewound the tape on my voice-activated recorder and checked the batteries. Restlessly, I loaded film into the camera and played with the light meter. What was taking so long? The phone rang as my hand hovered over the receiver.

"Hello?" a tentative voice croaked.

"Hello?" I waited. "Can I help you? Who are you calling?"

"Is this Clara Quiñones?"

"Yes, who's calling please?" I tapped a finger lightly on the console.

"This is Peterson, Alfred Peterson," he said. "I had a message that you called me." There was a note of injury in his voice and I guestimated his age at close to seventy or more.

"Mr. Peterson, thank you for calling me back," I gushed. "Can we meet? Where are you?"

"I'm at the club, cleanin' up the usual mess," he said. "Come over if you want."

The connection was disconnected abruptly and I stared at the receiver for a second. "Okay then," I said. "Let's get this show on the road."

I opened the door and looked around. A cleaning cart down the hall was the only sign of life in my wing of the hotel. There was a newspaper, a white business envelope with my name scrawled in red ink, and a single red rose wrapped in cellophane on the floor in front of the door. I sighed as I picked up the items and inhaled the promise implied by the rose. There was no note, of course, and I supposed that it must have come from Guy.

Behind the cover sheet, the fax was a single sheet of densely printed material that required a magnifying glass to decipher. Spike had an annoying habit of using the smallest, most dense font for his correspondence. The only item I could read with the naked eye was the invoice amount at the bottom of the page, but I barely registered the number. I started reading the report, pulling the lamp close.

The call was made from a private pay phone, such as you find in some areas of Manhattan and the Bronx. These lines have a distinct sound in the wire, usually because they are grafted onto the main telephone lines strung by NYNEX in New York. The call was made at night, which can be identified primarily by the background voice isolated to be a deejay commonly known as The Head who broadcasts every evening from seven to midnight in the city. The radio was playing in a car passing slowly by the telephone booth, and I can distinguish two male voices in the car, which, by the way, was a souped-up Jeep, probably a '95 or '96 from the sound of the engine and the squeaking of the shocks. I'll get back to the car in a second. From the tape of the show, the call was made at 8:43 p.m. The sound of a boat in the background places the booth at the waterfront, and when I checked shipping ports and ferry schedules, I found the most likely spot for the call is the lower Westside, probably just above Chelsea Pier. From his pattern of respiration, the caller's blood pressure was elevated and he was having an asthma attack or some other kind of serious breathing problem. The slight slurring of the speech suggests some kind of narcotic influence, and there is a minor problem with the pronunciation of the letter "r." The passengers in the Jeep are talking Spanish and I was able to make out only a few phrases in the short time they are in earshot, which, loosely translated, include "Look at that one," and "Pull over here." From the buzzing in the background, I can guess that he was standing fairly close to a crosswalk, probably an older stoplight that is on the way to obsolescence. There is a metallic sound, like keys or loose change being jangled in a pocket, and a clicking like two or three pieces of plastic rubbing together at the same rhythm. There are pedestrians on the street, some kids on bikes, and I can make out gears shifting just about three feet past his position. There are brake sounds and tire noises indicating that vehicles are making a turn nearby, and there may be some kind of incline that necessitates changing gears at that corner. A taxi was on the street, its meter ticking and the engine idling when the driver put it in park, as many of the foreign drivers like to do to save gas. There was some exchange coming over the radio, but I think it was Hindu because none of it was familiar. Someone was probably pulling together cash for the fare, and the call ended before I picked up any exchange between the driver and his passenger. A bus passed probably about a block away; just close enough to catch the air pressure sound of the brakes at a stop. There were no subway rumbles or telltale door opening tones, so the call was either not near a subway line or just between traffic below ground level. I did pick up the distant sound of a police car, but again, it must have been at least two blocks away and not close enough to pursue for witnesses. I examined a topographical map of lower Manhattan and have narrowed it to the meatpacking district on the lower Westside. Your best options here are (1) The Jeep with the two Spanish speakers, (2) the taxi, which might be hard to locate, and (3) maybe the phone records, if we can pin down the exact phone booth. I'll scope it out and let you know.

"Bless you," I whispered silently. I was always amazed at the things Spike could pull out of a noisy recording, amazed and fascinated. Now the question was whether this was going to give me any information that I could use. I stuffed the paper in my bag, took another deep sniff of the rose now teetering in a cloudy water glass on the bureau, and headed off to meet Mr. Peterson.

There was no vehicle in front of the Eagle's but I saw the back door propped open with a pool cue as I pulled slowly around the little stucco-covered box. A huge green dumpster was overflowing with large beams that looked like the remnants of a house fire, and I drove behind the box and parked.

The door creaked loudly as I pushed it aside and let my eyes adjust to the darkness. Peterson was as old and crooked as his voice on the phone and I cringed to watch him shove aside tables as he swabbed the floor with a dirt-brown mop. The reek of beer and cigarettes was intensified by the slurry he was sloshing on what was once a black and white checkerboard floor. A butt balanced precariously on his jutting lower lip, and I waited for the ash to drop on his stained white tee shirt, heavily yellowed beneath sleeves that hung loosely over the pasty white arms working the mop.

When he turned to answer my query, I recoiled from the sight of his marble-blue eyes, the pupils completely obscured by milky white scar tissue. "Mr. Peterson?" I asked. How valuable was a blind witness? I wondered, watching the little man turn to face me like a sunflower leans towards the light.

"Eh. You Clara?" he grunted.

"Yes, I am," I said. "I'm Raoul's sister."

"Humph." He turned towards the bar and grasped a stool with hands twisted by arthritis. "What do you want me for?"

"I heard that you were working the last time Raoul was in here," I began.

"Don't know." He cut me off. I watched, fascinated, as he rounded the bar and began unloading beer bottles from a case on the counter. "I'm always here, cleaning up, but I don't keep track of people comin' in and out."

"He got a call that day, and you answered it," I pushed. "It was about two weeks ago."

He shrugged. I had a bird's eye view of the top of his bald head, white wisps of hair over his ears swirling like a nimbus cloud that had been punctured by a lumpy, freckled bullet. The tee shirt logo featured garishly colored skulls and graffiti-style lettering of the word Hazmat.

"Please, Mr. Peterson, try to remember," I begged.

He looked up, not directly at me but to the left, the seat I'd been told was Raoul's usual place in the bar. He tugged on a long fleshy earlobe for a moment while I willed myself not to speak again. "Wahl, he was in here quite a bit, you know, and I mind my own beeswax, so I'd say no, I don't remember," he said slowly. "No," he turned to face me, rubbing his chin now in a parody of thoughtfulness. "I'd have to say I don't know anything."

"Okay, I get it," I said calmly. "If the police asked you, or a lawyer, you wouldn't have anything to say."

"Oh, no, no," he started.

"It's okay, Mr. Peterson. I know you would never betray a member, right?" I almost grabbed his arm but thought better of it. "There's no one here but you and me, and I need your help. Somebody killed my baby brother, and you may know something that can help me find out who did it. Please, Mr. Peterson, whatever you know, please trust me."

He walked to the end of the bar and heaved the empty carton over the top. I waited while the crash reverberated through the silent room. He stood there, kneading his hands and finally hiked up his green Dickie workpants before returning to me. "You want a soda or something?" he asked.

"Okay," I said, cheer ringing falsely from my grimacing mouth. I was determined to hang in with this guy until he told me something.

"Bud, right?" I saw a little grin as he ducked his head around. He placed the brown bottle in front of me. Okay, so he knew what I usually drank. I was definitely on the right track here.

"Thank you, Mr. Peterson," I said quietly. "Now, as I was saying, you were working here on the day Raoul was killed. And you took a call for him."

"Yeah? So?" He pried open another box and the clatter of bottles filled the air as he loaded the cooler. "I tol' you, I don't know nothing about it," he grunted as another box was heaved over the side of the bar.

I held my tongue and waited for him to continue. It was a little early in the day to start drinking but I massaged the bottle until he spoke again.

"You ought ta' watch it with that guy," he said. "Yer looking for trouble there."

"What guy? You mean the guy that killed Raoul?"

"No, GEE," he raised his voice to mimic the French pronunciation.

"Don't worry about me, Mr. Peterson, I can handle Guy," I almost laughed. "I really just want to know about Raoul."

"Dead. Nothing left to say about that."

My mouth opened to protest and it snapped shut again. I took a long swig of the beer to swallow the bile that rose in my throat.

"Yep, dead," he said again, hefting cans of soda into the giant refrigerator. "Just like what's-his-name there, the other one…ah, I forget."

"Who? Somebody else is dead?"

"Oh yeah," he shook his head and spoke to my left shoulder. "Same kind of thing, too, young one that."

"Can you remember his name?" I grabbed the bar. "When did this happen? Was he murdered?"

"Dunno about any of that," he turned away so I could barely hear him. "Found 'im hanging there in the back, pants down around his ankles, his business all cut up. Nasty stuff. Oh, it was a while ago now, yep."

I pulled out my cellular and started to dial Mark's number, but in a swift move, the old man grabbed the phone from my hand and madly pushed at the keypad until it was disengaged. He slipped the phone into his pocket and turned his back on my protests. "Hey, old man, what the hell are you doing?"

"You callin' the cops, eh?" His head nodded spastically, and I sat back in my chair and crossed my arms. "What you doin' girlie, goin' have me arrested or something?"

"No," I kept my voice level. "I was going to ask for some information about the dead body you mentioned before."

"Huh, sure," he waggled a finger in my general direction. "You think I don't know?"

"Know what?"

"What you're up to. Yer working with the cops, trying to close down this place, aren't you?" he poked his finger towards my face. "Your brother was the same way, poking around all the time, asking questions."

"Raoul? My Raoul?" Now we were getting down to it. "What kind of questions?"

He shook his head, then stuck a filterless cigarette in his mouth and flicked a white lighter. When he bent over it, the smell of burnt hair seared my nostrils.

"Are you okay?" I asked when he stopped slapping his nose.

"Damn kids think they're funny, always resetting the flame on my lighter," he grumbled. The tip of his nose glowed red and he puffed angrily at the cigarette. I finished my beer and waited for him to catch his breath. He splashed water on his nose and then wiped his chin gently with a filthy bar rag.

"Do you need a tissue?" I asked.

"Are you still here?" he whirled around and seemed to stumble. I watched silently while he grabbed the bar.

Both of us jumped when the cellular phone in his pocket trilled.

"It's the phone," I said quietly. I waited through another ring. "Can I answer it?"

He fished the device out of his pocket and placed it on the bar, then leaned back and inhaled deeply on his cigarette.

"Hello?" I turned slightly away from the bar, knowing full well that Peterson had an incredibly developed sense of hearing.

"Clara, where are you? I've been calling you," Robby said.

"This isn't a good time. Can I call you later? Thanks." I disconnected the line before he could answer.

"Sorry," I said to Peterson. "My boss, checking in."

"That's the way you talk to your boss? Humph. Figures. This isn't a good time, eh?" He snorted and ground the butt into a dented metal ashtray. "The old days, you'd never talk to yer boss like that."

"Listen, Mr. Peterson, let's cut to the chase here," I said quietly. "I would appreciate if you would tell me what you know about my brother. That's all I'm here for, and believe me, I don't have any hidden agenda."

"Just happened to be calling the cops, then, right?" he tilted his head coyly in my direction.

"Mr. Peterson, I am really impressed with your powers of observation, and that's why I'm asking for your help," I jiggled my foot impatiently. "I just want your help. Please. Help me. Please, Mr. Peterson."

He turned away and fiddled with the cash drawer for a minute, and then I heard the strike of a match and saw the glow rise behind his head. I looked at the old back rotary telephone and the equally ancient pay phone on the wall near the door. How could the old man identify the tones for the police department phone number, when the equipment in the bar was so outmoded? I nodded my head: someone here was a regular cell phone user, and Peterson was a regular eavesdropper.

After a long silence, in which we both inhaled too much tobacco, he shrugged and sighed at the same time. I watched his back straighten as he turned to face me again.

"What can I say?" he spoke slowly. "I heard some stuff, but I don't know what it means. Lotsa people talk, lotsa things happen here and most folks just ignore me or don't even see me. You'd be surprised."

"I'm sure you know a lot," I offered. "If you'll tell me everything, I'd really appreciate it. No matter how insignificant—just tell me what you heard."

"Thing is, I don't know you. And you were calling the cops before, and I don't want no cops poking around here," he sucked on the smoldering butt, his lower lip stuck out stubbornly.

"What're you trying to hide?" I asked, and then thought better of it. "I was just going to ask about the other murder you mentioned, to see if there could be a connection with Raoul."

"Cops wouldn't be able to help you none there," he grunted. "And anyway, that there happened a real long time ago, like over a year or so."

"Why wouldn't the cops be able to help?"

"Are you dense, girlie? Do you have to have ever thing spelled out? T'wasn't any cop called on that one, is all. No record, nothing." He leaned forward. "Like I said,

Missy, nothing happened here. Nope. No Thing Happened Here." He spoke slowly, and then crossed his arms tightly.

I stood up and circled around the bar.

"Where you at? Where you going?" he asked nervously. "Ayyyyi," he squealed when I grabbed his arm.

"Stop fucking with me, old man," I hissed in his ear. "Now tell me what the hell is going on here. And I Mean Now." I could talk in capitals, too. I squeezed his bicep just above the elbow and my fingers practically met through the loose flesh hanging there.

"Let me go," he cried. "What kind of person are you, beating on a helpless senior citizen? Help! Help me!"

I pushed his arm away and leaned against the bar. "I'm tired of playing with you, Mister," I said quietly. "Now either you tell me what I want to know, or I will call the cops and get them down here, digging up your backyard looking for skeletons. Is that what you want?"

"Just try," he massaged his arm. "We've got friends on the police force."

"Well, so do I," I pulled a dollar from my pocket and stuck it in his shirt pocket. "This should cover my tab."

Raoul

"YOU'RE NOT ON THE drug team."

"I know, I know. I started with this Pirate guy, thinking that if I'm on the water every night, I can see what's going out of the base. But so far, nothing. And now the guy has this new connection, bringing prescription meds into town and setting up pharma parties. They're probably targeting younger kids, and I think you should send someone in to stop it," Raoul said.

"This is not our jurisdiction," his handler said. "Just drop it, and get back to looking for weapons."

"But it's an easy arrest—next time the CVS guy is making a delivery, I'll let you know and you can pick him up. Simple! And then I'm off the hook with the Pirate, so I can continue doing my surveillance of the base." There was no reply, so Raoul kept talking. "And this other stuff, these Moslem guys, I think there's something going on there."

"We haven't picked up anything on that, so again—drop it."

"But—"

"Is that it?"

"Sir, I respectfully disagree with your assessment here—" Raoul started.

"Call in next week. That's all." The phone was disconnected.

He resumed dressing in the new clothes that the Pirate handed over when they finished the morning run, along with a ziplock bag full of colorful pills.

"What's this?" he'd asked, holding up the black shopping bag.

"Your new outfit, for the party tonight. Ten o'clock, room 215 at the Clarion," the Pirate said. "I'll be in the next room, so don't try anything funny."

"And this?" Raoul held up the bag of pills.

"What do you mean? That's the product."

"Well, how am I going to know what's what?"

"You don't. They take one, they pay five dollars. Some of these kids, they know what they want—so they'll pick out their choice. Anyone else, that's the fun part— you never know what you're going to get."

"What if they ask me?"

"Look, kid, no offense, but you don't look like the brightest bulb in the pack. If you don't know, just smile. You're not supposed to be a fucking pharmacist, you know. It's a party! Lighten up," the Pirate said. "Just remember, five bucks a pop, no exceptions. You see anyone start to have a seizure or anything like that, grab your stuff and high-tail it out of there. Got it? Now go."

The evening prayers at the mosque had left him in a reflective mood, and he scowled when he looked at his reflection in the mirror. Buttoning the black silk shirt, he thought about the men he'd befriended at the mosque. No one would believe he was going to be pushing pills in a hotel room tonight. The men in the mosque were quiet, respectful, almost shy with each other. The Imam radiated goodness, Raoul thought, but his gut told him there was something happening there, something that he felt compelled to pursue.

A core group was always together, and instead of leaving after prayers, they usually disappeared through a curtain at the side of the room. Raoul needed to know what was behind the curtain, and he had spent several weeks trying to get closer to someone in the group, someone who might invite him in. Metin, a quiet boy who also worked at the boatyard, was his best bet, and so Raoul would keep working that angle.

He waited for about forty-five minutes before the first group arrived at the party. Young kids, he thought, although they seemed to have plenty of money. One of the guys raised the volume on the light jazz Raoul had playing softly in the corner. The party was in a suite, and so he'd pushed back the chairs to open a potential dance floor, unsure of what the party-goers would be looking for. After collecting five dollars from each one, he watched to make sure they took one pill apiece, using the teaspoon he'd stuck in the middle of the ice bucket filled with pills. Two of the males handed over additional money and helped themselves to "the blues."

Raoul shook his head. What twenty-year-old guys needed with Viagra was beyond his imagination, but then he saw one passing a blue tablet to his date and he suspended all curiosity. After more than a dozen had come, and some had taken their pills and left, Raoul noticed a crowd of older men peering in the door. Most of them were well into their thirties, and there was not a female in the group, so he suspected the local gay network had been tapped as well. These guys were a bit more discerning in their picks, and Raoul found it challenging to keep tabs on the pills, the patrons, and the swirl of activity in the room.

"Hey, look who's here." Louie was close to Raoul's ear when he whispered the greeting. "What's happening man? When choo get back in town? And what the hell are you doing shillin' pills?"

"Louie Rapture." Raoul grasped his old friend's hand. "Hey. Didn't expect to see you here, man," he said. "You want something from the bowl? Go ahead, it's on me."

"Really, R., what the hell. I thought you was Mr. Lawman and all, and here you are. How long you been in Jerome, hey?" Louie reached into the pills and delicately picked out a gray and white capsule, which he popped into his mouth. "You got drinks or what?"

"Yeah, the bar's over there. Get something to wash that down with." Raoul was sweating, watching Louie walk away. The last thing he needed was to have to explain himself to someone, and to have that someone blab all over town that he was back—

and he was dealing. Dammit. He peered into the bowl. Wonder if one of these can erase someone's memory, he thought.

Louie and his friends began to dance, and Raoul was distracted by another group that came into the party. He could see couples disappearing into the bedroom, and hoped he could get out of the party without anyone getting arrested or hurt. Including himself. Wouldn't you think that the hotel would come and shut down the noise? He thought. After a while, he noticed K had slipped into the room and was counting heads by the bar. He nodded at Raoul.

At 2:00 a.m., the crowd started to thin. Several people were passed out in the corners, and Raoul (carting the ice bucket of pills under his arm) checked to make sure everyone had a pulse. A couple (or perhaps it was more than just two) were busy in the bedroom, and Louie was standing behind the bar, passing out shots of an amber liquid to his pals. The bartender was nowhere in sight. Raoul caught his eye and motioned for Louie to join him in the hallway.

"Hey man, how're you doing?" he asked. Louie's eyelids were drooping, but otherwise he seemed pretty chipper.

"I'm great, man. How are you?" Louie replied.

"I'm cool, man. Say, can I ask you something?" Louie nodded. "Can you keep it to yourself, my being here tonight and all? I'm not really here, you know what I mean? I don't want anyone to know I'm in town, and you know, about the drugs and all."

"No problem, bro," Louie said. "I do you a solid, you do me a solid, right?"

"Absolutely. What can I do for you? You need a ride home, place to crash, what?"

Louie smiled at him, his gaggle-toothed grin bringing back memories of their childhood. "So, you on the down low these days?"

Raoul looked puzzled, shook his head. "I don't follow you, man."

"You know, you and me—getting it on—oh, never mind. I can see you are still chasing pussy right? Too bad man, I could make you real happy." Louie licked his lips. "So maybe just another one of those de-lightful party favors you have there." Raoul held out the bucket, watching as Louie scooped up a blue tablet, something small and red, and another gray and white capsule. "Solid, man, right?"

"Yeah—just don't tell anyone you saw me here. Got it?" Raoul asked.

"Got it." Louie pulled a card from his pocket and stuffed it into Raoul's jeans. "Here's my number. Call me if you need anything. Anytime, bro. Anytime."

Louie gathered his friends and they tumbled loudly out the door. It was approaching 3:00 a.m. and the only revelers left were in the bedroom. Raoul poured the remainder of his pills back into the ziplock bag and closed the door as he exited the room. Tapping lightly on the adjoining room, he waited five minutes for either K or the Pirate to answer before shoving the room key under their door and heading for the exit. The wad of money in his jacket was probably not going to be enough to satisfy the Pirate, but Raoul was surprised at the number of pill poppers who'd found their way to the hotel. In three hours, he needed to be at work—stashing the bag in his basket, Raoul started bicycling home. Wonder if there's any uppers in that selection, he thought. Wonder if I could figure out which ones will help me stay awake tomorrow.

Clara

I WALKED OUT INTO the bright sunshine, filled with frustration and anger, most of it directed at my own inability to charm information from a blind old goat. "Dammit," I tossed my bag across to the passenger seat and slipped behind the wheel. In the shade of a large elm tree, I chewed my thumbnail and contemplated the tidbits I'd gotten from Peterson. The phone rang just as I ripped off a healthy bit of tissue and had to dig for a napkin to staunch the flow of blood.

"Clara?"

"Mark, I'm so glad you called. I had a question—"

"Wait a sec," he covered the mouthpiece and I could hear voices in the background. "Okay, sorry about that. I've just got a minute and I wanted to give you a heads-up on something. Don't go to your brother's place today."

"What? I, I was just about to head over there," I sputtered. "What's going on?"

"Well, we got a call about a break-in, and at first I thought it was you," he paused. "It wasn't you, was it?"

"No," I replied woodenly. "Was anything taken? Who called it in?"

"It looks like somebody got in there and, well, they tore the place up. So you'd better stay away."

"Dammit, what the hell is going on?"

"I don't know," he said. "I've got to go."

"Wait, wait," I hollered. The phone went dead. "Shit." I pounded the steering wheel and threw the phone in the bag.

I hit my head when something tapped on the car window. "Dammit," I opened the door and practically knocked over old man Peterson. "What the hell do you want?" I screamed.

He backed away, tripping over a large black trash bag. A gigantic black visor obscured his eyes, and the twitching of his scrawny face below the mask reminded me of a large fly.

I burst out laughing and he crossed his arms angrily. "You are a strange one," he said. "Wahl," he scratched his nose, now sporting an angry blister, his hand swimming in a giant blue rubber glove. "Jes' get out of here, now, go 'way."

"Okay," I tried to stop laughing, but the giggles kept bubbling to the surface. I was on the edge, it was clear, and this little man didn't know what to do with me.

"Git," he urged again. "Go on home now." With a grunt, he hoisted the bag over the lip of the dumpster.

"Git?" I giggled. I felt like a puppy, and as I stood there I realized an urgent need to pee. "Mr. Peterson, can I just use the bathroom for a second?" I asked.

"No," he turned and started to walk to the open back door. "You git now, girlie."

I followed him inside, not kidding myself that he was unaware of my presence shadowing his bent form. The lights in the bathroom were off and a strong scent of ammonia blasted my nose. At least it was clean, and after I finished my business, I gave the room a good going over. Nothing. I tried the men's room, looking for anything that Raoul might have hidden here, one of his emergency stashes. I did locate a little gun duct-taped to the backside of one of the porcelain sinks, which I dropped into a plastic evidence bag and placed in my shoulder bag. I did a cursory search of the storage area but decided that Raoul would never risk hiding anything in such a public space.

When I walked down the hall with the intention of giving Mr. Peterson one more go, I stopped abruptly in the shadowy doorway when I heard voices at the bar. A male I didn't recognize was berating Peterson. I quickly activated my tape recorder and positioned the microphone near the top of the bag.

"What the hell have you been doing here this morning, old man?" he yelled. "This place is a pigsty—you don't even have the bar stocked yet. Let me in here. Move over, dammit." I peered around the corner and saw a heavy-set man shoulder behind the bar.

Peterson cowered in the corner, watching the khaki work shirt open the cash register and start counting the bills. "What the hell," he roared. "You been dipping, old man? You been helpin' yourself to the profits?"

Peterson wrung his hands. "No sir, Mr. C, I never touched the drawer. I don't touch the money, you know that," he whimpered.

"What's this dollar bill stickin' out of your pocket, then? Eh?"

The henchman, Mr. C, slipped the money into his pocket and bent over the cash register. Muscles rippled under the crisply ironed brown shirt and I waited to catch a glimpse of his face. He was too far away for me to make out the name embroidered over the left pocket on a white patch. A large belly protruded over jeans coated with grease, but his face remained shadowed. It looked like the crew-cut hair was mouse brown, but it could've been gray, and all I could see of his skin was the thick red neck that puddled over his collar.

With a meaty hand, he swiped a thick wad of bills from the register into his pocket and then reached over to cuff Peterson on the shoulder. The old man stumbled, and then grabbed the bar for support. "You watch yourself here, Peterson," the man held him up by the throat. With a shrug, he tossed the frail bartender aside. "I've got my eye on you."

"Okay, boss, okay," Peterson groveled. His hands played nervously around his throat, straightening his shirt and smoothing the welts that must have been raised.

With a grunt, the larger man pulled a six-pack of beer from the refrigerator and walked to the front door. "I'm watching you, old man," he warned again. The door creaked shut.

I could hear Peterson's labored breathing as I approached the bar. He had slid onto the floor and was sitting with his head resting on the metal cooler. "You all right down there?" I asked softly.

"Ain't you gone yet?" Peterson feigned annoyance. He looked up suddenly. "Where's your car at?"

"It's still around back, behind the dumpster," I said. "Don't worry, he didn't spot me."

"What you talking about, smart-ass," he stood up slowly. I resisted the impulse to help. "You didn't see anybody in here, and nobody saw you. So you better git before that ain't true no more."

"I saw that man hit you, and threaten you, and take money out of the cash register," I said. "What is he, some kind of mobster?"

I was joking, but the old man's face blanched even whiter, and his blind eyes darted nervously in their sockets. "Hush, that's enough," he said. "We don't have nothing like that in this town. Now I'll kindly ask you to git before I call 911 and report an intruder."

"Huh," I sat on a barstool. "This is so interesting. I never would have imagined that there was a mob presence in town. But it makes sense, in a weird kind of way," I mused aloud and watched the little man twitch nervously. "I remember now that construction jobs all went to a couple of companies, and there were a few restaurants in town that were given all the big catering jobs, things like that. Hmmn, and here I thought it was a simple system of payoffs. But this looked like more than that to me, you know?"

"Ah, stop yer jabbering." He started wiping glasses and placing them on a rack below the lip of the bar. I noticed that his hands were steady again, and his breathing was less labored, so I slid off the stool.

"You okay now, Mr. Peterson?" I asked. "I can't force you to talk to me, but if you change your mind, give me a call."

"Why would I want to talk to you?" he asked. "Calling the police. You can't be trusted."

"You know, you did call me this morning, right? So I'm not wrong in thinking you might have had something to tell me. But it's okay; I'm not going to bother you anymore. I'll leave you alone." I walked across the room, praying that the tape recorder would not click to a stop before I could turn it off. With this man's acute hearing, I was sure he'd identify the sound, and that would be the end of any future help I might get from him. "Thanks again," I called over my shoulder. Without waiting for an answer, I went out into the light.

My car was still hidden behind the battered dumpster, and I slid behind the wheel gratefully. After clicking off the tape recorder, I pondered the cellular phone for a minute. I wasn't sure how Mark would react to a call from me, and I wished that we'd established some kind of signal so that he'd know to call me back.

The car flowed into traffic and easily maneuvered into a parking spot at the public library, directly across from Raoul's—and Mama's—apartment building. I looked for signs of a police presence but saw nothing obvious. Still, Mark had warned me not to approach the apartment, and I was frustrated with this delay in my plans.

Sitting back in the air-conditioned car, I watched the patrons entering and exiting the red brick library. Its white pillars looked the same as they were in the days when a library card was like a ticket to Disney World for us poor kids. The grass in front of the building was patchy and yellow, victim of the latest drought. As flush as the town now appeared, it seemed like the library was not a beneficiary of the economic boom. The formerly fine shrubbery that once skirted the base of the building was gone, leaving its foundation exposed and flawed, like an old woman's droopy slip whose lace hem escaped from the confines of machine stitchery and now fluttered freely around the thick ankles of its owner.

I checked the hotel for messages and wasn't surprised when there were none. I studied the windows in the apartment building, but from my vantage point on High Street, I did not have a clear view except for the occasional flutter of a curtain in Mama's window.

After reading over Spike's fax and making some notes on the little I'd gleaned from my talk with Peterson, I shut off the car and headed into the library. The marble steps, worn from the thousands of soles that had passed through the portals, seemed smaller just as the stacks of books seemed to have diminished, rather than grown, in my absence.

"Can I help you?" asked an attractive black woman, her hair smoothly pulled into a bun that perched like a dinner roll on the nape of her neck.

"Do you have old newspaper archives here?"

"Yes, of course," she replied. "Downstairs, some are bound and mostly the rest are on microfiche."

I was about to dive into a haystack without a clue. How could I find a murder without knowing the date? I was beginning to wonder if Peterson's tale of the hanged man was even true, and if so, maybe they had covered it up, and there was an actual skeleton moldering in the back lot of the Eagle's property. He had mentioned that it happened a year ago, but he also claimed there was no police report. Better to check on missing person's reports, and for that I had more reliable connections than the Jerome Daily News.

I veered over to the reading room and, in place of the wall-to-wall oak card catalog, was pleased to encounter a row of sparkling new computers. I leaned around the corner and caught the eye of the library assistant. "Excuse me," I waved at her. "Do any of these machines have internet access?"

She pointed towards the reference room. "Over there."

I entered the room, still lined with encyclopedias and atlases and all the accoutrements of learning that I'd reveled in during my last years in Jerome and settled in front of a new computer blinking cheerfully at me. No one else was in the room except an elderly man behind a heavily laden desk. His pasty complexion and sagging features could not disguise his identity as my former tormenter from the school orchestra. An image flashed of my failed attempts to master virtually every instrument with which Mr. Argent tried to unearth a musical inclination in me. I ducked my head down and prayed that he would not recognize me and was soon enraptured with the possibilities for information that a simple password was opening to me.

"Quiñones!" The voice called me back from what was starting to be an endless circle of "no response" responses to my queries.

I looked up; without even needing to check, I knew it was him, and that he'd recognized me. "Mr. Argent."

"Miss Quiñones, I thought that was you, but I wasn't sure until I checked your yearbook. My goodness, you haven't changed a bit," he proclaimed.

"You have my yearbook?" Un-fucking-believable. The man was still a weirdo.

"We have all the school yearbooks here, of course," he said. "I was so sorry to hear about your brother." He pulled a chair close to mine and leaned in to whisper "He was a special person."

"Oh." I tried to process the implied meaning. "Did you have Raoul in school?"

"No, no." He shook his head. "I left teaching shortly after you were in my class." He paused. We waited uncomfortably for a moment.

"I hope it wasn't because of me," I joked. "I really am tone deaf, you know."

"Oh my dear, you have no idea… Well, suffice it to say, I had a little problem and it was suggested that perhaps teaching was not the best use of my talents." He shoved his hands into his armpits and seemed to hug himself.

"I see," I pretended to see. "So, uh, how did you know my brother?"

"Well," I could feel his breath warming my cheek; the man was practically sitting on my lap. "We were introduced by a mutual friend, and I saw him around town quite a bit."

"Do you know what happened to him?" I asked.

"Of course, my dear, how horrible for you," he patted my knee.

"Mr. Argent, I mean, do you have any idea who did this? Who murdered my brother?"

"Oh. No. No, I …how could I? I just, no. How could you think that? Well, no," he fumbled.

"What about his friends, the people he was hanging around with? Can you tell me anything about them? Names, phone numbers, anything?" I begged. "I just want to find out what happened. Can you help me?"

"Oh dear, no," he shrugged. "Sorry. I have to get back to work now."

He pushed in the chair and I grabbed his sleeve. "Just a minute," I hissed. "You have to help me."

"I, I can't," he looked around the empty room. "My supervisor should be here any minute, and I can't be chatting with someone." He paused for a moment, and then almost whispered. "There have been military people sniffing around, too. Investigators, I think. I have to be careful."

"You're helping me find something on the computer," I said. I pulled out the chair. "Sit. Now, tell me who has been asking questions. Were they military police? Regular cops?" I was trying to stay calm, but it seemed like they were right on the trail, just as I had hoped. "Did anyone leave you a card?"

"I didn't actually talk to them," he said. "I hid in the stacks until they were gone. Sorry."

"Who did then? Who talked to them?" I pressed.

"Oh, Miss Macaroni, but I'm sure she had nothing useful to offer."

"Macaroni? Where is she?"

"That's just what we call her—her name is Mascolli, and she's off today," he said. "Wait a minute. You're not a cop or anything, are you?"

"No. You know me, right? I'm just Raoul's sister." I was getting tired of being mistaken for a police officer. It had never been like that when I actually had a badge in my pocket. "I'll give you my phone number, and if you remember something, please call me."

He took my card and scampered back to his desk. I had to wonder, what the hell had Raoul been doing with that loser?

Raoul

AFTER WORK, RAOUL WENT straight back to his apartment, climbed the back stair quietly, and collapsed on the unmade bed. Although it was a major disruption of the routine he'd so vigorously maintained for the past six months, he knew that without some rest, he was in real danger of making a fatal mistake. For the first time, he did not go to the club. He slept. Getting up at 1:00 a.m., he staggered to the bathroom, peed sitting down, and then collapsed back on the bed. A full moon outside cast strange shadows across the room, and he had a strange sense of foreboding that he shrugged off.

Hours later, once again awakened by the moon—or something outside—he slid out of bed and edged carefully along the outer wall until he was next to the fire escape. He waited a moment, heard the telltale sound of metal groaning. Someone was out there. He had never invested in window treatments, and the old paper shades were uneven and tattered, so it was fairly easy to watch the movement of a shadow.

He reached over and snapped the shade up, then leaned into the night air, pressing his nose against the rusty screen. "Metin, is that you?" he asked softly.

The quiet figure exhaled. "Yeah," came the reply.

"What are you doing out there?" Raoul asked.

"Checking on you. You didn't show up at the mosque tonight, and you looked pretty bad at work...so they sent me over to make sure you're all right."

"Yeah, I must have some bug. I needed to crash." Raoul rested his elbows on the sill. "You want to come in or something?"

"Nah," the other man whispered. "I've got to get going." Raoul saw the flash of a match and heard the inhale of a cigarette. "It's almost time for morning prayers, you know."

"Yeah." Raoul paused. "It's hard, without a muezzin, to keep track."

Silence. Another inhale, and then: "Yeah." The shadow moved. "Well, see you later," Metin said.

Raoul waited by the window until he was certain Metin was on the roof. Hopefully, he wouldn't disturb any of the residents on his way out of the building. Raoul walked back to his bed, picked up the alarm clock, and sighed. It was almost time to get going. At least he'd gotten some rest; the next few days promised to be intense. He closed his eyes and rested his head on the pillow. Thank God they didn't check on him when he made his first trip to Manhattan, he thought. He stood up abruptly. Or had they?

He showered, dressed, and was at the mosque when the sun started to brighten the eastern sky. Nodding at the others, he took his place in the middle row, near the wall. He hated to have his back to the rest of the men, but he needed to relax and trust that somehow, there was a God who had his back. Metin slid into place next to Raoul. He looked and smelled like he'd spent the night smoking on a fire escape. Raoul took some deep breaths and centered himself for the day to come.

Clara

I FELT THE SWEAT immediately bead on my upper lip when I left the air-conditioned building. I did not see my car, and I hesitated a moment before panicking. Could my car have been stolen right here, on the corner of Main and High streets, in broad daylight? What had this town come to?

I walked slowly down the steps, looking around. "Dammit." I pulled my cell phone out and walked to the shade of a tree before attempting to dial the police.

As I pressed the second "1," a car pulled alongside, and I heard the slick whir of a window descending and then my name, "Clara." A husky voice. I disengaged the call and looked into the window. Mark ticked a finger to pull me inside the car. "My car was stolen," I announced.

He looked at me, just a quick glance before pulling smoothly into traffic. His radio crackled with static and he flicked it off. He sighed.

"Okay, what?" I asked.

"Your car was not stolen," he said after a moment. "I had it towed."

"Oh." What the hell. "What the hell for?"

He turned down the boulevard, heading towards the hotel. "You need to get rid of that car," he said. "We have a car with out-of-state plates sitting outside the scene of a murder and break-in. That attracts a lot of attention. I had to take care of it."

"Well, what am I supposed to do?" I cried. "Do you expect me to sit in the hotel and wait until you find something?"

"Why don't you tell me what you were doing there? I told you to stay away from the apartment," he said. "Were you watching the building? Did you go in?"

"No. I was in the library, dammit, using their stupid computers to check on a stupid story that I wanted to ask you about this morning, but you hung up on me and so I decided to check it out myself," I yelled.

"Okay," he said calmly. "What did you find out? What story are you checking on?"

"Never mind," I pouted. "Where the hell did you put my car, and what am I supposed to do in the meantime? You sure as hell can't get along without a car in this town, and I am not leaving."

"Your car is in the impound lot, but I'd suggest that you trade it in for something with local plates." We stopped at a light and he looked over at me. "Even that won't last long, once people figure out what you're driving, but it will give us a little break."

"What the hell are you talking about? I went to the library, for God's sake. Is that a crime around here?"

"I had three calls in the time you were inside, with tips that there was a car from New Jersey parked outside the apartment building." He adjusted the visor when we turned the corner. "Far as I know, there were several other calls to the main number, with the same information. I had your car towed. You'll get it back. In fact, I'll bring you there now if you want."

I shrugged. "I don't remember this town being so, so small," I said.

"I tried to tell you."

"Aren't you worried that someone saw you pick me up? Isn't that going to be on the front page of tonight's paper?"

He didn't answer for a minute, and I fidgeted as the road to the hotel unfurled in front of the dark vehicle.

"It's an unmarked car," he said finally.

"And what good is that?" I sounded like a child, and I felt as frustrated as a five-year-old. "Doesn't everybody know everything? Don't all your fellow officers know what this car looks like, and who's driving it, and who the passenger is?"

"No, actually, they don't. I borrowed this car from a friend."

We pulled into the parking lot, and he drove to the backside of the hotel, near a service door. "Let's go." I followed him as he unlocked the door and led me up the stairwell. He stepped back while I opened the door to my room and followed me into the cool chamber.

I sat on the edge of the bed. "Now what?"

"You can get your car later," he said. He dropped into the armchair and laced his fingers together. "Tell me what you found out."

My stomach growled and I glared at him angrily. "I need to eat something," I announced. "You want a burger?"

He checked his watch. "Okay."

I called room service and watched him pull the photographs out of the folders stacked neatly on the bureau. My note cards fell on the table and he leaned over them, brow furrowed in thought. The gentle movement of his hands, the corresponding changes in his face, mesmerized me.

"Just help yourself," I said when I was finished with the phone call. "I mean, just make yourself at home."

He smiled. "You've been busy, but I don't think you have any real leads here," he said.

"Well, I know that." I sat heavily on the end of the bed again. "Did you get the phone records from the club?"

"Not yet," he admitted. "So what were you doing at the library? What story did you want me to check out?"

"I spoke with Peterson, the bartender at the Eagle's, and he told me some things. I don't know." I flopped backwards on the bed. "I think maybe he was just making stuff up, trying to send me on a wild goose chase."

"Let me be the judge of that," he said. "Tell me what he said."

I related the tale of the body supposedly hung behind the club. "What do you think?" I asked, resting my head on one elbow.

"Hmm," he came over to the bed. "Did he say when this happened?"

"Nah, he wouldn't give any real details. Have you ever heard of anything like this?"

He sat on the bed, near enough to touch. I studied the swell of his backside before swinging up to a seated position.

"I did hear something a few months ago, maybe longer. But we never found any proof so I figured it was just drink talk. You know? Urban myth and all that."

"But something about a body hanging in the woods?"

He nodded slowly. "I'll have to go back and check my old notebooks, but I'm pretty sure it was out that way, but like I said, I don't remember there being any substantiation. No actual body, nothing but rumors that popped up, now and then, around the jail and all."

"No actual body?" I asked. He shook his head. I related the apparent shakedown that I had witnessed at the Club and handed over the tape recorder. His eyebrows rose while the tape rewound. "This isn't legal, you know," he said.

"Just listen." I paced while he replayed the scene in the bar. "Well?" I asked.

"Well what?" he replied. "There is nothing for me here. I didn't even hear this tape." He handed it back to me.

A couple of short raps on the door and Mark scooted out of sight. He was behind the bathroom door before I could even move. When he came back out, we ate lunch in silence.

"Call this number, and you can get your car back," he said after wiping his hands on a napkin. "I think you should talk to the hotel management and arrange to rent a car, one with Connecticut plates, as soon as possible."

"Okay," I agreed. He moved the curtain aside and looked around the parking area below my window.

"I'd watch it with the tape recording, if I were you," he said. "There are some, how shall I put it, unsavory characters in the bar business. If one of them catches you—"

"I hear you," I said. "I'll be careful." He nodded slowly, looking at me through heavily lidded eyes. The full mustache barely concealed the lush red lips I remembered from our high school days.

"I've got to get going," he said after a moment. "I'll check on that body thing, and call you later."

"Oh, I forgot," I said. I jumped up and rummaged in my bag, pulling out the gun wrapped in plastic. "I found this taped behind a sink in the men's room at the club. Maybe you can check the prints on it, see where it's been."

"What were you doing in the men's room?" he asked, then shook his head. He took the gun. "Never mind. I'll get the lab to check it. Do you have anything else interesting in that bag of yours?"

"No," I said. I paced nervously. "Um, is it okay if I call you?" We almost collided in the small space between the bureau and the bed. "I mean, if I need to tell you something, can I call you on your cell phone?"

He looked at me strangely for a second. "Yes," he said. "That's why I gave you my number."

I felt the blood flush my cheeks. "Oh. Yeah, well, I didn't want to call you and cause, you know, any problems for you," I stammered.

"It's okay," he touched my shoulder softly and brushed past me. "Call me any time. Oh, and thanks for the lunch."

When he was gone, I flopped on the bed, my heart beating wildly. I must be losing my touch. Maybe it was being back here again, the land of the repressed and home of the narrow-minded. I groaned in frustration. What was it that had me so turned around? Death? Raoul's murder had affected me deeply, there was no question, but that was no reason to lose control. I jumped up and studied my face in the mirror.

"Get a grip, Clara," I said. I brushed out the tangles in my hair and called the reception desk to make arrangements for the car. I spoke with the manager and he arranged for a rental to be delivered to the hotel. Mark told me he'd move my car from the impound lot to a garage he rented, where I could retrieve it when I was ready to go back to New York. Talk about a sheriff offering to show someone the fastest route out of town, I thought.

I picked up the phone and called the Eagle's Club. It was shortly after 3:00 p.m., and as expected, Guy had just walked in. "It's that New York bitch," I overheard the bartender say as she handed the phone to him.

"Can we meet?" I skipped the preliminaries.

"Come here if you want." He said abruptly.

"Are you sure that's the best place to meet?"

"No, I'm not sure about anything," he said slowly. "Like what you want with me. But I do know that these are my friends here, and they won't do anything to hurt me."

"Like telling Binky what you're up to?" I sassed. There was silence, and I heard him breathing. Waiting. "Sorry."

"Yeah."

"I, uh, need a ride," I said after a moment. "My car got towed."

"What?"

"It's a long story—can you pick me up or should I call a cab?"

He laughed. "Call a cab?" he snorted. "First of all, you'd have to wait a few hours for the cabbie to get his ass over there—we only have one cab in town, you know—and then, well, you might as well take out an ad in the paper, because before he even drops you off here, everyone will know where you are." I could hear him scratching his chin. "I'll pick you up. Ahh, Christ, I can't do that. Too public."

I didn't mention his appearance in the hotel bar the previous evening, when discretion did not seem paramount. "Can you borrow a car from someone?" I was getting the hang of this clandestine thing.

"Perfect. Yeah, I'll take Joe's truck. Meet you out front in fifteen minutes, okay?"

"Sure. I'll be wearing a red rose in my lapel." I was tempted to add a hat to the disguise.

There was a short silence. "Uh, okay," he replied. "It's an old blue truck."

I pulled on a skirt and fresh tee shirt, leaving the remnants of my morning in a heap on the floor. I splashed a little cologne behind my ears—with a drop between the breasts for good measure—and was waiting by the door when a rattletrap vehicle pulled into the lot.

"Hey," I clambered onto a seat held together with duct tape. "Nice wheels."

He shrugged and pulled back into traffic. "What's going on, Clara?"

There was a coldness I hadn't expected, but it was understandable given our grappling the night before. I tried to keep a light tone. "I needed a break," I said. "It's been a tough day." I tried to decipher the look on his face, but dark glasses and a set jaw kept me on edge.

"Why didn't you just go to the hotel bar?"

"Okay, I wanted to see you," I conceded.

He didn't answer.

"I didn't like the way we left things," I said slowly.

He stopped abruptly at a yellow light and looked at me. "What do you want from me? You've been playing me for days now, on and off, and you're making me crazy. I can't sleep, I can't concentrate, and I don't know what the hell is happening."

I ventured a touch of his arm. Golden hairs glistening in the sun, heat rising around the road and vibrating around the idling truck. "I don't either," I said. "I really don't."

This was pure animal instinct, and I knew it, and when my hand found its way to his crotch I felt his resistance melt away. He shifted in his seat and opened his legs until my hand encompassed the softness of his balls. "Jesus," he said. He drove in silence after that, occasionally moaning as I moved my thumb up and down the length of his cock, straining by now against the rough fabric of his worn jeans.

By the time we pulled into the back lot of the club, and he found my hiding place behind the dumpster, we were both ready for the inevitable coupling. If he'd been a teenager, it probably would've lasted a minute, but the thrusts kept coming until we were both covered in sweat and I arched up to meet his orgasm with my own.

I felt the pulsing and tasted his salty shoulder, the acrid smell of sex surrounding us in the blazing truck cab. "Dammit," he grunted. "You're killing me."

I was melting into the lumpy cushions and shifted to signal his withdrawal. He knelt on the edge of the seat and pulled his white cotton briefs over the still-glistening hard-on. I pulled my skirt down and tried to find my panties amid the debris on the floor. "Here," he passed them to me. He traced a line down my thigh softly as

I tried to straighten myself in the seat. My shirt was rolled in a tangle under his leg and I tugged on it, his hand cupping my breast until I slipped the top over my head.

Roughly then, we embraced again, and he tasted of sweat and beer. Hands entangled in my hair smelled musky and I dug my fingers into his shoulder until we drew apart.

"No one's ever going to figure this out, right?" I grinned and turned to leave the truck.

"Where are you going?" he asked.

"Inside." I looked across the cab. He shook his head. "What do you mean? I'm dying for a drink."

"I'll give you a lift back to the hotel." He wouldn't meet my eyes.

"So what's this—wham, bam, thank you ma'am?" I tried to laugh.

He started the truck.

I jumped out of the cab and walked away towards the darkness of the bar, straightening my clothing along the way. Once inside I was relieved to feel the cold blast of air conditioning on my bare arms and legs. After a quick stop in the bathroom to wipe away the residue of sex, I slid onto a stool and embraced the cool brown bottle that appeared before me.

"Thanks," I said, and drank deeply. "Trudy?" I guessed at the name and her nod confirmed my recollection.

I greeted the familiar faces with a nod and looked around to see if Guy was in the room yet. He must still be stewing in the truck, but I pushed away thoughts of his fingers buried inside me and ordered a bag of chips.

The first beer was ancient history and I'd lost count by the time I noticed Guy draped over a chair by the pool table. Loud music and inane conversation revealed the attraction of this place for the locals, and I found myself dancing with an older man named Ike who kept ogling my breasts, which, in the absence of a support garment, were having an effect on the entire room. I was conscious of Guy's eyes following me around the room, the leering smile of his brother, and other faces blurred by cigarette haze.

I must have been there a while when I found myself lolling over the toilet, and a ringing in my bag snapped me out of the drunken stupor. "Yes?" I answered, struggling to sit up. The line went dead.

I smoothed my clothing and washed my face before heading out the back door. There were only a couple of trucks left in the parking lot. It took a moment before I remembered that I had no transportation, but I could not go back into the bar, and there was no friendly face to call for a ride at this time of night. I took a long look at the star-filled sky, straightened my bag on my shoulder, and started walking.

One of the unfortunate features of suburbia is the lack of proper sidewalks in towns where walking is what you do to get to and from your car. Dogs barked, cars slowed or speeded past, and I wished for a pair of anonymous jeans and a sweater. Having neither, I crossed my arms and walked furiously.

"Look like you mean business," we had been told in self-defense classes. Even Raoul, coming to visit shortly after I moved to the city, had admonished me to walk tougher. "When you're on the street alone at night, cut out the wiggle," he'd said. "You have a sweet little butt, but you better be careful here."

He mimicked my walk, exaggerating the sensual rhythm of my body with his own mincing steps. "See what you look like?" he'd said seriously, and I had nodded before bursting into peals of laughter and asking if he'd like to borrow my heels.

"Oh, Mijo," I muttered to myself. "Look what you've done. Why couldn't you just leave it alone?"

Raoul

A MUSCLE-BOUND KID, PROBABLY retired Marine, joined the group at the mosque on Sunday afternoon. Black skin glistening with sweat, he led the men in a series of exercises, then supervised hand-to-hand combat training. Each fight ended with the point of a rubber knife pressed against the jugular of one or the other pair. Sometimes both men had their knives engaged, sometimes one had a gun that he pulled from a hidden ankle holster.

"Don't forget about air marshals," the Leader warned. "You might be surprised by some middle-aged businessman with a pistol in his briefcase." In any event, he continued, even if one of the team was taken down, the goal remained to break into the cabin and take over the plane. "Don't stop, don't look back, don't take prisoners. Speak as little as possible. Just get up, push into the cockpit, and disable the pilot."

Raoul practiced with the others, tempering his previous skills so as not to appear too professional. However, he knew that the weaning process was underway, and he wanted to be sure to make the grade onto the final team. The closer he got, the more possibility that he could get real intelligence about the target and dates of the planned attack.

On a sultry Sunday in July, the training took a new turn. Instead of the rubber weapons, real box cutters were handed out. Several new faces were present, playing the role of bystander, and Raoul assumed these men were armed with real guns as well. Twice during the afternoon, he was forced to crack someone's rib: the snap was followed by a satisfying grunt and collapse of his adversary. In the final tussle of the afternoon, just before the group was dismissed to prepare for prayers, Raoul was paired with the trainer himself. Most of the other pairs stopped to watch the exchange.

The kid was fast, but Raoul had more than brute strength going for him: he knew the consequences of failure in this little exercise. Holding the Marine in a headlock, he reached for the knife strapped to his calf. Nothing. It was gone. Okay, he thought, tightening his hold. Improvise.

Slick with sweat, his opponent slithered out of the hold and once again faced off, crouched in position with a cutter in each hand. He flicked one, a smile flickering across his face in the second before Raoul landed a hit. Square in the center of his face, open palm jabbing upwards against the squat nose. Cartilage cleanly bisected the man's frontal lobe. He dropped like a sack onto the floor, knives falling and piss darkening the front of his camouflage pants.

Raoul turned away from the grinning men encircling the room. He wiped his face with a towel and added another body to his internal tally. Another one to account for when he met his maker. And this one harder to explain than the others; in fact, he thought dismally, as the kills got easier, the rationale became thinner. He turned back to the group, saw the Leader watching him, and did what he knew was necessary. He dropped the towel, threw his hands in the air, and yelled, "Allah akbar!"*

*God is great!

Clara

THE ROAD INTO TOWN was long and dark, and I caught glimpses of televisions moving behind closed curtains, air conditioners belching heat into the ozone night. A raucous party drove by and yelled obscenities, but I kept my head down and tried to disappear until they were gone. I crossed away from the West End Pizza and its scent of cheese, my belly rumbling and protesting its liquid supper. I could see the repair shop where my little black car was locked safely behind a barbed wire fence; no way to get it until morning, especially since I had no extra keys with me. I avoided the empty stretch of Center Street and cut through the mall parking lot to Main Street, where I kept in the shadows and slipped easily into the old apartment building.

Inside the door, I removed my sandals and walked barefoot past Mama's apartment and upstairs to the yellow police tape that announced Raoul's door. The key disengaged the lock and I was through the tape before anyone could have noticed the sound, but when the door closed behind and the smell hit my nose, I dropped to my knees.

Face down on the floor, I took it in. Although the place had been cleaned, in my half-drunken state I was overwhelmed by it all. Through my pores I absorbed the smell of death, the particular odor of blood, of my blood and that of my brother and sisters and all the lost relations mingled together on the floor. I envisioned the floor as a horrible mottled hardwood mess that must have saved the aroma of every evil thing that happened here, every drop of Raoul's blood that spurted, oozed, dripped, and soaked into it; my blood, my pain spilled there too, and it came out of my heart and twisted around my brain until I had to let it go, quietly sobbing, silently quaking, spewing my sorrow in the space where Mijo had fought for his life, where I could still feel his spirit and hear his angry words echoing once again against the scarred plaster walls, and I crawled then—tears and snot dripping onto my clothes— to empty my stomach into a toilet stained with scum and cigarette butts and God let it be rust and I retched it all back until nothing but spittle hung useless from my lips, lips that had so recently caressed another man and then so many bottles, now pouting, now angry. I slapped the side of the bowl angrily, over and over.

I flushed the toilet before remembering the need to be quiet, but once again it was too late to stop what was happening here. I sat quietly, listening for a sign that I'd been discovered, and when none came, I took a wad of paper and wiped my face, then the edge of the bowl. In another moment of weakness, I laid my head on the porcelain and cried some more. It had all gotten so out of control, and my best efforts to put things to right would never be able to erase the fact that he was gone. That could not be made right, ever.

I had to salvage what I could, or I'd never be able to move on from here. Part of me died in this room, too, just like the lonely child who still lurked in the walls of Mama's apartment, waiting for recognition, for the love that was never going to come.

One eye opened, I listened to the building tick. There was nothing left for me here. No clues—the place was clean. Mark must have sent in a crew after the break-in was discovered, and the place had been sanitized. This apartment was probably the only pristine spot in the entire city of Jerome, which wasn't saying much. I considered the characters I'd met in the last few days, the stories and threats and subterfuge. With a heavy sigh, I slumped against the wall and watched the sky lighten.

Just before 6:00 a.m., I dialed Mark's cell phone and when he answered, I could tell from the lilt in his voice that he'd been awake for a while. Probably out jogging or something physically fit like that.

"Sorry to call so early," I said. "I'm kind of stuck without a car and I was wondering—"

"Give me an address." His voice all business, probably the wife in the room. "I'll be there in twenty. Pick you up in the alley behind the building. You know where I mean?"

I waited a few minutes before standing up and trying to straighten my clothes and hair once again. I looked in the mirror and contemplated cutting off the mane that had caused me nothing but trouble. I pulled it back harshly and tried to secure it with an elastic band excavated from the bottom of my bag.

We hardly spoke for the mile ride to the hotel, but instead of pulling into the parking lot Mark drove past the hotel to the amusement park that decorated a spit of land extending into Long Island Sound. A gated back entrance opened to his plastic key card and we drove to what looked like a storage shed. The place was deserted at this hour, the park open only on weekends during the month of September. There was no sound here, just birds and the wind to punctuate the long silence between us.

"So," he said finally. "What have you been doing?"

"Have you ever noticed…" I hesitated, my voice trailing off.

"What? Noticed what?" I could feel his entire body shift in my direction.

"Never mind, I just saw something," I shrugged.

"You saw something—where, in the apartment?"

I cut him off sharply. "It's not what you think," I said. "Nothing about the case… the apartment was, well, clean. You ought to know. Your men did a good job."

He exhaled slowly. Waited for me to speak again. This was surely the sign of a good cop, this patience. Let the suspect fill the tense, dead air.

"It's not about the case. I was just watching the sun rise and, oh, this is stupid."

"Go ahead," he prodded.

I looked over at him for the first time, then back to the sky. "Did you know that there are faces carved in the Lorraine building on Main Street? Along the top, like the carvings you see on a church."

"Hmmn."

"I know, what's the big deal, right?" I nodded vigorously. "You must think I've lost it...and maybe I have, after spending an entire night alone in that apartment. Maybe I was seeing things. But they were beautiful, and strange, and when the sky started to brighten I looked up, and there they were." I opened my hands in wonderment.

"Okay. So, there are carvings on the building. That's nice," he said, his voice tense with frustration. "What else?"

His scrutiny made me nervous and I shifted uncomfortably in my seat, aware once again of my unwashed condition.

"What do you mean?" I stalled. "I was at the apartment, looking around. I don't think anyone saw or heard me—did they?"

He shook his head slowly. I watched his hands tap the wheel lightly, and I waited.

"I spoke with your former employer," he finally said. So, that was it. That I could handle, and I felt my heart slow a bit.

"Oh. So you know," I replied.

"Why don't you tell me your version," he said. "Maybe I've missed something, maybe you can enlighten me."

"Well, I doubt that. But sure, I'll fill in the blanks," I even managed to smile. "Do you want the short version or the long version?"

No answer. I saw the muscles in his jaw tighten. Okay, he must have gotten the full treatment from the bureau. "Do you think we could have a coffee or something?" I asked.

He crossed his arms and tucked in his chin in a stern look that had to be something taught at the police academy, or dog obedience school.

"Dammit," I said, then kicked off my shoes and stretched my toes. "Can we at least walk around? I'm having trouble keeping my eyes open." We both knew I was stalling, but after a long moment he reached over and unlocked the doors.

Barefoot, chilly yet refreshed by the reprieve, I walked along the path behind Mark, towards a secluded part of the shore. Behind us, ancient train tracks still carried the miniature cars up and down the beach and in a loop around the park, day after day, as they had for more than a hundred years. The water was icy when I tested it with one toe, but I splashed both feet around in an effort to cleanse some of the night's bad feelings from my body.

I remember the evening I'd spent here, waiting to see if the boy would be the kind to take me on the roller coaster, or if he was the romantic type who'd head for the train, its quiet ride around the periphery of the park the perfect place for making out—and then the Laugh-in-the-Dark, the stupidest ride, with the smell of old wet wood and the goblins that dropped from the ceiling. Skeletons dangled from the sharp curves and the cold wash of air was always an excuse to snuggle in the cars. As the night progressed, the necking started earlier in the ride until there were no more fake screams but instead the slurping sound of inexperienced lovers. I shook my head, then turned to look back at the park.

"Hey, where's the Ferris wheel?" I cried.

"Long gone," he shrugged. "Not much is left from the old days."

"Except the train."

"The train, and the carousel of course, and the original wooden roller coaster… but that's it," he said. "What are you smiling about?"

My brain was flooded with memories of the park in the old days. "Raoul and his friends used to come down here sometimes and jump out of the bushes onto the train…they got caught once, well, you probably know all about that."

"Yeah, that's why they stopped running the train after dark," he said.

I laughed out loud. "It didn't stop Raoul and his gang—you know, they used to hide in the Laugh-in-the-Dark and grab people when they came through."

Mark was quiet, waiting for my trip down memory lane to end.

"You know," I flopped on the rock next to him. I sat a little too close, our bodies touching calf to calf, thigh to thigh, hips and shoulders, but he didn't move away and so neither did I. "I saw those faces looking into the apartment this morning and I thought, my God, how could this be? I looked out of that same window literally thousands of times, hours on end, and I never saw them before."

I turned and looked into his eyes. We were so close, I could smell his aftershave and practically count the individual hairs sprouting between the unbuttoned top of his shirt.

"Clara," his voice was kind. "You lived on the floor below Raoul's apartment—maybe that's why you didn't see them."

"Oh, you're right," I was deflated. My grand discovery was not such a revelation, just more evidence that I'd been drinking too much. "Sorry." I pulled away from him and began rubbing my forehead vigorously, stopping only when I felt his hand on my shoulder.

"Take it easy," he said softly. "It's okay."

I leaned into him a little. "It seemed like an important discovery at the time," I said. "I guess I wanted to find something there, and all I discovered was a row of faces looking into the window."

He nodded. "I don't know if I should tell you this, but, there used to be a building in between yours and the Lorraine Building."

"Oh yeah," I said slowly. "I forgot about that. What's his name used to live there —Gary, Gary, dammit, I can't remember his last name. Oh, what difference does it make?" I turned to him, practically pleading. "When did they tear down that building?"

"Few years ago I guess. They've been dropping one after the other in the historic district. Nobody wants to take care of old buildings anymore." He removed his hand, but then I felt it lower on my back. "You've been through a lot, Clara, don't punish yourself," he said. "We all forget things."

"I'm a trained investigator, for Christ's sake," I said impatiently. "I'm not supposed to overlook these kinds of details. Details!" I jumped up, pacing in front of him. "I missed the fact that an entire building is gone. Christ," I shoved unruly curls back into their elastic restraint. "Christ!"

I started to shiver, my face muscles working over the idea of my investigative lapse. "You must think I am a complete loser—no wonder you called the bureau." My arms waved frantically as I felt myself losing control. I tried to catch my breath and rubbed my arms. "Sorry, my God, I am so sorry." I walked to the shore and lobbed a stone into the frigid water.

He came up behind me and I felt his warm arms encircle my shoulders. I leaned back and his body seemed to engulf mine. His breath warmed my neck.

"You must be exhausted," he murmured.

I choked back a sob and let him lead me back to the parking lot. "We'll talk later," he said. I knew he wouldn't easily forget whatever he'd learned from the bureau, but I was glad for the delay. At least later, I should be able to respond to his questions with a clear head. And perhaps a call or two might clarify exactly what he'd been told. No sense spilling more than he needed to know.

I tucked my legs underneath what little coverage my skirt gave and leaned on his shoulder lightly during the short ride to the hotel. Again, he went straight to the back entrance.

"Thanks." I was reluctant to leave the sanctuary of his car.

"You all right?" He straightened my hair and a long finger traced the edge of my chin, resting near my mouth. I shook my head, no, I was definitely not okay. Brown eyes met and held and I moved my head away before he could do what I was certain we both wanted.

I picked up my shoes and followed him to the door, where the magic key tumbled the lock. "Thanks," I said again.

I felt his eyes follow my passage down the hall but when I stopped at the door and turned back, he was gone. Message light blinking, several envelopes under the door, I tumbled into the bed and was asleep before the locks engaged.

Raoul

THE FAT MAN HANDED over a roll of cash that Raoul had trouble fitting into the hip pocket of his tight-fitting black jeans. He managed, though. No reason to let the money go to waste. He documented every dollar in his little moleskin notebook, using the elaborate code system that he and Clara had created during their "Mission Impossible" phase. Even if the bureau ignored his reports about the drug running, he wanted to be able to account for all the money when the bust actually went down. Mostly it was squirreled away in a hidden compartment under the van, beneath the spare tire. It was taking up a lot of room, being all cash and much of it small bills, so he moved a brick of it to Stagger Lee one night, wrapping the money in newspaper and taping it into an old White Owl cigar box.

Again, the transfer was documented, the box secured in the false bottom of one of the strong boxes he kept locked on the decrepit vessel. One lesson he learned the hard way, after Clara's inglorious departure from the bureau: never, ever bend the rules. Never. Once they'd finished investigating her, they went through his life with such a fine-toothed comb he felt like a chimp getting a lice bath.

Tonight, the money had to go directly to Stagger Lee. He hated to risk approaching the boat directly after leaving the Pirate, afraid that one day, they would be following him and all his secrets could be exposed. It was barely 3:00 a.m. and he was not even tired. Thank God for a fast metabolism, he thought. Papa was like this, barely needing to sleep or eat to survive. He had his girlfriends in the next town over, where he worked as a pastry chef on the weekends, in service to the city folk who summered in the luxurious cottages near Rhode Island. Once Raoul had followed the old man, gotten caught, and was made to wash dishes all weekend in the stinking back kitchen of a country club. The other workers joked about the old cook, who spent more time humping the rich bitches in the pantry than he did actually cooking. Raoul knew a lot about his father, and his definitions of how to be a man.

The old man liked to fish almost as much as he liked to fuck, and over the years Raoul had watched him stand for an hour in one spot, barely moving except to occasionally pull on his rod. From this he learned the kind of patience that made twenty-four-hour stakeouts a breeze. When they fished, if Raoul made a noise that Papa believed had scared off a big fish just circling his line at that very moment, he was immediately treated to a slap on the back of his head. Oh yes, the old man liked to teach his boy some lessons.

"You gonna be a man, not a pussy, eh? Your mama, she want to keep you home and dress you up like a doll. Not my son, no Miho. No, nada, nunca. Stand there and be quiet," he pointed to a spot. "You want to be a man? Stand there and fish." How many hours had they spent crotch-deep in some swamp or bay, looking for a fish that could feed seven people and that did not taste like the oily scum they caught on the Sound? Yeah, he learned how to be quiet, the old man made sure of that.

There was a certain poetic justice to using the old man's long-lost boat as a storage place for his ill-gotten money, Raoul thought. He remembered the night his father came home after losing the boat in a poker game, how angry he was and the way he threw Mama against the stove when she asked him a question. By then, Raoul was about an inch taller than his father, and so he stepped up, grabbed his father's greasy pony tail, and pulled him to the sink. Raoul's only advantage was speed, because he knew that Papa could still beat the crap out of him, so he quickly held the older man's head under the faucet while his mother screamed and the girls held her back.

"Hmmm," he mused. Never saw the old man again after that, never heard a word in the backrooms or kitchens. "Wonder where he ended up?" Snapping the heavy-duty lock shut, Raoul vaulted out of the boat in time to avoid the arc of a flashlight cutting across the yard.

"Anybody there?" A moment later, the sound of panting dogs reached his narrow hiding spot. Raoul pulled a couple of biscuits from his pocket and tossed them in the general direction of the Dobermans. Close call, but he remained the consummate Boy Scout: always prepared. After a few moments of waiting, the sound of footsteps fading away, Raoul climbed through the hole in the fence and readjusted his black cap. It was time to go back to his apartment. Metin would be waiting.

And he was, squatting in the alley, eyes gleaming in the light of the moon.

"Ismail," Metin said softly.

"Come," Raoul said, then opened the heavy steel door and led the younger man through the basement maze. Something metallic disturbed the white noise of the dryer, and Raoul spotted Mrs. Chen from the first floor, head lolling against the wall as she waited for her clothes to dry. Once inside the apartment, the two men sat comfortably on the prayer rug, backs against the wall.

"Why don't you have any furniture?" Metin asked again.

"Not planning to stay long," Raoul said. "This works fine for me." They sat quietly. A siren cut through the night and after it passed, Metin sighed heavily.

"Can I tell you something, Ismail? I have been thinking about going home," he said. "I miss my family."

"Then you should go. Why not? What's keeping you here?"

"Ismail, the Leader, you know."

"What? He only wants those who truly feel the call."

"He won't let me go."

"What makes you say that?" Raoul said. "Of course you can go. I already told you I will give you the money. I don't need it anymore. You take it and go."

"Why are you staying?" Metin looked at Raoul. "I don't mean to be rude but you don't seem very, um, inspired."

"Maybe I'm not. I don't know." Raoul rubbed his hand over his face. "I haven't got anything else, so I'm in. You, you have a reason to go home, you have a family. And you should go and have a life. Get married, have some kids, you know, the whole thing."

"You could, too."

"No."

More silence. Raoul fingered his prayer beads and Metin closed his eyes.

"He won't let me go," Metin said after several minutes. "They've invested too much in training me."

"What do you mean?"

"You know, they sent me over to a camp for a few months, and then they sent me to school here."

"Oh. I didn't know that. But, anyway, I'll get you out. I'll get you a plane ticket and drive you to the airport myself."

"I don't have a passport."

"What?"

"None of us do. He has all of them. You know that. So that's it. I can't leave." Metin got up and went into the bathroom.

Raoul listened to the other man's long piss, the flush, and then the quick burst of water from the sink. Good man: washed his hands.

"The sky is getting light," Metin gestured to the windows when he returned to the rug. "It's almost time to go to the mosque."

"Where did you go, for training, I mean?"

"Pakistan."

"Ahh. And then flight school, right? In Florida?"

"Yeah." Metin shifted. "Why are you asking me these things?"

"I'm curious. I never got any of that. I guess 'cause I came into the group so late." He bit a piece of skin off his thumb, picked at the cuticle and then bit again. "I don't even have a passport. And no one asked me about it. I guess that means I'm not as valuable as you."

"We're all on the same mission, and we're all going to the same place," Metin said. "That's what matters."

Raoul nodded. They watched the sky lighten and heard the birds begin their morning chorus. "You want to take a shower?" he asked. Metin shook his head. "I'm going to change my shirt. I can give you a clean tee shirt if you want one." Raoul started to rise, but then stopped. He put a hand on the other man's shin. "Listen, you tell me you want to go and I'll get you what you need. Just say the word."

"How can you do that? No, don't say it. No, I'm satisfied. I made the right choice. Really. My family will be better off this way. They'll be taken care of. Don't think about it. Don't mention it again. And I, I don't want to know anything. Let's just drop it."

Raoul went to the pile of clothes by the bed and pulled out a shirt. "Okay, my friend, I won't say anything. And I trust you, too." After changing and tying a clean bandana over his hair, Raoul turned back to Metin, who was still sitting quietly on the floor. "This training stuff, were there lots of guys? More than here? I mean, is everybody here now?"

Metin got up. He looked oddly at Raoul. "My friend Ismail, you're asking too many things now. But let me tell you this: There are many soldiers ready for this battle. We are just a small part of a much larger army that is ready to go." He walked to the door, then turned back to Raoul. "I'll pray for you, Ismail," he said. "I hope you'll pray for me, too."

Clara

THE SUN HAD LIGHTENED the room enough so that, pawing through the stack of manila envelopes, I could study what the cops had taken from Raoul's apartment, his "personal effects" limited to the change in his pocket and a couple of keys on a simple brass ring. I toyed with that, recalling the clunky chain he'd worn on his keys for years, and more recently the heavy ring full of plastic swipe cards from every supermarket in town. And his gym pass.

I leaned against the bed frame. Where were all those cards? Three brass keys snapped in my hand as I tossed them back and forth. Was this it? No mailbox key, either. Something was missing.

The computer hummed through its warm-up ritual while I studied again the transcripts Spike had faxed. There was another set of keys somewhere. I typed in the codes for access to my mail and scanned the list as new items dropped in from cyberspace. Nothing of interest, just urgent messages from the foreign land of work. I couldn't even speak that language anymore, so I ignored them and checked for something from the bureau. Nada. That could not be good news.

I pulled the inventory list out of the file and scanned it, then checked the photos. Where were Raoul's clothes? I was not interested in the lacy stuff in which he's been found, but the other things that had been scattered around the room—his black jeans, tee shirt, and denim jacket. I focused again. The expensive sneakers: they were black, too, except for the silver cylinder dangling from one shoelace. I pulled a magnifying glass towards the enlargement and studied it. At first glance, it seemed to be decorative, but then I flashed again on the key ring.

It was barely 7:00 a.m., but I knew Mirasol had already been up for hours. Despite her flighty appearance and questionable relationships with men, the girl was an early riser with elaborate exercise and grooming rituals. The phone rang only once before she picked it up. "Quien?" She was also the only one of us stubbornly hanging onto her Spanish.

"Mirasol, chica, it's me, Clara."

"What do you want?" she replied.

"Okay, listen, I know you all are mad at me, but I need to ask you something and it's important, okay?" Silence. I kept going. "Mirasol, I need to find Mijo's clothes, the ones they took from his apartment. Do you know where they are?"

"Why? What are you going to do now? You didn't help him when he asked you, and now you want his clothes? Dios mio!" I let her rattle for a minute, cursing me to all eternity, before I interrupted.

"Mirasol, please, can you just tell me? I think I can help the police find out what happened to him. Don't you want them to get the person who did this?"

"Oh sure, you are the great investigator, eh? I thought they kicked you out of the FBI after your last big bust. You think we don't know about you?" she jeered.

"I don't know what you heard, but I don't want to argue with you about it," I said. "I just want to find Raoul's stuff. Can you help me or not?"

"Are you going to manufacture evidence again? Maybe you'll be able to put some more of our friends in jail, eh?" I waited again for the imprecations to stop.

"Mirasol, don't get all high and mighty with me. You're not a saint, either, and I don't think you want anyone to know what I know about you. Especially mama." I let the threat hang in the wires between us. "Now, just tell me where I can find Raoul's clothes, please."

"The police still have everything, I think," she said. "He was not gay, you know. I don't care what they are saying about Mijo, he was not a faggot."

"Well, you should know." I hung up, dismayed with my childish comeback. *You should know?*

If the police still had the clothing, how was I going to get it? Mark might be less willing to help me if he'd learned about my problems with the bureau.

An hour later I pulled behind the police station in a utilitarian Chevy that drove like a tank compared to my sports car. When I spoke to the officer behind the desk, a tall handsome fellow with a thick blond mustache and eager manner, he listened attentively as I described the family's distress and desire to have Raoul's personal items.

"I can't give you anything from the apartment, ma'am," he said. "That's still considered evidence. Maybe the Chief—"

"I've already spoken with him," I replied. "I don't want the clothes he was wearing, officer, I just want to retrieve the other things from the apartment."

"I don't know. You'd have to speak with the detective on the case, or the Chief, like I said." He looked around furtively, and then offered, "You know, I think that anything that's not part of the investigation has already been returned. I saw someone in here the other day and she left with a big bag. Maybe that was one of your relatives?"

I did my best to smile. "Do you have a receipt? 'Cuz I'm not sure that you gave the stuff to the right person."

He reddened then, as I thought he might, and started tapping nervously on the computer. After about five minutes, he looked up. "I can't tell from this. Wait here a minute." He pulled a brown notebook out from under the desk. "The signature is kind of hard to read." He turned the log book so that I could read it. "Do you recognize this name?"

"Of course, that's fine then." I wiped my eyes and blew my nose, hoping to distract him. "I'm so sorry to bother you."

Before I could back the car out of the lot, Mark pulled his vehicle behind mine. I tried to catch my breath while he walked slowly to the window and motioned for me to open the door.

"Clara." There was a question implied but not asked.

"Hey, I was looking for you." I tried for lightness, desperate now for coffee and a chance to wring someone's neck. I did not want to have this conversation with Mark right now—actually ever, in fact, but I had to get my hands on that lying bitch Shelly, and retrieve whatever she had taken from the police.

"Are you coming or going?" he asked. He looked over into the car, and I was sure he'd already made a note of the license plate. Stop being paranoid, I told myself. He's just rabbity because he's got the hots for you and doesn't know what to do about it.

"Well, when I saw you weren't here I thought I'd just go catch some breakfast and come back later." My hand, seemingly of its own volition, touched Mark's wrist. "Care to join me?" I prayed the answer was no; it was.

"I've got a meeting," he looked at his watch. "Come back in about an hour, okay?" I kept smiling while he closed my door and returned to his own car, then let out a sigh of relief when I was back on the road. "Yeah, I'll be back in an hour," I muttered.

Peterson was once again engaged in his morning swill ritual and I could see his shoulders tense even as I tried to close the door quietly behind me. There was to be no fooling this man, I knew, but I had to distract him enough to get access to the membership list.

"What do you want?" he asked.

"It's me, Clara," I said cheerfully. I sidled over to the bar.

"I know who it is. I want to know what the hell you're doing here. Why are you showing your face back in this club, after yesterday?" He leaned forward on the mop handle, poking a knobby finger in my approximate direction.

"I wanted to ask you some more questions about that dead body," I said. I was behind the bar now, and he knew it.

"What are you doing? Get away from there—I'll call the police. You tryin' to rob me?" The wooden mop handle snapped like a bullet when it hit the floor.

"Listen, Mr. Peterson, I just need a coffee, can I make you one too?" I busied myself with water and clinked together some cups as distracting noise. My eyes skimmed the paperwork stacked behind the bar as my hands sought the coffee filters and rattled the can of Chase and Sanborn.

"I tole you before, girlie, that I ain't telling you nothin." He gripped the bar and sniffed. "Now get out of here or I'll call the cops."

"You're not calling anyone, old man, so just cut the crap. Relax, I'll have the coffee ready in a minute and we'll have a little chat." I reached over and patted the gnarled knuckles. "Sit, sit."

Muttering to himself, Peterson turned his back. I wasn't worried that he'd actually call the police, but I wasn't eager to have a confrontation with the thug I'd seen in here before. Quickly I came around the bar and snatched the cell phone from his hands. "No need to call anyone," I said, tucking the phone into my pocket. "Let's just have a private talk, okay?" I pushed him backward into a chair. "Now, tell me more about your hanging man."

I stood before the bent figure and crossed my arms. He clamped his jaw tightly and turned his face away.

"Okay, you don't want to talk about it," I said. "I understand. No one else seems to know anything either." I wished for a pair of handcuffs and looked around for a rope of some sort. "So maybe you want to talk about something else. How about Raoul? Can you tell me about him, what he was doing before he died? Do you know anything about that?" There, a shoelace—not enough to tie up the wiry little fellow. I could use his belt, however, but there would no doubt be a struggle to get it.

"I'm not talking to you," he said again.

There was a brown clump on the floor by his discarded mop. Oh precious, a dirty old sock. It would do. Before he could fight me, I had his hands tied behind the chair and securely fastened to one of the wooden spindles.

"What the hell?" he sputtered.

I returned to the bar then, poured some coffee and proceeded to flip through the various notebooks bulging with loose papers while Peterson tried to discern my location and what I was doing.

"Sorry, no coffee for you," I called out. "I tried to have a nice conversation with you and look what happened." I found a roster but without her last name. It was going to take a while to find Shelly's listing. Various fonts and handwritten changes made the inspection more cumbersome, but I did manage to jot down Guy's home address for future reference, as well as some interesting membership data on the Chief of Police. But no Shelly, and nothing on Raoul either.

She was probably not a member, I figured, but then I knew that Raoul had been a long-time Eagle and since I couldn't find his name, the list must be incomplete. More hunting, while Peterson vented his frustration at the chair, his bindings, and the indignity of being held hostage by a lowly female. Or lowlife female, perhaps. I wasn't paying attention until I caught him talking about Raoul.

I kept clanking things together, pretending not to be listening as the old man began recounting his problems with Raoul and the names of his friends. Pencil at the ready, I jotted down the names as best I could and waited. Perhaps Shelly was the Loren slut he referred to—and the name "Win" kept coming up. Winslow? Winston? I mused, checking back with the roster from time to time.

He stopped talking when the phone rang behind me, and we both listened as the message tape played and a voice cut through the silence hanging over the room like a halo of stale cigarette smoke.

"Peterson, pick up the phone," it demanded. "Peterson." Screamed this time. Then a curse, "Damned old coot, deaf as a post."

"I am not," Peterson yelled back. Again, the man shouted for the phone to be picked up, and then the dial tone bleated.

"He'll be here in a minute," he said.

I doubted that was true but wouldn't swear it, so I riffled through the last of the papers and folded the interesting ones into my back pocket.

"Thanks, I've got to run," I said. "I'll be back to talk with you later." I could hear his curses raining behind as I left the club and got into my car.

The fax from Spike was buried under the evidence photos splashed across my bureau, and I avoided focusing on the bloody pictures until I came across the one that included the shot of Raoul's sneakers. The magnifying glass was inadequate and I wished yet again for access to a developer so I could enlarge the shot.

I fumed about it for a few minutes and then reread the note from Spike. What the hell. I grabbed the phonebook and checked the yellow pages under "health clubs." Not so many in this little town, and only one with the high tech swipe key system similar to the one used at gas stations. I was willing to bet that Raoul's secrets were not kept in his apartment but in his locker, and without the silver passkey, I was going to have to talk my way through the security barrier.

Mark had arrived unexpectedly at my door, and he wasn't looking very friendly. "So do you want to tell me why?" he asked. I felt a trickle of sweat meander down the center of my back. Most likely, he wanted to talk about whatever he had learned from my previous associates in the FBI. Oh well. I knew how to distract him from that subject.

"Why?" I stalled. *Not a good idea to lose your cool here, chica,* I told myself. Get a grip. Mark had simply leaned back in his chair, arms crossed, and handed me a length of rope.

Normally, I'd have played, spinning a cat's cradle of a story for him, guessing and countering what I figured he must have gotten in the report from the Bureau. But that question—*so do you want to tell me why?*—echoed in my mind and I couldn't grasp it. It's a simple question, Clara, just make something up. I clenched and tried to look cool, studying him under lowered lashes.

My heart pounded. It was the question—how could he have known? It must be a coincidence, his using the same words that Raoul had queried me in our last encounter.

"So do you want to tell me why?" Raoul had asked, with more than a little mockery in his voice. His "I've got the goods on you and I'm going to tell" pose, the one I'd seen all his life, the one that got me into trouble with mama, with dear old departed dad, with the Bureau—and then my career, down the tubes, time to start over until that day, when Raoul came at me again, sneering, "So, do you want to tell me why?"

That time, the last time, was the last time I thought I'd ever have to explain myself to someone. And I'd taken care of it—given him the ultimate "butt out of my business" answer. No more explaining to do, no more "please love me do." But here it was again.

"You'll have to be more specific," I said to Mark. "Or should I just start at the beginning?" Not a flinch. Okay, I thought.

"Let's see, I was born the fourth daughter of a man desperate for a son, the fourth child in a family already living hand to mouth, on the paycheck of a low-level chef to a big-shot Navy man. That's why I hate to cook—can't boil water, if I do say so myself," I added. "But I digress—or are you interested in learning why I chose to divorce myself from the culinary arts?"

He continued to stare, so I proceeded with the jabbering, carrying on the non-sense conversation. My jacket fell open and I shrugged out of it, watching him watching me, using it. The move was the thrust and parry of my body against his mind.

He was carefully inspecting me, trying to unnerve me—me, the woman versed in the nuance of deception by its masters in the government. I knew the drill, though, and it made me hot for him, again. It'd been days since that need had blown up, demanding to be met. Days since the last fucking encounter with fucking Guy, the last fucking guy.

I had to smile at him then, smile and continue the story I'd begun to amuse us both. "So then we had Raoul, but I carried on the macho mantle for my papa," I said. "First the military, then the Special Forces, then the CIA and onto the Bureau when they called me in, but you know all about that."

No answer. "So why? I had to leave, that's all. I had no other spook mask to try on—oh sure, there's always the Secret Service, but you talk about boring, I'd rather be a museum guard than have to spend my days and nights guarding, well, you know."

"Why, why not?" I answered my own shrug. "I knew too much, maybe, I was expendable, definitely. We all are, in some way or another."

Hmm. Caught him in a sidelong glance at my blouse. Okay—progress. "I wouldn't fuck the right people, wouldn't take it in the ass, really, so I was shipped out—or back home, technically," I took a breath, pushing forward against the white fabric of my semi-sheer blouse. "But you heard all about the Contra stuff, I'm sure. And it wasn't just me—no, we all had to get out of there in a hurry. But the Spanish came in handy, and they found another use for it soon after. There's always another dirty little war going on."

"Why? Hmmn," I stretched again, trying not to be too obvious, but moving my legs slightly apart. If only I'd known where we were going today I'd have dressed for this little interview—I'm not above pulling down a Sharon Stone, especially for someone I'd been contemplating a good fuck with for days now. Oh yeah, it was definitely getting hotter in here.

"So you know all about the whole Puerto Rico fiasco," I lowered my voice. Better make him come closer to hear me. "I suppose everyone says the same thing—I didn't do anything wrong there. I just did what I was told, and they set me up to take the blame when it went down badly."

Too much of an act to put on crocodile tears now, I suppose. I decided to shut up for a change and contemplate the dampness of my panties. Your move. I studied my nails for a moment, waiting. When I polished the tips of my manicured nails against my chest, I know I heard him inhale just as I felt the nipple on the right side harden at the touch. Buff.

He sighed then and I raised my eyes to meet his look.

"Why can't you just tell the truth?" he asked.

"About?" A shaking of the head was my only response. "I'll tell you some truths, if you really want to hear them, but if you can't be more specific, I'll just have to decide what it is you're asking." I stood up and walked to the door, where I engaged the lock.

"No," he said. "You're not going to…"

He stopped talking when I straddled his lap and pressed my breasts in his face. "Yes, Mark, I am going to," I said. "And you are going to like it."

"Let me tell you why you're going to make love to me," I began, unbuttoning my blouse and moving slowly against his lap. "I can tell"—I reached down to adjust his erection—"I can feel that we're on the same wavelength here."

When I felt his fingers sliding up my ribcage, and around to loosen my breasts from the lace that tamed them, I knew we were done talking. My mouth found his, open and wet.

Raoul

LATE. NO MOON. CREEPING along the roadside, ducking into the underbrush whenever a car approached. By the time he reached the van, Raoul should have been exhausted, but his nerves were so tightly wound that he was hyper-alert. He unlocked the door and climbed in the back, checking to make sure all the windows were well covered before turning on the generator and switching on the lights.

It took five minutes to get the laptop unsecured from the floor and powered up, and during that time he pulled notes from inside his shoes, pockets, and hat. A wad of cash was carefully logged in and photographs of the night's drug sales downloaded from one of his flash drives onto the portable hard drive. Finally, he opened his log and transcribed his notes in careful code.

Another body to add, this time for the Pirate. He made a quick sign of the cross. "Jesus, forgive me," he whispered. "Dumb ass drug dealers." He closed his eyes for a moment and then shook his head, trying to get rid of the image of the man's pleading face as Raoul put a bullet in his brain.

"Do it," the Pirate had been screaming. "Kill him, or I'll take you both out!"

"He hates traitors," K explained, steering the boat closer to a cove where they could dump the body. "The estupido tries to trick the Pirate by handing him a bag of newspapers wrapped on the outside with money! Ha! Does he think we was born yestiddy?"

"Shut the fuck up," the Pirate said. "I didn't hear no shot yet. Is there a problem?" He reached for his own gun.

Raoul pulled the trigger then, easing the body over the edge of the boat. "Silencer," he said.

"Gimme the gun," the Pirate said, holding out his hand.

Raoul handed the weapon across the boat, then waited to feel a bullet enter his own body. He turned his head slightly and watched the last of the bubbles rise to the surface next to the boat.

"Go," the Pirate said to K. "Get us out of here." He smelled the gun. "Nothin' like the smell of cordite on a clear summer night." He put the gun in the holster under his arm. "So, what's your problem?" he asked Raoul.

"I don't have a problem," Raoul said. "I don't have one with you, and I didn't have one with that kid. So, I didn't need to kill him. In the future, why don't you take care of your own damn problems and leave me out of it?"

"Oh, squeamish, are we? Did I make you violate some kind of moral code or something? I mean, you do get that we're drug smugglers out here, not fucking Boy Scouts on a fucking outing, right?" The Pirate turned and spat into the water. "K, take this lady to shore. I don't want him to miss any beauty sleep tonight. And you —I don't want to look at your fucking holier-than-thou face anymore. Get the fuck off my boat. And tomorrow night, if you come to work with attitude, you're going to join your buddy in the deep over there. You get me?"

Typing in the stats for the kid, Raoul wondered how long it would be before the body would be found, and how much longer before the parents would learn that their child was dead. He was certain the boy was no older than twenty-five and was glad that he'd come alone to make the ill-fated exchange. There was probably a partner somewhere on the shore, waiting in a car for his buddy to arrive with the drugs that they were going to split, some for sale and some for their own use.

"I should go find him," Raoul said. He shook off the thought. He could never step outside his cover, even though he was working two investigations at the same time. No, the most he could do was record what happened and make his regular reports. Let someone else deal with the bodies and the fallout.

He was worried about Metin, he wrote, switching gears. The kid was on the edge of a breakdown. This kind of weak personality was just the type that could be taken over completely by someone like the Leader. Metin didn't know enough, or think enough of himself, to defend himself against this kind of cult of personality, he wrote. Maybe, if he was careful, he could get Metin out. But if he advocated too hard in that direction, it would raise suspicion and undermine his own place in the group.

A new file: Salim. This kid is the Leader's new pet, Raoul wrote. "He could kill me."

Clara

IT WAS QUICK WORK, dispatching the Chief. After a shower and return to my sleuthing outfit—tight jeans and a low cut black tee shirt—I worked some magic on the teenager at the health club and soon was headed back to the hotel, the contents of Raoul's locker emanating its musk from the backseat. Dusk was coloring the sky with dramatic swipes of purple and mauve. I hefted the keys in my free hand, paused at a stoplight. One large brass key, which I initially thought was just decorative, suddenly felt familiar in my hand.

"Could it be?" I shook off my hesitation and decided, once again, to follow my gut. I turned the car around and aimed it towards the docks. Well hidden in the shadow of the base, behind even the boat repair and storage places, a small lot held local fishing boats, mostly decrepit and balanced on blocks at this time of year. We'd spent some miserable hours here, scraping toxic paint and barnacles off the bottom of papa's boat, and my uncle's boats, and the boats of anyone else my father lost a game of cards to at one time or another. Later, when we were stubborn teenagers, we refused the assignments, but still haunted the boat yards looking for an open place to lie around and party.

It was pushed to the back, hard against a shed so flimsy it was difficult to tell which was supporting the other. But it was there. "Stagger Lee," stenciled in white on the side, looking more like the skeleton of a boat than something that once had been seaworthy. I climbed aboard, gingerly, my foot almost going through the first board I put my weight on. Someone bellowed nearby and I ducked down, crouching against floorboards slick with moss and animal droppings.

In the growing dusk, I sat and waited while sounds of activity lessened. Some car doors slamming, a few shouts and the squeal of a winch—for an hour I listened to the familiar noises and wondered how it was that this boat still sat here after all these years. Surely papa wasn't paying the storage; most likely one of the uncles had taken the title, or Crazy Leon now called the boat his own. Signs posted everywhere warned that Leon would own your property if any of the listed rules was violated, including "Dumping dirt" in unauthorized places.

"What's that mean?" I asked once, at the tender age of six or seven. Proud that I could read most of the sign, I didn't understand the dirt rule.

"That's for them fancy boats, the big ones there," he pointed. "The ones what have toilets inside—but they clean 'em out here in the yard and make a mess."

"Ugh."

"Rich people." Papa was quick to dismiss anyone with more money than he had —which was everyone, most of the time.

As far as I could judge from the dryness of the wood and the gaping cracks along the side of the vessel, Stagger Lee had not been on the water for a long while, probably more than a decade. The last time I was out on the water was probably before puberty distracted me from the glories of fishing. Sunbathing became my obsession, and papa did not allow what he called glamour girls on his boat. "If you come on the boat, you fish. That's the rule," he said. When Raoul was old enough to hold a line, papa no longer wanted females on his boat. "Bad luck," he said. "No more girls on board."

Papa had a lot of superstitions, many of them associated with the sea. The name of the boat, for instance. He called it "Swagger Lee" or sometimes "Swizzle Lee." My friends asked about the name so often, I hated repeating the story and often embellished it. "It was the name on the boat when he bought it and it's bad luck to change it," I explained. The truth. But later, I told elaborate tales of a Pirate named Stagger Lee, of a legendary folk song, of a woman lost at sea when she fell over the leeward side of the boat.

It was a simple boat, built mostly for fishing. At about twenty-five feet in length, it was small enough to tow with a sturdy truck but large enough to host one of my father's fishing jaunts. I remember watching him in the open cockpit, how different he looked when he was piloting the boat. Nothing like the broken man who returned home each night, reeking of cooking oil and dirty dishes. When he was the captain, my father looked taller. I wondered what kind of debt would have compelled him to give up his pride and joy. Maybe it was part of the reason he left Jerome so suddenly—never to be seen or heard from again.

His disappearance was just another mystery, one more chapter in the unhappy Quiñones family history—one that I was neither ready for nor interested in taking on. I shook my head, took a few mind-clearing deep breaths, and refocused on Raoul.

It was quiet when I got up and tried the key in the door. Nothing. I had been certain it would fit. Just wasted an hour, I grumbled. Turning around, I kicked at a black tarp piled on the end of the deck. My foot connected with something solid underneath, and after I recovered from the sharp pain in my toe, I pushed away the tarp to uncover a large storage trunk. The brass key slid easily into its fittings, and the lid creaked open.

Now it was too dark to see inside, and I had no flashlight to illuminate the problem. The box was too heavy to move, and I could not make out its contents although I could distinguish several metal lockboxes and some plastic containers that, when pried open, yielded paper—stacks of yellowing paper. I tried lifting the individual boxes out, but they were large and unwieldy and so I gave up. The lockboxes were all secured, and no doubt the keys were hidden in another location.

I slammed the cover and locked it again. The sound echoed through the empty lot and I sat on the lid for a moment. A low growl nearby was not my stomach protesting the late hour without lunch. The shining eyes of a black Doberman appeared over the bow. I could see the white teeth bared and recalled—too late—the owner's penchant for loosing his dogs inside the fenced yard every evening. How did we get around that, all those times we climbed into the boat with fat marijuana cigarettes, bottles of Reunite wine, and a handful of Trojan E-Z glides?

The answer was food, of course, but I was not prepared to bribe a guard dog and so my pockets were empty. The dogs used to be playful as kittens if you gave them some kibble. But Raoul knew that too—I turned and reopened the locker again, scrambling in the dark until I found a box that rattled comfortably when I uncovered it. Thank you, Mijo. I tossed a handful of kibble in the direction of the dog. He yelped and wolfed it down gratefully. I added more to his snack, closed the locker, and started down the ladder, the box tucked firmly under my arm.

"Where you going?" A voice floated at me above the sharp glare of a flashlight snapped in my direction. I tilted my head and tried to see behind the light.

"Sorry," I tried a smile. "I fell asleep on the boat and didn't realize it had gotten to be so late. I'll just be heading out now."

"What did you give my dog?"

I held the box up. "Just a little snack. I found this on deck, someone must have left it."

"Who are you, anyway? And what are you doing on that boat? That boat don't belong to you, it belongs to Leon."

"Oh, I'm sorry. It used to be owned by my…family, and I just was reminiscing about things and like I said, I fell asleep. No harm done. I'll just get out of your way now, if you can show me the way out of here. I'd really appreciate that."

"Nah, I think I better call Leon and check first. You come with me, come on this way." He turned and whistled for the dog. "Ralphie, come on now."

His hand was certainly leaving bruises around my elbow, as he shoved me forward like a mop jerking across an uneven floor. "Can you ease up a little?" I asked, trying to pry his fingers away.

He snorted. "Not so tough now, are you?" he muttered.

I tried to whirl around and face him, but he smacked my ear with the flashlight and continued towards the gate. I reached across to pull my bag closer, hoping to engage the cell phone inside, but he twisted it out of my reach. "What do you think you are doing?" he asked. "Just wait, now, and Leon will talk to you about things."

"What things?" I asked.

"Things. Things going on in this boatyard, things having to do with you snooping around here, things your brother was getting his nose into."

He knew who I was, and he knew about Raoul. Rather than make me nervous, I felt relieved. Now maybe I could get some answers. "Yeah, let's call Leon," I said. "I'm sure he'll remember me from when I was a kid."

He laughed. "No, you're thinking about Crazy Leon. He's long gone. This is his son, Leon Jr. He makes the old man look sane as a judge." He laughed some more.

"But don't you dare call him crazy. He'll kill you on the spot. He's sensitive that way, not like his father at all." More laughter. "This is going to be real interesting."

"And who are you, anyway?" I asked. Demanded, really.

"Never you mind about me." He laughed some more, pushed me into a filthy couch that was the high point of the boatyard's office. Dust billowed around me, and the dog sneezed, then shook himself and settled his head on my knee. A handful of kibble, and he was all mine. Mr. No-Name busied himself behind the desk, first calling Leon—"You better get down here, I caught me a live one on Quiñones' boat" —and then exploring the many features on my cell phone.

I tried again to engage him in conversation. "So, sir, what do you know about my brother's death? I've been trying to figure out who killed him, and I was hoping that you could maybe help me out a little. You know?"

"And why would I want to do that?"

"I could make it worth your while," He looked up from the cell phone, leering. "I mean, I can pay you." Jesus, I silently prayed, please don't make me have to give this guy a blowjob, please spare me. I talked faster. "So, how much? A hundred? Two? You don't have to tell me, just give me a clue and I'll figure it out. Really. Just a name—for two hundred dollars. That seems fair, right?"

He was back at the phone, not paying attention to me. "Woo-hoo, you got the Police Chief on speed dial," he crowed. "Ol' Leon is going to find that very interesting."

"We don't have to tell him, do we? We can make a private deal, right?"

He leered at me again, tongue wagging out of the corner of his mouth. "I heard that you was kind of loose. I guess it's true then." My phone rang in his hand and he read the caller ID. "Rapture. What the hell kind of name is that? You expecting a call from someone named Rapture?"

I shrugged. "I don't know. Answer it if you want to know who it is."

He put the phone down and waited until it stopped ringing. In a few seconds, it beeped to signal the receipt of a voice mail message. "I guess Rapture is looking for you," he said. The outside door slammed and the dog moved quickly into a corner. A large man entered the room, well over six feet tall with long black hair that he wore slicked back in a ponytail. His prominent cheekbones and dark eyes were the only resemblance to his father, who I recalled had been a full-blooded Indian from somewhere in Maine. Junior wore several large pieces of silver jewelry encrusted with turquoise, and he rested both thumbs on a huge belt buckle that was distinctly shaped like a mustang—the Ford, not the horse.

"So. Who the hell are you?" he said. "And what are you doing sneaking around my boats in the middle of the night?"

"It's only 7:00," I said. I struggled to my feet and stuck out a hand. "I'm Clara Quiñones. I was in town and I wanted to see the old boat. You know, memory lane and all that."

He ignored my hand and pushed my shoulder until I was once again engulfed in a cloud of dust from the couch. He leaned back on the edge of the desk, held out his hand and his deputy placed the cell phone in it.

"Quiñones. You know that boat is not your property any longer, right? Your pa lost it to my pa in a poker game. So what makes you think you can come onto my property and snoop around without permission? Huh?" He scrolled through the phone menu while he talked at me. "I should just let you go, seeing as how you have so many calls from the police station on here, but I'm curious."

He paused, looking at me slowly.

"Yes?" I asked.

"First I have your brother poking around here, and now you." He tossed the phone in my lap. "And you know what happened to him." He paused again. "So what am I supposed to do about this?"

"I don't know, sir, but maybe if you could just tell me what you know about Raoul, that would be really, really helpful. And then I'll just leave and get out of your hair and never bother you again." I tried a smile. No reaction. "Okay, I am here to try and figure out what my brother was doing, and so yeah, I would like to hear what you know, and I would be very appreciative of whatever you can tell me that would help me find out who killed my brother."

"She offered me money." The deputy chimed in from behind the desk.

"I don't like cops," Leon said.

"I won't tell them anything about you, I swear."

"Really?" He scratched an armpit. "I don't think I believe that. You being so friendly with Chief Mark and all. And," he turned to look at the man behind the desk, "didn't I hear something about you being a cop, too? Way back when?"

"Yeah, but if you know that then I'm sure you know that I was kicked out. So believe me, I won't go running to the Feds with anything you tell me."

He grunted, moved behind the desk while the other man scrambled to stand by the door. "I don't believe you." He looked at the guard.

"He don't believe you," the man echoed.

"Go do your rounds," Leon said. "And take the dog with you." Before the other man could leave, he added, "And don't tell nobody what you saw here tonight, got it?"

Nodding, the guard grabbed the dog's collar and backed out of the room. When the door closed, there was a long silence. I thought it best to keep my mouth shut, given the options here. Was he going to kill me and dump me in the Long Island Sound? It seemed a real possibility given the way he leaned back and stared at me.

"So," he said.

"So." I agreed. How I wished that I still had a gun strapped to my ankle. One of the bennies of being a cop that I truly missed. Sometimes a camera is not enough to ward off the bad guys.

"Tell me what you were really doing on the boat."

"I told you, I was just thinking. I'm trying to figure things out, and I remembered the boat and wondered if it was still here."

"Didn't occur to you that coming into a locked yard was illegal? And that you have no right to be here?" He inspected his nails; the beds were long and pink, almost manicured. I waited. He glanced at his watch. "What did you find?"

I shook my head.

"Stop playing dumb with me. I know there's something." He sighed. "I can't help you if you won't tell me the truth. But if you want to play it like this, that's fine with me. Tomorrow morning I'll go out to Stagger Lee and have a look around. And what I find there is mine. If I catch you coming back here, I'll have you arrested. Or maybe I will just let Ralphie have a go at you—without the box of kibble you conveniently brought along tonight."

"Look, I didn't find anything. It was too dark. So I just sat there and thought about things, until your goon came along and rousted me." I put my hands palm-up on my lap. "I was grasping at straws, because I have not been able to find out anything about Raoul. What he was doing here. Who killed him. I don't know anything, so I guess I'm just going to have to leave town without knowing what happened. I'll just leave it to the cops, I guess."

"Sure you will." He stretched. "Better make yourself comfortable then, cuz you're not going anywhere tonight. We'll just wait until morning and see what the sunshine brings."

He leaned over and opened a small refrigerator, took out a beer and opened it. "Want one?" he asked. "I heard you like to party. Maybe we can have some fun tonight, eh?" He tossed a can of Budweiser at me and I caught it smoothly.

Raoul

NOT **MANY PEOPLE KNEW** he was back in town, and Raoul wanted it that way. He saw his football teammate Henderson occasionally, usually just long enough to share a drink and some nonsense talk about getting high and scoring some good dope. In high school, that was Raoul's persona—the jock who could make you fly. Henny persisted in this fiction and so Raoul used it, convinced his friend that he was laying low and keeping clean for a while, "until things cool down." Henny bought it, the romance of the man on the lam, and tried to get Raoul to hide out in his apartment.

"Thanks man, I got it covered," Raoul always said, smiling. "I'm cool."

He was not expecting to be recognized in the Spanish bodega, either, but was actually glad to see Mary Kate, one of Clara's high school friends, sifting through the spice bin. He almost backed away, but she looked up and saw him. Her smile was so warm that he forgot any misgivings about being seen in town.

"Mary Kate," he said, taking her by the shoulders and studying her face. "How great it is to see you. You look terrific!"

She shrugged, smiled shyly and buried her face in his neck. "I've missed you, Cinco," she said.

"Cinco," he repeated. It was the name his father used when Raoul had misbehaved, which had then become his nickname with the other Spanish kids in school. "God, it's been so long since I've heard that, Mary Kate. Look at you. You're still in town then, eh?"

"Yeah, still here. Not going anywhere soon," Mary Kate said. "Mom passed and so me and Rose have the restaurant, and you know how that goes."

"And your dad? How is he? Are you still married?" he paused. "And the kids, you have how many?"

"Too many—two kids, one husband and a cranky father who still lives above the smoke shop. Spends most of his days there, sitting in front and chewing the fat with all the other old guys in town." She smiled. "You have to come over, come to the restaurant and have dinner with me. Come late, so I can sit and catch up with you."

"Is it still that fancy place, near the beach?" She nodded. "What are you doing here then? I'm sure you have better food than this place," he said.

She pulled a packet from under her arm and held it up briefly. "Secret ingredient," she whispered.

They parted with promises to get together soon but weeks passed, and it wasn't until he received an urgent message from her, via Henny, that Raoul finally went to La Corona for a visit. Crossing the bridge into the next town was almost like stepping through an enchanted mirror. Here, the houses were large and the cars were expensive. The beaches were private and so were the schools. The main drag was littered with restaurants that came and went, but La Corona survived because no one could serve a plate of seafood like theirs.

He arrived an hour before midnight, coming via water and stashing his dinghy between the monsters at the boat basin. He took off his jacket and hat, patted his hair back in place, and walked quickly across the street. From an alleyway, he checked to make sure no one he knew was in the area, especially not anyone from the mosque. He spent five minutes smoking in the shadows, watching, and when he was sure no one had followed him, he entered the restaurant. A few patrons lingered over coffee and plates of demolished tiramisu, waiters changed tablecloths in preparation for the next day's business, and Mary Kate sat behind the bar with a stack of papers and a calculator.

"Hey," Raoul said. He slid onto a stool.

"You got my message," she breathed. "Thanks for coming. I didn't know, I couldn't find out where you're staying and I needed…"

"What's happening?" he asked. He put a hand over hers. "*Calmate, calmate.* Relax—I'm here. Just tell me what's going on."

She sat up a bit straighter, running one hand through her short, choppy hair. "Sorry, sorry." She looked around. "You want something, a beer maybe? I'm going to have one, I think. Bud?"

Once she stopped stalling, serving their beer in icy mugs and placing a fresh dish of peanuts on the bar between them, Mary Kate took his hand again. "I'm sorry to bother you, but I didn't know who else to call. I mean, Joe, he's a good guy, and he's sick about this, but there's only so much he can do."

"Joe—your husband?"

She nodded.

"Okay, so just start from the beginning. What's this about?"

"It's my son, Cinco. The oldest one." She paused, looked at him meaningfully.

"What's his name?" Raoul asked.

"He's Silvio, like my dad. His friends call him Sal. He's eighteen now, just out of school. And he's been working, down at Frank's garage. He's a good mechanic, you know? He's not the smartest kid, but he's a good boy. Really," she said. Her hands twisted nervously. "He was always a good boy. But he's gone, Cinco…."

"Okay, slow down. Maybe he just went off with some friends, or a girl, or something. How long has he been gone?" Raoul asked.

"Well, he hasn't been home for two days," she said.

"Two days—that's nothing for a nineteen-year-old kid," Raoul said, trying to lighten the mood.

"Well, no, but the thing is, he's 'gone' in his head. I can't explain it. He's just… different lately. He doesn't talk, he doesn't shower, he doesn't shave. He spends all his time with his nose in a book, and when I ask him what he's reading, he ignores me, turns, and walks away. Doesn't even say a word. That's not my Silvio, you see. He's been gone for a while, and I need to find out what he's up to," she said.

"Has he ever been in trouble? Anything?"

"No, nada, he's a good boy. I'm just afraid—you know, about his genes—maybe he can't help it, and he's gone bad. Like his father—you know?"

Raoul was quiet, remembering the awful scene he'd come upon after Clara's high school graduation. "No, I don't believe it. You said he was a good kid, and I think he still is. You don't turn into your father overnight you know. I'm nothing like my father, and I grew up with him in the house so I should be just as mean and nasty as him. But I'm not, and Silvio's not," he said. "I don't think that one day he woke up bad. And you say he wasn't running with a gang or any street kids or anything?"

"Not that I know," she replied.

"Okay. So, what can I do for you? You want me to try and find him?" he asked.

"I know it's dumb, but I can't help but worry...."

"I need a picture of him, maybe the names of a couple of his friends," he said. "I'll poke around and see if I can find him. No problem." He took a napkin from the bar. "Here's my private number. You can always leave a message on this line and I'll call you back right away. Okay?"

She came out from behind the bar and grabbed him around the waist. "Thank you," she whispered into his shoulder.

The next day, and the next, Raoul looked for the boy. Two weeks passed, and Raoul was beginning to give up hope of finding him. But one Sunday night, the last week of August, Mary Kate called. The relief in her voice was tempered by a different tension.

"Silvio's back. He came home about an hour ago," she said. "But there's definitely something off."

"What do you mean?" he asked.

"All his hair is shaved off except for this bushy beard he's been growing. And he's wearing some kind of strange clothes."

"Is he talking? Did he explain where he's been?"

"No, he just said he was on a retreat. And that it was not my concern. Not my concern! He gets me all worried, walks in here after weeks with no word, and then he says it's not my concern? Joe is telling me to lay off, let the boy be, but I know something's up."

"Okay, I'll try to keep an eye on him, and if I can, I'll find out where he's going and what he's up to," Raoul said. "Just give me a day or two, and I'll see what I can learn."

The next day, Raoul worked his usual shift. Instead of heading to the apartment for a shower at 3:00, he checked to see if Silvio was on the job at Frank's, but there was no sign of him. So, the kid was not back at work—that was a bad sign. Raoul spent an hour checking the local clubs, bars, and hangouts, but as dusk approached he gave up and went to the mosque for evening prayers. There was a different kind of buzz in the room that night, some new faces in the front of the room, but Raoul could not make out any of the conversations there. After the prayers, when they usually headed downstairs, the Leader abruptly dismissed the men and told them there was no meeting that night.

Raoul checked back at the garage over the next couple of days, once going inside to inquire about Silvio.

"He quit," the owner said. "He went on vacation a couple weeks ago, and when I expected him to come back, he didn't show up. I called, you know, but he didn't call back for a couple of days, and then all he said was, 'I'm not coming back. Sorry, Frank.' That's it. Sorry—I have jobs lined up for the kid, people waiting to get transmissions, brake jobs, whatever, and he shits on me." He spat on the ground. "After all I did, training him…" He stopped, looked closely at Raoul. "Who are you, a friend of his or something? Does he owe you money?"

Raoul shook his head. "He come back for his pay or his stuff?"

"Nope. Told me to give it to the poor," Frank snorted. "Said something like, 'I don't need such worldly things anymore.' What the fuck does that mean?" He scratched his head, let another loogie fly. "I don't fucking know. Kids."

Raoul shrugged and walked away, his concern about Silvio growing. He called Mary Kate several times, asking if there was anything she could tell him about the boy, but she was as frustrated as he. "Have you found out anything?" she asked him on Friday.

"Not really."

"Well, does that mean maybe? Just tell me, tell me something."

"Has he been going to work?" Raoul asked.

"Yeah," she said slowly. "He leaves every morning at about 6:30, and sometimes he comes home to shower afterwards. Sometimes he doesn't come home until late, but that's not unusual."

"Interesting," Raoul said slowly.

"What do you mean? What's interesting?"

"I spoke with his boss. He hasn't been back to work since he returned to Jerome," Raoul said. He'd been reluctant to share this information with Mary Kate, afraid she'd go after Silvio and he'd disappear. "Don't get all crazy on me now," he said. He could hear her breathing heavily. "Mary Kate, are you with me? Don't go nuts. He's doing something, that's for sure, but we don't know anything concrete. I mean, he's still coming home at night, and he's doing something all day long—maybe he got another job and just didn't tell you about it. That's the logical answer. He's working somewhere else, but he hasn't told you. Yet. I'm sure he will eventually."

There was more silence.

"Mary Kate," he said. "Did something happen at home before he took off? Some kind of fight or anything—did he have words with you or Joe? Anything like that?"

"No." She sighed. "Maybe you're right. He must be ticked off about something, who knows what, and he doesn't want to tell us about it. Maybe he had a disagreement with Frank and he quit, and he doesn't want to tell us. It wouldn't be the first time."

"Well, I'll keep dogging him and eventually I'll figure out what he's doing, Okay?" he asked. "I'll keep in touch—and you just keep your cool." He ended the call and headed for the mosque. Things had been odd there; all week the Leader had been preoccupied and distant. It was a holiday weekend—three days without work that Raoul sorely needed; a chance to rest, catch up on his notes, and try again to get a message to his contact in Washington. Of course, the Pirate was still working—business usually picked up on long weekends, and Labor Day was no exception—so Raoul's nights would be spent on the water, ferrying customers to offshore boats.

Another group of new men was present in the mosque that evening, swelling the congregation until the room was packed. The women were told to leave, to make room for the expanded crowd, and the curtain separating their section pulled aside for the extra men. Raoul was curious, but everything else was the same, and the presence of a new cadre seemed normal given the transitory nature of the group in the months that he'd been attending. Most of the new men sat in the front, surrounding the Leader, and when the prayers were over they followed him into the basement meeting room. Raoul joined the others, staying in the back of the room, as per his usual behavior, and concentrated on listening to the men around him. He snapped to attention when the Leader stepped up and began to introduce the guests: one of whom Raoul thought might be Silvio, although his appearance had certainly been altered so it was hard to be certain.

He was introduced as Salim, a special student of the Imam and someone the Leader proclaimed was "destined for great things" in his lifetime. Raoul scarcely noticed the rest of the men who were introduced, although he was certain that none of the others were locals. Salim had just returned from intensive training in Florida, the Leader said, and he asked the younger man to demonstrate the use of a small signaling device.

"With this small transmitter, you can disrupt the signal on a radio or radar system, or many other devices," Salim said. As he continued to describe the device, Raoul sighed. He was sure that it was Silvio. He recognized the young man's voice, which was almost identical to the distinctive nasal tone of his father.

"Damn it," Raoul muttered. Mary Kate was right—her boy was in trouble.

It was September 1, 2001.

Clara

ONE THING ABOUT INDIANS is that they can't hold their liquor. I can. It only took four beers, which gave me an urgent need to pee, which I did as soon as I got past Leon, snoring loudly in his reclined desk chair. I had no idea how I was going to get back in to retrieve the boxes from the boat, but I was happy to be back on the road to downtown Jerome with most of my dignity and all of my secrets intact. I had no doubt, however, that Leon would be tearing up the boat at first light, and so I needed to get back in there before he did.

Changing into a black tee shirt and jeans, I swiped a flashlight from the linen closet of the hotel and replenished my supply of kibble at the 24-hour market. On the way back to the boat, I redialed Rapture. "Louie, what's going on?" I chirped.

"What time is it?" he mumbled.

"I don't know, two or three? What difference does it make? I'm returning your call. What's up?"

"Clara, please, I have a job. You can't be calling me in the middle of the night."

"Sorry. You used to be up all hours. So, what can you tell me?"

He sighed. I could hear the bedcovers being shifted. "Clara. You're such a pain in the ass."

"Yeah, I know. But you're awake now, so you might as well talk to me." I slowed the car to allow a police cruiser to pass.

"What's that noise?" he asked.

"Oh nothing. Just the television."

"What are you up to?" he asked. "Spill it."

"Nothing, really—so. Tell me. I need to know what you know about Raoul." I downshifted, switched off the lights and pulled into a parking lot across from the boat yard. "You said that he was into bad stuff, drug dealing. What can you tell me about it?"

"I don't know Clara, I really can't say anything. I don't want to—Look the guy is dead, and I'm sorry about that. But isn't it best just to leave it alone? Move on, forget about it? You really don't need to know."

"I do, Louie. I need to know. And don't worry. Nothing will come back on you."

He laughed, and I could hear the snap of a lighter and his lungs drawing hard on a cigarette. "Chica, I don't trust you for a second. What kind of dope do you think I am? I know what you did, and I'm not going down for you or Raoul. Sorry, babe, but I don't owe you anything anymore. I took care of all those debts when I bailed your brother's sorry ass out of trouble—and not just once. I am even with you, and I'm done."

"So, why did you call me? If you're done with me?"

"To tell you—just to tell you that you better be careful. You got into something down there at the Eagle's and I heard that folks are pretty teed-off about it. So be careful."

"Thanks."

"You're welcome. Now, I'm going back to bed, and you're not going to call me again."

"Okay, Louie. I get the message. If you change your mind." He hung up on me. I cursed, turned off the ringer, and hooked the phone on my belt. Taking a Swiss Army knife from the glove box, I slipped it in my sock. I had no idea how I was going to cart all that material from the boat, but I knew that time was limited and so I swung the car around the back alley, creeping in darkness until I spotted the edge of the main building. Turning right, I tracked close to the fence until I came to a tangle of shrubbery and trash bins. This was as close as I was going to get, still a hike from the dead boat area. I turned off the overhead light and slipped out of the car. If memory served, the daunting fence gave way to a less-than-secure mish-mash of old cedar fencing that was easily moved aside. If only Ralphie responded to my presence, I could handle it. My pockets were bulging with kibble. If his keeper was still attached to the other end of the leash, I was probably spending the night on the couch in Leon's office.

The fence still gave way, and I was able to make my way to Stagger Lee with a minimum of confusion, only getting turned around once. When I swung my legs into the boat, however, Ralphie greeted me with a drooling tongue. A lighter revealed the guard, sitting on the locker.

"I thought you might be back," he said.

"Jesus." I leaned against the boat. "You scared me." I handed Ralphie some kibble to stop him slobbering all over my pockets. "Who are you, anyway?"

"Name's Jack. That's all you need to know. So. What's in this locker? I was going to break the lock, but I figured you'd be back so I saved myself some trouble. Sides, the only thing worth a damn on this tub is the locker, far as I can tell." He stood up and waved his flashlight at me. "Go on, then. Open 'er up."

I had no option, so I slid the key into the lock and pushed the top back. Illuminated, the scope of the cache was larger than I expected. "Listen, can we make a deal?" I said, turning to face Jack. "I'll pay you—"

"Never mind," he pushed me aside and started opening boxes. "What the hell. This is all paper. Where's the stuff?"

"What stuff—oh, I know. You thought Raoul was stashing his drugs here, right?" I crossed my arms and watched him rifle through the boxes. "You're not going to find anything there," I said. "My brother was not dealing drugs."

"Sure, sure." He held up a metal lock box. "So, what's in here then? Where's the key?"

"I don't know. All I have is the brass key for the locker."

He rattled the box. It didn't make any noise.

"Doesn't sound like drugs…" I ventured.

"What do drugs sound like?" he asked. "Idiot. I should just shoot the locks off these things."

"Wait, you don't want to do that—it's a small box, don't you think a gunshot would, like, destroy whatever's in there?"

"So what do you suggest, genius?"

"I'll keep looking for the keys. And if there're drugs in there, I promise, they're all yours. I don't want anything to do with drugs."

"Forget about it. You're not taking these boxes. No way. You can have the ones with all the papers in them. Hell, I'll even help you carry them out. But I'm keeping these locked ones. When you find the key, you bring it to me. If you find the key. I'll give you—two days. That should be enough time. And if you don't come back, I'll get 'em open the old-fashioned way." He aimed an imaginary gun at the locker and said "Pow."

Between the two of us, it only took three trips to get the other boxes into the trunk of my car. There were four metal lock boxes left in the locker. I moved to pick one up.

"Uh uh uh!" he said. "I'll take care of those. You better just get out of here before I change my mind and turn you over to Leon."

"Jack, I don't think Leon would appreciate knowing the deal you just cut with me. You have just as much reason to cooperate with me as I have with you."

"How do you figure? It'll be my word against yours, and believe me, you will be the loser in that game. Just get out of here and remember: the clock is ticking. If I don't hear from you in two days, I open the boxes my way."

"How do I know you won't do it sooner?"

"You don't," he said. "I got these lock picks that I been itching to try out, so I'll see what I can do. If I get in, all bets are off."

"All right, all right. So, how do I get in touch with you?" I asked.

"I programmed my number into your phone. Just give a call to 'Stud'."

I rolled my eyes, glanced once more at the precious boxes, and descended the ladder. Ralphie thrust his nose into my butt, and I shooed him away. The last of the kibble distracted him as I made my way out the back of the boat yard. The sky was beginning to brighten when I started the car and rolled onto the main drag.

Raoul

MUCH LATER, AFTER THE moon had risen and crossed the sky, the bars emptied and the crickets had taken over the night, Raoul walked out to the pier and called his sister. Her machine picked up, and he did not leave a message. If he had a car, he could get in and out of the city in a couple of hours, and no one would be the wiser. He did not like to move the van from its hiding place, except in an emergency, which in his mind meant leaving an assignment for good. Since he wasn't ready to leave Jerome yet, he needed to borrow a vehicle, and he needed it quickly.

"Louie," he said when the call was answered.

"Who the hell is this?" grumbled his old friend.

"It's Raoul. I need a favor."

"Of course. Why else would you call me out of the clear blue—at two in the morning—after how many years?" Louie shouted.

"Look, there's no need to be testy—"

"Testy? I'm not testy. Believe me, I know testy and this is not it."

"Louie, you are such a character. I mean it," Raoul spoke lightly, trying to jolly his friend. "I just need a car, for a couple of hours. I'll owe you big time," he said. "I need it right away, and then I need you to forget you've seen or heard from me. Can you help me?"

"Of course I can. And really, I haven't seen or heard from you in a dog's age. A car. Give me a sec." Raoul could hear the phone being dropped on a table and footsteps across a floor. Louie was breathing heavily when he picked up the phone and spoke again. "This is nothing illegal, right? Oh, don't answer that. I'll put the keys under the driver's seat. A silver Ford, parked in back of the Polish Club. You know where I mean?"

"Yes, thanks. I owe you!"

"Yeah, you do. Just have the car back in one piece by 8:00 a.m. And—oh never mind. Just be careful." Louie sighed and hung up the phone.

Raoul walked quickly across town, cutting across the marsh on his way to the parking lot. He was smiling grimly as he thought about Louie, the old friend whose crush on Raoul had not abated over the years. By the time he reached it, the keys were exactly where Louie promised. In five minutes, Raoul was on the highway, the little car juddering as the speedometer reached eighty.

It was well after 3:00 a.m. when he reached the city, and he pulled over near the meat packing district. Groups of twenty-somethings gathered at the corners near former warehouses that now pulsed with lights and music. Cabs passed over the cobblestones and Raoul crossed carefully, heading to a pay phone near the West

Side Highway. Traffic never stopped on this road, and Raoul wanted to make sure no one had followed him out of Connecticut.

He dialed Clara's number again, and once more, the machine picked up. Was she never home, even in the middle of the night? He grimaced, trying not to think about where she might be, or what kind of thing she could be involved in. Again. He checked his watch. There was no time to waste, waiting for her return. He left a message. As he spoke, a jeep passed by and Raoul hesitated, thinking they were coming for him.

He tried to modulate his breathing, but a sense of panic was causing his lungs to spasm. A bus groaned to a stop nearby, and he cut the call short. One last look around, and he ran across the street to the safety of the car. His hands were shaking as he turned the key, expecting the ignition to blow up the vehicle, or the police to block his U-turn back to the highway. Those would actually be preferable to the scenario he most feared, the Leader and his men catching him sneaking back into Jerome.

"I have got to get some sleep," he decided. On the road, windows open and radio blaring, he struggled to stay awake until the lights of the shipyard loomed ahead and he turned off the noise, extinguished the lights, and slipped back into the city. The sky was turning pink as the dawn broke over a new morning and as he walked away from the Polish Club, he debated about skipping work. It was too risky, he decided, and so he donned the worker's costume for another taste of the daily grind.

The foreman watched him all morning, approaching several times to inquire about his ailment. "You okay today?" he asked. Raoul nodded.

"Well, you look like crap," the man commented. "You better not be spreading some flu around here—go on, take the rest of the day off."

Clara

I WAS TOO KEYED up to sleep, although it had been a long and rather stressful night. Somehow, the combination of sex and danger was a real turn-on for me, and the discovery of Raoul's cache added to the energy that propelled me into an immediate sorting frenzy. Some of the boxes held paper that was so dried up and yellowed, I feared it would disintegrate in my hands, and I placed the older stacks carefully on top of the bureau. Soon, the room smelled like the cellar of a hoarder, and I cracked the window open to even out the moldy perfume.

What was I looking at? Records of surveillance dating back several years, meticulous recording of movements for several characters known only by initials. Dammit, that was not going to help. Then a stack of transcripts from phone conversations, equally daunting since the subjects seemed all too aware of the possibilities their discussions were under scrutiny. Lots of pauses and enigmatic phrasing; pages filled with the garbled street language that characterized police communications.

I had to get this stuff out of here, but I also really wanted to get my hands on those lock boxes. I tried Shelly's number again, called the Eagle's and got nowhere there, too. Even with disguising my voice. The place seemed clamped down like an oyster shell, protecting its own.

"Paper, paper!" I muttered, sorting through another carton. The key, it seemed to me, had to be in the lock boxes. That must be where Raoul kept his notebooks. He had one the last time I saw him, shoved carelessly into his back pocket. Small, pages curled and dirty, bound with an elastic that secured a ballpoint pen to the vinyl cover. I could see it in my head, but I could not put my hands on one. I dug deeper into the boxes, feeling along the edges with my hands, trying to come up with an old one or two. Nothing.

Halfway through transferring the boxes back to the trunk of my car, the cellphone rang. It was 6:00 a.m.

"Sam." I answered. Nothing but air on the other end. "Are you there?"

"Yes. You called?" she said with clipped precision.

"Yeah, yes, sorry. I wanted to talk with you." More silence. "And to apologize. You know what an idiot I can be. Sorry."

"Sure. Whatever." More ice through the receiver. "Anything else?"

"Look, can we get together?" I asked. "I need to talk with you."

"I told you, get a shrink." She hung up.

I called back. "Sam, listen, really, I am heading back to the city today and I want to stop by. Will you be there?"

"No. I can't be your sounding board anymore."

"What do you mean? I thought you were my friend." I could hear her breathing. "Listen, I said I was sorry. There's a lot going on…."

"I heard. And yes, I have been handing out sandwiches to the volunteers. I guess that makes me an idiot, right?"

"Sorry—I just, you know, my brother was killed and there was the attacks, and now I'm here in Connecticut and it's been a lot. That's all. I didn't mean to criticize you."

"So, what do you want? Who's the guy?" I didn't respond to that one. "Or is it more than one? Have you gotten yourself mixed up in something again?"

"You know me." I huffed. "Never mind then. I'm sorry I bothered you."

"Clara," she said. "Get some help."

"Sure, fine."

"I am sorry about your brother. He was a good guy." And she hung up. My last and only friend, who knew all my secrets. I sat heavily on the bed. More than ever, I was alone in the world.

I finished packing, checked the room thoroughly for any wayward undies, and turned my key in at the desk. I was leaving Jerome, hoping not to return. I had a few quick stops to make before I could go, however. I was not willing to leave those lock boxes in the greasy hands of Leon and his friends, and I had come to a dead end. I had to wait for the rental office to open, and then for someone to drive me over to pick up my car where Mark had stored it. Transferring the boxes, I spotted Raoul's gym bag, still ripe with dirty clothes. I hadn't bothered to look through the bag, but now, waiting for the clerk, I dumped the ripe mess into the trunk and sifted through the socks, sweats, and stained towels.

There was an old paperback book at the bottom of the bag, its pages dark and curled. I looked at it—an old Tom Clancy spy novel—and tossed it aside. Under everything else, I found a workout notebook. It was heavily used, pages filled with reps and muscle groups and pounds, written in a shorthand that I did not want to understand. I'd spent my fair share of time in the weight room at Quantico and other macho places, and I knew that only the hard core and OCD guys kept these journals. I had been banking on the fact that Raoul was an obsessive note-taker. I stopped, picked up the Clancy book again, and stood for a moment, weighing it in my right hand. I flipped through a few pages. Jackpot: he'd cut out a section from the center of the book, glued it to create a hidey-hole, and wedged a set of tiny keys in the cache. I pried them out and pocketed the prize. Time to return to Stagger Lee.

It was good to be behind the wheel of something that had some juice, and I turned the radio high enough to rattle the windows and get my heart racing. When I got close, I snapped off the radio and glided into the alley behind the boatyard. Far from the busy office, I chose the unofficial entry through the fence. I silently prayed that Jack had left the boxes in the boat locker, and that he was not going to be any-where near the place when I climbed aboard. Keeping low, I moved quickly between the older vessels until Stagger Lee was in view. I waited in the shadows for a few minutes to make sure no one was on the boat, or working nearby. It was quiet, most of the sound echoing from the work being done closer to the water, where the sea-worthy boats were being hauled onto solid ground and prepared for winter. There were some construction noises, an occasional plane buzzed overhead, and a steady hum of traffic soon became white noise.

Slowly I climbed aboard, trying to keep low and invisible. No sign of dog or man. The brass key was not necessary, since Jack had left the lock dangling open. I took a breath and opened the locker. Three of the four boxes were still there. "Asshole," I hissed. He probably took one to try and open without the keys.

As quickly as I could, I tried and rejected several keys before opening the first box. Its contents were quickly emptied into a black nylon tote bag I pulled from my pocket. The notebooks, some other papers. Another set of keys, quickly pocketed. I repeated these moves twice, and in less than ten minutes I had finished my job. Replacing the contents with a couple of old paperbacks and some magazines I'd lifted from the car rental waiting room, I restored the boxes to their original position and scrambled back to the car. Once safely away, I would assess what I had found, and see if I needed to return for the contents of the fourth box.

Good plan. Half a mile away, near the entrance to I-95, I pulled into a gas station and parked in the shadows near a public telephone. Thank God for Sherlock Holmes, our hero. Raoul had learned from reading all the stories featuring the master detective. I imagine there would be a veritable treasure trove of secrets hidden in his bookshelves, if I could ever find the place he called home.

The bag yielded a dozen notebooks filled with dense, tiny handwriting. Some kind of shorthand, but much of it was comprehensible. This would explain a great deal, if not everything, I needed to know. One smaller notebook, a tiny three-ring binder that had several thick elastic bands securing its bulging contents, was the real prize of the cache. I bet this was the code that would help unlock the boxes of tran-scripts, notes and perhaps, some of the mysteries contained in his daily jottings.

There was nothing, however, that provided any clue about where Raoul was living. I assumed he was camping out locally, maybe sleeping in a van somewhere, but there had been no car keys with his belongings. I returned to the gym bag. With a Swiss Army knife, I sliced carefully along the seams and pulled apart every piece. Under the cardboard bottom, I found what had eluded everyone: his credentials were duct-taped to the flimsy floor of the bag, along with his real ID cards and a couple of brass keys pressed into a small segment of foam board.

"Yes," I shouted, pounding the steering wheel. I had his keys, proof that he was working an FBI job, and more information to dissect on some kind of high tech gizmo with a function I could only imagine. But if it was new and cool, Raoul was certain to have it. Similar to the cards inserted into digital cameras to collect data, this long, thin metal stick was certain to be the key to something big.

"Yeah, now I just have to figure out where he kept his computer," I muttered to myself, pulling back into traffic. As the car raced back to the city, I contemplated the mysterious life my brother had chosen. The cell phone buzzed as I approached the tricky New Haven interchange, and I slid the phone between my ear and shoulder to answer.

"Mark," I said.

"Hey," he replied. "Where are you? You checked out of the hotel. I hope it's not because, well, listen. I'm sorry about that, it should never have happened, and I swear I won't let it happen again."

"Mark, no, it's not that. That—our little conversation—that was wonderful," I said. "It's time for me to get back to work, though. I'm sure I'll be back, you know, to check up on the case and all."

"Oh," he paused. "Anyway"—back to the business voice now—"We picked up someone you might be interested in talking to. Shelly Loren. Seems she pretended to be a member of your family, and helped herself to Raoul's belongings. I thought you might want to chat with her."

"Oh, yeah. What did she have, anyway?" I asked.

"Well, his clothes, you know, what was spread around the room. His wallet, but there was no money in it, no credit cards or anything like that. She swears that's how she found it. I don't know whether to believe her about that."

"I wouldn't. You picked her up—for what?"

"It was just a regular traffic stop, one headlight out and no registration, that kind of thing."

"Whose car was she driving?" I asked.

"I don't know. Wait a minute…" I could hear muffled voices. "Some kind of old van, a Chevy. Not clear who owns it. I'll have to ask the arresting officer…They have it at impound."

Dammit. "Okay. Can I take a look at it?" Silence. "Mark, why did you call to tell me this, if you aren't going to let me near the investigation?"

"I just thought you should know."

"Fine. I know. Thanks." I hung up. Signaled and shot into the passing lane, and then had to brake back to seventy. It's almost impossible to satisfy the need to speed on a road as crowded as I-95. I pounded the steering wheel. Checked the mirror. Should I turn around? Or just go with what I had collected so far? The phone rang again, interrupting my argument with myself. It was Mark, calling me back.

"Yeah," I said.

"Sorry about before. There's no way I can give you access to this right now— Maybe after the guys have a run at it."

"Do they know about the connection with Raoul?"

"Well, they didn't, until they were here in booking and realized she was carrying his wallet. Then some red flags came out." He lowered his voice. "I don't think there's anything to this. She's not connected to the murder, I'm pretty sure of that."

"Really?" I was losing my patience. "Why did she go to the police station and pretend to be a member of the family so she could get Raoul's stuff? That doesn't sound so innocent to me."

"Yeah…I dunno. I think maybe she was just looking for drugs. That seems to be her primary interest. But why would she go and do that? I don't have a clue." There was silence. "Clara, you sound upset."

"I'm not upset. I just don't think you guys have handled this very well, that's all."

"Well, I'm going to personally supervise the interrogation and see what we come up with. Thanks for telling me that she got the stuff by posing as a family member. I'll work that angle and let you know if she says anything of interest."

"All right," I said. "Thanks."

"Are you really leaving?" he asked.

"Mark, I'm already gone." There was crackling on the line.

"Clara, there's something you should know," he said.

"What?"

"The Coast Guard fished a body out of the river today. It was a young man, probably Middle Eastern." He paused. "He didn't drown, his throat was cut. As far as we can tell—and this isn't definitive because the body was in the water for over a week—it was the same type of wound that killed Raoul. Just not, you know, in the same place."

"So you think these two deaths are related?" I asked. "But how?"

He hesitated a minute. "There's a third one—"

"What? So, you've been holding out on me. What else haven't you told me?" I shouted, pounded the steering wheel.

"I didn't think it was related, but now, I'm not sure," he said. "We found this guy caught on a pile in the river about a week ago. He was another young man, but this one had a bullet in his temple. So I really didn't think it was connected to Raoul, but now, I don't know. That's a lot of dead young men in a short period of time. You know, we don't have this kind of crime in Jerome."

"Do you think these are vigilante killings, some kind of reaction to the Trade Center attacks?" I asked.

"Nope, I thought about that too. But these guys were clearly killed before September 11. And so was Raoul. So that's not it," he said.

I swore silently. Listened to the dead air crackle between us. "I'm losing the signal, Mark. I'll be in touch. And I'll be back."

"Wait," he said. "I need help here. I can't handle this kind of thing—murder, maybe a serial killer. I'm going to have to get the Staties involved."

"Don't do that," I said quickly. "Not yet. I'll help you—Just don't call the State Police yet." I disconnected the call. I had to think. But first, I cut across two lanes of traffic and screeched off an exit. I couldn't leave Jerome, not yet.

Raoul

LATER, OVER A LUNCH taco that hit his sour stomach like an acid bath, Raoul felt the eyes of several of the other men on him. As they returned to the loading dock, Metin fell in step next to him.

"So, Ismail, you going swimming tonight?" he asked. He lowered his voice, leaned in closer. "Going to fuck some girl at the club?"

Raoul shook his head. "How do you know what I'm doing?" he asked. "Have you been following me?" Although it was pretty obvious that the answer was yes, the big question in his mind was why the Leader had not intervened yet. If they knew he was having sex, and trying to get to New York, why wasn't he locked in the basement of the mosque?

Metin shrugged. "I just do what I'm told. They want me to keep tabs on you, I keep tabs on you. Nothing personal."

The foreman yelled for them to get back to work, but all afternoon Raoul felt Metin's eyes on him. How soon before they came to question him?

When he left work at 3:00, he could hardly keep his bike on the road as tiredness overtook his legs. Not taking his usual care to be quiet, he climbed to his apartment, dropped his bags on the floor, and crawled into bed. It was hot, but he'd never minded the dog days of summer in Jerome. After a couple of hours, he awakened, drank glass after glass of cold water standing over the sink, and finally noticed a figure sitting in the living room.

"What do you want?" he asked, stepping into the dusk-shadowed room.

"Ismail, we heard you were sick today, so I decided to come and check on you." The Leader rose from the folding chair, looked around the empty room and walked towards the kitchen. "So, have you lived here long?"

"A couple of months, I guess," Raoul replied. He scratched his bare chest, embarrassed to be undressed in front of this man.

"You don't plan to stay long, I see," the older man said.

"No. I, I guess I'm not sure of my plans."

"Living this way, without many material possessions, it's good for a man, good for your soul. Ismail, I hope you are not troubled by anything. Are you? Do you have anything you need to share? Any doubts, or confusion? Any questions? You can ask me, or you can ask the Imam."

Raoul nodded. "Thank you."

He watched the other man walk around the kitchen, opening doors and grunting at the nearly empty refrigerator. "For a young man, you don't eat much, do you?"

"I eat out a lot. I don't know how to cook, so." Raoul held out his hands. "It's my life. I like it this way. No complications."

"Ismail, where are you from?" the Leader asked. Without waiting for an answer, he continued to speak while quietly looking into closets and cabinets. "You know, we checked on you. Couldn't really get a handle on where you come from, how you got to this country, nothing. A complete blank slate. It's as if you were born here, working at the shipyard. Before that, there don't seem to be any records of your life."

Raoul shrugged, kept silent.

The Leader stopped, crossed his arms, and rolled back and forth on the balls of his feet. Their eyes were locked in a long stare that felt neither threatening nor uncomfortable to Raoul. He focused on relaxing the muscles in his jaw. Finally the other man spoke. "It's not a problem, just a curiosity. In fact, we find it quite convenient."

The Leader took a final look around the apartment. "Are you feeling better now? I was surprised to see you sleeping so early."

"Yeah, I think I picked up some kind of virus, I was really achy and tired. But now I do feel better. After a good night's sleep, I should be fine tomorrow."

"Not coming to mosque tonight then? No, you should stay here, get some more rest. We'll see you tomorrow." He opened the apartment door and then turned back. "Be careful, Ismail," he said. "We wouldn't want anything to happen to you now. You should stop working at the shipyard. It's time to devote yourself fulltime to prayer. Good night."

Clara

I PASSED THE EXIT for Jerome and crossed the bridge into its well-heeled sister city. Here, the houses were huge and the yards manicured, the stores over-priced, and the only people with Spanish surnames were the housekeepers and landscapers. There was a large inn at the center of the downtown, right on the boulevard, which had been converted into a more modern use, perfect for my needs. Studio apartments were available rented by the month, for executives on extended business or relocating their families to this part of the state. I signed the agreement and carried my stacks of boxes to the second story room with a view. From here, among the wealthy, I could see rows of yachts and the twinkling lights of the pier.

I entered the apartment prepared to get to the bottom of things. Where this would lead, I had no idea. I figured that my only chance to make sense of what was happening in Jerome was by studying Raoul's notes. I might be able to discover what he'd been working on, and then—hopefully—something that might lead me to his killers. Without the distractions of Jerome itself, I thought I might be more productive.

I set up the crime scene photos and maps by tacking them to the grass-covered walls. Working steadily, I arranged all the visuals in some semblance of order. I was deep in the boxes of notes and covered in dust. I sneezed, smeared a black streak across my cheek, and sneezed again.

"Oh, Mijo, what the hell is all this stuff?" I exclaimed. Stretching, I realized that it was dark outside and my stomach grumbled its complaint. I headed to the kitchen, although I don't know what I expected to find in the empty fridge. My cell phone jittered, and I listened to messages after washing my hands in hot soapy water.

Nothing of interest popped up, until an abrupt message from SA Boyd, calling to "check in" with me. What? I replayed that one. This guy—whom I had not seen or heard from since the day I handed over my badge and received my threat papers. It was officially a separation agreement, which was kind of humorous given the implicit warning that if I ever spoke about anything I knew to anyone outside—or inside for that matter—there would be consequences "not limited to incarceration." Not exactly a golden parachute. And Boyd was my contact. Except for the threat he whispered into my ear before he closed the door behind me, I had not heard from or even thought about Boyd for a long, long time. Now it came back, a reminder that any violation of our agreement was going to have a steep price tag.

"Crap, crap, and more crap," I muttered, jotting down his phone number and hitting the delete button. The phone rang again as I was performing some stretches to loosen the knots in my neck. I checked the caller ID and dropped into a chair before engaging the phone.

"Hey," I said. "What's up?"

"Nothing much," Mary Kate said. "Where are you?"

"Oh, decided to get out of Jerome for a while. I needed to take care of some things and, you know, I need to get back to work." No point in telling Mary Kate I was less than a mile away.

"Ha," she grunted. Silence shouted the airwaves between us. "So, I guess you don't want to get together then."

"Oh, sure, yes I do, I really want to catch up with you," I said. "I'll be back soon, you know? I just needed to get out of Dodge, do a little work to earn the paycheck, you know how it goes." I was trying to be jolly, quite an unusual effort for me. She wasn't rising to the occasion. More silence. "So, Mary Kate, is there anything you want to talk about? Something come up?"

She cleared her throat a couple of times. "Yeah, well, you being back and all, it kind of brought up a lot of things for me, about you and Raoul. Just some memories, you know."

"Sure, yeah," I agreed. "It's hard to go back there. I mean, for me, to be back in Jerome, it's not easy."

"Well, just imagine how hard it is to live here then. You know, with those memories right inside your life all the time," she said.

"Are you mad at me for something? 'Cause I'm not following you. What's this about?"

"You know, I thought it was buried. I thought it was all over, but just hearing your voice made it come back. I mean, I knew Raoul was here in town. I saw him a couple of times, just around, you know? And he seemed okay, like he used to be. We spent some time together, actually, and he, ah, he helped me out with something. And it was great. Until the last time I saw him. He was acting all strange, wouldn't look at me, you know? He was kind of jumpy. I was worried about him, asked how he was doing, but he brushed me off, said he was cool, and then, he disappeared. And now, he's dead. I don't know. It just isn't right. He didn't deserve that. Of all people, not Raoul." She blew her nose loudly. "It shouldn't have been him," she said again.

"I'm sorry, I didn't realize you were friends with my brother," I said after a pause.

"Not friends exactly," Mary Kate said slowly. "I just knew he had my back. He was always around, and I felt safer knowing that. And like I said, we had gotten together in the past month, and he helped me out with a family problem." She signed heavily. "I don't know why I called you. I don't want to have this conversation with you, I really don't."

"What is this about? Just tell me, was it something to do with Raoul's death? Do you know something about what happened?" I pressed. "Mary Kate, you know me, right? Whatever it is, you can tell me."

"I wish I knew what happened to him, honestly I do. But I have no idea. Like I said, he was good, it was good to see him, and then something happened. I don't know what," she said. "Oh, Clara. It's hard to talk to you. I know you, all right. But the thing is, you don't know me. And you haven't for a long time. You did some things that hurt a lot of people here. And they don't forget."

"I know."

"You know, I don't think you do. I think you are so wrapped up in your own little life that the rest of us—we're expendable to you. We're just subjects for you, isn't that right? We used to be suspects, and now we're the subjects for the great photographer." Mary Kate's voice rose a pitch and wavered like a wire about to snap. "You know nothing about Jerome, about the people here. You don't even really know your own brother. And you don't know anything about me."

I sat on the floor, pulled my legs up, and listened. I could hear her breathing heavily, then her voice was muffled, and then she came back on the line.

"You still there?" she asked. Without waiting for my answer, she continued. "You know, this goes back even to high school, when we graduated. You were in such a hurry to leave, remember? You and that hot-shit car you had, what was it, an old beat-up Chevy or something. But you treated that car better than you treated your friends." She took a swig of something with ice cubes that clinked against her teeth.

"Just spit it out, Mary Kate. I really don't know what you're angry with me about. I never did anything to you," I said. "Did I?"

"Well, maybe it seems like nothing, and with us being all grown up now it probably seems like child's play, but it still…it's still…it's my life, dammit. You left here, you got away, but I got stuck and it's because of you."

"How is that my fault?"

"Remember the night of graduation, we all went to that party on the beach and there was a bonfire and music and beer—and we went together, right? Except halfway through the night, you took off. You left with some stupid jock and you left me there."

"You weren't alone, there were a hundred kids there."

"I had to walk home. I had a curfew, remember? My pops would have skinned me alive if I came in late—didn't matter if it was graduation, or if I was 18-years-old. I had to be home. I didn't want anyone to know that I had a curfew, so I ducked out of there. And I started walking. It wasn't bad, it was a nice night. But dark, no moon at all. I shouldn't have gone the back way, but I was in a hurry and what the hell, right? So I did, and I came across a couple of guys and they were doing something—I couldn't really tell what—and I guess they were afraid that I had seen or whatever but anyway," she stopped, gulped some air. "So they grabbed me and they raped me, right there in the picnic area. I got slivers all in my behind, they were so rough and I tried biting one on the hand so he shoved my own panties in my mouth and I just wanted to scream or throw up or die. I kicked and fought them, you know? But you can't win when there's two of them…. The second one got on me and the first one grabbed my hair and tried to stick his dirty cock in my mouth and I squirmed and then it was over—I saw a dark shape come out of nowhere and the guy was knocked off me and the other one got hit too. And he ran, pulling his pants up. And then Raoul was there, and he pulled down my dress and he took the cloth out of my mouth and, I turned away and threw up all over. And he was so nice, he helped me get up and he cleaned me up and he brought me to the donut shop so I could fix myself enough to go home. He wanted to go back and find those guys and teach them a lesson, he wanted me to call the police, but I just wanted to go home and be in my own bed. And so he took me there. He was so kind, and gentle, and he never said a word to anyone. I made him promise, and he kept that promise. I always felt that he had my back."

"Oh, Mary Kate, I am so sorry that this happened to you. Why didn't you ever tell me?"

She laughed, the sound brittle. "I tried to tell you, but you were full of your own plans and you wouldn't listen. You left town, but I had to stay and so I tried to forget." She made a strangled sound that was full of tears. "But I couldn't let it go. I have to deal with it every single day of my life."

"Why?" I didn't follow.

"I was pregnant. One of those assholes left me pregnant. And what the hell could I do about it? Nothing. I didn't even know which jerk was the father. And once my parents found out, well, that was the end of me. I've been atoning for that sin ever since," she said. "Hell, Pa even blames me for my mother dying, and Rose—well, we don't speak anymore."

"It's not your sin," I objected. "You were the victim. Why didn't you get an abortion? Why didn't you go to the police…?"

"I don't believe in abortion, and I decided I wasn't going to be a victim. So I had the baby. And I raised him the best I could. And when I had the chance, I got married so I could leave my parents' house and get some control over my own life. I had a couple more kids, took some classes and got a decent job at the hospital, and that's it. I never told anyone about the rape. Until now. Until today, the only person who knew was Raoul. He saved me, I truly believe that. They would have cut my throat or something—that was what they were saying when they held me down and raped me."

"Oh my God." I didn't know what else to say. "I am so sorry. Mary Kate. You should've told me. I am so, so sorry."

"What could you have done?" she asked. "Anyway, it's been hard. I reconnected with Raoul, and he was great—and then he was gone. And with Raoul being dead and then hearing your voice again—it all came back."

"What can I do? Tell me, anything."

"No, I don't want anything from you. I just wanted you to know what kind of guy your brother was. He was special, and I will always be grateful to him for saving me, and for keeping my secret. And you know, when I needed help, he came and he helped me. That means a lot to me."

"Oh, Mary Kate," I began.

She cut me off. "Don't get all crazy on me. I probably will regret this in the morning, but I needed you to know. That's all. I don't want you to ever mention it again. I hope you can be as honorable as your brother, and keep my secret. Can you do that? I'm not sure that I can trust you today, any more than I could trust you back then. But I hope you can prove me wrong." She hung up the phone softly, leaving me listening to the whoosh of time passing.

I hung up the phone when it began honking at me, picked it up quickly and dialed Mary Kate's number again. "Listen, I know you don't want to talk about it but I need to ask you something," I said quickly.

"My God, Clara, does it always have to be about you?"

I stopped breathing. "No," I said softly. "I, I just want to know, was I always such a bad person? Like this, like you just said? So self-centered? Was I ever a friend, a real friend to you, ever?"

She exhaled loudly. "Oh for Christ's sake. Sure you were, like in grammar school, you protected me from all the bullies and shit. Everyone thought you were a dyke, you used to fight all the boys who came near me, remember?" She sighed. "Okay, feel better now? You're not a monster. So leave me alone." She hung up.

Mary Kate was wrong, I was a monster. I'd fooled myself into thinking that my toughness was built from training in the bureau, from years undercover. And here was the truth: I'd been like this all along.

Raoul

THE PIRATE WAS BECOMING more demanding, and Raoul was less interested in the drug running exploits as he realized that these small-time operators had nothing to offer him: no connections to big drug suppliers, and certainly no insight into the fencing of guns that was his original assignment. One night, tired from lack of sleep and fed up with the abusive Pirate, Raoul leaned back in the boat and said, "So. You guys just small time, eh?"

"What do you mean?" the big man replied. "You think you're better than this, punk?"

"Well, yeah, I do. I mean, I thought you guys were going to be doing some big scores, you know."

"So what. Maybe we are, and you ain't getting a piece of it. What do you think of that?"

Raoul scratched the thin growth of whiskers on his chin. "Listen, Leon, I think I had enough of being an errand boy for you," he said.

"What did you just call me? How do you know my name?" the Pirate snapped. "Hey stupid, did you tell him my name? And anyway, it's not my real name. So don't think you have anything on me. You just keep your trap shut and we'll be fine. We got a lot of business coming up, things get busy in the fall, believe it or not. So just shut up and maybe I'll let you keep working. And maybe I'll keep paying you."

Raoul shrugged. "No man, I'm tired and I think I'm calling it quits. It's not enough money to make it worthwhile for me—so I'm done."

"Nobody quits. I might throw your ass off this boat, but I decide who fucking stays and who goes," the Pirate said. He looked over at his henchman. "Get my gun," he said. "I need to teach this boy a fucking lesson."

Before either man could move, Raoul was over the edge of the boat. The big man held on to his seat as the vessel rolled. "Get him," he hissed. "Where's my damned gun?"

Raoul slid quietly the length of the boat, the water barely moving in his wake. He stayed away from the engine but almost completely submerged. It was very unlikely that Leon would start shooting, since he was so paranoid about attracting attention from the Coast Guard, but Raoul figured it was better to lay low and wait for the boat to move.

A bright light was shined across the water, and both men grumbled about the poor visibility that night. "Too much fog," the younger man said.

"Keep looking—over there, something moved," Leon said.

"Just a fish."

The sound of another engine echoed in the gloom. "Cut the light," he gestured. "There's somebody out there—they probably think we were signaling. Dammit."

The two men were quiet as the smaller boat approached. "Ahoy there," Leon called out cheerfully. "What can we do for you tonight?"

Raoul took the opportunity of the noise and the wake from the other vessel to slip into the shadows and paddle towards shore. The rise and fall of conversation—a probable deal in the works—covered his escape, but Raoul had no doubt that Leon would be looking for him. Another predator to avoid, he thought. At least this one rarely sees the light of day. Cold comfort as he jogged towards the van, eager to shed his wet clothes and find a new parking place for his home away from home.

The van started and Raoul tried to keep its rumble low as he moved from the shadows of the junkyard. He aimed it towards the other side of town, near the railroad tracks and the abandoned industrial park. He needed some quiet time to think about all the different threads of his investigation, and he wanted to make another attempt to contact the D.C. office about what he'd found.

But what had he found? He wondered. A group of Muslims about to launch an attack on New York? Improbable, but not impossible. He'd seen the damage at the World Trade Center in 1993, knew that it was an attractive target. But since that attempt had failed, and the buildings were obviously not vulnerable to a car bomb any longer, was that really a logical plot?

Raoul scratched his head again as he flipped through pages of notes. The planes, that was a new element: all this pilot training, talk about hijacking. Just because it hadn't been done for a while didn't mean that it couldn't happen—but what was the objective? Would they hold hostages in exchange for the release of prisoners here, or abroad? Again, possible, he thought. After about an hour skimming notes and jotting new thoughts on a sheet of butcher paper, Raoul stood up and scratched. Dammit, he must have picked up some kind of fungus in the water. He drove the van back to his former parking spot in the woods behind the Eagle's Club, grabbed his gym bag, hopped on his bike, and headed downtown for a hot shower.

The route took Raoul close to the entrance to the naval base. Its security fences bristled with electricity and Raoul slowed down enough to contemplate the stone-faced sentry at the gate. The sun was warming the sky already and a line of cars waited at the checkpoint. If there's a naval base, and a bunch of potential terrorists organizing in the town where it sits, wouldn't that be the logical target of an attack? he thought. Why airplanes and not scuba gear?

He brought the bike to an abrupt stop, barely missing a car crossing the intersection. The guy waved a fist in his direction and shouted some blessings at him. Of course, Raoul thought. More than one group, more than one target—and more than one mode of attack. He crossed the busy avenue and peddled furiously towards the plaza where his gym was located. Next door, at Radio Shack, Raoul purchased a pre-paid cell phone with a slightly damp fifty dollar bill.

Around the back of the storefronts, he parked his bike, locked it up, and ripped open the plastic encasing the phone. Quickly, he dialed several of the contact numbers that he'd memorized over the years, hanging up as soon as the operator's voice announced that the numbers were no longer in service.

"Dammit," he said. The back door opened and a muscle-bound trainer stepped outside.

"Hey," he said, bending over to light a cigarette. "How's it going?"

Raoul chucked his chin at the guy and focused on dialing another number. Another pre-recorded message played, and Raoul stepped away from the building. He was tempted to hurl the phone into the woods, but instead called his own phone to check messages. Nothing there. The other guy opened his cell and started an animated conversation about vitamins, and when Raoul looked over at him the lifter walked away.

Finally, Raoul dialed Clara again. A mechanical voice informed him that her answering machine was full. Great. He stuck the phone back in his bag and went inside to take a very long, very hot shower. He needed to go back out on the water tonight, to change the way he'd been surveilling the naval base, but he knew it would be tricky to avoid Leon's boat. Maybe he needed to watch from a different perspective, he realized, soaping his armpits thoroughly. There were a few small islands— large rocks, really—that offered a vantage point to the shipping lanes. It would be a challenge to elude the security systems around the base, and then the more primitive threat posed by Leon, but he thought it might yield some answers.

Clara

LATE THAT NIGHT, I texted Mark and arranged to meet him at the boathouse by the amusement park. I needed to know more about these murders, and how they could be connected to Raoul's death, and I guess my self-imposed isolation was more than I could handle at the moment. Sam was refusing to return my calls, Mary Kate had pointed out the depth of my self-absorption, Robby from the office kept calling and leaving messages, and I, burned out from twenty-four hours looking through my dead brother's notebooks, had come up with nothing.

At low points like this, I historically found a penis to console myself with, but this time, that was not the first thing I thought of. Perhaps the toss-off from Guy had made an impact; whatever it was, and however attractive I found the Chief, sex was the last thing on my mind as I paced the shore waiting for his car. The night was dark, and it was definitely coming onto fall. Leaves changed slowly around here, due to the warmth from the Sound, but the night was damp and so was my mood.

When he pulled into the parking lot, I got into his car and immediately turned sideways to face him. "So, what have you got?" I asked, impatient for information.

He reached over and pushed a curl away from my mouth. "Clara, just a minute. Let me look at you," he said. Jesus, this guy was going soft for me. "How are you doing? I'm so glad you came back."

"I'm great, just great. When you told me about the other bodies, of course I had to come back," I leaned against the window. "Have you been able to connect them in any way?"

He sighed, put both hands on the steering wheel. "No, nothing yet. Two kinds of kills, no ID, no apparent links between the two men."

"You mean three men—Raoul was probably killed by the same people," I interrupted.

"We have no way of knowing that," he said. He sighed again. "Clara, I haven't been able to stop thinking about you, about what happened between us…."

Oh, that. Crap. "I know Mark, and I'm sorry about that. It will never happen again, I promise," I said.

"No, that's not—look, I'm not sorry it happened. It was great, and then you were gone. I just want to make sure you're okay."

"Yes, of course, I know." I had to take this slowly—I needed to continue to work with Mark, to access the information he had, but I was not going to get tangled up in an affair with him. "I respect that you're married and the Chief, and so I understand that it was a one-time thing. And it was wonderful, but I know it can't happen again." I held my breath, kept my eyes steady and hoped for the best.

"Clara, if only…" his hand snaked around my back and pulled me closer. Well, okay, maybe just a short make-out session, I thought. Next thing I knew, my ass was naked on the vinyl back seat and Mark was sliding his delicious cock in and out of me. I admit, being a bad girl has its perks. We spent a solid hour in the back, working out various positions and marveling at the chemistry between us. When he stepped out of the car, turning away while I slid back into my jeans, the sound of a motor offshore rumbled. I closed the door and extinguished the light, and we leaned against the car companionably as the boat puttered into the distance.

I waited for him to speak, but Mark had always been a man of few words. Eventually, I shivered and he heard my teeth start to chatter. "Cold?" he pulled me closer and rubbed my arms.

"A little."

"Want to sit inside?"

"Yeah, that would be a good idea." He opened the door and I slid under the steering wheel, retrieving and pocketing my panties along the way. Once inside, he turned on the engine and the radio crackled to life. "I hope no one is looking for you," I said.

"I'm off. But my phone is always on. I don't listen to the radio at night. Not anymore. They'll call if they need me for something," he said.

"So."

"So."

"Can we get back to the bodies? I hate to keep going back to it, but there has to be a connection," I said.

"I know, I agree with you," he said. "But so far, we're not coming up with anything. I mean, it looks like the cuts on the one guy were made with a box cutter. And the wounds to Raoul, they were more, um, surgical. Like with a scalpel. Very clean. So they seem to be a different method. And then there's the guy with the bullet in his head. Totally different."

"But three young men in such a short time?"

"I know. I asked the M.E. to pull up all the unsolveds for the last six months or so, and he came up with a few others. But these are even stranger—they all look like deaths from fights. One strangulation, two broken necks, and one nose shoved into the brain. All young men again. Maybe it's a fight club or something, I don't know."

"Or training for something."

"What do you mean?"

"It almost sounds like a training camp, where hand-to-hand combat is being trained. Are any of them military?"

He shook his head. Absently, his hand played with my hair. "No, they're all unidentified males. No links to the community, that we could find, and nothing from any database. It's strange."

"Strange, but I think you have enough to go to the Feds and get them involved."

He exhaled. "I hate to do that, Clara. They never help, they just come in and push everybody around. And we never get answers. Never." His hand slid down and cupped my right breast.

"What if there was a terrorist cell operating right here in Jerome? And Raoul was onto it? They would have killed him and anyone else who got in the way of their mission."

"Clara, you have a vivid imagination. Nothing like that happens here, believe me. With the base here, and the military police all up in everybody's business, I would know if something like that was going on." He chuckled a little, gave my boob a squeeze, and leaned over for a kiss. "You are really special, you know that?"

I smiled. I was special, but I wasn't some dumb broad who was going to take a kiss-off. "Mark, given what just happened in New York, I think you'd be foolish not to take this seriously. You could have terrorist activity right here, operating under your nose, and you can't ignore it. How many bodies do you have to have before you take this to the Feds?"

He straightened up. "Are you threatening me? Are you planning to go behind my back to the FBI with this?"

"I'm talking to you right now, aren't I? If I wanted to, I would have already contacted people in D.C. But I'm trying to work with you on this. You just aren't taking it seriously. And I think you should."

He resumed rubbing my arm. "Yeah, I see that. I do. I just want to be sure—"

"I know, you don't trust me. I get that." I took a deep breath. "No one trusts me, but in this case, I am being straight with you. I'm not going to go to the Feds, but I really encourage you to reach out and see if they are interested in what you've uncovered. Maybe they have some similar information, and together, you can make a case. I don't know. And I don't blame you for not trusting me. I get that."

There was silence in the car. I broke it. "This is my brother I'm talking about. I know that my family thinks I betrayed them, and even Raoul was angry with me for a while about what happened, but believe me, I would do anything to find out what happened to my baby brother. And I hope that you'll help me do that."

The windows were steaming up and he reached over to open them a crack. Another boat puttered by, or was it a low-flying helicopter. The radio crackled and the zzzzzzt zzzzzzt of a phone vibrating broke the calm inside the car.

"Yeah," Mark spoke into the phone. "What's your twenty? Okay. At the station. Out." He put the phone back into the holster, leaned over and kissed me deeply. Juices flowed again. His hand slid inside my shirt, fingers played the nipple. "I gotta go," he breathed. I felt the hardness of his erection against my thigh.

"Are you sure?" I teased it a bit with my finger.

He groaned. Unzipped and unsheathed, ready to go again. He could drive with the windows down for a week, but I was certain that the musky scent would be there quite a while. When he was done, I climbed off, slid back into my jeans, and grabbed my bag.

"Call me tomorrow, and let me know what you decide," I said. He nodded, sleepy now. "You okay to drive?" I looked pointedly at his exposed genitalia, shining in the moonlight.

"Ah, yeah," he tucked back into his boxers. "Good to go." Zipped up the pants. He started the car. "G'night."

I waved him on, walked over to the water and hugged my jacket close. When would I learn? I shook my head, looking at the stars and a slice of moon.

After a few minutes I turned back to my car and headed to the apartment. I had to pee. And get back to work.

It wasn't long after sunrise that the phone rang, interrupting my reading of a dense passage in Raoul's third notebook. I wasn't surprised to see Mark's name on the caller ID.

"Good morning," I said. Trying for cheerful, yet full of self-loathing.

"Hi, how're you doing?" he asked. Not waiting for a response, he continued. "I happened to run into the base administrator at the gym this morning and I mentioned that we've come across a few unidentified male homicide victims. Well, he was a little evasive but I did get him to admit that they had a few unexplained things going on too, so we're going to meet and compare notes. All off the record, for now, but I thought you'd be pleased."

"Yes, that's great," I agreed. "Can I tag along?"

"Uh, no, not a good idea. The guy is already a little skittish, but I can see he's in a tough spot. You know, like me, he's got this stuff happening, and everyone breathing down his neck, so I think we can help each other. Just that you'd be, you know, a distraction. So, no. I'll let you know what I find out."

He hung up before I could protest about being called a distraction. But I knew what he meant. Dammit. Back to the notebooks. But not for long. Another call, this one from Robby. Christ.

"Hello," I answered after the fifth ring.

"Hey Clara, wassup? How you doing? Listen, I know you needed some time and all but I really need you to get back to work. I got an assignment, a real easy shoot, you know, that I need you to do for me. What do you say? Can I count on you?"

"Hi Rob," I slowed him down. "What kind of assignment? I told you I wanted to take some time off, can't you get someone else on it?"

"Listen, I can't protect your job forever, and I need you to do this one. It will be good for you, therapeutic and all. I need someone to cover all these memorial services, and there's a lot of them up near you, in Connecticut you know, so I figure you're already there you can go and shoot some stuff for me this week. I'll fax you the list of times and places, okay? Just do this for me, would ya?"

"You think going to memorial services will be therapeutic? Are you shitting me? Honestly Rob, I don't know if I can do it. I mean, how intrusive, taking photos at somebody's funeral? How low are we going for this story, anyway?"

"Don't get all preachy with me. And you can get in there, because your own brother just got killed and so you can relate. You can," he said. "I'm not asking. I need you to do this. What's your fax number?"

"I don't have one set up," I said dully. "Email it to me."

"Great," he said. "You'll see, this is good. Get back on the horse and all that. You know. Work is what keeps you going. So, I'll need this stuff asap, right? You on it?"

"Asap, I got it," I said, then disconnected the phone. "Son of a bitch."

Raoul

AFTER A GOOD WORKOUT at the gym, Raoul showered and was ready to spend some quality time at the mosque. If the Leader trusted him, and saw him as a good candidate for this mission, he would find a way to make a report to D.C. and stop whatever it was from happening. All the endorphins swimming through his bloodstream confirmed that this was a good plan, and so he combed his hair, brushed his teeth, and got ready to pray.

A new face greeted the men in the meeting room after prayers that night. After a brief introduction, he started lecturing them about the meaning of jihad and the necessity to destroy Israel, the United States, and any other Zionist countries. This political lecture was entirely different from the focused training imparted by the Leader, who was not in the room. Most of his important lieutenants were missing as well, and no mention was made of the obvious change in leadership. Raoul sought out Metin after the men were dismissed.

"So. What's happening?" he asked.

"Ismail. You ask too many questions, you know?" Metin said.

"Hey, I'm just asking how you're doing. You know, the American way—'Wahs happ'nin?'" Raoul replied.

"Nothing."

"Okay. So what did you think about the meeting tonight?"

"I don't think anything. I just listen." Metin walked along the road towards the block of cheap apartment buildings in which most of the men lived. "Gotta go."

Raoul watched the other man's back as he skipped up the steps. His affect was withdrawn, but his body language was energetic. He wondered if Metin had made some decisions about his own future, but he wasn't going to pursue it. He had his own agenda for the evening. Once he saw the light go on in the apartment Metin shared with three other men, Raoul jogged to his van, hidden in the woods behind the Eagle's Club. Changing into a black cap and grungy tee shirt, he entered the bar, slipped onto his usual stool, and set up an alibi.

The bartender, always soft on the skinny man with the long eyelashes, pushed a Budweiser towards Raoul. "How you doing tonight, sweetie?" she asked.

"Good," he said. "I'm doing pretty good. Hell, it's Friday night—who wouldn't be feeling good?" He lifted his beer and took a long drink from the cold bottle. "I got paid, I'm goin' get laid—life is good!" he shouted. The bar erupted in cheers. Raoul managed a smile. "How about a round for the bar, beautiful?" He pulled a wad of money from his hip pocket and threw five twenties on the counter as another cheer went around the room.

He ducked his head down, had another swig of beer as a second bottle was placed before him. Alibi firmly established, he nodded at the men who raised their brown bottles in his direction. Now, to get out of there—"Hell, yeah!" he shouted. Slamming the bottle down, he pressed the phone to his ear and then grinned before snapping it closed. "Gonna get me some pussy now. See ya'll down the line." Amid the hoots and hollers of the men and cries of disappointment from the women, he sidled out of the bar and into the darkness.

Once inside the van, he quickly donned the wetsuit and stowed his scuba gear and provisions in a waterproof pack. Rubber-soled diving shoes proved efficient for picking his way through the underbrush until he arrived at his former hideaway. There was no sign of the Pirate's boat, but Raoul sat for thirty minutes waiting for a ripple or flash of light. When he was reasonably sure that it was safe, he slipped into the water, fitted the mask and goggles over his face, and dove into the murky waters of the Sound.

The swim would have been easier if the water were clearer, or perhaps in the daylight, but Raoul relied on his knowledge of the area as well as his instincts to lead the way. Pulling himself up a rocky shore, he scampered for cover just as a searchlight skimmed past. In another minute, the light swung around again. He had landed precisely where he'd hoped: one of the small outcroppings with a direct view of the naval base. He planned to check the area to see if any other surveillance was underway, especially conducted by the terrorist cell, and then scout the other islands for similar activity. Hopefully, he could find something without attracting attention to himself, but in the meantime, he stowed his scuba gear under some rocks and put on a pair of night vision goggles. If only he had access to the heat detection technology, his task would be easier. But then again, he thought, if the idiots in D.C. would turn a satellite in this direction, they could save everyone a lot of time.

He didn't pick up anything on the shore, so he found a tree to climb where he might be able to take in most of the outcropping. Nothing. Crouched in the armpit of a scrubby old tree, Raoul took binoculars and scanned the water and opposite banks. The naval base was lit up and activity obvious from his vantage point. The searchlight swept around regularly and he didn't see any boats on the water, nor other signs of surveillance around him. So. The target might not have anything to do with the base, but then the nagging question kept coming up: Why Jerome?

Suddenly a light was trained on his position and he froze as a voice ordered him to come down from the tree. In very short order, he was handcuffed and riding a Coast Guard speedboat towards the shore. Naturally, he had no identification on him, or in his gear, and he assumed that he was in for a rather unpleasant night.

It wasn't as expected, however: he was placed in a cell and left alone for several hours. Aside from the cold, he managed to get a few hours' sleep. In the early morning, after being fingerprinted and issued a verbal warning for trespassing, Raoul was released. He walked out to the main road, shaking his head. What kind of security was this? He'd asked the officer to call his contact in Washington, and the man merely laughed.

"Sure, 007, I'll give them a heads-up that you were here," he chuckled. "Now get your skinny ass out of my sight. And don't let us catch you around here again."

Clara

IT HAD BEEN A while since I'd been out for a drink, after my overindulgence at the Eagle's Club. I was crazed, however, after too many hours spent in front of my laptop, sorting and searching for clues. These men, these dead Middle Easterners, were proving to be a bit of a puzzle for all of us, including the top law enforcement agency in the nation.

Not surprisingly, I found myself back in the parking lot of the Eagle's. Guy's truck was already there, so I hesitated a moment before getting out and going in. I was curious about him, but more interested in talking to Shelly. I wasn't buying the story she told Mark about why she took Raoul's belongings, and I wanted to have a turn asking the questions.

She wasn't at the bar, but the room was full and the night was young. I decided to sit down and see what happened. Peterson was behind the bar and visibly cringed when he saw me. "You, get out of here, you," he shouted, pointing at me. "I won't serve you. You're not a member here." He looked around the bar. "Where's the club president? Where's the sergeant-at-arms? I want her thrown out."

I put up my hands in mock surrender. It wasn't worth the attention, I decided; I'd just wait in the parking lot and catch Shelly coming or going. Guy stepped up to the bartender and whispered something in his ear. The old man shook his head, but Guy patted him on the back and he retreated to the other side of the bar.

"What can I get you, beautiful?" Guy asked, smiling.

"I'll have a beer. Thanks," I replied. Sat back on the stool, plopped my bag on the floor.

"So, how've you been? I haven't seen you around," he said, placing the beer in front of me.

"Yeah, well, the last time I was here was kind of….unpleasant," I said.

"Oh, yeah, that. Hmmm. Sorry. I thought you were the kind of gal that liked it rough like that," he leaned across the bar and whispered. "So, you want to dance or something?" He traced a line on my hand.

"I guess your wife's not here tonight then, eh?"

He shook his head. "Nope. I am all yours, free as a bird." He came around the bar, leaning against the counter near me.

"Well, thanks, but I just stopped in to talk to Shelly. And maybe see if anyone else might know something about my brother."

"Are you still harping on that?" He crossed his arms, frowning.

"Yes. He's my brother, and I'm still trying to find out what happened to him."

"Hmmph." He looked across the room. "Nobody here's gonna tell you anything, I just want you to know that. So you're pretty much wasting your time. If that's really what you came here for." He pushed between my legs with his hip, slid an arm around my backside and pulled me closer. "But I don't think that's what you're here for. Is it, baby?"

I tried to turn away from him, but I was trapped. I smiled, brought my knee up sharply and saw the color drain from his face. "No thanks," I said. "I think I've had enough of what you have to offer."

I pushed him back and twisted off the stool. "Thanks for the beer."

I walked into the room, looking around at the patrons to see if I recognized Shelly or anyone else who might have some information, but to my surprise the only face I knew was Mark's. He sat at a table near the back, bent over a pitcher with several other men who looked like cops. I knew he was a member, but figured it was one of those political things to demonstrate that he was one of the guys. I didn't think I'd find him actually patronizing the place, but I knew better than to approach him here.

No one held eye contact with me for very long, so I decided to retreat to Plan B and wait for Shelly in the parking lot. From my vantage point in the back corner of the lot, I saw most of the traffic entering the bar, and Shelly never showed. Perhaps she'd moved on to one of the other animal houses in town: the Elks, the Moose, or the Fish & Game Club. In any event, the wine and heavy meal were making a strong impression: I needed to get some sleep, and soon. I aimed the car east and headed back over the bridge.

Raoul

HE WAS AT THE end of his rope, not a place that he liked to be but one that was beginning to feel very familiar. Back at the van, Raoul pulled his laptop from the wheel well and prayed that the battery was not dead. The bigger computer was left behind. He'd welded the CPU to the floor of the van, hidden under metal panels, and no one was going to be able to break into it. Without the keyboard and monitor provided by his laptop, Raoul figured it was secure. He tossed the titanium-clad laptop into his gym bag and hoofed over to the apartment on Main Street. It was light out, but with his hoodie and his unshaven, filthy appearance, no one looked twice in his direction. He powered up the laptop and waited to get online with the bureau. If this didn't work, he was truly alone.

From the apartment below, Raoul heard his mother yelling in Spanish. From the decibels and the pauses, he figured she was on the telephone with one of his sisters, but he could not make out any of the conversation. Just as well. He missed that, the connection with his family, but it was the life he'd chosen. He called up the secure screen, typed in his password, and nothing happened. He'd been cut off and denied access to the website. Okay, he nodded. It was time to throw in the towel.

An hour later, he had showered, changed into something slightly less rank, and packed as many of his belongings as he could fit into the rucksack. Although he hated to give up, Raoul had come to a realization: he could not single-handedly stop this group from their terrorist plans, and he was not going be forced to participate in a suicide mission. There had to be a different way to go—and it was to Washington, he decided.

Shouldering the bag, he crept down the back stairs and paused briefly on the landing outside his mother's door. Closing his eyes, he said a small prayer, "I hope I live to see you again someday, mama." Soon, he was cutting through to the railroad tracks, heading toward the van. When he arrived there, he dropped his bags and fell to a crouch. All four tires had been neatly removed, and the vehicle was sitting on cinder blocks.

"Dammit," he swore under his breath. "Goddam Leon." He went inside, checking for a booby trap before carefully opening the door, and then made sure that nothing of value had been discovered or stolen. Everything he needed to make his initial report was in his bag, so he left the van, secured the doors, and hit the road. He planned to walk south until he reached an intersection where he could hitch a ride. But first, he detoured to the boat yard, slipped through the dilapidated fence at the western edge of the property, and quickly made his way to Stagger Lee. With the large brass key that everyone thought was a decoration on his ring, he opened the wooden storage trunk and then. using one of the small silver keys on the ring, opened one of the small lockboxes. The box was overflowing with notebooks, so he opened two more until he found one with room enough to fit his latest notebook and cellphone. He grabbed his old wallet, so worn it was curved to the exact shape of his butt cheek, and checked to make sure his FBI badge was inside. No more joking around with MPs, he was going in armed with proper credentials this time. Looking at the laptop, he considered leaving it behind. Too risky. Although he'd been using the boat to store his secrets for decades, this time the stakes were higher. He secured the boxes, threw the tarp back over the locker, and started his trek out of Jerome.

The day was getting warm, so he took off the hoodie and shoved it into the over-full bag. At the rear of a convalescent home, he pulled out some of his belongings and dropped them in a dumpster. Along the way, whenever he had the chance, he discarded another piece or two of clothing, his coffeemaker, his ditty bag, his work shirts. As the bag became lighter, with only the laptop weighing it down, he gained confidence.

The rumble of trucks meant he was approaching the highway. He wiped the sweat from his face, tied a bandana across his forehead, and ditched the last of his clothes, a pair of heavy work pants that he stuffed into a shopping cart that was obviously filled with the belongings of another man. "I hope you can wear these," he said. "If I never have to put on another pair of green Dickies in my life, I'll be a happy man." He scrambled over a fence already bent in half from the weight of many previous travelers. The highway shimmered in the distance. He paused, looking around to determine his precise location: not too far from the New London exit, he thought. Perfect.

He stayed away from the road until the exit loomed ahead. Then, fishing in the bag, he pulled out a Yankees cap and put it on. If that didn't garner him a ride, nothing would. It was approaching noon, and the sun was hot on his face. "Next time, bring water, idiot," he said aloud. He ran across the exit ramp, cut through the brush to the entrance loop, and jogged to the other side. Hopefully, he could catch a ride from someone before they sped up to join the flow of traffic headed to New York City.

Not long afterwards, a red pickup truck slowed down and Raoul jumped in the cab before the vehicle came to a complete stop. "Where're you heading?" the driver asked.

"New York," Raoul said. "Appreciate if you can take me as far as you're going."

"No problem, man. Name's Jim."

"Hey Jim, thanks for the ride."

"Solid. You want to toss that bag in the back? There's room behind the seat."

Raoul had placed the duffel in the floor between his feet. "Nah, I'm good here."

"No really, man," Jim said. "Put it in the back. Make yourself comfortable."

Raoul looked over at the guy. He seemed normal enough, so Raoul turned and stowed the bag. Reaching for the seatbelt, he was startled by the presence of a strong hand on his leg. "What the hell..."

"Why don't you just pay for your ride right now," Jim said, squeezing and then releasing Raoul's leg. When Jim unzipped his own fly, Raoul realized this was not the kind of ride he'd been looking for.

"Hey man, I'm not, I don't go that way, sorry," he said, edging closer to the door. He tried not to look at the other man's junk as he exposed himself. "Shit," he muttered. "Let me out—pull over, would ya?"

With that strong right hand, Jim grabbed Raoul by the hair and pulled him towards his lap. The truck had attained its full cruising speed now, at least sixty miles per hour, but it remained in the right lane. Raoul was inches away from Jim's crotch and so he made the only play that came to mind—he grabbed the other man by the nuts. "Let go of me," Raoul said through clenched teeth. "Let me go or I'll rip 'em out."

Jim smashed the side of Raoul's face into the steering wheel, then screamed. "I'll kill you, bitch," before he slammed on the brakes. The truck swerved to the left, then to the right over the rumble strip. Screams filled the car: both men yelling, "Let me go!" Raoul dropped the other man's genitals and reached for Jim's face. He was turned completely to the left, tangled in the seatbelt and struggling to release the catch with his left hand, while his right hand pushed Jim's chin towards the window. The truck careened off the road, and both men were jostled as it bucked over the uneven shoulder.

When it came to a stop, Jim reached into the space between the door and the seat and pulled out a bowie knife, which he pointed at Raoul. "I should just kill you," he hissed. Raoul fumbled for the door handle. "Get the fuck out of here!" Jim screamed. He did.

When the truck fishtailed back onto the highway, Raoul realized that his laptop was now in the possession of an idiot. Fortunately, with all the security and encryption, the machine would be of little more use than a doorstop. But that didn't take away the sting. It had been too long since he'd hitched, and so he forgot the rules of the road. Well, he'd gained a mile and lost his computer. Lesson learned. He stuck out his thumb and started walking.

Clara

APPARENTLY THE RESIDENTS OF Fairfield County in Connecticut sent most of their men, and some of their women, to work in Manhattan every day. A significant number of them worked on the lower part of the island, around Wall Street and the World Trade Center. Despite the fact that many bodies had been pulverized during the collapse of the towers, those confirmed dead were being buried in ceremonies across the tri-state region. Robby emailed me a list of what he had, and where I could find more scheduled funerals to disrupt with my camera.

Sure, I'd done this in other places, but usually in times of war and never in my own backyard. There was a difference between shooting a burial in Israel or Bosnia, and filming one in Darien. It just felt wrong, but I sucked up my objections and strapped on my camera bag. In many ways, it was a distraction from the slog of going through Raoul's belongings, and from the frustration of dealing with the police.

Shelly, who had helped herself to Raoul's personal effects, apparently wanted only to find drugs or money. Figuring that she looked a little bit like me, Shelly swore that her misrepresentation was not criminal; she just wanted to get some stuff that Raoul owed her. Mark let her go, despite my lobbying to have her charged with impersonation or forgery. He gave her a written warning.

I pressured him heavily to repay me by allowing me to participate in the meeting with the naval base commander. "He's going to walk," Mark protested. "Then we'll have nothing."

"I promise you can throw me out, if you let me sit and listen in the next room," I said. I was not above batting my eyelashes at the man, and I got what I wanted.

Commander Hammer, an extreme pole-up-the-ass naval officer, barely registered the interpersonal vibes around him. He had no time for this, we were told several times.

"Then let's get on with it," Mark said. "Here's what we know: four young men, all apparently from the Middle East, were found dead in the last three months. Two were just found in the past week. We think that the death of Raoul Quiñones may also be related to these murders, and so that makes a total of five." He pushed five photographs across the table. "Do you recognize any of these men?"

Hammer (whose name was actually Krauthammer, I think) shook his head after briefly looking at the pictures. "No, I don't know any of them. Do you have ID?"

"Not yet. Except for Raoul, we have no idea who these men are or what they were doing here."

There was silence. The commander aligned his pen and paper, while Mark looked through his notebook. I fidgeted.

"Sir, you said that you had some 'unexplained' events on the base. Can you tell me what you mean?" Mark said.

Hammer looked at me, then back at Mark. "What's she doing here again?"

"This is Clara Quiñones, she's the sister of one of the deceased men and she's helping with my investigation."

"I know who she is. I don't think she should be here. I'm not comfortable speaking to a civilian about these matters, particularly one who is related to a victim," Hammer said.

"Fine. Clara, would you step out? Please?" Mark asked.

Instead of protesting, I glared at the two men and exited the room. I went directly into the observation room that Mark had unlocked before bringing Krauthammer into the "conference room." I listened.

"Sir, we had an incident a couple of weeks ago, which could be potentially embarrassing to the Navy should it reach the press."

Mark sat back in his chair. "I totally understand. This is completely off the record, believe me. I don't want the Feds breathing down my neck any more than you do. But if we can put the pieces together and there's something that will help us track this down, well, that's worth trusting each other, isn't it?"

More silence. I waited, as did Mark, for the Hammer to relax his sphincter a bit.

"Historically, we try to keep a very tight rein on the base. But we have been having some trouble... some weapons have been missing, and we've been investigating to see if there's some kind of smuggling ring. And we've got some drug trafficking happening on the water, and we're working with the Coast Guard to get that under control, and so these bodies are... disturbing. Possibly related to one or both of those activities. We don't know."

"I see." Mark kept cool.

"We have picked up a body on the perimeter of the base, and two weeks ago there was one that seems to have been dropped onto an offshore location."

"One of the little islands?"

"Yes. Both as you describe, young apparently Middle Eastern men. We didn't connect them, since both causes of death were different, but now... It seems they must be related. Someone is definitely killing off these young men."

"What were the causes of death?"

"One was electrocuted, the other had a broken neck."

"Any photos?"

The Hammer opened his bag and removed two color photos that seemed eerily similar to the five Mark had put on the table. "Here. The one from the island had been in the water for quite a while, as you can see, so he was pretty decomposed. But, like yours, there was no ID on any of the victims, and none of their prints came up in any system. So they are unknowns."

"Autopsy?"

"Yes, nothing remarkable there. Clothes all cheap, Wal-Mart stuff. No distinguishing marks."

"Okay. So what are we looking at? This started well before the attack, so it can't be retaliation. Although I know the Middle Easterners around town are being harassed quite a bit. But so far, the only violence has been a rock thrown through the mosque window and a cross-burning at the international grocery store. No bodily harm or direct physical assault."

"Right. We have nothing like that on the base, although the Muslim personnel have been separated from the general population—for their own protection."

"So I don't get it. Why did you insist that Ms. Quiñones leave the room? You have nothing that relates to her brother," Mark said.

"Ah. Yes. That," Hammer said. "I do have one other thing. There was an incident, about a week before the attack...let me see. Here it is." He pulled a red file folder from his briefcase. "Now, this is entirely off the record, you agree?"

"Of course," Mark said.

"We had a person... we discovered a man, Raoul Quiñones, it turns out, who was captured on Rock Island, watching the base from a position in a tree."

"What?" Mark almost smiled. "You caught Raoul on your secure island. When was this?"

"Like I said, we identified an individual sitting in a tree on the island. He had night vision gear and he was performing some kind of surveillance of the base. He was detained and questioned, and released. That's it."

"That's it. Really? What did he say? How did he explain what he was doing there?"

Hammer adjusted his collar. Coughed a little. "Well, he claimed to be FBI and asked us to contact his handler. But he had no identification, and when we ran his prints, nothing came up except an arrest for some juvie offense. So we cut him loose." He leaned across the table towards Mark. "It's a little embarrassing, you know? I think we should have kept him in custody and done a little more checking on the guy. After all, he was after something. Maybe he was working for the terrorists. I don't know anything about the guy. But we caught him, threw him back, and now you show me a photo of his corpse."

"Yeah." Mark tapped the table. "What do we make of this? I don't see it. I really don't know what the connection could be. But I can tell you that Raoul Quiñones really was with the FBI. So whatever he was doing, it was legit."

"We had no way of knowing that."

"Did anyone call D.C.? Check his credentials?"

"Well, apparently not. I think that my officers didn't take him seriously. They cut him loose before I even heard about it."

"So I assume you've tightened your security now, right? You aren't catching people on a secure naval facility, running their prints and just 'cutting them loose' anymore, are you?" Mark shook his head.

The Hammer sat up straighter, if that was possible, and his face reddened. He straightened the papers in his folder.

"Look, don't get all self-righteous with me," Mark continued. "I know shit like this happens all the time. Hell, we had these bodies popping up and nobody put two and two together until now, so I know it happens. But what it means, I don't know. And that's what we need to figure out."

"Yes, I think that's the right approach. What does this all mean?" the Hammer said. His left eyelid twitched. Behind the glass, my fists clenched. I could kill him with my bare hands. Good thing Mark made me leave the room. I guess.

"I think it means that we screwed up. And I'm not sure, but maybe we're going to find a link between all of this and what happened at the Trade Center," Mark said.

"So. What do we do next?"

"You have resources that I don't have," Mark said. He held up his hand when the Hammer started to object. "I know you don't want people to know what happened. We don't have to talk about Raoul, and the fact that you let him go. But we can maybe figure out the connection between all these men. You have access to labs and national security data and we can try to figure out who these men are, where they came from, and what they were doing here."

"How do you think we can do that? I can't just call the Secretary of Defense and say, hey, we found these bodies—"

"Why not?"

Silence. "Oh," Hammer finally said. "I guess, I mean, I can make a call."

"I'm sure that the folks in Washington will be very interested in learning more about the people who master-minded the attacks, and if this can provide some insight, then all the better. Right?"

"Yes. But what I know, well, this can't leave the room—what I know is that they have traced the suicide bombers to Florida. They seem to have been based in Florida. So how can these bodies relate...?"

"I don't know." Mark sighed. "I honestly have no clue. I just know that this is important, and we need to follow it to see where it leads."

"All right." The Hammer put his files back in his briefcase. "I'll make a couple of calls and see what I can do."

"Great." Mark pulled out a business card, scrawled on the back. "Here's my cell phone. Call me, anytime, and we can meet again."

"Sure." The Hammer took the card. "I won't be coming here again. We can meet outside somewhere."

"That's fine. Let me know if there's something I can be doing."

"I assume you've got DNA samples, prints, everything?"

"Of course."

"Send me what you have, we'll feed it to the database and see what we come up with."

Mark stood at the same time as the commander, offering his hand across the table. It was not reciprocated.

"And Ms. Quiñones, I better not read any of this in a newspaper," the Hammer said, addressing the mirror. He returned his steely gaze to Mark. "Captain, I would appreciate if you could messenger a copy of your files to me this afternoon."

Mark opened the door. "I'll get it right over to you. Thanks."

"Discretion," Hammer said. "Please remember to use discretion."

"Absolutely." Mark nodded solemnly. "Word of honor."

The Hammer sniffed and walked out. Mark turned to the mirror and shrugged.

I let the air out of my lungs and closed my eyes. They could have saved Raoul, I thought. And possibly all those people killed in the attack. "Discretion my ass!" I said aloud. "The damned Navy fucked up, and they want us to keep it quiet."

Mark stood next to the open door, catching the end of my exclamation. "Clara, I promised we'd do this his way. Please don't go off half-cocked and screw this up. If they don't cooperate with us, we'll never stand a chance of getting to the bottom of it."

I rolled my head around, easing the kinks in my neck. "You agreed to that, not me."

"Clara!"

"Well. You did," I turned to face him. "I'll keep quiet for now, but not for long."

"Good. Otherwise I'd have to lock you up," he said.

"You wish."

He laughed, nodding.

Raoul

IT TOOK A COUPLE of hours before Raoul found another ride, and the driver was only going as far as New Haven, so at that point he decided to try another mode of transportation. A train to New York had just left the station, so he was forced to sit and wait for the next one. Well aware that his last train trip had been interrupted by the Leader, he decided to walk around outside rather than risk being spotted inside the station.

There's not a whole lot to see or do around the train station in New Haven, and Raoul felt very exposed walking along the busy street. He ducked down a side street, near a housing complex, and stumbled upon a hippie couple sitting on the sidewalk with a box full of puppies. He stopped, petted the little black and white pups, and tried to converse with the pair.

"What kind of dogs are these?" he asked.

"Mutts, mostly, I guess," the girl said. She couldn't be much older than eighteen, dressed in what seemed to be an outfit constructed of dirty rags pinned together. "You want one?"

"No, I can't take care of a pet right now," Raoul said. "I'm kind of between homes at the moment."

"Dude, that's cool," the boy said. "We're, like, living off the land. You know? Use only what you need and leave the rest behind. You sure you don't want a puppy? They are really good dogs, and you get lots of dinero when you—"

Raoul stood up and walked away.

"Hey, man!"

Raoul kept walking. The dogs had triggered something, a memory that caused his heart to race and he needed to get away. He turned quickly down another street, entered a parking garage, took the elevator to the roof and rested there, leaning against the wall. To his left, the water of Long Island Sound sparkled in the sun. To his right, the silhouette of New Haven pushed at the blue sky. He took out his cell phone, dialed quickly and held it to his ear.

"Mama," he said when the call was answered. "It's Raoul. How are you?"

"Mijo!! Where are you, how are you, my boy, I have missed you. Why haven't you called me? Where have you been, I've been so worried. Mijo?"

"Yea, Mama, I'm fine. I've been working. I'm, I'm in New York. I was thinking I might come up and see you, maybe in a couple of weeks. How would that be?"

"Oh, Mijo, it would be wonderful. I hope you mean it this time. It's been months and months—I can't even remember what you look like anymore. Why don't you ever call me? You're getting to be just like your father, Mijo, you're breaking my heart. Don't you feel sorry for your poor mommy? All I have is your sisters and you know they are all selfish, they just take-take-take, and no one cares about me. I am getting so old, and I have no one here to take care of me. Mijo, why don't you come home and stay with me? You can get a job here, and I'll cook for you, and you can find a nice girl to marry. Yes, I know, Mrs. Caro has a daughter, she's about your age, she'd be perfect. So, Mijo, when you come home I'll invite them to come over and you can see, she's a nice girl."

"Mama, no, I don't want to meet anyone. I just want to see you," he said.

"Okay, not that girl, but we'll find one for you and you can settle down. It's time for you to settle down, Mijo, you need to come home. Si? You call me and tell me what day and I'll have everything ready for you. I'll get your bed ready and make your favorite food, eh? You let me fatten you up a little, okay?"

"Okay, mama. I'll call you and tell you when—or maybe I'll just show up on your doorstep one day real soon."

"Any time, Mijo, you come home any time."

"I love you, mama," he said.

"Mijo? What's the matter? Are you crying? Are you hurt? Is something wrong?"

"No, ma, I just wanted to hear your voice. Everything's okay. I'll see you soon. Okay?"

"Okay, then, you be good."

He hung up the phone and looked at it for a minute, then dialed again. "The mailbox you have reached is full. Please try again—" he disconnected before the message ended. "Dammit, Clara."

A car squealed around the ramp and sped onto the roof. Raoul stepped back into the shadows, watching a young couple walk hand-in-hand to the elevators. Raoul followed them, waiting until the doors had closed and then pushing the button again. Time to get back to the train station, and to reality.

He bought a newspaper at the kiosk and found a seat against a wall, where he could see all the entrances to the station. Holding the paper open, he watched the people come and go. No one noticed him, and no one intervened when two young men approached him, lifted him by the arms, and escorted him to the door.

"Metin!" Raoul exclaimed when they were on the sidewalk. "Thank God you found me!"

"Get in the car," Metin said tonelessly.

"Okay, great, thanks," Raoul chattered nervously. "This is terrific," he said as he slid into the backseat. Metin's companion, a silent, serious man named Ahmet, got in the other side of the car and the pair sandwiched Raoul.

"Go," a voice from the front seat instructed the driver, who promptly veered into traffic and narrowly missed hitting an oncoming car. Raoul recognized the voice of the Leader.

He started to speak. "I am so glad—"

The Leader's hand went up.

"Really, I don't know how—" Raoul tried again.

"Pssshhht." The hissing noise meant "quiet" among the Pakistani men. "Ismail, if that really is your name, you would be wise to keep your mouth shut right now. Or we will shut it for you," the Leader said. He did not even bother to turn his head.

"I understand, but I can explain. See, this guy picked me up and attacked me, and —"

"Pssshhht." The Leader flicked a finger at Metin, who reached under the front seat and removed a roll of duct tape. He cut off a length with a box cutter, turned, and slapped it on Raoul's face, cutting off his protests.

"Now, if you wish, we can also tie your hands and feet, and we can put a blindfold on you." The Leader turned and looked at Raoul, one eyebrow raised. "Or would you prefer that we throw you in the trunk? No? Then sit quietly and pray. That's all you have left, young man. Prayer."

Clara

MARK CALLED WITH NOTHING to report, and I was not in a hurry to see him anyway. I needed to gird myself for funeral duty the next day, and since I was on the other side of the river, I decided to visit one of the finer establishments in town. Maybe I would visit Mary Kate and see how badly that relationship was screwed up. I was truly batting a thousand.

She was there, of course, behind the high counter that separated the open kitchen from the dining room. I was seated in a small booth by the bar, perfect to watch the crowd and appreciate the success Mary Kate had made of her parents' restaurant. I ordered the house salad and the special, a linguini with clam sauce that sounded like the perfect accompaniment to my glass of cold Pinot Grigio. The patrons were smoother here than the ones I'd gotten used to in Jerome: the voices were softer, the clothing better, and the talk was about museums and books and sailing at the club. A long, long way from Jerome indeed.

Mary Kate headed to the entrance, checking the reservation book and speaking quietly with the maitre'd. The next time I looked up, she was behind the bar, mixing a drink and smiling at one of the elderly gentlemen who were seated there. Either she had seen me and chosen to ignore me, or she hadn't seen me, which was impossible. The woman was literally everywhere in the room. I was working my way through the linguini and a second glass of wine when she pulled out the opposite chair and sat down.

"So, you slumming or what?"

I wiped my greasy chin with a thick white napkin. "No, I thought I would check out how the other half lives. This is some place you've got, Mary Kate. Congratulations."

She smiled. "It's pretty good. It's a lot of work, though. I have no life when the place is open. We close down for a couple of months after Christmas, and then open again in March. So I get a little reprieve."

"Is Rose a partner with you?" I remembered that Mary Kate's parents always talked about how the two sisters would take over when they were old enough.

"She's not a partner, in the way you mean. She takes her cut though. We haven't spoken for years, but she gets her share—without doing any of the work," she said. "I guess she was the smarter one, after all."

"Why do you give her money? If she doesn't help out?"

"She's entitled to it. And she holds me hostage."

"What?"

"Aside from the fact that Pa would never let me cut her off, she has half of the sauce recipe. You know, Mom's famous sauce? That everyone comes here for? Before she died, she gave each of us one half of the recipe. So neither one of us can make it without the other. And so Rose comes in here with her jar of spices, already mixed, and we make the sauce every Monday afternoon for the week. I've tried to make it without her, believe me, but whatever is in there, makes all the difference. I guess she got the critical 'secret' ingredient." She paused, checked the room, and then crossed her arms. "But I'm sure you didn't come here to talk to me about Rose, or about marinara sauce, or the cultural differences between Old Stonefield and Jerome. What do you want, Clara?"

"Honestly, Mary Kate, I just needed to get out of Jerome and have a decent meal. I was hoping I'd see you, but I understand if you are still angry with me. So you don't have to talk to me if you don't feel like it. I'm still processing what you told me the other night, and I totally get why you're mad."

"I will always be angry with you," she said. "But that doesn't mean I won't talk to you—or take your money at my restaurant." She laughed. "I have a 'no discount' policy for friends and family. Otherwise I'd never make a buck." She was interrupted by a waiter who came over to get her approval to honor an old gift certificate. "So, Clara, have you found out anything about who killed Raoul?"

I shook my head. "It just gets curiouser and curiouser, Alice. The more I find, the less I know." I sipped the wine. "When you saw him, did he tell you anything about what he was doing in Jerome? Anything at all?"

She looked at the table for a moment. "He did help me out with something. My son was missing for a while and Raoul was looking for him. And then when Silvio came back, Raoul tried to connect with him, see what was going on, that kind of thing. I guess that my son had found religion, and he went a little weird for a while. But now he's okay. So I don't know."

"What kind of religion?"

"What?"

"I mean, was he going to church a lot, or was he part of a cult?"

"I don't see what difference that makes."

"It could be important. When was this?" I asked.

"In August. He took off for a couple of days and I got nervous, but then he came home and it was okay, that's the whole story," she said. "Raoul was really supportive, and I appreciated that he was here. My husband, he's kind of useless that way."

"Mary Kate, Raoul was working undercover, and we think that might have been what got him killed. Anything you know could be really helpful to me. Anything."

"I really don't know. You should talk to Silvio, then, and maybe he'll tell you. I haven't been able to get him to talk to me since he came back. And since September 11, he hasn't left the house. I don't know what's going on with that kid." She sighed. "You're welcome to give it a try. I can't guarantee that he'll even let you in his room, though."

"Great. Thanks. When can I come over? When do you get out of here?"

"Hold on," she said. "You can come over in the morning. I will be here late and quite frankly I don't have the strength to deal with him when I get home."

I tried to protest, but she cut me off. "Tomorrow morning, no earlier than 10:00 a.m. Here's the address." She scribbled on a card and pushed it across the table. "So, enough about my family," she said. "What was up with your mother at the funeral? I don't mean to be crude, but what the fuck? Throwing herself into the grave? I mean, I know she loved your brother and all but…"

I had to smile despite the horror that her comments brought back to mind. Mama, jumping on the coffin as it was being lowered into the grave—It was like something out of a bad soap opera. But it was still my mother, and I felt her pain acutely.

"Yeah, she went over the edge there. Literally."

"But why? I mean, crazy's crazy, but that was something else." She shook her head. "If you don't want to talk about it, that's okay. I was just curious."

"No, it's actually an interesting story," I said. If you can separate from the fact that this is your mother you're talking about. "When she was born, on the island, Puerto Rico, you know, her mother died during childbirth. And I guess my mother didn't cry, so they figured she was dead, too, and they laid her out in the casket next to her dead mother. That night, when some family came around to pay their respects, the baby cried. So they took her out before they closed the box. She's had a fear of coffins ever since, and I suppose she just wanted to make sure Mijo was not alive in the coffin, crying to get out." I paused, took a gulp of wine. "So crazy, yes, but actually not unreasonable."

"Wow. I never knew that. But she can't possibly remember…"

I shook my head. "She swears that she does, but I'm sure it was just hearing that story all her life, she transformed the facts into a memory. We tried to convince her to have Mijo cremated, but she's even more afraid of being burned alive—and she wasn't listening to anything I had to say anyway. So. That's the story. Now you know yours is not the only screwed up family in Jerome."

"Hell, I knew that a long time ago," she chuckled. "Too bad I'm not speaking to Rose. She would freak out if she heard that story—she's got this thing about being buried alive, too. Ha. Might be worth breaking the silence just to see her reaction." Mary Kate laughed quietly. "Well, that's too much of a break for me. I have to get back to work. So, come over in the morning if you want. I don't know if you'll get anywhere, but you're welcome to try."

We agreed that I'd see her in the morning, and I left her contemplating the tarot of credit card receipts on the bar.

Raoul

THEY DROVE FOR A while and took Raoul through some neighborhoods even he'd never traversed before. At a nondescript cape, they parked and strong-armed him into the house. It was sparsely furnished, just some mismatched chairs and an old metal card table in the living area. He was shoved into a metal folding chair where his arms and legs were taped. He watched the men, their silence more frightening than any tirade would have been. One was sent to the back, Metin was stationed outside the door, and the driver was told to guard the front of the house.

The Leader sighed heavily before he sat down. "Ismail, I am very disappointed in you today," he said. "I think you know why." The older man reached over and removed Raoul's wallet from his back pocket. As he opened it, Raoul began to sweat. He had never been caught with his identification before; it was an amateur mistake.

"So, Mr. Quiñones. Or excuse me, Special Agent Quiñones. What exactly have you been doing here in Jerome, coming to my mosque and pretending to be one of my men?" Although he spoke calmly, Raoul could see the veins bulging in the other man's temple. Abruptly, the Leader kicked Raoul's chair, toppling him to the floor. Metin rushed in at the crash.

"Step outside," the Leader said to him, not taking his eyes off Raoul. "So. You are going to tell me everything that you have done, and what you have been reporting, and to whom."

Raoul closed his eyes. The Leader kicked the seat of the chair, then came around and kicked Raoul in the head. He blacked out after the third kick.

When he awakened, he was in a small, dark space. The dirt floor, dampness, and lack of light—he was in the basement. Maybe the same house, maybe not. There were no windows, and when his eyes adjusted to the light, he saw a single door. Stacks of wooden crates were piled along two walls. His feet and hands were tightly secured with plastic fasteners, but Raoul managed to crab across the ten-foot span and look into one of the open crates. Guns. Ammo. Cell phones. All packed in straw, with wine bottles pushed aside. It was kind of stupid for them to leave him in here with all these weapons, he thought. If he could get one assembled—

The floor creaked, and the door opened, casting light on Raoul leaning over the boxes.

"Pretty impressive, isn't it?" the Leader said. "Shipping weapons under wine. Just one of the ways we have been moving things around. Getting ready for action. You could have been part of that, part of something bigger than your pitiful little life. Serving the man. You are just a tool of the American devil. And you had a chance to serve Allah. Pity." He shook his head. "You had potential. But we thought you were too good to be true. Coming out of nowhere like you did, and we couldn't find out anything about you."

The Leader grabbed Raoul by the hair. "Are you going to tell me what I need to know, or are you going to make this difficult?"

Raoul shook his head, and the Leader tightened his grip. "We'll get it out of you, don't worry. I don't have time for this, but if you want to do it the hard way, that's fine." He dropped Raoul's head and shouted to the other men, "Get him up in a chair."

There's many different kinds of torture, Raoul thought. Although his head rang from being kicked, he was still quite aware of what was probably coming. The nerves in his body tingled with adrenalin. *These guys are not going to be subtle*, he thought, recalling the various killings he'd witnessed during the past few weeks. If he was lucky, he'd get a bullet to the brain or a knife to the throat. Even the hanging seemed preferable, now, to what he expected to be limb-severing, blood-gushing, teeth-gnashing pain. Bracing himself, he was surprised to see Metin approach with a syringe. Another man placed a thick arm around his neck and held out Raoul's right arm while Metin jabbed the needle into a bulging muscle. Heat instantly rushed through Raoul's body and he gave a surprised yelp before his head fell forward.

This was not what he expected. It was a drug, something more powerful than anything he'd ever tried. While his heart leapt in ecstasy, Raoul tried to slow his racing mind enough to contextualize the experience. He heard the door close and the rumble of voices in the other room. They'd left him here, hands unbound and feet loosely tied to the chair. If only he could summon enough strength to stand up, he was certain that he could get out of the window before anyone noticed. But he was unable to move and slowly gave in to the feelings of warmth and wellness. He slept.

Clara

IT WAS HARD TO sleep that night, so I gave up after a very short time lying on the bed. The night was chilly, the undertones of fall beginning to push aside the heavy blanket of summer heat. I sat on the screen porch, wrapped in a light blanket, and read through some of the obituaries that Chris had sent over. At noon tomorrow, I needed to be at a service in Darien, where several families were gathering to mourn their lost son, father, and brother. Most of the grieving families had no bodies to bury, so the rituals stayed away from funeral homes and cemeteries. Instead, groups threw flowers into the sea or created altars of photographs and mementos. I dreaded the assignment, hated to be the one to interrupt such a private time with a camera in my hand. But these deaths belonged to the country, it seemed. We were all mourning the loss of these innocents, so there was a role that I needed to play.

I was fidgeting in my rental, sitting across from Mary Kate's house by 9:00 a.m. No movement could be seen; I supposed the children were long gone to school and the husband must also leave the house early. I saw the curtains flick open and then the door: Mary Kate was waving me in. Her hair wild, a bathrobe tied loosely around her waist, she did not look happy to see me.

I held out a cup of Dunkin Donuts coffee. "Too early?"

She looked at me, grunted, and took the coffee. "I am not entertaining you at this hour. Silvio's room is upstairs, second door on the right. Good luck." She waved a hand in the direction of the stairs and disappeared towards the back of the house. "Let yourself out afterwards, would you?"

"Thanks," I said. I clenched the coffee cup and knocked on the closed door. "Silvio? Can I talk to you for a minute?" No response. "My name is Clara Quiñones, and I'm Raoul's sister. I know you met him, and I just want to talk to you about him. Can you open the door please?"

More silence. I waited, sipped the lukewarm coffee. The house sighed around me.

"Silvio, are you in there?" I knocked again. "Look, I know you don't know who I am, but if I could just talk to you for a minute—"

I heard the creaking of a mattress. "Go away," he said, voice muffled by blankets and sleep.

"I'm not going away. I'll sit here until you talk to me."

A clock chimed in the living room. Water ran somewhere in the house. I sat on the floor and leaned against the door. "Silvio? I'm still here." Silence. I finished my coffee. Trying to remain calm, I practiced counting my breaths. I am breathing in, I am breathing out. "Fuck."

I got up, banged on the door five times, and then reached for the knob. It was unlocked. "I'm coming in," I said, pushing open the door. The smell hit me first, the unwashed smell of homelessness, decaying food, and illness. The room was so dark I could hardly make out shapes, but then I realized that everything was covered in something else, like a forest covered in ivy. Clothes, blankets, newspapers—every surface was piled with stuff. In the middle, a bed whose unwashed occupant seemed buried beneath an entire wardrobe of clothing. I waved the door a little, hoping to bring in some fresh air from the hallway.

"Silvio?"

"Get out." More of a growl than a human response.

"I just need a few minutes—"

"Get out before I kill you."

"Wait a minute, I just want to ask you about my brother…."

I heard the distinctive thwak of a switchblade springing open, and I instinctively took a step back into the door jam. A shadow passed behind me.

"I told you," Mary Kate said. "Leave him alone."

"I need to talk to him," I replied. "I think he might know something about who killed Raoul."

The figure on the bed leapt to a standing position. He was big, well over six feet tall, and completely naked. In the light from the hallway, I could see that while he still had the musculature of an athlete, weeks of hibernating had taken a toll on the young man's physique. Although his semi-erect cock was much more impressive than the shiv, the knife slicing the air between us held my attention.

"Get the fuck out of here before I cut you both," he growled. "I don't know who the fuck you are, or who your fucking brother is, and I want you to leave me alone. Get out." He waved the knife and lunged closer to me.

"Jesus Christ, Silvio, cover yourself up. Put down the damned knife. Honest to God, I don't know what happened to you!" Mary Kate stepped forward, took the knife from her son, and folded it into her back pocket. "You know Raoul, he visited you a couple of weeks ago, after you got home. Remember?" She pulled a sheet from the tangle on the bed and handed it to him. "Cover yourself." He did. "Now why don't you take a shower and come downstairs for some breakfast. You must be hungry."

His head hanging, Silvio crossed the hallway, sheet dragging behind, and went into the bathroom. Almost immediately, the shower began running.

"Look at this room," Mary Kate said. She flung open the shades and lifted the windows, allowing some fresh air to penetrate the stench. "I don't come upstairs, I've been leaving him alone. I had no idea he's been living like a pig up here. I hope there are no bugs…" She avoided my eyes as she started heaping clothes in a mountain, separating dirty dishes and newspapers into two separate piles on the floor. "Can you give me a hand here—he's going to be a while in there—take this stack of dishes into the kitchen for me? Thanks."

When I came back up the stairs, the water was still running, but a strange sound was coming from the bathroom. "Is he all right in there?" I asked Mary Kate. She was making the bed with fresh linens.

"That noise? Yeah, it's pretty awful, isn't it?" She shook her head. "He's been crying like that on and off for weeks. I can't figure out if he's singing, or praying, or really crying." She shrugged. "If you grab that trash can, I'll get the clothes and we can bring everything downstairs. I'll refill your coffee for you."

We waited, silently, while the clock chimed again and the water still ran upstairs. "The hot water should be gone by now," Mary Kate said, checking her watch.

I tried to make polite conversation. "So, what does Silvio do? Is he in school? Does he have a job?"

"Well, before this summer, he was working at a garage, but then all hell broke loose with him. I don't know if he's sick in the head or what." She stood up, looking towards the ceiling. "I'm going to run the vacuum around in there while I have the chance. I'll send him downstairs when he gets dressed. Let me know if you get anything out of him, would ya?"

I listened to their raised voices for a few minutes and then heard heavy footsteps coming down the stairs. The young man, now wearing a pair of sweat pants that barely clung to his hips, came into the kitchen and poured coffee into a huge mug. Three large scoops of sugar and two splashes of milk told me this was not his usual drink. He stood in front of the sink, looking out the window, and drank most of the hot beverage in one gulp.

"What do you want?" he asked finally.

"I want to hear whatever you can tell me about my brother, Raoul," I said. "Your mother told me that you spoke with him a couple of weeks ago. He was murdered, and I am trying to find out what happened to him."

"I can't help you," he said. Another sugary mixture was blended in his cup. He turned and looked at me. "I don't know anything." He could not meet my eyes, and his voice was heavy, a bit slurred.

"Are you on something?" I asked him.

"Just leave me alone," he said, turning to leave the room. "Leave. Me. Alone."

I followed him upstairs, watched as he ripped the vacuum plug out of the wall and pushed his mother out of the bedroom. The door slammed. She looked at me. "Anything?"

"Nope." I turned and went back into the kitchen, discarded my Styrofoam cup and headed to the door. She stood at the bottom of the stairs. "If I were you, I'd get him to a doctor. He's on something, and I don't think it's good."

Raoul

THE MAN THEY CALLED Doctor came back later, another syringe at the ready. This drug, rather than provoking a warm response, chilled Raoul to the core and he began to shiver uncontrollably. Two men tied his arms and legs to the bed frame. After several minutes, his teeth chattering, sharp pain began flashing across his brain and his vision was obscured by light and dark floaters. He lay thrashing on the bed panting, his tongue swollen and throat constricting.

The Leader stood next to the bed, dropping ice cubes onto Raoul's chest. "Do you feel like talking yet?" he asked.

Raoul rolled his head from side to side. "Stop," he croaked.

"Ah, my friend Ismail, we will not stop until you tell us what you have done." The Leader gestured to the Doctor standing near the bed. "Okay, give him another dose," he said.

"We'll talk more later," he said to Raoul.

The blast of drugs from the next syringe lifted Raoul's body in a single spasm, his back arching more than an inch over the soaked bedding. He lost control of his muscles and the smell of urine and feces filled the room. Darkness enveloped him as the two drugs dueled within his system, and he strained to remain alert and tried to listen to the voices raised in the next room.

"We have no idea," the Leader spoke into the phone. "Metin, come here. You were responsible for shadowing Ismail. Tell me what you saw. Who did he speak to, where did he go?"

"I told you everything; I wrote it in my daily reports," Metin stammered.

"Did you leave out anything? Think! What did you miss?"

Metin hugged himself, rocking forward and back on his feet. "I don't know sir," he said. "If I missed it, how would I know that I missed it?"

The Leader struck Metin across the face, using the phone as a weapon. Blood ran down his cheek as Metin rested his forehead on the floor, awaiting the next blow. He began to pray.

The Leader threw the cell phone at the wall, turned away as its pieces flew in all directions. "Allah, Allah, what have we done?" he addressed the ceiling. "See how one man can destroy the good work of many? Do you see?"

Moving into the kitchen, the Leader reached into a cardboard box and removed another cell phone. He put on small reading glasses to consult a list of numbers, and he began dialing.

"We may have been compromised here," he said. "I have no idea. The cell is corrupted." He listened, nodding, and then switched off the phone. Handing it to the man at his side, he picked up another and repeated the message. While he spoke, the other man removed the SIM card and smashed both the card and the phone with a hammer. The trash was swept into a bright yellow bag from Shop-Rite.

"Get the Imam," the Leader muttered at one point. "We've got to leave this town. Have everyone gather at the mosque for evening prayers." He jotted some names on a scrap of paper. "Bring these men here this afternoon," he said. "Go."

When they returned to his bed, Raoul was staring unblinking at the ceiling. "Is he dead?" the Leader asked.

"No," the Doctor said. "He's alive."

"Get rid of this stink," the Leader turned to another young man hovering in the doorway. "Take him into the shower and rinse him off—and burn those sheets. In fact, get rid of the mattress. Just tie him back on the frame. Metin, stop weeping like a child over there. Get up and do something helpful for a change." He clapped his hands together. "Doctor, give him another dose. We're running out of time."

Clara

CONNECTICUT'S "GOLD COAST" HOUSES many of Wall Street's movers and shakers, and the numbers lost in the Trade Center were still being tabulated when the memorial services started. All of the employees of Cantor Fitzgerald, a brokerage firm that had had offices on the 101-105th floors of 1 World Trade Center, were presumed dead, many of them having left widows and children in luxurious homes in Greenwich, Darien, and Westport. The families clung to each other and glared at the reporters following them day and night.

I clicked away, looking for the one shot that would make this intrusion worthwhile to my editors if not to my own sensibilities. When I hid behind the camera lens, I could usually maintain enough distance from the subject of my work. In this case, I felt my hands shake and my eyes gloss several times. The numb faces of the children were the worst, and I lowered my camera a couple of times when the sorrow reached a crescendo. I stared at one teenaged boy and zoomed in to capture the animal rage that lit up his eyes despite the impassive thrust of his chin. Silvio. He had the same fire in his eyes this morning, I thought, but there was something else. I scanned the crowd, searching for it.

Fear. That was it. Silvio was afraid. I doubt it was me he feared—no, suddenly I was sure of it. He was afraid of something, or someone, that he had seen. Perhaps it was related to Mijo, but maybe not. But that was definitely why he'd been hiding out.

When the speeches ended and the crowd broke into smaller groups, I knew that I should wander around and look for the candid shots of family grief that we all knew sold magazines. First, though, I stepped away from the other photographers and took out my cell phone. Punching in Mary Kate's number, I got the machine. "Mary Kate, it's Clara. Call me when you can. Thanks," I whispered the message, then turned the ringer to "vibrate" so I would not miss her call.

A middle-aged woman tapped my shoulder. "Excuse me," she said.

"Yes, can I help you?"

"What are you doing? Have you no respect for these families? How can you intrude like this, take pictures, make phone calls? What kind of monster—"

"Lady, I appreciate your opinion. I truly do. But I'm just doing my job here. I'm sorry." I backed away from her finger-pointing anger, stepping on the well-shod toe of an elderly man standing close behind me. "Excuse me, sir," I scooted away, pressing my camera to my chest in case someone had the bright idea of trying to take it away.

My cell phone rang as I was backing out of the crowd, prompting more muttering about intrusive journalist scum. It was Mark.

"Clara, where are you? You checked out of the hotel..."

"Yeah, I told you, I needed to get some distance. Is there anything new? Have you found out anything?"

"No, we're still trying to run down the identities of the dead men. So far, we're drawing a blank," he said. "Where are you?"

"I'm at a memorial service in Darien," I said.

"What? For who?"

"I'm working," I hissed.

"Oh, sorry," he said. "Are you coming back? Can we....meet later?"

"Sure," I said. "I want to track down Shelly and see if I can get anything out of her —Say, what do you know about Silvio Rossi?"

"Who's that?"

"Kid went missing during the summer. Raoul was helping the mother locate the boy."

"We didn't have any missing kids reported. Who's the mother?"

"Mary Kate Flannigan. I guess it's Rossi now," I said. "Her son is over 18-years-old, so I guess he's not a kid anymore. She owns a restaurant in Old Stonefield, we went to high school together. Anyway, she asked Raoul to help find the kid, and it seems like one of the last things he might have done. So I wanted to see if the kid could shed some light on what Raoul was doing around town."

"And?"

"Nothing. Kid is closed up like a clam, seems to be scared of his own shadow. I couldn't get anything out of him."

"Hmm." I could hear him breathing. The silence vibrated between us like a taut string connecting two tin cans.

I shifted gears. "So what were you doing at the Eagle's last night?"

"I was going to ask you the same thing. I thought you were done with that Guy person," Mark said. "Not that it's any of my business—"

"You're right on both counts. I am done with him, and it's none of your business. I was looking for Shelly. You?"

"I go in there once in a while, listen to what's going on, that kind of thing. I was trying to see if anyone noticed strangers around, and of course that was the wrong place to ask that question. I got an earful about all the strangers in town, most of them not speaking English—well, you know the drill. But nothing that seems to be related to all the John Does that we have popping up."

"Have there been more?" I asked.

"I'm not sure. Seems like the hospital has had a couple of drop-offs recently, guys without ID who didn't make it. One was stabbed, the other one OD-ed."

"So all together, how many are we talking about?"

"At least ten so far," Mark said. "I put out a query to the surrounding towns, see if any more have shown up. Or washed up."

"We have stabbings, hangings, one shooting, and now one overdose. Interesting array. Aside from the fact that they're all young, Middle-Eastern men, these killings have nothing in common."

"Nothing except that all the victims are unknowns."

There was silence. The air crackled between us.

"So, are you around later? Can we catch up?" he asked.

"Sure. Meet me at La Corona, around 8:00."

I resumed my stealth photography, trying my best to disappear into the crowd. I think I got a few good shots, and after uncomfortable encounters with the principals —I did have to get the names if we were going to print the photographs—I decided I had enough. In the car heading back to Jerome, I called the club, hoping to catch Peterson. Some man answered, told me Peterson had been fired, and hung up on me. Okay. When I got to my apartment, I called Mark back.

"Do you have any kind of relationship with old man Peterson at the Club?" I asked without prelude.

"Not really. I know who he is. Seems to be blind as a bat. Why?"

"I still think he knows something, and I couldn't get anything out of him, as you know. Why don't you give it a try?"

"I could—not sure what I could get, and whether it's worth drawing attention to the old guy."

"Well, he was just fired. I called over there and they said he was gone," I said.

"Oh. So how am I supposed to talk to him?"

I sighed. Did I have to do this guy's job for him? "Maybe you can find out where he lives and pay him a little visit," I said patiently. "Just try not to spook him out, he seems kind of skittish."

"I'll see what I can do," Mark said. "Anything else you want from me, boss?"

"An address for Shelly Loren would be very helpful," I said. "I'm heading to the library now, so call me if you get something. Please."

While I was talking to Mark, I had tacked up a map of the shoreline on the wall, and marked the locations of the bodies that had been discovered. The earliest, the hanging behind the Eagle's Club, seemed to be unrelated to the rest. Perhaps that had more to do with the thugs running the club than any international espionage, but at this point, everything was on the table. Until it wasn't.

I went directly to Mr. Argent's desk when I arrived at the library. The smile on his face vanished as soon as he recognized me. "You didn't call me," I said.

"No," he stammered. "I haven't had a minute."

"I want to talk to you now."

"Uh, sorry, no can do." He looked past me towards the checkout desk. "I really can't help you. Go away."

"You will help me. I need you to tell me where you met Raoul and how you came to spend time with him."

"I can't talk to you here. I'll get fired. I'm on probation, and if Macaroni sees me —"

"Cut the crap, Argent," I said. "You should have called me like you promised. Now, you're going to take me into the stacks and show me what I'm looking for. And when we're away from your co-workers, you're going to tell me what I want to know."

"Miss Quiñones, really, there's no need to threaten me," he said.

"Let's go."

He crossed his arms and looked away.

"Do you want me to go and tell your Miss Macaroni that you fondled me? I will, you know. If you don't help me, I'll make you pay."

He chuckled. "She'd never believe you. You're the wrong gender and about twenty-five years too old for my taste." He stood up. "But all right, just to get rid of you, I'll tell you. Come on."

I followed him upstairs into the far reaches of the non-fiction books. When he was sure that we were alone, he turned to face me again. "I heard that you were a real bitch; that you'd sell out your own mother. I didn't believe it, but now I've see it in action." He shook his head. "You're nothing like your brother."

"So do tell: How is it that you know so much about Raoul? I find it hard to believe that he would spend time with a worm like you."

"Hmph. You know nothing about me…. Anyway. There's not much to tell. I met Raoul at a single's event a few months ago. We shared some recreational drugs together in a hotel room, and occasionally I would seek him out to purchase more of his wares. That's it."

"You're telling me that my brother was dealing drugs?" I asked.

"Nothing bad," he said. "Nothing like heroin or even pot, just some prescription-grade stuff. No harm."

"And you met him at a singles dance? You don't mean to imply that he was gay, do you?"

"No, he was definitely straight. But a very reliable guy, no judgments, very solid. Everyone liked him."

I shook my head again. "I don't believe you."

"I don't care. I certainly don't feel a need to satisfy you. So, that's it. Now, will you please go away and leave me alone?"

I waved him off as I moved towards the stairs, already dialing Mark's number on my cell.

"No cell phones in the library!" Argent called out imperiously, following me to the door. I heard him stage-whisper to the clerk at the desk: "I found her on the phone in the stacks, so I just escorted her right out of the building!"

"Mark, Clara. Can you run a report on a man named Vincent Argent? He claims to know Raoul, says he was selling prescription meds. Let me know what you find." I left the message and sat in the car for a moment, thinking about this new piece of information.

What did I know so far? Raoul had been chasing gun runners, supposedly. He had stumbled on something else, that was certain. All along, we'd assumed it was related to terrorism. What if it was drugs? The connection, given the body census, seemed to be Middle Eastern, but what if it was drug smuggling that he'd uncovered? Although I remained skeptical, my training told me to pursue every lead and not draw conclusions until all the evidence was collected. This new information just added another dimension to the confusion surrounding the investigation.

I called Louie. Now there was a drug connection, as well as an underworld contact—and I did know that Raoul had been talking to Louie. Time to find out what they had shared. I woke him up.

"Christ almighty Lou, it's two in the afternoon. Don't you have a job? What do you do, sleep all day and party all night?"

"Did you call me just to criticize my lifestyle choices, or do you want something from me?" he grumbled. "I thought I told you not to call me again."

"Let me buy you breakfast. I can bring you a bagel and coffee—"

"Make it a Big Mac and large Diet Coke, and you've got a deal," he said.

"Oh, and a healthy diet too," I said. "Give me an address."

"You know where I live. I'm still in the house on Lillian Road," he said. "Oh, and don't forget the fries."

When he opened the door, dressed in a pair of plaid boxers and a filthy gray tee shirt that said "For Sale" on the front, Louie said, "I do have a job, bitch. Today's my damned day off." He took the bag I held out and left me to follow him into the townhouse. From the kitchen, I could hear the scrabbling of dog claws on linoleum, and the whimper of a caged pet. When the food bag was opened, and the scent of beef was released, the dog began to bark.

"Shut up," Louie yelled over his shoulder. He'd plopped into a recliner that looked like it was held together with packing tape and prayers, and arranged the food on a coffee table covered with porn. "Damned dog," he muttered. "So, what do you want?" he asked me after his third bite and second slurp.

"Tell me about Raoul and the prescription drugs."

"What about it?" he spoke with his mouth full of fries. Charming.

I sat on the easy chair across from him, pushing a pile of questionable laundry onto the floor, where it joined a similar stack. "You know about it. Just tell me what he was doing, whatever you know," I said.

"He was working at the shipyard, and selling some recreational pills on the side," he said. "That's all I know. He'd show up at a party, pour some pills in a bowl, and charge you $5 to pick one. It was fun. You never knew what you were going to get.

Later, I heard that he'd take orders for specific things, but I never dealt with him that way. Just pill party stuff."

"That's all?"

"As far as I know, that's all."

"Where was he getting the stuff?"

"How should I know?" he took a mouthful of soda. "One time, he asked to borrow my car, and I don't know where he went or what he needed it for: the car was back where I left it the next day, and I never saw him again."

"Do you remember the date?"

"What date? Today is the twenty-eighth, right?"

"Not today, you asshole. What day did he borrow your car?"

He shook his head, loaded up on fries again. The sight was nauseating. "Don't remember."

I was seething. "What about Mr. Argent, what do you know about him?"

"That perv?" he snorted. "Nothing. And I don't want to know anything about him."

"Seems like you know something, if you know that he's a perv and you don't want to be associated with him."

Louie stood up, tossed the wrappings from his meal into the vicinity of the kitchen. "That's it, your time's up."

I didn't move.

"Clara, get out. I've told you what I know, and that's all I have for you. Don't make me throw you out." He paused, scratching his armpit. "I will, you know. Or maybe I'll just call one of your old friends. How'd you like to see Rico again?"

"Louie, I don't know why you're acting this way with me. I brought you lunch, and I asked you a couple of little questions. Why the hostility? What did I do to you?"

"Let's not go there, Clara. I am trying to live my life here. You, you come in from New York City all important-like and you want us to drop everything to help you. That's not how it works here. Sure, we was friends growing up. But that was a long time ago. And I got no obligations as far as you and your brother are concerned. So, get out and don't come back." He walked towards the kitchen, where I could hear the dog ripping apart the MacDonald's papers. "Stuey, you hungry, boy? I got a friend here that you can meet." He looked back at me, smiling. "Wanna meet my pit bull?"

I decided to leave then, not eager to defend myself against another guard dog. When I got into the car, it still smelled like fried food, and I decided to stop at the grocery store for some produce. My guts were in a jumble, and it was probably due to a steady diet of tension and fast food. It was apple time in New England, and some Macouns with a hunk of cheddar would be just the thing to tide me over until I met Mark at La Corona.

Raoul

HE NEEDED TO GIVE them something, enough to make them back off on the drugs, enough to give him a small window through which to escape. Raoul decided to share some of his activities undercover with the Puerto Rican Revolutionary Guard, the group he'd infiltrated and eventually bought down. Although it was against policy to ever reveal the details behind an operation—no matter how long ago—in this case Raoul knew he had to give up something real to buy himself some time. And, he thought with a cringe, if he got fired, that would not be the worst thing that could happen.

"Ismail," the Leader crooned his name. "Have you thought about your options? I'm afraid that we are a bit pressured for time, and so I can't let you rest any longer. The doctor here has something nice for you, something that is guaranteed to make you talk. Doctor?"

Raoul winced as he saw the needle approach. "Wait," he said. "I'll tell you whatever you want to know. Just wait."

The needle punctured his skin and silenced the pleading. Warmth shot into his chest and he felt the vessels in his neck expand. His eyeballs felt hot.

"Ask me your questions!" he gasped. Sweat poured off his forehead and stung his eyes.

"Ismail, tell me about your work with the FBI," the Leader said. "Or should I call you Raoul? We can let go of that other identity now, can't we? No one is going to be looking for Ismail, no one will notice that he's gone. But Raoul, let's assume, has been in contact with some people in Washington. You were reporting on all our training, weren't you? Our little exercises?" The Leader lit a cigarette, held the hot match to Raoul's inner arm. The smell of burning hair filled the room, and Raoul strained against his bindings.

"It has nothing to do with you," Raoul said. Every word was agony to release, but he took a breath and continued. "I was sent here to find out who was smuggling weapons out of the naval base. That's it. No one is interested in you or your plans."

"More."

"I have made friends with some Puerto Rican nationalists, they work at the shipyard, and I've been getting closer to them in order to find out how they have been getting the weapons out."

"And?"

"And, I have been working on some connections. Mostly from the Eagle's Club, some guys at the gym, lots of different leads. Nothing about you, I swear. I have not told anyone about what is happening at the mosque," Raoul said. "I swear."

"Really? Well, let's see. What is happening at the mosque? What do you think?"

"I'm really not sure. I think maybe you are training some guys to go back to Pakistan and run some guerilla operations there."

"That's all. And you 'swear' that you haven't told anyone about it? Not about the hand-to-hand training? That you killed a man with your bare hands last week?"

"Nothing. Why would I tell anyone that? I'd get thrown in jail."

"Ah. I see." The Leader sat on a chair pulled close to the bed. Occasionally, he flicked his ashes onto Raoul's naked limbs, but he was beyond feeling that pain. Whatever the medication had been intended to do, it was having a definite impact on the heart and breathing rates of the young captive. "Tell me, Mr. Secret Agent, what have you been doing at the mosque every night? If your real work was with the Puerto Ricans at the club, why spend so much time with our little group?"

Raoul gasped as the Leader ground out his cigarette on Raoul's thigh muscle. He shook his head from side to side, grimacing and gasping for breath.

"Nothing to say about that? You spend months with us, praying and eating our food, and participating in our training. Why waste your time? Why create a false identity if you were not trying to infiltrate our group?" He looked at the doctor. "Hit him again."

"No, no, wait," Raoul said. "I joined the mosque because it was a place for me to go and—you know—pray. I liked the guys there. I liked the feeling of belonging somewhere. That's all. I swear that's all I wanted."

"And the name? Ismail? Who needs a fake name to join a religion?"

Raoul winced as a second needle was inserted between his toes. Icy tendrils shot up his leg, constricted his belly, and caused him to shudder. His bladder and bowels loosened again, and the Leader stood up. "Get the hose," he said to the guard at the door. "Clean him off—and then bring the jumper cables in here." He turned to Raoul. "I'll be back. Think about your answers carefully. I don't have time for your fairy tales any longer. I want to know who you talked to, and exactly what you told them."

A garden hose was used to rinse the feces from his body as Raoul panted on the bed. A tarp was dragged from under the metal bed frame, replaced by another. The guards, silent when the Leader was in the room, chatted in a combination of Urdu and English, mostly using the English to comment disparagingly about Raoul's physique, especially the shriveled junk they liked to flick with blasts of freezing water.

"Ismail, look at your shrunken dick," they taunted. "Pretty soon, it will disappear entirely and you'll be just like a woman." They streamed water up his nose until he retched and passed out, choking.

"You two, take that out. It's almost time to leave, so get rid of this mess and go pack your things. Your group is leaving in an hour," the Leader said when he came back into the room.

Ali, the younger boy, nodded and grabbed the corners of the tarp. The other young man hesitated, and then turned back to the Leader. "Sir, where are we going?"

"You don't need to know. We will be relocating everyone until we know for sure what this traitor has told his bosses. Now move!" The Leader returned to Raoul's side, jabbed him with one of the clamps hanging from a battery on a cart. He attached one to each of Raoul's toes, and then flicked a switch. The current jolted Raoul from unconsciousness, and he screamed.

"Duct tape," the Leader said, and the doctor handed him a piece to slap over Raoul's mouth. He fiddled with the gauges and flicked a switch to administer another burst of power.

"How do you feel now?" he asked. "Ready to talk more?"

Raoul nodded, and the duct tape was ripped off. "I told you, I was sent here to look for gun smugglers," Raoul said. "There are a whole lot of weapons missing from the naval base, and I was assigned to find out who is taking the stuff, and how, and where it's going. That's it. And so far, I haven't gotten anything. In fact, they called me back in because I have nothing to report. That's the truth." His statement was garbled by a scream as the doctor injected another solution into the webbing between his splayed fingers.

"That doesn't answer for me why you kept coming to the mosque. And if it was just for the religion, then why the fake name, Ismail? I'm not buying it." The Leader ground another cigarette into the soft tissue under Raoul's arm. "No, I don't believe you. I need to know exactly what you reported to your superiors about our activity at the mosque. And you will stay here until I am satisfied. Doctor? Let's give your patient a little excitement, shall we?" The two men removed the clamps from Raoul's bloody feet and placed them higher, one on the ball sack and the other on his erect left nipple.

Raoul passed out after the first jolt.

"What do you think?" the Leader asked the doctor.

"I don't have much left—and I think it might take you a while to get him to break. He's really good. I don't think anyone else could hold out this long."

"You think he's telling the truth?"

The doctor shook his head. "No, but I think you've run out of time on this. I'd move everyone out, and get rid of him."

"This one has connections with people in town. He won't be a simple body dump like the others. We need to make his death look like something else. And discredit him with his superiors, in case he has told them about our plans."

"Well, he's loaded with drugs, so it could be a dispute between dealers. Or that he owes money.…"

"Okay, that's what we'll do. Send one of the boys out to get some heroin. We'll fix our friend up right." The Leader called out. "Yusuf, pack him up in something. Try that big duffel bag. We're bringing him to his apartment. Tonight."

Clara

I HEADED TO MY apartment and started making calls. Shelly had a mailbox that was not set up—what a surprise. Petersen was not in the phone book, and Mark's cell went straight to voicemail. I gazed at the map, hoping that the colorful pins would show me the way to look. We'd found Raoul's apartment, and it was clean. He had hidden some papers on Stagger Lee, and those were in an elaborate code that I had yet to break. His gym locker yielded nothing, so far, and yet here I was given evidence that Mijo had been running drug parties. Where were the drugs? Where did he keep them, and where was all the money he'd collected?

Undercovers are just people, with homes and families and a somewhat different job: they assume another identity and go off to live that other life for a period of time that may end up being years. Needless to say, most marriages did not withstand this kind of pressure. I was certain that Mijo had no wife or girlfriend, but he must have had a place where he could be himself. To call in and report, to make notes and store evidence, even just to be able to nap without worry. Where was his place?

It had been a while since I'd been on active duty, in fact, but I remember that there was an entire office staffed with people who kept the lights on when you went under. Paid your bills, watered your plants; basically, they maintained your life while you were playing someone else's. I called my contact in that office to see if they had Raoul's file.

"Shaniqua, how are you girl?" I said.

"Who is this?"

"It's me, Clara Quiñones. Remember?"

"Sorry, you've got the wrong number."

"And the wrong Shaniqua? I don't think so. Listen, don't hang up. I just need a tiny bit of information from you. Remember my brother Raoul—you always said you wanted to turn down his sheets. Remember him?"

"Uh-huh. Maybe. So?"

"Well, he was under and he got killed, and I need to find out where he was living. For the family, you know. For my mama." I was laying it on thick, but I knew the way into Shaniqua's database was through her heart. "We just want closure, you know? And to get his belongings back would be a wonderful thing for my mother."

"I hear you, girl, but I can't help you," Shaniqua said. "I'm sorry for your loss. Your brother was one fine man."

"Wait, what do you mean you can't help me? You don't have access to his file?"

"There is no file. Dude was the only agent I ever heard of who didn't keep a crib somewhere. He was off the radar completely. No apartment, no post office box, nothing."

"What about bank accounts? You must have been depositing his paycheck somewhere," I said.

"No. He told us to keep it 'on account' in house. When he came in from a job, he'd stop by and sign for a check. Sometimes big money. Then he'd supposedly go and rent something until the next gig came along. That's what I hear anyway. I never talked to him personally, since I'm the scheduler and he ain't had nothing to schedule. You dig? I'm sorry about this, but I shouldn't have even told you what I just did." She hung up.

Damn. I studied my phone, idly scrolling through the list of names. "Stud?" I read aloud. Who the hell—oh, I remember: Jack, the guy guarding Stagger Lee. He had the fourth lock box. Maybe there was something in there that could help me, if I could just get it from him. Since I had stolen three of the boxes, it was pretty likely he would not want to share the last one with me. I knew it was a gamble, but I had to go back there. This time, in addition to kibble, I strapped a gun to my ankle.

As soon as it was dark enough, I headed to the back side of the boat yard. "Damn," I hissed when I saw that the fence had been repaired. I rattled around looking for another possible entrance, and then arrived at my least favorite conclusion: I had to climb over to get inside. I tossed some dog biscuits over first, hoping to distract the dog long enough to avoid getting bit in the ass. Like clockwork, when the fence began to rattle, the dog came bounding out between the hulking shadows of rotting wood, and greeted both me and the kibble with equal affection. That's not true—he was happier to see the kibble.

By the time I found Stagger Lee, Jack had found me. Tonight, he held a shotgun casually over his arm while he smoked a cigar with his free hand.

"Well, lookie here. See what the dog dragged in. You forget something, girl? You forget that you promised to come back? To help me open those boxes and divvy up the take?"

"Yeah, well, you already took a box, I noticed. There was nothing but more notebooks in mine. And the one you kept? What was in it?"

He laughed. "Nothing for you. I shot it open; found a plastic bag full of pills and some cash. Which I am keeping. Both of them. And you're going to give me the rest."

"I told you, there was nothing in my boxes. You really found pills, huh?" I was disappointed, despite all the evidence to the contrary: I hoped they were wrong about Raoul selling drugs.

"You really found pills, huh?" Jack mimicked me. "Yep, and I want the rest. You opened those boxes and took the stuff for yourself, and that was not the deal. So hand it over."

"If I had already gotten what you say, why would I be coming back here, climbing over the stupid fence? Huh? And we had no deal. And if we did have a deal, you broke it by taking one of the boxes out of the boat." I paused, took a breath. "Look, I don't care about the pills, or the money—you keep whatever you found. I just want to know if there was anything else in the box. That's all I want. If there was a notebook or another key or anything like that. Please, give it to me. You have no use for it, and I need it."

Jack climbed aboard the boat and sat on top of the locker. "Come on up," he gestured with the gun. "I'm not going to hurt you."

Once I was in the boat and settled by leaning against the side, Jack relit his cigar and took a puff.

"You're not supposed to inhale those, you know," I said.

"Won't make fuck-all difference to me," he said. "I got cancer anyway, might as well live it up while I can still inhale." He took another drag. "The pills I found will come in very handy," he said. "And the money—whoa, there was a lot of money in there. All wrapped up and hidden in the bottom of the box. I'd a never found it if I hadn't broken the box with a sledgehammer."

"Anything else?"

He reached into a back pocket and took out a moleskin notebook. "Something like this?" he asked.

"Yes. Can I have it?"

"Say 'pretty please'," he said.

"Pretty please, Jack, with sugar on top or cocaine or whatever the hell you want. Can I have the notebook, Jack?"

He tossed it at me. "Now get lost."

"That's it?" I scrambled to my feet.

"Get out of here before I change my mind," he said. "And don't send any of your cop friends in here to look for those drugs, either. Then I won't be so charitable about letting you get away."

"Thanks," I said. "Good luck with that cancer thing." I didn't have time to figure out why he was letting me go. I jumped off the boat and jogged to my car. My phone went off as soon as I started the engine: Mark.

"Hello," I said.

"Hey, Clara. We've got something. Where are you? How soon can you meet me?"

"Where? What's happening? What did you find?"

"Come to the station, I'll fill you in there."

"On my way." I threw the car into gear and made it to the station in record time. Mark was standing at the reception desk when I walked in. He buzzed me through and I followed him to his office. Once the door was closed, he turned and smiled. "We hit pay dirt, finally," he said.

"What did you find?"

"Remember I told you they arrested Shelly driving an old van. Well, it was Raoul's. I think it was where he lived. It sure looks like his headquarters."

"What took you so long to find it?" I sat down and watched him pace. "You guys arrested Shelly more than a week ago."

"It was sitting in impound, just a rusty heap. The guys looked around, didn't see anything of value, and locked it up. Finally, the forensics guys finished another case and went over to look at it. Raoul had the entire thing rigged with all kinds of secret compartments and special features. The damned thing had a hemi engine in it, solar panels hidden on the roof that produced enough juice to run a computer and lots of other equipment. And we found money. Lots of money, stashed under the floor-boards along with notebooks and pictures. Dozens of photos, most of them from inside some kind of meeting room. We started running the pictures, but just by looking at them, I could ID two of our John Does. So he was involved with them."

"But who is 'them'?" I asked. "Any clues about who the hell these people are, and what they were planning?"

"No, but we just started going through the stuff…. If he wrote it down, it's got to be in there. Maybe there's a log on his computer, I don't know." He stopped and sat on the edge of the desk. "Isn't this great? Aren't you happy? We're finally getting some answers."

"Yeah, yeah, it's great," I said. "Can I have a look at the stuff?"

"Well, that might be a problem," he said. He held up a hand when I started to protest. "How about this—when the guys get off shift tonight, I'll take you in. Around 11:00. Okay? I can't bring you down there when everyone's around. I told you, you can be involved, but not out front."

I shrugged. "Eleven. Should I come through the back door or what?"

"I thought we were having dinner tonight. We'll come over after that," he said.

I agreed and slipped out of the office, eager to get back to my apartment and start deciphering the code in the notebooks. These cops, I thought to myself, they are never going to be able to figure anything out without my help. I was the only one who was going to be able to make sense of it. That, at the very least, was what I could do to honor my brother. *Mijo.*

Raoul

THEY UNTIED HIM. THEY dropped him on the floor and rolled him in a tarp. He was still breathing, barely, but no one seemed to care either way. The entire household was in an uproar, laundry being done, floors and walls scrubbed with bleach, and car by car, groups of two or three men leaving for destinations unknown. They prayed together, in the empty living room, before the Leader sent each group off with a map and a blessing.

The doctor injected a sedative into Raoul shortly before he was bent and fitted into the duffel. Although he was five foot eight, he was thin, and, it turned out, very flexible. His body was tossed into the trunk of a sedan and left until the sun fully set. It was a hot day, and wrapped in the tarp, sweltering in the duffel bag, closed up in the trunk of a car, it was a miracle that Raoul did not die. It would have been a mercy if he had, but the sedative slowed his heartbeat to hibernation levels and so he floated, tethered to life by a thread.

When the house was empty and all but four men were gone—to Florida, or Mexico, or Canada, to wait for another opportunity to serve Allah—the Leader looked around satisfied that they had left no evidence. "We bring him to his apartment now," he said. "You two will watch over him and I will visit the mosque to pray one last time. I'll be there soon to finish our business with Ismail."

When the limp body had been carried upstairs and transferred onto the bed, the Leader left the men alone. "Metin, you stay at the door. Keep this gun. Do not let anyone in the apartment," he said. "Do you understand?"

Metin looked wide-eyed at the weapon and stuck it in the waistband of his pants. He nodded.

"I will call you from the car to let you know when I am coming upstairs," the Leader continued. "I have a key, so I will let myself in. Make sure you don't shoot me."

Metin nodded again. The Leader placed his large hand on Metin's bony shoulder.

"Don't worry, my son," he said. "We are almost at the door to paradise. Keep calm and pray to Allah. You will meet the virgins in heaven very soon." He turned to Salim. "You, stand guard over the body. Do not let him move. If he tries to break his restraints, give him a dose of drugs with the syringes that the Doctor left there, in the bag by the bed."

Salim nodded and assumed a military stance inside the bedroom door. "Do I get a weapon?" he asked.

"You don't really need one, do you?" the Leader said and half-smiled. "You are a weapon, one of the best I've ever trained." He snapped a salute at the young man. "I'll be back in an hour, and then we'll get on with our mission."

After the door closed, both Metin and Salim listened to the kitchen clock tick. Noise from the street penetrated the apartment, and they could hear car traffic as well as the sound of pedestrians on the sidewalk below. The corner was infamous for its drug peddling activity, and occasionally the loud bass from oversized speakers vibrated the windows in their panes. Once, the scream of a siren caused Metin to pull the gun from his belt.

After it passed, he hissed, "Salim, you there?"

Salim stepped into the kitchen. "Where would I be?"

"Did you hear that?"

"What, the siren? How could I not hear it? Believe me; no one is coming after us. No one is going to rescue this guy, cuz no one knows he's even here. Don't be so jumpy. And put that damned gun away before you shoot one of us by accident. Damn." Salim walked over to Metin, took the gun from his shaking hands, and put it on the kitchen counter. "Just relax. Take some deep breaths." He looked around. "Man, it's hot in here. I'm going to hit the AC, cool things down. Maybe block out some of that sound."

"How will we know if someone is coming then?" Metin said.

"Believe me, if they are coming for us, they're not going to announce their arrival with sirens," Salim said. "Chill man. We're almost done here."

Once the air conditioner was on in the living room, Salim stepped back into the bedroom. From his vantage point, he could see Metin's back, his eye pressed against the peephole in the door. Speaking softly, he said, "Metin, can you hear me now?" There was no response.

He directed his gaze to the man restrained in the bed. Raoul was staring at his captor; his eyes clear despite the days of drugs and torture. Salim cocked an eyebrow.

"I suppose you know who I am," he said.

Raoul nodded.

"I used to look up to you. I wanted to be just like you," Salim paused. He smiled, shaking his head. "Look at us now. Two guys who couldn't cut it, never finished the job we started out doing."

Raoul knitted his brow questioningly.

"You know, the whole 'Eagle Scouting' thing. You never finished your project. And I had some crazy idea that I was going to do it, yeah; I was going to pick up where you left off—Huh. Never did it, though." There was silence while Salim checked his companion in the other room. "You know, I always thought my mother had a thing for you. Like, maybe, you might be my father or something crazy like that. But then one day she told me what happened, so now I know. Yeah, my dad's no hero FBI man; he's just some asshole rapist dude. Cool, right? That your mom tells you one day, by the way, the only reason you're here is cuz I was raped and I don't believe in abortion, but I love you. Really?"

He cracked all the knuckles in his hands one by one, and then cracked his neck, left—right, and walked to the window. The room was steamy and the smell of urine was overpowering.

"Mind if I turn on the air? It's getting funky in here, man." Salim looked at Metin, then at Raoul, and turned on the AC in the bedroom. "You want me to take off the gag for a few minutes? Promise not to scream or anything? I mean, I really did admire you growing up and all, and I hate to see this but you know, we got no choice here, it's got to be done." He pulled the wad of rags out of Raoul's mouth, and checked Metin again.

"Okay, it's cool. So, like, tell me, who did you tell about this mission? I mean, you can really help me out here, man. I'll be like a hero with the Leader if I can give him something good when he gets back here, you know?"

"Why should I help you?"

"I—Man, you don't get it. You are going to die in, like, thirty minutes or something. So why not help a dude get ahead, you know?"

"And you, Silvio Rossi, you're okay with being a part of a mission to kill thousands of people?"

Salim shook his head. "What do you want me to say? I'm the son of a rapist, man. I got no moral fibers or nothing. I can relate to these dudes, their country is being raped by the American devil, you know?"

"I'm sorry you believe that," Raoul said. "Your mother loves you, and she is a wonderful person. You are the son of a beautiful, loving human being who would do anything for you. She has done everything for you."

"You ain't got much time, here, man, so let's cut to the chase. What can you give me?" Salim paced back and forth between the door and the bed, huffing impatiently. He stopped abruptly, picked up Raoul's hand and twisted it behind his head. When Raoul struggled, Salim placed the rag back in the other man's mouth. He checked on Metin—still facing the peephole—and moved Raoul's hand against the headboard of the bed where he quickly snapped the bone in Raoul's ring finger.

Raoul bucked and struggled until Salim clamped his hand over the older man's mouth. "Shut up," he hissed. "Settle down." He pushed Raoul's head hard into the mattress, letting up only when the fighting abated. He watched while Raoul tried to catch his breath.

"Dammit, I told you we could help each other," Salim said. He fumbled through the bag of syringes on the floor next to the bed. "Why can't you just do what I say? Do I have to give you one of these shots? The Leader wants you awake when he gets back, so settle down." He stuck a needle into Raoul's bicep and injected a small dose of fluid into the muscle.

"There, just a little hit to take the edge off," he said. "Now. You are going to give me a name."

He stood back and waited. Raoul's eyes were closed but gradually he opened them and stared at Salim. After a solid minute, he nodded. Salim reached over and removed the gag again. "No yelling," he cautioned.

Raoul nodded. "But you have to do something for me, too."

"Why should I?"

"I guarantee if you do this, and for some reason you get caught, you will not get the death penalty. In fact, you'll be able to argue that you were being coerced by the Leader. If you help me get a message to my sister, you can use it as proof that you were an unwilling participant—"

"Why would you think I would want my legacy to be that? I want my death to have a meaning. I want to be a martyr for the cause—"

"Oh, cut the crap," Raoul said. "You're just an opportunistic kid. Believe me; I recognize it when I see it. You deliver a message to my sister, and she'll take care of you if for some reason you don't end up dead."

"That's all you want? And you'll give me a name? You'll tell me who you told about our plans."

"Yes."

"For sure?"

"Yes. Scout's honor." Raoul grimaced. "Get me a pen, and hurry before I pass out again."

Salim went into the kitchen. "Metin, my man, how's it going? Any movement in the hallway?"

"No man. All quiet."

"Good job. It's almost time. You stay put." Salim took an index card from an open package on the counter and found a pen in the drawer.

"What are you doing?" Metin asked.

"Writing my will," Salim said.

"Should I do that?" Metin asked.

"Just keep praying," Salim said. "You can do yours later."

"Okay."

Salim took the card into the bedroom and shook Raoul. He had drifted off and was hard to rouse. "Hey, wake up, it's almost time."

Raoul looked at Salim. "Silvio, what are you doing here?" he asked.

"Come on, just write your note," Salim said. "Quit fooling around."

Raoul looked at his hand; the third finger ballooned to twice its size. "I can't write. You do it."

Salim sighed. "What do you want to write?"

"Just put these letters: C, colon. That's the two dots on top of each other. Right. Then capital A, capital B, period, capital R. Let me see. Yes. That's it. Make sure she gets it."

Salim looked at it for a moment before he stuck the card in his back pocket. "You're a strange one, man. What kind of message is that? Some kind of code? You're not setting me up, are you?"

"Nah, don't worry. It's from our childhood. Just means, you know, I love you."

"All right, then," Salim said. "So now, tell me. Who did you talk to? Who knows about the mission?"

Metin's cell phone rang.

"What do I do?" Metin called from the kitchen.

Salim went to the door. "Who's calling?"

Metin looked at the phone. "It's the Leader."

"Answer it."

"Hello?" He said. "Yes. Yes." He hung up. "He's here. Coming up now. Make sure the prisoner is ready." He picked up the gun and stood at the door.

Salim went back into the room. "Tell me now!" he hissed.

"I'll tell you this—your Leader is going to kill you. Be ready. Once you've done his dirty work, he's going to get rid of you. Be ready to defend yourself."

"That's bullshit. I'm his right-hand man. Now, tell me what I want to know."

Raoul shut his eyes.

The door opened. The Leader entered the room.

Clara

I BUSIED MYSELF IN the hours until dinner studying Raoul's code book and the entries in his daily logs. I couldn't wait to get to the van, to see the reality of Mijo's life as an undercover here in Jerome. I knew he was a hero; I was certain that he'd been on the trail of something large. If they'd listened to him, the idiots on the naval base, would he have been able to stop the attacks? Or even, could he have saved his own life? I knew that these investigations rarely wrapped up as neatly as we'd like, but I felt that the pieces were going to vindicate my baby brother. In this spirit of optimism, I called my sister Carmen.

"Hey, it's me," I began.

"Who?"

"Your sister, Clara."

"Oh. Hi. Are you still around? I thought you went back to New York," she said.

"No, I'm still here. I found out some things about Mijo's murder that I thought you should know. You can decide how much to tell Mama," I said. No reply. "Well, okay then. So, you know he was murdered?"

"No shit," she said. "Thanks for telling me that."

"Just listen. It wasn't anything bad that Mijo did. He was working undercover and these men—"

"What? He was undercover here, in Jerome? No."

"Yes, he was looking for someone stealing weapons from the base. He was in Jerome for a few months, I guess. We haven't got an exact date when he started this assignment."

"I can't tell Mama that he was here and he never came to see her; that would be worse for her. And you don't know how long—so maybe he just got into town, and he hadn't had the chance to get over to the apartment yet." She sounded hopeful, spinning a yarn to make things better. That was a family trait I had not inherited.

"Whatever. That's not what I was calling to tell you."

"Of course you don't think that part is important, because it was never important to you to stay in touch with family. Your own mother—when was the last time you called her? Or came for a visit? He wasn't like that. He was nothing like you."

How little she knew about us, after all, and it wasn't going to be my job to tell her. "Listen to me, I'm just going to tell you once and you decide what you want to do about it. I think that Raoul stumbled onto a group here in Jerome that was part of the plot to attack the World Trade Center. He tried to stop them, he tried to alert the authorities, but they didn't believe him. And then, before he could convince anyone, the group killed him."

I heard her exhale slowly. "Don't tell anyone else," she said eventually.

"Okay, you tell the family in your own way," I said.

"I'm never going to tell them, and you shouldn't either," she said. "Can you this one time keep your damned mouth closed? No press, no 'hero' shit in the newspapers, okay? Can you do that?"

"But why?" I asked. "He was a hero—he tried to stop the attacks. He was killed because he tried to stop it. Why shouldn't we tell everyone?"

"He failed. That's why. Once again, you don't get it. He's no hero. He'll be a laughingstock. 'The man who could not stop the terrorists from killing thousands of people.' Big deal."

"I can't believe—"

"Oh, cut the crap. You, after all, you figured you'd get a big fucking parade when you came back to Jerome, didn't you? Miss Special Agent, bringing down a big gang all by herself. Remember that?" she asked, voice reaching new heights. "Well, you didn't live here. You didn't hear the insults and the threats. Those people you arrested back then, they were our neighbors. Our friends. They had kids, and mortgages, and lives. And you ruined them. So no, I don't think Jerome would embrace another Quiñones hero."

"And Mama, shouldn't she know that her son died trying to save people from the attack?"

"She already thinks that. In her mind, Raoul died in the towers. And she already believes he was a hero," she said. "So you leave her alone. Leave all of us alone." She hung up.

I couldn't wait until 8:00, I called Mark. "Did you find a gun in the van?" I asked without preliminaries.

"Yes, it was taped under the driver's seat. Why do you ask?"

"How about his credentials? Badge?"

"No. Why?"

"He was made. His badge should have been in the van with his gun. He'd never have his credentials with him. Never."

"How would we know the importance of something we didn't have? Shelly took his stuff, remember, but there was no badge."

"They made him as an undercover, that's why the elaborate killing scene. Otherwise, they'd have dumped him in the river like the others."

"Okay," he said slowly. "What difference does it make?"

"I don't know," I said. "I just think we're missing something." I paused. "See you at 8:00, then."

Point by point, painstakingly, I went over what we had. There were an awful lot of holes, but it slowly became clear that Raoul had been juggling two investigations, and maintaining two different identities. Which of those had lead to his death? That was the question I could not answer yet.

Raoul loved code, and so I spent an hour trying to separate things into two categories: drugs and terrorism. Nothing indicated that he had any success tracking down the missing weapons, although I would not be surprised to find another notebook with that information coded an entirely different way.

The drug dealing was recent, that I could tell from the date coding. It started in July, or possibly June, since both months could have been coded as '10.' We'd argued when developing that code as kids: problems with January and April also presented themselves.

"January is easy," Mijo had argued. "Since it's a J-A and not a J-U. What if we do J-Y and J-E? that would make their codes 11 for January, 15 for June, and 31 for July. Simple!" He had been pleased, but, as usual, I argued against the solution.

"It's too high. How can we have 31 as a month code? Won't that mess everything up?"

"Exactly. If you don't really know the code, you'd never get it. It's perfect."

I remember trying for days to find another solution to the January problem, but Raoul had been satisfied with his solution. And here it was. He'd reversed the dates after all: His first pill party was June 13, 2001: 101315. He had the weight of the bags of pills before and after the parties, and a dollar amount shown as a timestamp. Bless Mijo and his gadgets: the fishing scale on his all-purpose tool must have come in handy. How else would he be able to account for the volume of drugs? No way could he take the time to count hundreds of pills, and knowing my brother, spend precious minutes separating them into types and looking up their composition in the PDR. So he weighed the bags.

Some parties were better than others; obviously, once the word spread, they became more popular. From twenty-five to five-hundred grams at one little soiree. That's a lot of pills to sell at five bucks a pop.

It appeared that he had documented all the drug dealing activities meticulously. He was careful like that, always.

Most of his entries were titled COD, and I spent an hour trying to figure out what that meant. Coding can be fun, but not if you don't create a key. What was fun in childhood had evolved into a professional system, one he probably didn't have to think twice about. I wondered again how his superiors felt about his improvisations. COD: could it be as simple as cash on delivery? It nagged at me, but I moved to other things.

The lists of numbers in his battered little notebooks were probably daily logs. JD was probably his day job, since it appeared five times a week with what seemed to be straightforward time records. He worked, ate lunch with different guys at the FT—must be food truck—and went to the gym (OW) most afternoons. Receipts for bike shop purchases and repairs confirmed that he either traveled by foot or bicycle: smart, keeping the van hidden from sight. But why borrow Louie's car when he had his own transportation? Somehow, he must have felt that there was a possibility he was being followed. "Always respect the gut," he said. In time, that had been shortened to "gut," a golden rule that we both respected. In this case, his gut was right, but he didn't get out in time. Or did he?

I stopped reading and leaned back in my chair. What if he knew that his cover was compromised, but he still went back? Or what if one of the operations had been compromised by the other—say the Muslims found out about the drug smuggling? They might have killed him, but probably not in the manner they chose. I'd wager they would have dumped him in the Sound like all the other no-name bodies that had come ashore later, if he'd been a mere sinner in their eyes and not a potential threat to their entire operation.

If there was something he thought he could stop, or someone he needed to protect, Mijo would have stayed undercover. I had no doubt about this. This was the kind of thing that drove supervisors crazy—why they insisted on absolute obedience, and seldom got it: if an undercover had a gut and refused to walk away, the collateral damage to others in the field could be high. But most of the agents I knew had at one time or another refused to come out. Could be they turned, that they liked the life inside more than out; could be they believed that only they could solve the case or stop the bad things from happening. And once in a while, they stayed in to save someone, to get someone out of the life or remove them from possible harm. In this case, which scenario fit? Had he gone back to rescue Silvio, or had Silvio been the one who identified Raoul and turned him in as a prize catch?

I headed to the restaurant early, my head spinning with code. It was about 7:00 and the parking lot was jammed, so I found a spot on a side street and walked over. The night was sultry, with a hint of the coming autumn in the air. The lobby was packed with patrons and I slid through the crowd into the bar, which was uncharacteristically raucous. The woman behind the bar was crazy-eyed, slopping wine into glasses and pulling beer taps randomly. A waiter came to my side as I watched the chaos.

"Miss," he spoke into my ear. "Are you a friend of Miss Mary Kate?"

I nodded. "What's happening? Where is she?"

"We don't know—some kind of family emergency."

"Oh, I should go...." My first instinct was to go to the hospital; maybe her dad had taken ill.

"Please, Miss, just a moment," he said, holding my elbow. "It would be more help, perhaps, if you could stay here." He lifted his chin towards the bar. "She cannot handle this, she tries, but—"

I shook my head. "What? You want me to bartend?"

"Yes, can you?" he nodded eagerly. "You are friend of Miss Mary Kate, and you can help, yes?"

I found myself propelled gently behind the bar. My bag was stowed under the register and before I knew it, my hands were sticky with beer glasses. Anyone who ordered a mixed drink was encouraged to reconsider, or wait until I could get to it, and so mostly the crowd turned supportive and stuck with beer and wine. My companion behind the bar, a lovely woman named Rita who usually helped at the reservation desk, stayed until we caught up with the orders and then washed her hands before returning to the door. "Thank you," she whispered.

"Wait," I said. "Do you know what's happened to Mary Kate?"

She shook her head. "She got a call and ran out of here a few hours ago," Rita said. "No one has heard from her since."

I continued to fill orders for the waiters and managed to keep satisfied the thirsty group clutching buzzers and waiting for tables. I had no idea of the time when I looked up and saw Mark grinning on a barstool. "What can I get you?" I asked, wiping the counter in front of him.

"I'll take a Bud," he said. "What are you doing back there?"

I poured the beer and explained the crisis, and asked him to see if he could find out what happened. Before I finished pouring, he was on the phone with the EMTs. I watched his expression as I poured a Chardonnay and mixed a gin and tonic. When I could, I leaned across the bar and tried to hear his conversation, but he held me off with a raised finger. From his face, I knew it was not good.

I filled a glass with club soda, chucked in a lime, and leaned against the back counter, assessing the crowd. It was almost 9:00, and while most of the patrons had been seated, I still had a solid group enjoying their libations. Funny, I didn't think of this as the kind of restaurant where the bar was a main attraction, and the last time I'd been here, there had been just one lonely guy sitting here.

I saw my captor and called him over. "So, what gives?" I asked him. "Why are there so many people here tonight? Something going on?"

"Oh, yes, that's for sure, Miss." He nodded. "The place down the street, Pisa, it was raided today and the door is locked tonight. That's where most of this bar crowd usually goes. So we have a big chance tonight, you know? But then Miss Mary Kate is not here and we have no real bartender, and so Miss Rita tries to do it—but you, Miss, you have saved the day!"

"Well, I was happy to help. You don't have a bartender, really? Okay, so who can take over for me? I'm supposed to have dinner…."

He looked panicked. "Can you stay just a little longer, Miss? I will ask the waiters. But you know, they are making more in tips, so I don't think anyone will want to go behind the bar. But I will ask," he said.

When I turned back, Mark was off the phone. He looked glum.

"What? Is it her father?" I asked.

He shook his head. "Her son, Silvio. The one you asked me about? He attempted suicide tonight. It's a real mess. He held his little sister hostage until Mary Kate got home, then threatened to kill the whole family, said he had a bomb. He did have a knife and a gun, but that's all. She was able to get the other kid out, but he stabbed her."

"Is she alright?"

"She'll be fine, I think. Physically at least. She went down; he got the gun and shot himself in the head. He's still alive, I guess, but I don't know how bad it is. They're both at the hospital. Do you want me to take you there?"

"I do, but—" I looked around. "Maybe I can help her more by staying here. Do you mind? You can eat at the bar. I'll bring you a menu. When things calm down, we can go to the hospital."

"That's fine with me."

"I wonder… I know Silvio was having problems. I still haven't figured out his connection to Raoul, if there was one. I mean, Mary Kate asked Raoul to find the kid, and then Silvio was home but he wouldn't leave his room, and now this. What do you think?"

"I've seen this before, and I don't know what to tell you. It's pretty common. Kid gets messed up with drugs or gambling, goes crazy. Sometimes it's more, they'll be diagnosed with schizophrenia or bipolar or something bad like that. But mostly it's drugs. And when they get a hold of guns, it gets ugly." He shook his head. "I don't know what to tell you. I've got two daughters, and I think about sending them away to boarding school every day. To a convent, if that's what it will take to keep them safe. But my wife—"

"Ah, your wife. How did you explain being out on a Friday night? Work? Meeting with a snitch? Or is it a snatch?"

"Don't be crude," he said. He looked at the menu. "So, how long do you think you have to stay here? I can have an appetizer, and we can take something to go later, bring it back to your place—"

I walked away. I was suddenly angry at him, angry at myself: frustrated at the entire world. What was wrong with men, that they couldn't stay home and fuck their wives? Why did they always want someone else—and what was wrong with me, for always being that someone else? Damn. I cleaned the counter, dried some glasses, and poured more gin. From the corner of my eye, I saw Mark waving his menu.

"Can I order something?" he called.

I took a pad, walked over. "What can I get you?"

Raoul

THE MAIN ROOM OF the mosque was empty; the congregation that had once felt so powerful now was diminished and sad. A few older men and a couple of women with their heads covered in colorful scarves sat on the floor waiting for the Imam to begin the prayers. The ones left behind, the locals who never asked about the meetings after prayers, remained calm and steady in their lives, running convenience stores, sending money to relatives abroad, and hoping for a better life for their children. A single child, a ten-year-old named Ali, sat with the men and visibly brightened when the Leader arrived. He'd been watching the others for weeks, fantasizing about the day when the Leader would look at him and invite him to join the other men after prayers.

The Leader stepped to the front of the room, spoke briefly with the Imam, and lowered himself slowly to the floor. To his surprise, the boy saw the Leader turn and look at him, then pat the carpet to his right. Without hesitation, he boy scampered forward, shaking off his father's hand reaching out to stop him. The prayers began.

It was a sorrowful service: even the boy felt the difference. Like a long good-bye, a mourning for the missing, and yet the boy felt energized. The Leader gave off energy, sparks of something like hope and certainty. The boy slid his eyes to the left whenever he could, inhaled the scent of the man as they stood, and knelt, and chanted together. He had a good nose, the boy did: he got sweat, blood, and antiseptic. He picked up bleach, latex, and a tiny hint of urine.

The Leader, for his part, enjoyed knowing that he could take this boy along on a majestic ride to glory. He wouldn't, of course—his work here in Jerome was done, and he was bound for glory in the completion of his mission. But he would not take a boy from his parents, the way he had been taken from his. That, if nothing else, he would give to the child. And perhaps when the boy was a man, he'd remain a pious believer. Perhaps the world would be different by then, and he would not need to hide or apologize for his faith. Perhaps.

The Leader rose heavily at the end of the service. Again, he shook hands with the Imam and said his farewell. The boy, reluctantly returned to his father's side, watched with big eyes as the older man approached. "Study hard, and obey your father," the Leader said, tousling the boy's hair. "God willing, we will meet in paradise someday, praise God. God is good."

When they returned to the car, the doctor appeared, carrying a package.

"You got it?" the Leader asked. He took the brown bag without looking inside. "Go then, and Godspeed to you. Take Ali and Shem with you. Here's the map." He turned away and got into the car. He would meet Metin and Salim at the apartment to finish the interrogation of Ismail. When it was done, they would disappear, too, like wisps of fog swirling into the wind, burned off by sunshine.

Clara

MARY KATE WAS SLEEPING when I arrived at her bedside. Although it was late, I snuck past the nurse and into her room. Mark had given me the room number when he left the bar, a take-out bag tucked under his arm.

She moaned in her sleep, and I reached for her hand. The right hand was heavily bandaged, but the left was free and so I held it loosely, waiting for morning. She woke long before the sun rose, startled into consciousness by something in her dream.

"Where is he?" she asked me.

"Down the hall," I lied. I actually had no idea where her son was, but I knew he was still alive. "Just get some rest. I'll wake you if anything happens."

She shook her head, tried to straighten up. Wincing, she grabbed at her midriff. "Yow, that hurts," she said. She looked at her bandaged hand, held it up. "What's this?"

I shrugged. "I don't know. Do you remember what happened?"

She closed her eyes, sighed. I thought she was going back to sleep, so I relaxed back into my chair. After a moment, she started talking. "He was talking crazy, yelling, waving a knife around. And he had Beth in the room with him. She was so scared, I could tell. She was trying to be brave. But when I called her to come to the door, he grabbed her. Held the knife against her neck: his own sister. He was going to cut the throat of his own sister!" She opened her eyes and looked at me.

"That's not my son. My son would never hurt his little sister. He loved her. He loves her." She started to cry, tears running down her cheeks. "He's still alive, right?" I nodded. "And Beth, she's okay. She's fine, right?"

I didn't know, but since Mark had not mentioned her, I took the safe bet. "She's fine, don't worry," I said. "I'm sure she's shaken up, but you know kids. She'll be fine." What the hell did I know about this? I decided to shut up and let her talk.

"Thanks," she said, breathing deeply. She clutched the bandaged hand to her chest.

The sky was lightening when she woke again, another little cry. "What?" she asked.

"Mary Kate, it's me, Clara. I'm here. You're all right."

She looked at me, her eyes wild. "You. What are you doing here?"

"I heard what happened and I came over to see if I could help."

"You can't help me. Where's Joe? Where's my husband?" She covered her eyes with the bandaged hand. "Oh, he's never going to forgive me. He's not here. He's probably taken Beth and left town. Oh my God—"

"Joe wouldn't do that," I said. "He loves you. He knows this was not your fault. It's nobody's fault," I corrected myself. "Silvio's sick, something went wrong in his head. But he's in the hospital now and he'll get better. You'll see. It'll be all right."

She looked at me again. "Who the hell are you?" she asked.

"Mary Kate, you know me. It's Clara."

"Yeah, the Clara I know would never dish out this kind of crap. Tell me the truth: Silvio is dead, isn't he?"

"Not as far as I know. The last I heard he was okay. And that's the truth. The other stuff, you're right, I have no idea what I'm talking about."

"So why are you here? Really."

"I went to the restaurant—"

"Oh my God, I just ran out of there. Oh my God. I gotta get a phone, Clara, hand me that phone."

"Would you shut up and listen?" I said. "I'm not giving you the phone, you're not calling anyone. It's the middle of the night. Just listen. I went to the restaurant around 7:00, things were a little crazy there so I helped out for a couple of hours and then I came here. No problem. Your assistant Lester, he closed up. Everything is fine."

She looked at me again, accusing. "You helped out? Doing what? Washing dishes?"

"Har har," I smiled. "I tended the bar. I did some bartending back in college, so I was a little rusty, but I must say, I think I did pretty good overall. Except for one bad martini, I think it was okay."

"Figures you'd end up behind the bar," she said.

"That's gratitude, huh?"

She shrugged, closed her eyes again. "But no sign of Joe, right?"

"He wasn't here when I came in, so no, I haven't seen him. But that doesn't mean anything, Mary Kate."

"Okay, shut up now."

An aide came in to check vitals and glared at me. "What are you doing here? It's not visiting hours yet."

"Don't bother trying to throw her out," Mary Kate said. "She won't leave."

"I can make her leave, you just watch," the woman said. She did have at least a hundred pounds on me, but I doubted that she could move very fast. I stayed in my seat.

"It's okay, don't bother," Mary Kate said. "I need to talk to the doctor. Can you tell me about my son?"

"I don't know anything about your family, Miss, and the doctor will be here later," she said. "You just rest now. You'll get some breakfast soon, and we'll get you out of this bed in no time." She glared at me. "I'm going to keep an eye on you," she said. "One word from the patient and you're out of here."

I gave her my sweetest smile. "Thank you!"

When she was gone, Mary Kate sat up straighter. "Give me your phone," she demanded. "I need to call Joe, make sure everyone is okay. See if he knows anything about Silvio. Give me. Hand over the damned phone or I will have you thrown out."

"Mary Kate, it's not even 6:00 in the morning."

"Joe gets up early. Give it."

I handed over my cell phone, stood up and looked out the window while she dialed. "Joe, pick up, it's me. Joe? Dammit, he must not recognize the number. Joe? Beth? Pick up the phone…. Okay, when you get this message, call me back. The number is….well, just call the hospital. You can come and get me." She hung up. I didn't turn around, and she dialed another number.

"Can you give me the condition of Silvio Rossi? Yes. He was admitted last night. Yes, I'm his mother. Correct. Oh. Okay. Thank you. Here." Mary Kate held the phone out to me. "Silvio's not even in this hospital. They took him to another hospital last night. Can you find him? Please?"

I took the phone and checked the internet for the nearest psychiatric facility. "Did they tell you anything?" I asked. She shook her head. I continued to search, and the phone in the room shrilled to life. I picked up the receiver and handed it to her.

"Joe, yes I'm fine. I'm waiting for the doctor to let me out. Are you okay? Beth? Oh, I was so worried. Yeah, that's okay. Sure. Bring her too, no it won't be scary. Oh, she's with your mother, that's good. I'll see her later then…I'm fine. Joe, what about Silvio? Do you know anything? They said he's not here. What? Where? Oh. Oh. Okay. See you in a while. Okay. Love you too." She paused. "He's in the psych ward at Yale."

I looked up the number and jotted it on the back of an old receipt. I handed the paper to Mary Kate, waited while she waded through the dialing options, and then tried unsuccessfully to make sense of her side of the conversation.

"Thanks," she hung up. "His condition is stable. He's in a locked ward, on a suicide watch."

"The gunshot?"

"Blew off a part of his ear. I guess when I lunged at him, I was able to turn the gun away from a direct shot. That must explain this," she held up her bandaged hand. She blew out a huge burst of air. "It's not as bad as I thought."

"So he'll be fine," I said. "No permanent damage?"

"Yeah, he'll be okay. Physically anyway." She paused. "Get me my clothes, will you?"

"I don't think so. Wait until they tell you that you can leave."

"I know, I know," she huffed. "I have to wait for Joe anyway, so I'm not going to make a break for it. I just remembered something. Silvio gave me a card, said to give it to you. I just remembered that I stuck it in my pocket. He was screaming at me: 'Take it! Take it!' And he was waving the gun around, and I was holding my side, and I grabbed the card. I said, 'Fine, Sil, I got it, I'll give it to her,' and he was shouting, 'Don't forget, tell everyone I'm sorry,' and then he pushed the gun under his chin. I'll never forget that moment. You know how they say time slows down? It really does. I felt like I was moving underwater; I could hardly get to him fast enough." She closed her eyes. "The noise of that shot, and blood everywhere. I was holding his head, trying to keep him from falling apart. I thought he shot himself in the head. Oh, my baby." She turned away from me and I watched as her shoulders shook. I sat back in the visitor chair and watched the sky lighten.

"Did you find it?" she asked eventually, her voice muffled by the pillow. "The card?"

"Oh, no," I replied. I got up, went to the closet and looked for her clothes. "There's nothing here."

"What do you mean? Where's my stuff?"

"I bet the police took everything." I grimaced. "I can make a call. See if I can get that card. And you can call Joe and ask him to bring you some clean clothes." I was already dialing Mark's number, although I was reluctant to talk to him after the fuck-off speech I gave him last night. I hope he didn't misinterpret my call.

"What?" Okay, so the friendly greeting answered that question.

"I'm calling about Silvio."

"What about him?"

"Mary Kate told me that Silvio gave her a card and told her to make sure I got it. She shoved it in her pocket and apparently the police took her clothes after she was admitted here. Can you get me the card? I hate to ask you for another favor, but it could be important." I could hear him breathing.

"Fine, I'll see what I can do." He paused. "Is she okay?"

"Yes, she's fine—" He hung up as soon as he heard "fine." Good, I thought. I was happy. Finally someone was listening to me. Finally I was going to be done with married men.

On the other phone, Mary Kate was having an emotional talk with either Joe or Beth; I couldn't tell which. I sat and checked my email. Seventeen messages from Rob; the first ones were good, all nicey-nice about my work on the memorial services. Then the usual: "Where are you, why aren't you coming to work, why are you avoiding me? Do you want this job anyway? Call me as soon as you get this. I have another assignment for you." The last one: "As your friend, I have to say that I am very disappointed in you. Please do me the courtesy of calling me back or responding to this message." Yikes.

I sat quietly, thinking about everything that had happened since Sept. 11. Although my mind encouraged me to look back further in time, it was all I could do to think about my brother, dead, and all those innocent lives blown to bits by terrorists. I thought about my own life, selfishly, and how out of control it had become. I think both Mary Kate and I fell asleep, lost in our own pain, and we were awakened by the cheerful greeting of a young doctor.

"Ladies, good morning! And how are we today, Mrs. Rossi? Any pain? Feeling okay? Let me take a look—do you mind stepping out, Miss?"

I held up the wall in the hallway for a while, trying hard to stay out of the way. It was morning, and the smell of steamed breakfast permeated the halls. Doctors in white coats flipped through giant blue binders, dodged in and out of patient rooms, spoke to nurses who nodded and sometimes asked questions. I was glared at by the heavy-set woman who'd tried to throw me out earlier, and I smiled at her. I felt Mark coming down the hall before I saw him, and I braced myself.

"What are you doing out here?" he said.

"The doctor's in with Mary Kate," I replied. "Did you get it?"

"Yes." He handed me a small index card, sealed in a plastic evidence bag. Written in block print were four letters: C:AB,R. I sighed and handed the card back to him.

"I suppose you know what this means," Mark said.

"Yes," I said. "It's our code. His way of saying goodbye to me."

"That's all?" he asked.

"Yep. Can I have the card when you're done with it? As a memento, you know."

"When you tell me what it really means," he said. We stared at each other a moment, but he looked away.

"Say, any chance I can see the van today?" I asked.

He shook his head. "Not until you tell me what the note really means."

"Oh." I stepped aside to allow the doctor to exit Mary Kate's room. "Is she going to be okay?" I asked.

"Yes, she was very lucky. It's just a flesh wound, no organ damage. She can go home; just has to watch out for infection. Any sign of a fever or redness, well, you know the drill," the doctor said. "Bring her to the E.D."

"And what about her hand? What happened to it?" I asked.

"Third degree burns from grabbing the gun as it was being fired," he replied. "She'll have to get that checked, change the bandages, keep it clean and dry—but her own physician can take care of it."

"Thanks," I said, turning back to Mark. "So, when can I look at the van?" I asked again.

"Not today." He entered the room, then turned back to look at me. "You coming in?"

"Sure." I did, although I couldn't wait to get out of there; to go and follow the last instructions from Mijo.

I waited, quietly, while Mark went through some questions with Mary Kate. He seemed satisfied with her version of events and quickly closed his notebook.

"We'll deal with any charges against your son later," he said. "Do you know where he got the gun? The serial numbers were burned off with acid."

Mary Kate shook her head.

"Do you have a gun in the house? At the restaurant?" More negatives. "What about his friends, his boss? Anyone?"

She choked out, "No."

"Did he give you any indication why he was doing this?"

Another shake. "Honestly, I have no idea. When I got home, he was ranting. My husband could maybe tell you more about what happened before…. Before Silvio grabbed Beth and hid upstairs. I wasn't there yet." She paused. "Have you talked to Joe?"

"I haven't, but I know my officers were with him for quite a while last night. I'll talk to them. I hear you're going home. Please don't take this the wrong way, but we'd appreciate it if you didn't leave town for a while, until we get this whole thing cleared up."

"I have to leave town—Silvio's in the hospital, and as soon as I get out of here, that's where I'm going. I need to see him," she said.

"Mary Kate, they won't let anyone see him right now. He's in a locked ward. You'll have to wait until they let you know he can have visitors," I said. "You should go home and get some rest, and spend some time with Beth. And Joe."

She gave me that "don't tell me what to do" look and I backed off again. Mark left his card and asked her to keep in touch. He met Joe on the way out the door, and I was treated to a visual inspection of Mary Kate's husband: he was tall, well built, and sported a full head of wavy black hair. I could tell he had dimples, but he wasn't smiling. His dark eyes snapped with anxiety as he looked past Mark to see Mary Kate. I decided to leave the reunion and stepped out as soon as I saw him bury his face in her lap. No, Joe was not going to leave Mary Kate, no matter what her son did.

But I was. I walked slowly enough so that I didn't take the same elevator as Mark, and he was already in his car when I came out into the fresh air. I had no illusions that he was not going to watch where I was going, and so I took my time merging into traffic and heading to the shore road. I was craving a good breakfast, and so I pulled into the deserted parking lot at Angie's on the Sound. While I wanted to see what Raoul had in his van, I was certain that the key to understanding came from whatever he'd hidden for me. AB indeed—the asphalt beach had been our rooftop alternative to Jerome's private beaches and swimming clubs. I needed to go there, but I did not want Mark to follow me. In time, he'd realize that he could not decipher Raoul's codes without me, and he'd call. Of that I was certain.

Raoul

THE CAR SMELLED, AND even with the windows open it was a hard ride. The Leader breathed shallowly during the two miles to Main Street. The Leader emptied the contents of the glove compartment into the brown paper sack and entered through the unlocked back door of the apartment building.

"He's awake," Metin said when the Leader came into the apartment.

"Good," the Leader said. "I want him to be awake for his last moments. I'll give him one more chance to tell the truth, and I need him to be awake for that."

The Leader clipped price tags from the silky garments he removed from the paper bag. "Gloves," he said, loud enough for the other two to pull latex from their pockets and pull on the gloves.

They straightened Raoul on the bed, and the Leader held up the silky panties. "Lift his leg, there," he said. He pulled the panties up around the knees, and then nodded for the others to drop him.

"Now this. Pull him up," he said. With a man on each side, they pulled Raoul to a sitting position. One arm at a time, the brassiere was placed across his chest. The Leader struggled to fasten the hooks in the back, and Salim took over. When it was done, they dropped him back onto the mattress. The Leader pulled the bra into place and removed four silk stockings from the bag.

"Tie him to the bed with these," he said. While the two young men tied him to the bedpost, Raoul tried to pull his hand away.

"What happened to his hand?" the Leader asked.

"Must've been injured coming upstairs," Salim said.

"No matter," the Leader said. He grabbed Raoul's jaw and shook his head. "Have you anything to say?" he asked. "This is your last chance."

In response, Raoul closed his eyes and lips tightly. The Leader grabbed a syringe and administered a dose of heroin through an exposed vein in Raoul's arm. When his head lolled to the side, the Leader turned to the others.

"Search the place one last time," he ordered. "Check everything—we don't want to miss anything. But keep it quiet—I don't want the neighbors to hear us. And we haven't got much time, so be quick. I want to be out of here in an hour."

The two divided the small apartment, one taking the bedroom and the other going through the living room. The Leader checked inside every kitchen cabinet, under every drawer, and squeezed every parcel in the refrigerator. There was nothing hidden there. He returned to the bedroom, turned the air conditioner to its highest setting, and spoke quietly to Raoul. "You had a chance at paradise, you know? Now you will burn in hell for all eternity."

The other men joined him at Raoul's bedside. He was barely awake, eyes jumping from side to side.

"Metin, put on the apron," the Leader said. "You too," he gestured at Salim. He waited until they were covered in protective plastic.

"Now, who wants the honor? Vengeance is mine, sayeth the Lord." He held out the blade. "Salim?"

Clara

WHEN I'D EATEN HALF of my bagel—a luscious cornmeal treat, toasted and loaded with cream cheese, lox, onions, and a dribble of caviar—I took out my cell phone and called Rob. The morning newspaper was spread out before me, a photo I took at the memorial service taking up a quarter of the page above the fold. Not bad for a reluctant photographer. Good composition, I thought as I waited for Rob to pick up the phone. He didn't, so I left a message on voicemail. "This is Clara T., your star photographer, returning your message. Your turn."

In the time it took to fill my mouth, savor the combination, and prepare to swallow, Rob called me back.

"Hold on," I choked, swigged some water and tried to wash the remainder away. What a waste! "Hey, Rob. Saw the photo this morning, looks good."

"Yes, it does. You do good work, Clara, when you put your mind to it. Any chance you might feel like working again this week?"

"Actually, Rob—"

"Wait, I just emailed you a list of the next set of services. There's quite a few in your area, and then you can head back here to cover some of the local ones."

"No, I don't think so, Rob. I have to take a leave, and then—"

"What? What kind of leave? You're barely back to work as it is. How long this time?"

"I don't know."

"Well, you get a week off for a death in the family, and that shit passed a long time ago. I need you here, Clara. Shit, we're all grieving. We all lost someone. We all need a break—I can't let you go right now."

"You have to. I can't do this stuff anymore. No more chasing widows around cemeteries. I'm not kidding." I took a deep breath. "Rob, there's going to be a war, and I'm going."

"Seriously? Not for this publication, you're not. We don't send females into combat zones."

"Yes, seriously. I'll go over your head if I have to, or I'll go to another paper, but I am taking my camera and I'm going over there," I said.

"What the fuck." There was silence. "Is there anything I can say to change your mind?" he asked finally.

"I don't think so, but thanks. I know I've been a handful, as an employee and a friend. And I thank you for putting up with that."

"At the risk of repeating myself, it's our company policy, so it's not up to me—"

"I'll make the calls," I said.

"Well," he said. "Come to the city next week and let me buy you lunch."

"That would be great, Rob. Really great. But you're not changing my mind." I hung up as Mark slid into the booth across from me. "Don't you have an office you should be in?" I asked him. He picked up the paper, saw the byline on the photo, and looked quizzically at me.

"This yours?" he asked.

"Yes. My professional name is Clara T. Get it? Clarity?" I signaled the waitress for a check. "So, you got tired of waiting for me in the parking lot?"

"What's the note from Raoul about, Clara?" he asked.

"Let me see the stuff in the van, and we can help each other," I replied.

He sighed. "All we found so far is lists. Your brother was a major list-maker. And most of the lists are codes. I think the numbers are letters, and the letters are numbers, and God only knows what else is mixed in there. How do you think you can help?"

"We made those codes together, most of them. I'm sure he got more sophisticated over the years, but I should be able to break most of it down for you. What about his computer?"

"Can't get in. We have guys working on it. Password-protected up the ying-yang. I mean, the thing was welded underneath the floor of the van. We had to use a blowtorch to cut it out of there. Fortunately, it has one of those titanium shells so the heat didn't damage anything. But damn, we even had the fibbies look at some of the stuff and they just shook their heads," he said.

"Okay, let me at it. I know most of his passwords. I can give it a shot. And if they don't work, I can use some variants. I can get in."

"Fine," he said. "They're working until about 4:00 today. I'll come and get you around quarter to."

"Pick me up on Main Street," I said. "I'm going to pay my mother a little visit this afternoon."

He had no idea that was an unusual event, so he readily agreed and prepared to leave. He looked at the paper one more time. "Can I take this?" he asked.

"Sure. You like the photo?"

He nodded. "Is this the job I just heard you leaving?"

"Yes."

"Too bad. You're pretty good." He smiled and stood up, newspaper tucked under his arm. "Ah, about last night…"

"Yeah?"

"You're right, I should know better. I have a wife, a wonderful wife really, and two kids, and I have no business running around with you. I'm sorry about that. I got carried away."

"I have that effect on men, I guess." I smiled. "Water under the bridge." In my head, I continued the thought as he walked to the door: *And I was just using sex to get information from you.* I cringed. What a cliché I'd become.

I looked down on the sparkling blue of the river emptying into the Long Island Sound as I drove across the bridge and returned to my apartment. I took a quick shower, jotted some notes, and headed back to Jerome, eager to find whatever Raoul had hidden on the roof. I parked on North Main Street and hoofed it over to our apartment building. The back door was unlatched, as usual, and I walked quietly up the stairs to the roof. The noonday sun was warm, and I put on sunglasses before crossing to our beach area. How many summers had we spent here, lazing on chaise chairs with duct-taped webbing? We had a bunch of beach towels stolen from backyard clotheslines. I wore mismatched bathing suit hand-me-downs and Raoul cut the legs off his blue jeans and fringed them with an open safety pin. Sometimes one or two of our sisters joined us, bringing Tab and Coppertone, and shiny silver platters that they held under their chins to make sure they were totally tanned.

My father had come up to the roof once, on a Sunday afternoon, and sat with us for a few minutes, a beer and cigarette in his hand. His leg bounced more and more the longer he stayed, and when the beer was done, he stood up, announced, "I don't know how the hell you can stand the boredom up here," and left us alone. A few minutes later, we heard the steady putt-putt of his motorbike as he headed to the club. Papa spent very little time at home, and most of it when he was asleep.

Raoul had looked at me and shrugged. Papa's approval meant a lot to him. "Should we go and do something?" he asked.

"We are doing something," I said. "We're shipwrecked on Asphalt Beach, and we've got to devise a way to signal for help." I pulled him closer. "What about this?" We devised all kinds of elaborate machines, and codes, and stories. Not just in the summer; throughout the year we spent many nights on the roof, passing binoculars back and forth, watching the neighborhood and taking careful notes of the movement of each household. All of it in careful code, written on sheets of unbleached newsprint that Mama purchased in reams from the newspaper office. Once she came home with a huge roll of brown paper, and it took us months to fill it with maps, code, and drawings.

There was one spot that constituted Asphalt Beach: it was the eastern side of the building, overlooking Main Street. Perched there, we could see anyone approaching for a mile in every direction. Old man Konopka kept his pigeons on the back side of the building, and we watched them all take off together, following their progress through binoculars until one of them pooped on my bare back while I was sunning myself. Little Dickie was with us that day and he vomited in the corner while Raoul smeared the thick white shit off my back with his tee shirt.

The chimney rose from the corner, and the elevator shaft rose next to it, creating a private wall where we could stay out of the wind and avoid the neighbors who came up to hang clothes and gossip. Once we caught Ramona with a boy, his bare butt working hard between her legs. I remember her face: she looked bored, and she jerked her head to the side in that "get out of here" gesture all kids know. So we went to our side of the beach and waited for them to be done. We had loosened some bricks in the walls, and as we got older, we created storage space behind them for things like cigarettes, money, and pot. Once, when I was babysitting, I lifted a couple of airplane bottles of liquor and they stayed in the wall for years. Raoul and I were not interested in using the stash, we just wanted to have it for emergencies. We also collected maps and kept our binoculars in the largest opening.

As I ran my hands over the bricks, searching for openings, I wondered what I would find, and I was not disappointed to discover the two whiskey bottles, their contents all but evaporated, and the crumbling remains of rolling paper and tobacco. There was a shiny foil packet that I didn't recognize: condoms. So, Raoul had used the Asphalt Beach for other things. Quickly, I moved and replaced each brick, searching for a notebook or plastic bag full of index cards. He should have been a librarian, my brother. He so loved to index things: his possessions, especially all the comic books, were cross-referenced and tabulated. The card Mark showed me was no different from hundreds I'd seen before with its careful printed message. Where was it?

Our usual places were not yielding any secrets. I leaned against the wall, studying the beach area. The chairs were long gone, as were the beach towels. The array of antiquated antennae swayed in the light afternoon breeze. I let my eyes relax and waited for something to stand out, some brick misaligned or out of place. The floor was covered with many layers of tar, sheets of asphalt repairing the leaks that acid rain and dog urine had created over time. One corner looked warped, as if the roof had been peeled back. I jumped up and looked underneath, but only saw a jumble of trash and what looked like a bird's nest. Crouched on the floor, though, I spotted it: a metal plate screwed to the outside wall. There seemed to be no reason for this rusted metal rectangle to be there and in fact I had no memory of it. The screws appeared to be rusty, but on closer inspection I realized the sham: he'd used some kind of rust-colored paint to make the entire thing look old, but the camouflage easily gave way to my Swiss Army knife and its screwdriver implement.

I found a metal box fitted neatly into the hollow where a brick used to be, and pried it out. This was trickier: I needed a key. Nothing in my knife worked on the lock, so I pocketed the box and replaced the metal plate carefully. I respected Raoul's ingenuity and made sure that everything was pristine before I headed back to my car, my apartment, and his set of keys.

I started down the stairs and something made me stop and go back. I looked over at the abandoned pigeon roost and sniffed the air. When the wind died down, there was a smell that I previously attributed to years of pigeon droppings, dog pee, and the accumulated grease lining the central ventilation shaft for the building. But there was something more in the roost, I could tell as I approached. There was a large pile of what looked like guano, but on closer inspection it seemed to be unmixed cement. Lime, perhaps. I kicked one of the walls until a piece of wood splintered and I was able to twist it off, and then I stuck it into the center of the mound. I encountered something solid. I poked again and tried to sweep away some of the gray powder.

Rain had solidified some of it, but the more I poked, the more certain I was that there was something rotten under this gray shroud. I had to call Mark, but I wanted to get the box hidden before he arrived so I hopped quickly down the stairs, jogged down the street, and started dialing his number as soon as my car was in view.

"Mark, there's something funky on the roof of my mother's apartment building. I don't know what it is. I didn't want to disturb it too much, but I think there might be a body in the pigeon coop."

It took a moment for him to reply. "At this point, I suppose there's no reason for me to ask why you were poking around on the roof of your mother's apartment building, right?" he said. "Nothing I need to know, right?"

"I told you I was coming to visit, and before I saw her, I decided to go to the roof. Memory lane and all that, you know. So I was walking around, and I looked to see if there were any pigeons left in the old coop, and voila," I said.

"Right." He sighed. "I'll be there in five."

"Oh, I'm not staying," I said. "I forgot that I promised Mary Kate to help her with something this afternoon, so I have to go. Call me later?"

"Sure. Whatever. How do I get to the roof?"

"I'll prop the back door open. Then, you use the stairs." I was itching to get off the phone. "Okay?" I started the car with one hand while I ended the call with the other.

Back at my apartment, one of the little keys on his ring opened the box. When I saw the IBM logo on the side of a small device that was about the size of a matchbox, I whooped with joy. I assumed that this thing contained whatever I needed to unlock all of the information Raoul had been collecting and hiding. I powered up my computer and waited. I'd seen these sticks before, mostly on lanyards hanging from the necks of the tech geeks at the newspaper. I never used one myself, and while the computer was coming to life, I inspected the various options available to plug it in. "USB, that looks right," I matched the pins, slid the device in, and immediately encountered Raoul's security wall.

I typed in several of his favorite passwords, but the computer beeped its rejection of each. I tried my name, and its numerical equivalent. No go. I looked at the device, closed my eyes, and let my mind wander back to the roof. My fingers typed Mac-Gyver. I hit enter, and I was in.

The data was neatly arranged in directories: Daily log. The Pirate and K. Masked Men. Naval Gazing. What was he doing, writing sitcoms? I wondered. I started with The Pirate and K, a category I found too alluring to pass up.

He'd attached some photos, but I started with the narrative files, which were arranged by date. They contained lists of numbers and some names, which I eventually figured out were boat registration numbers. In the event the numbers were covered up, he tried to list the name or at the very least, the type of boat and engine. In some cases, he was unsuccessful, but for the most part, I could see he retained a great deal of valuable information. These must be the drug smugglers, I thought.

Based on that assumption, I was able to identify amounts of money and type of drugs exchanged. I backed out of the file for a moment, looked at the directory, and found the jackpot. A file named, appropriately, The Jackpot. My brother had a great sense of humor, which I was appreciating more and more every day.

The Jackpot was indeed a gold mine. The key to the codes, of which there were many. There was the dollars for donuts code, as opposed to the dialing for dollars code. Some related to drug deals, others to payments he received for services. Or at least that's what I figured. His was the donut money, clearly the lesser of the two types of payment. A late arrival on the list: Dollar Daze, which coincided with Raoul's gig as host of the prescription parties. He made a great deal of money for The Pirate, whoever that might be. Time to look at the photos.

I was taken aback briefly when I opened the file entitled "Matey" and recognized Leon from the boatyard. He was the Pirate? Made sense, in a way, but I had not attributed him with enough intelligence to expect that he was capable of organizing such a lucrative drug smuggling operation. But here it was and down to the penny: the dates, the places, and the drugs. The other man, called only K, was no one I recognized, but I assumed that Mark could run him down.

On cue, my phone rang. It was Mark. "Well, you called it," he said. "Body covered in lime, so ID will be tough but we can pretty much tell his neck was broken and he was dropped there. I don't think it was very long ago, but that's just my guestimate."

"Wow, that's amazing. Maybe he was involved in killing Raoul?"

"That's pretty certain, since we found Raoul's badge in a car parked nearby that has his prints all over it," he said.

I was quiet.

"Clara, are you okay? What are you doing?" he asked.

"I'm fine. I'm just looking at Raoul's notebooks," I said. "It's all coming together, isn't it?"

"Yes," he said. "We're getting close."

"Hey Mark," I asked. "In the van, did your guys find anything odd?"

"Define odd."

"You know, out of place."

"You mean aside from the computer welded to the floor?" he asked. "Can you be more specific? I don't know what you're looking for. I've got the inventory list, let's see. There was clothing, a sleeping bag, some personal stuff like shaving cream and hair gel, lots of black clothing, a couple of bags of empty cans, some old magazines, and stacks of money. Your usual stuff. What are you thinking?"

"Did you look at the empty cans?"

"Not really. Why?"

"I think he might have been collecting fingerprints. Same with the magazines. He was on the job, you know, and so I think he gathered whatever he could to help make a case later."

"Hmmm."

"Just run 'em for prints. So, can I still see the stuff? I'm back at my apartment and I can come over any time."

"Sure, meet me at the armory at 4:15," he said.

I hung up and returned to my computer, opened another directory called Naval Gazing. There were very few files here, mostly photos of the naval base taken from the water and varying distances away. Most of the photos were taken at night, several with night vision technology and heat mapping. Gee, he'd had some good toys on this job. The file entitled "A Shot in the Dark" was very cryptic, mostly Raoul's musing about ways to approach the base and possible avenues for personnel to remove weapons without detection. Like I said, it was a short list.

The last directory, the largest, was labeled "Masked Men." I quickly surmised that "The Mask" was actually the mosque, and it was here that Raoul spent his most valuable time. There were fewer photos, probably because of the danger of being detected with anything resembling a camera. But he did create maps, lots of them, and sketches of many of the individuals he had encountered at the mosque. I thought I recognized a couple of them and figured that they might match up with the bodies that had been popping up all over town. Names were sketchy; he had only first names for most of the men, and estimates about age and country of origin. Lists of vocabulary words, quotes from the Koran and someone he called the Leader.

The Leader was obviously very important, and Raoul had taken his photograph many times. Most of them were dark, or taken from a distance, or very shaky. It was going to require someone with a really good computer to be able to find some usable pictures of this elusive fellow. He'd also sketched the man and noted that the Leader had twice handled his copy of the Koran, a paperback that was presently held together by an elastic band after the man had ripped it in two. I dialed Mark again.

"Did you find a paperback copy of the Koran in the van?"

"Yes, I think that was in the inventory. Why?"

"Raoul's notes said that the Leader of the group meeting at the mosque ripped it in two with his bare hands, so it will have his prints on it. Maybe they are readable."

"What notes are you talking about?"

"I found something—I'll give it to you when I see you later. Just get the prints, and let's try to find this guy." I hung up.

I kept searching. There was a file that did not seem to fit the "Masked Men" directory. Labeled "Eagle Scouting," the document opened with the Boy Scout motto: "A Scout is trustworthy, loyal, helpful, friendly, courteous, kind, obedient, cheerful, thrifty, brave, clean, and reverent." The next page held a list of names. Next to each name, he'd listed an approximate age and the date of death. Raoul noted what he knew about each man: country of origin, family ties, length of time in the U.S., employment, training, specialty, and other details (one man was allergic to shellfish, another was a vegetarian). He had some sketches of each man, one or two photographs, and a detailed description of each man's death. At his hands.

A third page was simply labeled "Silvio" and contained notes from his conversations with Mary Kate, when Silvio was missing. I did not bother to read beyond the first couple of lines.

I left the daily logs until I returned from looking at the van. To be safe, and fair, I copied the entire memory from the flash drive into my hard drive. And then I made another copy on a CD, just for good measure, which I stowed in my underwear drawer.

Mark seemed exhausted when he opened the back door to let me in. I followed him up the stairs, around a maze of corridors, and into the massive open space of the armory.

"This is the only place we have that's large enough to take apart a vehicle," he said. "Sorry it's so cold in here." The van was literally in pieces, and the contents arranged by category, laid out on a grid with plastic numbers next to each item. "If you touch something, make sure you put it back in the same place," Mark said. "Everything's been catalogued and photographed as it lies, so we don't lose anything during the forensic process."

I took the gloves he held out. "Very thorough," I said.

He grimaced. "The last thing I want is the Feds coming in here and accusing us of fucking up the investigation. I'm being super careful about this one."

"I appreciate that, and I'll be careful too," I said. "Here's what I found on the roof this morning. I wanted to look at it before I handed it over. It's got all the codes, his daily log, and some photographs and sketches of the men he worked with. I didn't erase anything, it's all there." I handed it to him.

"I knew you were up to something this morning," he said. "So, you don't trust me. Is that it?"

"I do. It's just—he's my brother, and I wanted to see if he left me any messages. So far, there's nothing personal on it," I said. "Sorry if that upsets you. But it's all here. Promise."

He stuck the drive in an evidence bag. "On the roof, eh?"

I was already walking in the rows separating the material from the van. "Yeah, that note from Silvio. It was a code—C is Clara, which was an easy one, AB is asphalt beach, and R is Raoul. Asphalt beach was our rooftop getaway when we were kids. We used to spend the summers up there, and we hid things behind the bricks all the time. So I knew he had left something there. And here it is. End of story."

"Thanks," he said. "I'll need you to make a statement...."

"I know. And, you're welcome." I turned to face him. "You're going to need help with all of this. It's bigger than we think. You'll see when you open the file. He had a lot of irons in the fire, and you're going to have your hands full trying to chase all of them down."

"For example?"

"Have you looked at the mosque at all?" He shook his head. "From what I can tell, that's where the terrorists were being trained. In the basement. By someone Raoul called 'the Leader,'" I said.

"Okay. We'll look at it. I know the Feds have been all over that place since September 11," Mark said. He pointed towards the far side of the room. "His computer is over here. Want to give the password a shot?"

It would have been too much for MacGyver to work a second time, but I tried that one first. Nope. None of the other obvious words worked either: Holmes, Sherlock, and Watson. I sat with my hands on the keyboard, eyes closed, willing Mijo to send me a sign. My hands moved. "Clairvoyant." The computer beeped, and I was in.

The hard drive was massive, loaded with documents, all of which appeared to be encrypted in gobbledygook. "I think you're going to need tech assistance from the bureau," I told Mark. "They have some kind of encryption key that they type in and it unscrambles the whole shebang."

"Once they know we have this, it's gone," he said.

"Well, that's true." I had to agree. "But they don't know about the flash drive. He left that for me, and I think it has the important bits on it. Saved in a way that I could access." I stood up and we both looked down at the computer. "Call the Feds, Mark. This is bigger than us, and you can let them chase down the terrorists while you nab all the drug dealers in town."

"You really want me to step back and let the Feds take over this case?" Mark asked.

I looked at the room filled with evidence Raoul had collected for the past year, and thought about my apartment, filled with more paper and photographs and maps. "Yes. You said yourself this is too big for the department. I can't help you anymore—and you're going to need a lot of help."

"I thought you wanted a piece of this—to vindicate your brother, to chase down the bad guys?"

"So did I. Until I saw this…this room. How many identities did Raoul have? And what kind of life? I did that before. And it cost me. And it cost Mijo and my family. I think I'm done."

"Why do you think Silvio was involved?" Mark asked.

"It's just a feeling I have. Raoul had a file on him, but it didn't seem to have much in it. I didn't go through everything yet, so who knows. Silvio could be part of the drug running thing, or the mosque group. I mean, we need to have an explanation for how Silvio had the note from Raoul for me. To me, it means he was close to Raoul while he was being held. I'd like to find out when he got it, and why he didn't give it to me before. I think that Silvio was involved, and I'm not really sure how. Anyway, maybe that's why he went berserk," I said. "There's a lot we don't know yet, but I think we're going to find out enough to fill in most of the blanks."

I peeled the gloves off and handed them to Mark. "I'll box up the stuff I have at home and bring it to your office."

"I can send someone over to pick it up. Or I could stop by..." he said.

"No, I'll get it to you. No trouble at all." I hesitated. "Just out of curiosity, did Shelly tell you where she found the van? Where did he have it hidden?"

"It was deep in the woods behind the Eagle's Club. Maybe that was why he spent so much time in there—it was close to his base and he needed a cover in case someone saw him coming and going."

I nodded. "I wondered about that, why he was hanging around at the club. At first I thought he was undercover there, but he wasn't looking for gun smugglers there after all. Although, maybe the drugs—Ah, who knows? I'll leave that part up to you."

"So, are you heading back to New York?" he asked.

"Not yet. I've got some things I still need to do here," I said. "I'll be around for a few days. Call me if you need anything, and I'll try to help you."

"Thanks," he said, holding open the door. "I will call."

I looked back at the array of items in the garage. Another time, I would have combed through every piece myself, but I felt good leaving it behind.

"One more thing," I said. "There's a file in the Masked Men directory called Eagle Scouting. The descriptions there should match up with a couple of the John Does."

"How would Raoul have that information?"

"Because he killed some of them," I said. "It was part of the training at the mosque, apparently. But he kept a record. So we would know what happened."

"What do you want me to do, erase it?" he asked. "I don't think I can do that."

"That's your decision, not mine," I said. "Do what you need to do."

His hand came up, softly wiped away a tear from my cheek. "It'll be okay," he said. I nodded and walked away.

I took a walk on the beach, thinking about my decision to let Mark take over the case. Was it the right move? I'd spent weeks here, chasing down leads and trying to figure out what happened to Raoul. I think I was really close. I had a couple of questions, and there was only one person who could give me the answers. I'd just wait for the opportunity to talk with him and decide then what else needed to be done.

I headed back to my apartment and started packing up Raoul's notebooks. There was a lot to dissect, but the basic facts were coming clearer: Raoul had infiltrated a terrorist cell in Jerome, posing as a worker named Ismail. To remain in the group, he'd killed several other men during training exercises. Somehow, his cover had been compromised and the group left Jerome, but not before torturing and killing him. I tried to read his daily logs but they made me jittery and so I closed the computer, changed into a white button-down shirt, black pants and conservative shoes. My shift behind the bar at La Corona started at 6:00.

Around 9:00 p.m., Mary Kate came in. I saw her stop and wince as she accepted hugs from most of the staff and some of the patrons. She took a seat at the bar. I slapped a coaster down and smiled.

"You look like hell," I said.

"Thanks. That sums up where I've been very nicely," she agreed. "Give me a club soda, would you? With a lime."

I returned with the beverage. "So, how are things? How are you feeling? How's Silvio doing?"

She sighed. "Silvio—I don't know. I think he'll survive. And I'll be fine. My hand hurts like hell, but I deserved it. Didn't see what was going on under my own roof. My kid was going crazy. And when you came over, it just pushed him to the edge."

"I'm sorry. I never meant—"

"No, it's not your fault. If it wasn't you, it would have been something else that triggered it. He was a time bomb, hiding in his bedroom." She sighed, took a sip and looked at me. "And you did warn me that he needed professional help—I just didn't listen.

"It's coming out slowly, so we don't have the whole story yet," she continued. "Silvio apparently joined that mosque in the summer, and they sent him to Florida for 'special training.' They were training him to be a terrorist. He actually learned how to fly a plane into a building. Can you believe that? My little boy...anyway, he's not saying much else yet, but I think something happened and the group fell apart. He could have been on one of those planes that flew into the Trade Center. Or the Pentagon. I don't know what happened, but I thank God he wasn't part of that attack."

"Really?" I felt my heart racing. "He told you all this? Did he say how he got away from them?" I asked.

She shook her head.

"Mary Kate, do you know where he got the note for me? Did he say anything about Raoul?"

"No. I don't know. He talks a lot about someone named Ismail, but so far he hasn't mentioned Raoul. Why?"

I heard a buzzing in my ears and felt dizzy. Raoul was Ismail. I held the edge of the bar to stop the trembling in my hands. "Didn't you tell me that you asked Raoul to talk to Silvio when he came home?" I asked.

"Yeah, why?"

"Oh, I don't know." I shook my head. Inside, I felt like sparks were flying. Outside, I felt my mask lower into place. The muscles in my face were tight; my jaw ached as I refilled Mary Kate's glass and continued to listen to her chat with the staff. My gut churned. I wrung water out of the bar cloth, smiled when Mary Kate directed a comment in my direction.

"Yeah," I said. "I love bartending. Who knew?" It hurt to smile. My mind was racing as I filled in the blanks I'd been missing. Silvio knew Raoul, knew him as

Ismail. Silvio could be the one who exposed Raoul as an agent. I turned away from Mary Kate. "Can you watch the bar for a minute? I need a bathroom break," I said. I needed air.

Raoul was Ismail, and Silvio had known it. If this, if that…it was hard to see a resolution that didn't end with Raoul's death, given that his handlers in D.C. had dismissed his discovery of the terrorist cell as "unfounded." If they had listened, everything would be different. But what happened was not going to change. Raoul was dead. And Silvio—the kid had been caught up in this web—would pay for it the rest of his life. He'd rot in prison, if the people who trained him didn't get to him first. Silvio. My gorge rose.

I couldn't tell Mary Kate what I knew or suspected to be true. I did want to know what Silvio's story was, and I was going to make him tell me. I went back inside after splashing water on my face. A large party was getting noisy in the dining room, and Mary Kate was still sipping her soda at the bar.

"You okay?" she asked.

"Sure," I said.

"You know, Silvio always looked up to Raoul," she said.

"How well did they know each other?" I asked.

"Oh, no, they just met recently. But Silvio was in the same Scout troop that Raoul had been in, and the troop leader always used Raoul as his example. When Sil wanted to get his Eagle Scouting badge, he was going to pick up the project that Raoul started a few years ago. He never finished it, and Silvio wanted to do it."

"I had no idea…What was the project?"

"He was going to build a small lighthouse on the point—you know, where the park ends. He was going to put solar cells on it, for the lights. It was a good project…."

"Maybe one day he can finish it, Mary Kate," I said. The phone rang and she picked it up. A waiter approached with a list of drink orders, and I was busy for a while before I noticed that she was gone. I used the slow moments to replace some glasses and restock the beer. I watched a family toasting a child's birthday and I thought: What path were we on as a nation, when Eagle Scouts could become terrorists, where innocent children could grow up to be killers?

I had no answers, only questions upon questions.

A waiter dropped an order on the bar. I took down a glass and filled it with beer. Into another glass, I mixed a Cosmopolitan. Dropping a cherry into the pink drink, I smiled.

This, I can do, I thought. And later, I would take care of the rest.

Salim

THE ROOM WAS DARK when he woke. A metallic taste accompanied the frisson of cold that flowed through his veins with the injection that the figure in the white coat added to his IV. He looked up, his vision clear for the first time in days, but her back was turned. She took off the coat and placed it carefully on the rolling cart, next to a clipboard. She was wearing green surgical scrubs, with booties covering her shoes and latex gloves that felt soft when she touched his cheek.

He smiled when she lifted her face and he recognized her. "Oh, thank God," he said. "I was afraid it was them. The others. They're coming for me. I told the people here and they just think I'm crazy, they give me drugs. But you know. You know they are going to come for me, and they're going to kill me for what I did."

"Yes, they will," she said.

"Will you tell them?"

She nodded. "But you need to tell me everything first."

"Oh yes, I will. I know I owe you an explanation. I want you to understand what happened," he said. "I'm so sorry. But I had no choice, you see…"

She nodded again and then pulled up a chair.

His wrists were loosely bound to the bed by thick fabric restraints. "Can you untie me?" he asked, raising the arm closest to her.

She shook her head. "No."

"Should I begin at the beginning, or the end?" he asked.

"Just give me the basics for now."

"All right, all right," he said. "I met the Leader in the spring when I was working at Frank's garage and hanging around at the Whole Donut, you know it? Lots of Pakistani guys hang there. He invited me to come to the mosque. Eventually, I went to Florida with a small group to learn how to fly a plane into a building. We never learned how to take off or land a plane, just how to take the controls, and steer the plane to the target.

"We came back to Jerome in August and started drilling with the rest of the team. I was living in the dormitory, eating with the others and totally into the mission. I remember seeing this man called Ismail in the mosque with some of the others. He didn't seem to belong there. He was clearly not a Pakistani, he was Hispanic, and while it didn't make sense to me that they would have someone like him on the mission, I would never have questioned the Leader at that point. I felt like he wasn't one of us. I know how stupid it must sound, but by then, I didn't think of myself as an American anymore. I was one of them. I didn't say anything to the Leader about him, I swear. I didn't realize it was Raoul, not until later.

"I don't know how long the Leader had been suspicious of Ismail, or how long he had been having him followed. I only became involved at the end, when they picked him up for interrogation. The Leader found out that Ismail was working for the FBI, and he needed to know if our mission had been compromised or if we could still go ahead. I think I was chosen to help because of my size, mostly, but also because of my devotion to the Leader. But when I realized that it was Raoul, I…"

He paused. "May I have some water, please?"

She poured a glass and held it to his lips.

"Thanks. I'm not looking for excuses. Knowing I was carrying Raoul Quiñones didn't stop me from helping the Leader. I didn't expose Raoul, even after I realized who he was. I didn't rat him out if that's what you think. But I didn't save him. I…. I gave you his note, right?" He coughed, closed his eyes.

"I did what I was told," he continued. "I was a good soldier. I followed orders, and then, when it was over, I saw that it was all for nothing. I was nothing, just another dead body."

He paused again. She sat silently, waiting for him to finish.

"When it was over, when Raoul was dead and everything was cleaned up, we went downstairs. I went first, carrying a trash bag filled with bloody aprons and gloves. Metin was behind me, and then the Leader came down last. When we were in the alley, I turned around and saw the Leader break Metin's neck. I looked up at the Leader and he just nodded. 'Metin's work on this earth is complete,' he said. 'Toss him in that dumpster with the bags.' So I did."

He grimaced. "The Leader was watching me, and I knew right away that I was next. I knew that the Leader was going to tell me to get into the dumpster myself so he could just reach over and kill me too. I could clearly see it happening, and I could see his logic. But dammit, I wasn't going to die in a filthy dumpster like that. The hell with him! I was more than a tool for this guy, wasn't I? And so after I rolled Metin into the dumpster, I ducked down and turned around before the Leader could get me, too. I grabbed him by the head and twisted, just once to the left, just like he'd done to Metin, just like I was taught, and he dropped like a sack of potatoes. It was that easy. The toughest part was that I had to get rid of him, so I picked him up and carried him to the roof. I couldn't leave him with Metin, because I knew the others would find him instead of me and they'd know what I'd done. He's buried in the pigeon coop, covered in lime. I figured that would buy me some time… and so I ran home, and I hid like a child in my mother's house. Until you came to see me."

It was quiet in the room. Machines whirred, things ticked and shifted.

"What are you going to do now? Will you tell the doctors that I'm not crazy or paranoid or whatever? That there really are people coming to get me?"

"I have to go now," she said. "You rest."

"No," he said. He screamed over and over, the sound echoing in the room after she closed the door behind her.

When he awakened, hours later, she was there again. "You're back," he said.

"Yes," she replied. She pushed a syringe full of liquid through his IV and waited for it to take effect. "Do you remember what you told me before?" she asked.

"Uh huh," he mumbled. "Did you tell the doctors? Will they protect me from the people coming to get me?"

She stood up and looked down at him. "What would make you think that I would help you, after what you did to Raoul?"

"You have to help me," he said. "I killed the Leader, I got justice for you. I did it. Please, I'll do whatever you want." He closed his eyes, squeezing a tear from each corner.

"How long did they torture Raoul?" she asked.

"I don't know, I wasn't there…."

"I don't believe you. I think your 'transportation' services must have been used before the last day. I'm guessing you helped capture him and take him to whatever safe house they held him in. It looks like he was tortured for days, and I think you watched all of it."

"No, I didn't."

She looked at him for a moment. "In fact, I bet you did some of it too. You might have even enjoyed it, right?"

"No, not really." He was crying in earnest now.

"How can you live with yourself?" she asked.

"I don't know, I don't think I can," he said. "Won't you help me?"

"No," she said, quietly leaving the room again.

When he awakened again, his bedclothes had been pushed aside to expose his legs and arms.

"Did you put the fancy underwear on Raoul?" she asked him. "Did you torture him?"

His head rolled violently from side to side.

"No?" she asked. "So you didn't watch while they injected him with drugs and zapped him with electrodes and burned him with cigarettes? You didn't help with any of that, even though you were the Leader's 'favorite?' His 'right-hand-man'?"

"They would kill me if I didn't do what they said," he protested weakly. "They're going to come for me any time now, you know."

"How did it feel to hold another man's cock in your hand?" she asked. "Did you like it? Or was it repulsive?"

"I'm sorry," Silvio cried. "I didn't want to do it, I swear."

"When your friends from the mosque find you, what do you think they will do to you?" she asked. "Do you think it will be a quick slash across the throat or a bullet to the temple? Or do you think you'll lie on a bed, kind of like this one, and spend some time thinking about the brilliant Leader whose life you ended with your bare hands?"

"I don't know," he said. "I don't care."

"If you were in the Middle East, in Pakistan where your buddies come from, you know what they'd do to you? First they'd cut out your tongue. Then they'd cover you with a thousand small cuts, and stake you out in an ant hill and let the insects suck you dry."

He thrashed around in the bed.

"They are coming for me, you believe me, right? Why won't you tell the doctors?" he asked.

"Do you want me to do that?" she asked. "Do you think you should be saved so that you can spend the rest of your life in prison, or maybe in a mental institution? Or do you believe that they'll let you go free?"

He closed his eyes.

"You're guilty. You'll get the death penalty, one way or the other. By your friends from the mosque or the U.S. Government, your life is going to be ended."

"You do it," he said.

"What?" she asked.

"You kill me. Do it. You deserve to take your revenge for your brother. So go ahead. Do it," he said. "Do it," he screamed.

She left the room silently while he shouted over and over, "Do it."

Clara

MARY KATE WENT TO see Silvio each day and reported that while he was improving physically, the doctors were not sure when he would be rational enough to speak about the events of the past month. She took her daughter to another therapist, and spent time with her husband, and tried to mend fences all around while the rest of us maintained the business. Mark was busy with the Feds and the notebooks, and I appreciated that he kept me up to date on their progress.

"Listen to this," he said, stuffing a piece of garlic bread into his mouth and reading from a printout. "They matched prints from this Leader guy to someone on the terrorist watch list. And all along, he's living here in Jerome, nice as can be. One of the prints might match someone on one of the planes—There's still a lot of forensic work to do. So much DNA to process, it might take weeks. But they're expediting everything, so hopefully we will get something back soon."

"I'm glad," I said. "Can you tell me, what about his handler? Did the guy get reprimanded at least?"

I hated the fact that Mark looked at me with something approaching pity in his face. "You know they are never going to tell an outsider something like that," he said gently.

"I'll find out," I said.

"I'm sure you will," he laughed. "I'd hate to be the guy trying to stonewall you..."

I nodded, folded my arms across my chest. You betcha.

"What about the case against Silvio?" I asked.

"What about it? We aren't even allowed to talk to him. There's nothing we can do until the kid is out of the loony bin, and then he has to be declared competent to stand trial, and then, who knows? We don't even know what he'd be charged with right now, except that he was involved."

"How about treason?" I suggested.

"Oh, sure. Can you prove it?" he asked.

"Look in the notebooks," I said.

"No photos, no direct implications. Mostly Raoul was speculating about the whereabouts and activities of a kid named Silvio. Then he started writing about someone named Salim, but are we positive they are the same person? No evidence yet—and even if there's something in the book, there's no physical evidence against the kid yet." He paused. "We need more. Do you think Raoul had more stuff hidden somewhere?"

I sat quietly. "Maybe. Let me think about it...."

Mark wiped the residue of sauce from his plate. "I have to get back to work. Thanks for dinner," he said.

"Not so fast," I said, handing him the bill. "We have a 'no friends or family discount policy' here, remember? And don't forget the tip."

"Humph," he grumbled, placing a credit card on the bar. "I'm going to have to stop eating here so often. I'm getting fat and poor at the same time."

When Mark left I sat behind the bar and scribbled on a piece of paper the places I'd found Raoul's belongings: the van, the gym, the boatyard. Asphalt Beach. It was a pretty small list for someone who loved his "bolt holes." There had to be more.

After the bar was closed and I changed into my regular clothes, I headed back to Jerome. Parking in a shadowy corner, I entered the Eagle's Club land from the southern end of the property. Raoul's van had been discovered in the dense foliage back here, and I could see the tracks were it had been towed out. How many times had he risked moving the vehicle, and how had Shelly known where to find it? I wondered. She was a bit of unfinished business that I had to follow as well. But for now, I sat quietly amid the trees and let my eyes adjust to the darkness.

Despite the best efforts of our parents to dissuade us, all the Quinones children loved to read. Some of us (the other girls) liked the Harlequin romances. But Raoul and I devoured first the Nancy Drew and Hardy Boys mysteries, and then we graduated to the Sherlock Holmes stories. We created tests for each other, experiments using different kinds of dirt and perfumes and rocks, so that we could solve cases. We took books from the library to identify trees and flowers, and once I accidentally poisoned our neighbor's cat by feeding him something I thought might be catnip that turned out to be deadly nightshade. Raoul saved the scrawny thing by making it throw up and then carrying it on his bike to the vet's office, claiming he found it eating from the garbage can.

He was meant to be a spy, he told me. His costumes for Halloween, legendary among our classmates, were nothing compared to the disguises he'd create and the junk he hid all over town in his friends' basements—his bolt holes, in the Holmesian style. I had no doubt that he lived in Jerome for months without being recognized, since when we were kids, I'd once watched our own mother hand him a tip for carrying her groceries to the car without even realizing that he was her son. Somehow, that day, he'd figured out how to make his face look Asian using Crazy Glue and eyeliner. Mama gave the retard a quarter, she told us afterwards in the car, because he couldn't help himself—but otherwise she'd never tip for something she expected to get for free. When I snickered, knowing that boy was Raoul, she slapped me for being insensitive and made my father drop me off in front of the church so I could go to confession immediately.

The lights from a car pulling into the club parking lot illuminated something shiny in a large tree a few feet away. I tried to dislodge it using a long stick, but I couldn't reach it, so I marked the base of the tree with a fluorescent tag and moved back. There were thousands of shiny things in the woods, and this was going to take all night, I thought after a few more attempts. Better to resume this particular search in the morning.

Back in the car, I studied my list of hiding places: the boat, I think I had already covered. His workplace, I had to assume, had been a hot zone where other members of the group could access anything he might try to hide. I'd found very little at the gym, which might be another hot zone for Raoul. I reconsidered my approach. What if I stopped thinking about the present and looked back at the hiding places he used in the past? As I knew, one major advantage he had was that he knew this town better than anyone else—better than the terrorists, for sure, and certainly better than the Pirate who tried to exploit his knowledge of the water for his drug trafficking. What else? Most of his friends were gone, but the high school and the library were still here: Two of his favorite places to hide things. I could go hunting there later.

And then, of course, there was the apartment building. The place he'd rented using the name Ismail had been scoured by the police and I'd gone over it as well. I'd checked the roof, but I could go and look behind every brick in case I'd missed something. I'd do the same in the laundry room and the boiler room. One of Raoul's favorite hiding places had been the empty space under the dryers. It worked well until the time when he hid a very flammable vinyl bag there that melted and caught fire after too much continuous dryer action.

And then, I knew I needed to check Mama's apartment. I hadn't been there very long, and so I hadn't really looked there, but I wouldn't be surprised if he had hidden things right under her nose. The question was how could I get access to the place, without the family going crazy on me? I could wait for my sisters to take Mama to church, or I could speed things up a bit. I dialed Jack at the boatyard and he picked up on the second ring.

"Yeah," he said.

"Are you still alive?" I asked.

Silence. "Ask me something you don't already know," he said.

"Can you arrange a decoy for me?"

"What?"

"I need to have an apartment exterminated," I said.

"Look, who are you trying to call?" he asked. "We don't do that kind of job. We're just delivering pharmaceuticals. Not exterminating anybody."

"I don't need real exterminators. I just want to have access to an apartment for a couple of hours, so I need someone to show up with a decoy. You know, a truck, equipment, paperwork—the whole nine yards. Get the folks out of the house for a while, you dig?" Silence. "Never mind."

"Oh, I can do it," he said. "But what's in it for me?"

I frowned. "How much?" I asked.

"Not money. I don't need that."

"What, then?" I asked. "I assume you have all the drugs you need, so what is it I can get you?"

"Relief," he said.

Oh for God's sake, I thought. *Another horny guy.* "Can you be more specific?"

"I need you to kill me."

"Jesus H. Christ," I said.

"Turns out I can't do it myself and I don't want to wait around anymore. So you do it, and I'll arrange your decoy for you," he said.

Shit, hell, and damn, I thought. *Just call me Clara Kevorkian.* "Fine, you get me in the apartment tomorrow, and I'll take care of your problem," I said.

"I knew you would do it," he said.

"Sure, Jack," I said. "There's just one thing I need to know."

"What?"

"Do you want to know it's coming, or do you want me to take you by surprise?" I asked.

"Oh, surprise me, definitely."

"Cool," I said. "I need the exterminators at 215 Main Street, apartment 3B. Just let me know the exact time they'll be there, so I can be ready." I paused. "And Jack. Thanks a lot."

"My pleasure," he said.

"Likewise, I'm sure," I said.

He hung up laughing.

Salim

HE WAS MORE SEDATED the next evening, but awakened abruptly when he felt the pressure of a sharp blade against his throat and the rush of warmth traveling his bloodstream.

"Good drugs, eh?" she asked.

"Mmmm," he replied sleepily.

"Still want to die?" she asked. "Or are you going to wait for the assassins to come for you?"

"No," he slurred. "I'm telling."

"What? They're waiting outside. I saw them when I came up the back stairs. They have some nice things for you. Do you want me to tell you what they brought?" she asked.

"No," he said. "Just kill me, and leave me alone."

"I want you to tell me some more about Raoul. Did you rat him out? Did you expose him to the Leader, and have him killed?" she asked.

"I am done talking. Just get it over with, why don't you?" He struggled to sit up.

"Did you show mercy to Raoul, and put him out of his misery? Did you even bother to speak to him, to warn him that he'd been compromised, to give him a chance to save himself?"

He snorted. "Are you stupid, woman? I was in a war, and he was a traitor who was discovered in our cadre. Why would I 'talk to him' or 'warn him'? Dumb bitch." He spit at her and she slapped him hard across the face.

"You know, it's very tempting. I'd like to cut off your penis, I really would, and leave you to die the same way you left my brother. But that's too easy for you."

"You're going to leave me here?" he asked. "You're not going to help me?"

"No."

She left the room.

The next time she returned it was dark. He was not sure if it was the same day or another. He was hot and agitated in the bed, having soiled himself. The nurse call button was not working.

"Please," he said.

"Are you asking me for something?" she said.

"Let me go."

"Tell me, where do you think you're going when you die?" she asked.

"Heaven."

"Why is that? Why would you deserve a place in heaven?"

His mouth worked awkwardly to form the word: "Martyr."

She slapped him across the face again. "No."

They stared at each other. The scar on his jaw was a jagged purple line from the shooting accident, and the pale cheek above it bore the red imprint of her hand.

"You are not a martyr. You are a sinner and a coward and a murderer," she said. "I will not help you." She left the room.

Clara

I **DROVE TO THE** library next, calling my buddy Spike from the road. Knowing that he didn't sleep during the dark hours either, I expected him to pick up but had to leave a message and wait for his return call. In the meantime, I jogged through some backyards to the back entrance of the dark building. The phone eventually vibrated against my hip.

"Spike, thanks for calling me back," I whispered.

"Didn't recognize the number, had to verify the incoming," he said.

"Cool."

"Cool."

I outlined briefly what I needed. "So, can you help me with this one?" I asked.

"Clara, I'm way out there with you, messing with the Yale security system and all. That's been a real gas, you know. But this municipal stuff, you know, that's like child's play. Why don't you just do it yourself?"

"I don't mean to insult you, Spike. I just don't have any equipment here and what would take you like, a minute—"

"Not even," he interjected.

"A few seconds then," I said, "It would take me, like, all night. So can you just zap it and let me in, please?"

"Oh, all right. But we're almost done with this, right? I mean, move on, man, you know?"

"Yes, just another visit or two and it'll be all over."

"And then you'll tell me what it was all about, right?"

"Absolutely. When I come back to the city, you will be my first stop. Anything I can bring you from the boondocks?" Please, do not ask me to off you, I thought. And no sex.

"Um, like, a Yale hoodie would be cool," he said. "Don't tell anyone, though, okay?"

"It's between us."

"Okay," he said. "Your alarm is off. When do you want the other one?"

"Give me an hour in here, then I'll call you with the next location. Thanks."

I picked the lock on the library door once I saw that the red light on the alarm had changed to green, and I made my way to the second floor. The building had undergone a major restoration in recent years, so it no longer had the same configuration—or the same bolt holes—as it did when we were children. But I decided to go for the obvious, and searched the adult fiction stacks for Sir Arthur Conan Doyle, where I found a musty copy of "The Complete Sherlock Holmes."

I took it down from the shelf and blew the dust from the pages. Raoul would never deface this book, his "Bible," but perhaps he may have left something inside. I flipped through the pages and was disappointed. The other books on the shelf were treated to the same, less gentle inspection, and yielded the same result. I picked up the original again, recalling how often we'd check out this book. Maybe not even this one; maybe it had been replaced because we had worn out the older copy. The plastic cover was firmly attached but that didn't mean anything.

"You didn't," I said aloud. I carried the book to the checkout desk and searched for a pair of scissors. When I found an exacto knife, I slit open the bottom of the cover and a piece of almost transparent paper dropped out. "Mijo! You made me deface a library book," I murmured.

"But I did it first," I could almost hear his reply.

I looked briefly at the contents of the letter, then looked again. This was no alphabet I'd ever seen. Why couldn't my brother ever do anything the easy way? Another code I'd have to break...I sighed.

I returned the knife to its sheath, the book to its shelf, and my body to the car. After calling Spike, I turned my attention to the high school across town. I had only a couple of hours before the janitorial staff would arrive to open the building, so I hurried to get there and gain entry.

This time, I knew exactly where to go. My only obstacle was the small locks on the trophy cases, but those were easily opened and I began the tedious process of checking the bottom of each sport trophy with Raoul's name engraved on it. I collected a variety of keys before securing the door and standing back to survey the case. "Am I missing anything?" I asked myself.

I bent down and tapped the lower part of the display. It was hollow, and it took me a few minutes to find the opening. Snapping on a flashlight, I looked underneath and pulled out a dusty duffel bag. Inside, I found file folders, stacks of blister pack prescription pills, and rolls of cash.

"Jeez, Raoul, leaving this here where the kids could get into it. Bad karma, hombre," I said aloud. "You must've been hard up for hiding places, eh, Mijo? To stash this stuff here?" I clucked a little bit, shaking my head and trying not to think about how desperately Raoul must have been trying to get in touch with someone for backup. To get a message to me.

I dragged the bag to the back door and left it there, then checked the base of all the cabinets before determining that this was the only bag Raoul had stored here. I looked at my watch and raced down the hall: One more stop.

In the boys' locker room, there was a special place, a room with a couple of deep hot tubs where the boys soaked off their ailments. Raoul had liked to stay behind after the other boys were gone and think. Since he lived in a house filled with women, he particularly enjoyed spending time in the masculine stink of the locker room at school. During his bad time, when I visited him in Bellevue, he told me about some long-ago nights when he laid soaking in the tub and looking up at the pipes beneath the high school. There, he had been able to figure it all out.

"All the questions I had, everything I wondered about—I got the answers just looking at the maze of pipes overhead," he told me. I thought he was nuts back then, but on this night, when I found the room and the tub, I climbed in.

"So look who's nuts now," I thought. Above me, there was a congested highway of plumbing. Different sizes, different colors—different functions, I was sure, as all the water for the massive building flowed from the street to various destinations upstairs. It was dark, pipes creaked and groaned, and my flashlight sputtered. My phone rang, but I ignored the call. I had just fifteen minutes left in my allotted visit to the school.

"I'm not getting any insights here, Raoul," I said. "No big revelations. No answers from above—Oh, wait a minute."

I stood up abruptly and looked around. There were some benches, but nothing tall enough for me to reach the lower level of pipes. I needed a ladder. I pulled out the keys from my pocket. Most of them had been stuck to the underside of the trophies with old chewing gum, but one of them, a relatively new and shiny one, still had a piece of double-sided tape attached to it. I looked around for a door with a lock that might match it and found one right outside the steam room. A ladder awaited.

It was tight, but I managed to wedge myself between some pipes and located another duffle bag, this one filled with high-powered rifles with scopes, ammunition, and silencers. The best part, however, was the black moleskin journal in which Raoul listed all his contacts with the agency, his reports and their responses. Dates, times, and information: everything he had provided to his contacts in D.C. was here. His handlers had been provided intelligence about a terrorist plan to fly a plane into the World Trade Center—and they chose to ignore it. And now I had the proof in my hand.

I left the school, hefting the two duffle bags and sliding the latex gloves off my hands before sending the "all-clear" to Spike and then listening to Mark's message. The urgency in his voice prompted me dial his number before the voicemail was finished.

"What's happened?" I asked.

"Shelly," he said.

"What about her? It's so strange, I was going to ask you to bring her back in for questioning. I had some things I wanted to ask her," I said.

"Too late," he said. "She's dead. Her body was dropped off in front of the Emergency Room tonight."

"Let me guess—unidentified vehicle, no license and no clear visual on the driver, right? And Shelly—was it an OD?"

"No, she was raped and then assaulted pretty badly with a metal pipe," he said. "Nasty stuff. Where are you? Are you home? Did I wake you up?"

248 • Dawn Leger

"Nah, I couldn't sleep. I'm just driving around," I said. "So, what do you think? Who's responsible for Shelly's death?"

"Unclear. Could be a boyfriend, who knows? It's probably completely unrelated to anything we're doing. Why did you want to talk to her again?"

I stopped at a red light and recognized his car parked in the shadows near the police station. "Hey, is that you?" I flashed my lights. "Do you want to follow me? I'll explain everything when we get there."

"Where are you taking me?" he asked. "Oh, never mind, lead on. I got nothing better to do than go home and pretend to sleep for a couple of hours."

When we pulled into the back of the Eagle's Club and parked, I saw him shaking his head. "You're kidding, right?" he said as he got out of the cruiser.

"No, do you have a couple of good flashlights in there?" I asked. "It's getting light, but in the woods, we'll still need 'em."

He tossed a flashlight at me and followed my lead. When I spotted the fluorescent tag, I stopped and turned my light towards the multiple tire tracks where Raoul had parked his van.

"So?" Mark asked.

"I know the tow truck and others made some of those tracks, but I was wondering how Shelly knew the van was here, and how many times she took it out. And what, if anything, she helped herself to from the contents of the van. I mean, Raoul didn't have a lot of stuff, but Shelly might have taken something that's important to the investigation. She wouldn't know it, she might have just wanted to sell it, or who knows, keep it for sentimental reasons. But we need to check out her residence and see what she took."

"Okay, I follow that," Mark said. "What else?"

"What do you mean?" I asked. He waved his flashlight as a signal to continue. "All right, so I was sitting here looking around, you know? Raoul was a big fan of hiding things— like on the roof, you know?"

"Yes, I got that."

"He must have hidden things here in the woods."

Mark looked around. "But, why?"

"Why not? In case his van was discovered. Or he was followed, so he could grab stuff on the run. Or just because. Like, if there's a cave around, I guarantee we'll find some of his stuff there. That's just how he was. He had bolt holes."

"Like Frankenstein?"

"No, like Sherlock Holmes." I illuminated the shiny object that I had spotted earlier. "See that, up there, the shiny thing? I bet that's something. I couldn't reach it though."

"Probably something a crow hid in his nest."

"I think we should check."

"Go ahead."

"You want me to climb this tree?"

"Did you think I was going to climb it for you? It's your discovery and your idea, so go ahead. I'll give you a boost." He put down his flashlight and laced his fingers together to provide a step for me, and before I had time to think, I was halfway there. An interesting intersection of branches had created a platform that someone augmented with a couple of pieces of plywood. "I found something," I shouted.

"Before you touch anything, can you take a photo? For chain of custody?"

"Oh, now you want police procedure?" I chuckled. "Sure! Send up a camera. How about I put on some gloves before I touch it, too? Got any on you?"

"I've got gloves," he said. "But the camera's in the cruiser. Just bring it down, whatever it is."

It was a briefcase, a metal one, with handcuffs attached and some sophisticated technology keeping it secure. I snapped on some latex gloves pulled from my back pocket, stuck my hand into one of the cuffs, snapped it shut, and headed back down the tree.

"You handcuffed yourself to it?" he asked. "Are you freaking kidding me?"

"Yes, and good job, Clara," I said. I reached into my right hand pocket and brought out my cache of small keys. "One of these will fit, I'm pretty sure."

"Where did you get these?" Mark took one and started trying the lock.

"Another bolt hole," I said. "Let's go to the cars where you can see better."

"Just wait a sec," he grumbled. After several tries, he opened the lock. "Now what?"

I looked at the lock mechanism for the briefcase and shrugged. "No idea," I said.

"What should we do with it? Give it to the Feds?"

I shook my head. "Not yet."

He crossed his arms. "Why not?"

"Let me try to open it first," I said. "In the meantime, how about you come in here when it gets light with some officers and some ladders and see what else you can find?" I put the briefcase in my trunk. "Oh, and how about that cave you mentioned?"

"You mentioned a cave, not me."

"So where is it?"

"There's a ton of them—"

"And I bet you're going to find stuff in at least one or two of them."

"But wait a minute," he said. "What are we looking for, anyway? Isn't this what the Feds are going to do?"

"Why let them have all the fun?" I said.

"I thought you said you didn't want to investigate this? You said you were going to step away. What happened?" he asked.

"I don't know—I just can't let it lie," I said. "Look. We know the when, where, and how. And now we know the why, more or less. And I am pretty sure about who —Silvio. I know you're not convinced about that, and some people maybe think he was just a kid following orders or whatever. But somehow there has to be more. Somebody was responsible for this, and I want to know who."

"So this is about revenge?"

"No, not exactly. I don't think so. It's more about truth."

"You're going in a dangerous direction," he said.

"Why is that? Because I want to know who's responsible for my brother's death, and I want some accountability? Why is that dangerous?"

"We have laws. We are not vigilantes. I'm not going to let you go off on some mission—"

I got into the car and started it. When I took a breath, I lowered the window. "I know you think I'm going to go rogue like I did when I was an agent, but this is not the same situation. I just want to gather all the clues that Raoul left behind, and figure it all out. That's all."

Mark leaned into the car and studied my face. "There's a chance that Shelly was killed by the terrorists, that there are still members of that cell in this area and they are after the same information that you are. So I know I can't stop you from doing whatever you are doing. But I can ask you to be careful, and to call me if you need help. Okay?"

I nodded.

Salim

"I'M SORRY," HE

She stared at him. "Are you?"

"Yes."

"Truly?" she asked.

"On my honor."

"I don't think you have any honor," she said. "I think you would say anything to manipulate people. I think you're a liar, and a manipulator, and you're trying to trick me now."

"No, I am telling you the truth."

"You don't know the truth, you're just trying to save your own sorry life," she said. "You're contemptible."

"Give me a knife, I'm ready to die." He looked away.

"Really?"

"Yes. I'm done. I'm ready to go and face the punishment for my sins."

"You're just afraid of the torture."

"Yes, I'm not ashamed to admit that I'm afraid."

"Tell me again, who are you afraid of? Who was left behind in your group that is now coming to get you?"

"I don't know the names," he said. "I just know that they're coming."

"How many? Where are they coming from?"

He shook his head.

"You were supposed to be on the plane, right? Or at least that's what you were trained for."

"I was trained to get into a cockpit and fly a plane."

"Who taught you this?"

"I can't say," he said, closing his eyes.

"What makes you think any members of this group are still alive? And that they are around here, waiting to come and get you?" she asked.

"They told us it was so," he whispered. "Once we made our pledge to fight, there was no going back. No changing our minds, no running away. They will find me and kill me."

"And so you believe this is going to happen."

He nodded. "Why don't you just do it? Take your revenge. It's your right. Do it!"

"I'm offering you a way out, why won't you take it?"

"I can't. You must have your revenge. What's wrong with you? I killed your brother—I sliced off his dick and shoved it in his throat. Doesn't that make you want to kill me?"

"It does," she said. "I admit that. But I want to watch you do it, and to know that you'll suffer—and my hands will be clean."

He sobbed.

"Do you want the knife?" she asked again. "This is a one-time only offer. I am never coming back. Take it or leave it—and wait for your friends to arrive with their offer."

He shook his head.

"Fine," she said. "I'm done with you."

She was at the door. Silence. She left.

When she returned, another day had passed.

He was weeping. Tears mixed with snot ran down his cheeks.

She stood by his bedside. "What's the punishment in Islam for suicide?" she asked.

"Glory," he said.

"No," she said. "I did some research. If you take your own life, you spend all eternity reliving your death. Over and over."

"No," he said. He closed his eyes.

"You will never see the face of God, never get relief," she said. "Do you want to wait for your friends to come in and play torture games with you? I can leave the door unlocked for them."

"No, I want you to help me die," he said. "You kill me."

"I am not a killer," she said. "You are."

"I am a soldier," he said. He gritted his teeth. "I am fighting the jihad."

"So, you fight alone." She left him.

Clara

AFTER LUGGING THE BAGS home, I called Jack to arrange the extermination and took a long hot shower. It had been a long night, but the adrenaline was still keeping me hopping so I was ready to tackle the apartment when I received the call. Armed with gloves and some evidence bags, I drove across town and hid my car behind the decrepit mall structure. When I heard Carmen's squealing Blazer engine idling outside the apartment building, I waited on the back stairs for its departure.

Carmen, take the car to Mario and get the belts checked, I admonished her in my head. *Don't wait for this engine to catch on fire or fall out like all the others!* When I no longer heard the whine of the car, I climbed the last flight and met Jack on the landing. He looked pale.

"I thought you were sending a crew over," I said. "You look like shit."

"Nice to see you, too," he said. "I figured I'd give your job the personal touch, since you're going to do the same for me."

I smiled. "Absolutely. Now get out of here, so I can get to work. How long did you tell them to stay out of the apartment?"

"Four hours," he said.

"Perfect." I passed by, entering the living room just as Jack reached out and tapped my backside.

"See you soon," he said, giving me a squeeze.

I shut the door. I had no idea how I was going to handle Jack—I had no intention of killing him—but I didn't have time to dwell on that issue now, so I just said a small prayer that he'd fall down the stairs or get hit by a car on Main Street. "Thank you, Jesus," I swiped my hand across my chest in a quickie version of the sign of the cross.

Raoul smiled at me from his photo atop the television set. Mama had not washed away the drop of blood that had fallen on the glass like a tear, and it was heartbreaking to look at. No wonder the woman was going crazy sitting in this apartment day after day, looking at that face. The giant blood stain on the ceiling above had been painted over, but not well, so it looked like the sky was about to drop at any moment.

I went into his room. Starting in the closet, I went through every item of clothing, checking pockets, emptying everything onto the bed without studying what I found. I did the same in the drawers, pulling them out completely and looking for envelopes taped behind or beneath the drawer. But that was too predictable for my brother, so I didn't find anything there. In his shoe boxes, stuffed inside an almost-new pair of Adidas soccer shoes, I found a small gun with an ankle holster and a brown envelope filled with unidentified pills. I tossed them on the bed.

My phone rang. "Hey Mark, what's up?"

"I was just going to ask you the same thing," he said. "What are you doing?"

"Just housecleaning," I said. "You make any progress today?"

"Sort of," he said. "We found some more stuff up in the trees, and a couple things in the caves."

"Such as?"

"Scuba gear, night vision stuff, some extra clothes, some guns."

"That's it?"

"No, there's a box of journals. At least I think that's what they are. It's all in code. So we'll need you to take a look at them," he said. "Maybe this afternoon?"

"Sure," I said. "I have to work at 4:00, but I can stop over before then."

I disconnected the phone and continued my excavation of the room, now taking apart the bed, knocking on the frame and searching the mattress for any openings. I couldn't find one, but that didn't mean anything—I went out to the living room and found Mama's sewing kit. She always kept a large magnet in there, in case she dropped a needle or pin on the floor. I took the magnet and ran it up and down the mattress methodically, until it clicked on something hard.

"A-ha!" I slit open the cover and pried out another small gun. "I wonder how long these have been here?" I said aloud. Finishing the search, I replaced the sheets carefully and put the magnet back in the basket as I found it. When I returned to his room, I stood in the doorway. It was a small room, created by sectioning a part of the master bedroom because, as my father put it, "the boy needs his own space." There was room for a twin bed, a bureau-closet combination, and a small bookcase. In our family, the only purpose for a bedroom was to sleep and dress—and endure punishment. We spent no other time in our rooms growing up and had no entertainment or study materials in them.

The bookcase, however, did offer a big opportunity to me. I started checking each book, and found a variety of notes, keys, and cut-outs in almost every volume on his shelf. In fact, there was no unaltered book in his room. However, most of the alterations seem to have been made back in the "Hardy Boys" days, so I was not getting anything of value from this search. I gathered the pile on the bed and swept it into a plastic bag. There was $3.63 from his pockets, thirteen different pills, and too many pieces of paper to count. I'd take them back to study.

I went into the bathroom and searched the toilet tank and all the other available hiding spaces, but came up empty. The kitchen yielded the same, although I found a large roll of money in an old sugar tin in the pantry. I wonder if Raoul had left it for Mama, or if it was her "insurance" money.

Again in the living room, I surveyed the opportunities for hiding things. "May as well just do it," I muttered, and began patting down the furniture, removing pillows, unzipping covers, and using the magnet to check every item. I looked in the cabinet housing the ancient liquor that my father had kept in the house "for visitors" and discovered only empty bottles there. Mama's Bible held only photographs of Raoul and her grandchildren, some pressed flowers, and a card from his funeral. Standing behind her chair, I was ready to give up.

The RCA was an ancient piece of furniture. I was astonished that it still worked, but then I realized that the actual television had been replaced with a flat screen inserted into the old cabinet. "Clever," I said. I walked over and knelt in front of it, then pried open the bottom speaker compartment. Inside, I found another duffel bag. It was filled with more notebooks, money, and a pair of binoculars. "Really?" I asked. "This is what you leave me?"

I put everything inside the bag and dragged it onto the landing. Before I left, I looked around to make sure I had left the apartment exactly as I had found it. As a decoy, I pulled a bottle of vetiver oil from my pocket and left a few drops in each room. My family would not recognize the scent and would believe it came from the exterminator. *Maybe it would help them find peace,* I thought, taking a deep breath. And we can all use a little bit of that.

I met Mark at the station and he asked me for the little keys. They had found another briefcase, this one with a chain wrapped around and locked to its handle. "Any luck opening the other one?" he asked.

"I haven't had time," I said. "I found some other stuff. I think we should bring it over to the armory, spread it out near the van and see what we've got."

"Holy Christ," Mark said when all the bags had been opened and the contents tagged. "He really had a lot of hiding places."

"And this is just the ones we found," I said. "There may be more." I sat heavily on a chair next to a table stacked with journals and files. "The problem we have here is that I can't read most of these pages. He used some kind of strange alphabet to write most of it."

"I know," Mark said. "We've been avoiding this, but we're going to have to turn it over to the feds. No way can we handle this."

"I have a feeling the answer is right under our noses," I said. I walked between the rows of tables, surveying the weapons and gadgetry that Raoul had hidden in his bolt holes throughout Jerome. The most valuable information, so far, had been the thumb drive hidden on Asphalt Beach. "Wait a minute," I turned abruptly. "Where is that duffle I just brought in, the one I had in the backseat of my car?"

Mark pointed to the table nearest the door. "Where'd you get that one?" he asked.

"Right under Raoul's nose—beneath the television set where his photo was on display in my mother's apartment," I said looking over the items. "Here they are." I picked up an old leather binocular case and opened it. Despite its weight, there were no binoculars inside. "When I picked this up, I wondered, 'Why would Mijo leave a pair of binoculars under the RCA?'" I said. "But there are no binoculars in here." I reached for a pair of gloves and then stuck a finger inside, sliding out a sheet of red vinyl. It was thick and filmy. "What the hell?" I reached in and pulled out another, orange this time, and more, virtually every color of the rainbow, curled carefully inside the tubes of the binocular case.

"What do you think they are?" Mark asked.

"It has to have some kind of data on it," I said, holding one of the sheets to the ceiling light. "But I can't see anything." I looked around. "Give me one of those files." When Mark handed me a sheet of the encoded paper and I held the red transparency over it, words became legible although hard to read. "We need a light box," I said. "I bet these sheets are the decoders."

Salim

IN THE DEAD OF night, perhaps the same day, she injected his IV with another substance that awakened him abruptly. His heart raced.

"Are they here?" he asked. "Is it time?" He looked around the room anxiously. Finally, his eyes settled on her face. "You came back," he said.

"Yes," she said. "It's time."

"All right."

"Are you ready to die?" she asked.

"Yes. Just one thing," he said.

"What now?"

"Will you tell my ma I love her?" he whispered.

"Sure I will," she said. "You betcha."

He breathed deeply. "How will you do it?" he asked.

"You're going to do it yourself," she said. "I'm not."

"No," he said. "You agreed."

"This is all I can do for you," she said. She placed a greeting card on the table next to the bed. The front was a bright yellow happy face.

"What's that for?" he asked.

"See this orange dot?" She pointed to a small orange spot on the bottom corner of the yellow circle.

"Yeah."

"That's poison. You pick it up with your tongue, and you'll be dead in less than two minutes."

"Painful?"

"Quick," she said. "Just don't leave it hanging around for anyone else to touch, or they'll be the ones to die. Like your ma, or your little sister. Don't kill anyone else, you hear me?"

"Yes. Okay, I'll do it."

"If you don't, if you're still alive when I come back, I'm going to tell them where you are, so they'll come and get you. And it won't be this easy when they kill you, believe me."

"Don't do that." He cried. He pulled against the restraints. "Loosen one of these, will you? How am I going to reach? Leave the card where I can get it. Move the table closer, here, next to me. Okay."

The door locked behind her as she turned and walked quickly down the hallway. On the basement level, she removed the blue scrubs and tossed them with the white coat into a laundry bin. She exited the building via the service entrance, removing

258 * Dawn Leger

her gloves as soon as she released the handle and tossing them into a trash bin on the corner. Wearing jeans and a Yale sweatshirt, hair tied back and covered with a Yankees cap, she blended easily with the college crowd on the street in the wee hours. No one noted her coming or going from the building; no camera captured her departure.

Clara

I WAS POLISHING A glass when Mark came in, looking like he hadn't slept in days or shaved in a week.

"Coffee?" I asked. "You look like hell."

"Thanks." He nodded and slid onto a stool. He paused for a minute. "Silvio is dead."

"What? How the hell did that happen?" I asked. "Does Mary Kate know?"

"I just came from her house," he said. "I got a call from the hospital this morning."

"What happened?" I asked again. "Wasn't he still on suicide watch?"

"Well, he managed to get a pair of scissors and cut his own throat last night. Or someone did it for him." Mark stretched.

"What?" I sat down on the stool next to Mark. "He did what?"

"What a mess. Do you know what a bloody mess it makes when someone cuts their own throat?"

I felt lightheaded. "I think I need a drink. You want something?" I asked.

"No, I'm on duty, but I'll take some aspirin," he said. "The case won't be mine for long, but at least until I hand it over, I've got to keep a clear head. What a mess," he repeated.

"Wow," I said. I took a deep breath. "I never would have guessed he had the balls to do something like that." I stepped behind the bar and mixed a Bloody Mary, heavy on the vodka, with a large celery stalk and very little ice. Before sitting down, I went to the front door and shakily printed a sign that announced the restaurant was closed due to a death in the family. I returned to my bar stool, handed Mark a bottle of Excedrin, and took a long sip of my drink.

"Why are you handing over the case?" I asked, breaking the long silence.

"The Staties have already been here and they called in the FBI. They're assuming that the terrorist group Silvio was involved with came in to finish him off, to make sure he wouldn't tell us anything about their operations. The staff said he's been ranting about needing protection, but they figured it was just part of his psychotic break."

"Uh-huh," I said. "So, they don't think he did it himself then?"

"Nope. Because of the scissors."

"Oh, yeah," I said. "Then, the thinking is that someone came in and offed him?"

"Yeah," he said. "They're interrogating the staff now, figure it was probably someone on the janitorial staff who let somebody in after hours to do the job. It was definitely an inside job. All the cameras went off for about fifteen minutes, but apparently that's been happening on and off for about a week so no one thought much about it. But last night, when the screens came back on in the nursing station, they saw blood everywhere and Silvio was dead."

"Sounds like pros." I turned away from him. "You said Silvio was asking for protection. Maybe he recognized someone on the staff and knew they were coming to kill him."

"Like one of the maintenance guys or something?"

"Yeah. So they found him, and cut his throat, as a lesson for betraying their Leader," I said. "In fact, maybe it means that Silvio was the one who actually killed Raoul."

"I think you're reaching," he said. He shook his head. "But then again, when you think about it, Silvio was just a kid. Why would he be so important that they had to come in and finish him off?"

"Exactly. He was probably like a prodigy or a special project for this Leader guy. You know how they like to turn Americans—and then if he betrayed the group, they'd have to use his death as an example. Otherwise, why not just leave him locked away in the loony bin?"

"I don't know, and in about an hour, it's not going to be my problem anymore," he said.

He stood up and watched as I sipped my drink.

"So. You okay? You looked a little green around the gills for a minute there," he said.

"I'm sorry for Mary Kate. What a terrible thing for her, losing her son like that," I said. "You think I should go over there? What's the polite thing to do?"

He raised an eyebrow.

"What can I say? I'm not very good with this kind of emotional stuff. Am I sorry that my friend's son just died? Well, of course I am. I'm not a monster."

"Of course not."

"But I can't pretend to be sorry that the person who killed my brother is dead."

He paused. "Why are you still so positive that Silvio was involved in Raoul's death?"

"The card, obviously. He had Raoul's message for me."

Mark reached over and squeezed my shoulder. "Maybe you should try to let that go."

"It's not that easy," I said. "And I know that we're going to find proof somewhere in Raoul's files." I took a sip of my drink. "I guess I should call the staff and tell them not to come in to work. And then I'll go over to see Mary Kate. I don't know what else I can do."

"You'll figure it out," Mark said. He stood up. "Oh, I forgot," he said. "I went to close out the mailbox we rented, and there was something in there for you."

"What?" I looked at the envelope in his outstretched hand. "How could this be? No one but you and I knew about that box."

He shrugged.

"Is it from you?" I asked. "Is this some kind of joke?"

"No. It's not from me," he said. "I don't know where it came from, I just know it has your name on it." He put the envelope next to me on the bar. "I'll catch you later."

I listened to his footsteps crossing the parquet floor, the door shut softly. After taking another sip of my drink, I picked up the envelope. My name was printed in all capitals, of a uniform size similar to the writing on architectural drawings. When I held it up to the light, I could see the yellow circle and the black smiley face through the thin white paper, along with some dark marks that were probably blood spatter from Silvio's "suicide." I dropped it carefully on the bar and turned my head aside to exhale slowly.

"What the hell," I said aloud.

I held my breath and moved in closer, squinting eye-level at the envelope. When I smoothed my hand over it, I could feel the slightly raised circle of the orange dot within the yellow circle, where I had glued it just the night before. It was still there. I lifted my hand carefully and moved back a step before breathing in. Standing there, a hand over my nose and mouth, I studied the writing on the envelope for a long time. Who had sent this to me, and why?

I realized the urgent need to get out of town—but before I ran, I had some decisions to make. Raoul's moleskin notebook with the record of all of his calls to D.C. was in my back pocket, my passport was in the glove compartment of my car, and I had several options. I could use the notebook to expose the intelligence community that had ignored my brother's warnings—intel that could have saved him and thousands of others on that brilliant day in September. I had evidence of their failure right in my hands, and a whole warehouse of proof just down the road in Jerome.

I paused and drank the dregs from my glass. I had stayed in Jerome these past few weeks to find out what happened to Raoul, and to get closure. And in the process, it seems I had placed myself in danger, too. Did I still want revenge, or should I just try to save myself? Maybe if I exposed the people who were behind this, it could also slow down the folks who were now gunning for me. *Maybe it was for both of us*, I thought. I stood up and paced. *And what was wrong with revenge?* Exposing the failure of the government to act, to listen to its own agent, and to protect him when he was sounding the alarm: That needed to be done, didn't it?

I stepped up to the bar and gazed at the envelope lying there. It was pretty clear that I needed to disappear, but I felt compelled to finish what I'd started on Raoul's behalf. Was there a way I could do both? I'd have to do something before Mark transferred all the evidence to the feds.

My cell phone rang. My hand shook when I picked it up. On the third ring, I answered.

"Jack," I said. "I was just about to call you. I have something I want to mail to the *Times*, maybe a couple other newspapers. Do you have any medium-sized envelopes laying around? Good, that's great. I'll be right over; I might need you to lick some stamps for me. What did you say your address was?"

I gingerly picked up the card and headed out the door.

OUR MISSION IS TO publish new literature, including fiction, poetry, memoir, and criticism, with a focus on contributions that best serve to enhance and represent the intellectual life of the New England region.

Lefora Publishing seeks to support a vibrant community of writers

...by stewarding writers through the editorial and marketing process,

...by working with emerging talent as well as seasoned writers,

...by sharing in the development of their careers,

...by hosting an online journal,

...by sponsoring writing contests,

...by offering speaking opportunities.

and we will do each of these as we create the *Lefora Publishing* legacy.

The porcupine depicted in our logo represents the character of New Englanders; in fact, the porcupine is a mammal unique to the New England states. Additionally, the quill has a long history as a writing implement commonly utilized by writers in New England and elsewhere.

For more information about *Lefora Publishing*, including author submission guidelines, please visit our website, www.leforapublishingllc.com.

Lefora Publishing